FORGET ME NOT

A. M. Taylor lives and writes in London. When not making up stories, she writes copy for a living and can most often be found drinking coffee, watching Netflix, and trying to keep up with a never ending TBR pile. She's been obsessed with mysteries ever since Nancy Drew first walked into her life and would probably have attempted to become a private detective at some point, if only it didn't involve actually having to talk to people. She has a cat called Domino, ambitions of owning a dog one day, and is as obsessed with *My Favorite Murder* as you probably are.

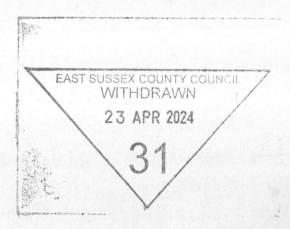

FORGET
ME
NOT

A. M. TAYLOR

**KILLER
READS**

KillerReads
an imprint of HarperCollins*Publishers* Ltd
1 London Bridge Street
London SE1 9GF

www.harpercollins.co.uk

First published in Great Britain by HarperCollins*Publishers* 2018

A catalogue copy of this book is available from the British Library.

ISBN: 9780008312923

This novel is entirely a work of fiction.
The names, characters and incidents portrayed in it are
the work of the author's imagination. Any resemblance to
actual persons, living or dead, events or localities is
entirely coincidental.

Set in Minion by Palimpsest Book Production Limited, Falkirk, Stirlingshire

Printed and bound in the UK by CPI Group (UK) Ltd, Croydon CR0 4YY

MIX
Paper from
responsible sources
FSC
www.fsc.org   FSC™ C007454

This book is produced from independently certified FSC paper to ensure
responsible forest management.
For more information visit: www.harpercollins.co.uk/green

For Ruthie (big sister, best cheerleader, and all-round super woman)

CHAPTER ONE

Madison Journal

Ten Years Gone: Family Mourns Missing Daughter

By Angela Cairney

January 7, 2018

Ten years ago, the family and friends of Nora Altman woke up to find themselves living in a nightmare. Tomorrow marks the anniversary of her disappearance when the 17-year-old's car was found abandoned by the side of Old Highway 51 on the road between Forest View, WI, and nearby Stokely in the early hours of January 8, 2008. The car was locked, with no sign of a struggle; the only indication that anything was wrong with the car was the empty tank of gas that had presumably halted the teen's drive.

The case has long since gone cold, and the local police department have been criticized both by members of the

1

community and Nora's family for not acting quickly enough when she was first reported missing. But Chief of Waterstone Police Department Patrick Moody claims he hasn't given up. "We're always on the lookout for anything relating to Nora's disappearance. This is the kind of case that defines your whole career, but its impact has been much more far-reaching than that. It's affected the whole community and I feel the full weight of that responsibility daily. Even now."

Three years after the teen first went missing, her father, Jonathan Altman, almost launched a civil suit against the Waterstone Police Department. "There are no hard feelings," Moody said, "he was just doing everything he had to do to find out what happened to his daughter. As a father, I would have done the same."

Chief Moody was planning on joining the family and close friends of Nora today to mark the ten-year anniversary of her disappearance. "We've done it almost every year since Nora went missing. It's good to get together and remember her, and also to remind ourselves that there's still work to do."

For the family, though, the nightmare still goes on. "We'll never have closure," Nora's younger sister Noelle said. Only 7 when Nora went missing, Noelle regrets not having had a big sister to grow up with and guide her along the way. "My brother Nate tries his hardest, but it's not the same. Even though I know I barely really knew her, I still really miss her. I just know she would have been the best big sister."

CHAPTER TWO

I was dreaming of the sheet of glass again.

I was carrying this huge plate of glass that was beginning to crack, tiny spider webs of distortion spreading fast, and as it did the pane shifted in my heavy arms and slipped from my grasp. I woke just as it should have been shattering into a million pieces on the floor below me. I carried that great big sheet of glass everywhere I went, my arms straining with the effort, my forehead shining with sweat, the glass itself slowly, slowly cracking as I shifted it slightly from hand to hand, arm to arm. It was exhausting and debilitating, cumbersome and controlling and, I thought, so, so obvious to everyone I met that I was struggling. People recognized the struggle of course, just as I knew they would, gave it a name, and either pushed it to the back of their minds or worried about it endlessly depending on who they were and what they were to me. They all made the same mistake, though: thinking that pane of glass made me weak. You try carrying something like that around with you wherever you go. You get tired, sure; but you also get strong.

There was nothing particularly special about waking up to that shattering glass. I'd done it a thousand times before and no doubt it would continue to haunt me after; it wasn't a portent, or an omen, I didn't have to write about it in my dream journal, or put a black mark in my diary so that in the years to come I'd be able to look back and say "ah yes, the dream. I should have known something terrible was going to happen." Because there was no way anyone could have known.

Because when the worst has already happened, you don't expect it to happen again.

But this story doesn't start with a dream. What story ever does? No, this story starts with Nora.

Nora's parents had chosen Sunday for the memorial because more people were available. The day was white and gray, the sky thick and heavy even though the snow didn't come until nightfall. It had been the same on the day Nora disappeared but then that should have hardly come as a surprise. January has a way of making every day look and feel the same, the month lasting forever and then suddenly over. I don't know why we gathered at the lake house rather than at the Altman home, although I was glad we weren't huddled around the trees by the side of the road where her abandoned car had been found that morning, so many years ago. Too many impromptu vigils had happened there in the days and weeks following Nora's disappearance for me to feel anything other than nausea when I drove past. At least the lake held some happy memories, long gone but still just about holding on. So, Nora's dad, Jonathan, spoke, and then her older brother, Nate, did, and then we all just stood looking at the lake for a while, no one really knowing what to do, what we were expected to do. That's something I've learned over the last ten years; no one ever tells you what to expect or what's going to happen next because no one knows. You're on your own.

I waited for a while, wanting to get Nate on his own, but Leo and Bright were stood with him, their faces pale and maybe even a little drawn but talking to each other as animatedly as you can at a memorial. They were trying to draw Nate into the conversation, trying to coax him out, but wherever he was it wasn't with them. I had a feeling he hadn't been with them for a while.

"Hey, Maddie," Leo said as I approached. "Nice to see you." Leo had just graduated from the police academy when Nora went missing. Three months on the job and he was investigating the disappearance of his best friend's little sister. Whenever I saw him back then the image of him in his brand-new uniform would shock me all over again; he looked so young, too young to be in a position of such authority, as though he'd put the uniform on for Halloween and never taken it off.

Bright, or Michael Brightman to give him his full name, was a year older than Nate and Leo; the same age as my older sister, Serena: They'd gone out for a while, in fact, back in high school. He'd had a year longer on the job than Leo, a year or so to prepare for something neither of them could ever have seen coming when they decided they wanted to be cops in the same small town they'd grown up in, where nothing ever seemed to happen. I could still see his face, stark, stretched and stunned, when he told me they'd found Nora's car but that there was no sign of Nora.

"Nice to see you too," I said, leaning in for awkward hugs with both Leo and Bright before stopping at Nate whose eyes were turned towards the lake, or where the lake would have been if it weren't blanketed with snow. I had lain my hand on Nate's arm in an attempt to get his attention, and he finally turned towards me.

"Hey, Mads. Good of you to come," he said, his voice scratching the cold air around us.

I looked at him, trying to make sense of what he was saying before just nodding my head slowly and saying: "I wouldn't miss it."

Nate sucked in a breath, still not really looking at me, and I turned back to Bright and Leo, the latter of whom met my gaze and shrugged. "Can you guys give us a minute?" I asked, the two

5

of them sharing a look before wandering off towards the lake house without another word.

"How're you doing, Nate?" I asked.

Nate shoved his hands into his pockets and turned towards me with a sigh. "I don't know, Mads. How do you think I'm doing?" He was facing me but not meeting my eyes, his gaze wandering across the snowy landscape, taking in the fractured group of people who had gathered to remember Nora.

His younger sister and brother, Noelle, and Noah, were walking together towards the house, looking for warmth; his aunt stood with her arm around his mom as she quietly cried. My oldest friend, Ange, was talking to Bright and Leo now, while our parents stood in a small knot, joined by Nate's dad, Jonathan, and the Winters family. It was a scene familiar to me, too familiar, and I wondered if that was what Nate was thinking too: How many times had we done this, how many times had we stood here, if not exactly in this precise spot, then one very much like it, thinking about Nora, remembering her, trying to keep her with us even while she was taken further and further away from us?

Ten years. I tried to take it in and couldn't. Ten years was a lifetime, an entire decade. What was there to say about an entire decade that, for the most part, had been marked only by absence? For some people if there's something missing, if there's a hole in their life, they fill it; I tend to fall down it.

"How's work?" I asked, searching his face, desperate for something, anything. "How's Texas?" Nate had moved to Austin almost four years earlier, and I'd barely seen him, barely spoken to him since, the distance between us so much bigger, so much wider than those thousands of miles.

Nate took another long breath, looked like he was readying himself for something and ran a gloved hand over his face before batting my question away. "Texas is fine, work is fine."

"Wow, that's really illuminating stuff, thanks, Nate." I wanted to smooth out the edges of my words but, for some reason, even that day, I couldn't. They were sharp and cold, like the weather, like the day.

"That's all I have for you right now. How about you? You want to tell me all about your great, interesting life?" Sarcasm shaded his voice, adding an unfamiliar arch to it, and he was looking right at me then, his eyes dark and hard, like a dare. I shrugged off his question, trying to pretend it slid right off my back, and he decided that he'd made his point. "See, that's what I thought. Good to see you, Mads, be sure to have a slice of the coffee cake before you go."

And then he was walking away from me, hands deep in his pockets, shoulders hunched.

Nate and I used to be able to communicate with each other even through silence. Despite it, because of it, whichever way you want to look at it, neither of us had the words available to talk about Nora and that was how we communicated, through the understanding that she was there, always, in every word we said and every word we didn't, every word we couldn't. But it had been years since that was the case and, by then, whenever we saw each other, whenever we spoke, the silences in between had no give to them. They felt like gaps, misunderstandings, another hole to fall down, another hole to be filled.

I didn't have any cake. I'd long stopped eating at those kinds of things. The food was a necessary distraction, it gave your hands something to do while you tried to figure out exactly what it was you were meant to be doing, but I could never take a bite, my stomach twisting and turning, my throat closing up as soon as I raised anything to my lips. Inevitably I just ended up carrying a loaded plate of food around before finding somewhere to stash it. No one stayed too long that time though. No one wanted to. We'd had ten years of these things after all, and were just marking time now. When she first went missing, even in the year or two after, there was still something close to hope at the vigils and memorials but, after ten years, that was just a way of saying *look at how much time has passed, look at how we're still thinking of you*. Nora was gone, and it was simply something we had to do to remind ourselves that we were still here.

Eventually I followed Nate and the rest of the party into the lake house where everyone had decamped to. I would have preferred to have left without even a goodbye, but my parents had attempted to raise me better than that, and besides, they'd driven me there. I helped myself to a coffee in the small kitchen, wishing it was a little later in the day, wishing there was wine instead, or better yet, vodka, but grateful for the pocket of extra time it gave me away from everyone. The cabin was small, just one large room with a utility room off the kitchen, the front door opening onto the living room, and even though there weren't that many of us, it was still too many. I clutched at my coffee cup, waiting for my hands to warm up, waiting for the crushing feeling inside my chest to ease up.

Noelle was sat on the arm of one of the couches, picking at a thread that was coming loose on the sleeve of her sweater. Ten years younger that Nora, she'd turned seventeen just a few months earlier, the same age Nora had been when she went missing. I stared at her, looking instinctively, automatically, for the similarities between the two of them as I always did when I saw Elle. I didn't have to look for long. Her hair was lighter, and she wore it longer than Nora had, and her eyes were the same brown as Nate's rather than Nora's arctic blue, but Nora was there still. They had the same mouth and jawline, the same shaped eyes and long neck. I knew that when Elle stood up she'd be almost as tall as Nora was, but for now Leo was leaning over her, talking intently as Elle refused to meet his eye. I joined them with my coffee, maneuvering carefully around Nate as I did so, neither of us saying a word.

"Maddie," Elle said, her eyes meeting mine, looking grateful, I thought, or maybe even a little pleased.

"Hey, you. How you doing?"

We hugged and her body felt small in my arms even as she pulled quickly away.

"Oh, you know. Not great."

I don't why I kept asking people how they were, to be honest. I hated that question even on a good day, let alone that day.

I nodded and slid my gaze towards Leo, who raised his eyebrows at me and asked: "How long are you in town for, Mads?"

"I have to get back tomorrow."

"How you finding being back in Madison? You're doing a PhD, right?"

Yet another question I dreaded even more than "how are you doing?"

I coughed through my coffee and shook my head. "No. I quit, actually. A while ago. I'm working in the communications department now. At the university."

"Oh. How's that going?"

"It's fine. It has its moments."

"Sure," Leo said nodding, polite, polite, "well, it's a job, right?"

I looked at him, trying to decipher his words but he just smiled, nice and easy, his face wide open.

"They all have their moments. Last call out we got was to save Mr. Hetherington from himself. He'd locked himself out of his house and decided it was best to just sleep off whatever he'd drunk in his car, but the neighbors were worried about him, so they called us. Probably almost died of hypothermia, but what are you gonna do, that's the job, right?"

It would have been too generous to describe Hetherington as the town drunk. He was simply a guy who got drunk and happened to live in town. I wondered at what Leo was complaining about though. You become a cop in a small town, and what else do you expect from life except fishing drunks out of ditches and pushing cars out of snow drifts? Apart from a former classmate who'd been missing for ten years, of course. It took me a while to realize that he was throwing me a tentative bone. I wasn't where I'd expected to be in my life, but there had been days, hell, there had been months and years, where getting to even where I was then would have looked like something close to a miracle. And when it came down to it, none of us were really where we had expected to be.

I returned Leo's smile, or at least tried to and said: "Well, you'll be running the place soon though, right?"

Leo rolled his eyes towards the other side of the room where his father, Patrick Moody, stood, replete in his chief of police uniform, too big for this room. "Yeah, just as soon as the boss retires."

"Hey," I said to Elle, grabbing at her bicep, "is Jenna here? I haven't met her yet."

Elle shook her head. "No, she couldn't make it."

"That's a shame." Talking to Elle felt like talking through a mask or as though I was trying on another character. I tried so much harder around her than anyone else. Not because I wanted her to like me or anything, but being around her made me act the way everyone else seemed to act around me. Drawing me out, pushing for information, wide concerned eyes, forced cheer; I went the whole nine yards with Elle even as I knew how much she must have been hating it. I couldn't help it though, the blanket of concern that overwhelmed me whenever I saw her. I so desperately wanted her to be okay, even while I came to accept the fact I never would be. Hypocrisy doesn't always come from a bad place, just a confused one.

My efforts normally paid off with Elle though. It would be a stretch to describe her as bubbly and I hate the word vivacious, but her infectious energy was hard to ignore normally. She'd been all of seven when Nora disappeared and, in some ways, I think her youth had shielded her from the worst of it. Sometimes I wonder if it would have been easier—better—if it had happened when we were all younger. Or older. There's something about seventeen, those soft teenage years when you think you're made of sterner stuff but are really still filled with cotton wool. It imprinted itself so hard, so firmly into and on to me because I was so malleable, so yielding. At seventeen you think you're done, fully formed; but really you've barely even got started. It was like a handprint in wet concrete pushed in at just the right moment and then made permanent.

"You talking about Jenna Fairfax?" Leo asked, and Elle nodded.

"How do you know Jenna?" I asked.

"I've been coaching the hockey team for a while now. Me and Bright. Fairfax is one of our best players. On the girls' team, I mean."

I raised an eyebrow. "Of course."

"Elle's getting pretty good too these days. Most elegant player on the ice what with all that figure skating," Leo said.

Elle's face seemed to pale even further, and her lips pulled back in a grimace as if she was about to speak before she stopped herself.

"Elle, you OK?" I asked.

"Actually I'm feeling a little sick. I might go upstairs and lie down."

"Okay," I said, watching as she placed her glass of water on the coffee table and pushed through the crowd to the staircase.

"She's taking this pretty hard, huh?" Leo said.

"I don't know. Maybe she's really just not feeling well."

"What about you?"

"You'd think I'd be used to it by now," I said.

"It's a rough thing to have to get used to, Mads."

I shook my head, not disagreeing with him, just trying to shake something loose. To get to the root of what made it all feel so disturbingly empty. "It's just not getting any easier. Sometimes I wish we'd stop with all the commemorations and memorials. It's not like any of us have to be reminded, right? It's like we're trying to prove something, but what are we proving? Look around, there's what, sixteen, seventeen people here?" I was talking in a strained rush, my voice low and jagged, and Leo had to step towards me to hear properly. "What good does this do any of us? All I see is us getting older and Nora staying the same."

Leo's brow was furrowed as he leaned over me, his hand stretching out to rest warmly on my shoulder; but someone behind me spoke before Leo had a chance to answer.

"You can go home whenever you want, Mads. No one's keeping you from leaving," Nate said, his voice stripped of emotion, warmth.

My hands tightened around my mug of coffee which had started to go cold. "That's not what I meant. I want to be here; I just wish we didn't *have* to be."

"That's not what I heard."

"Well, maybe you shouldn't have been eavesdropping."

Nate's jaw clenched as his gaze shifted almost imperceptibly so that he was now staring just to the left of my face.

"All I'm saying is, I wish one goodbye was enough. Or I wish we even got a goodbye. But we don't even get that luxury, so we have to keep saying goodbye over and over and over again and it just feels less and less real the more that time passes," I said in a rush.

"It's been ten years. You think we should have just ignored that? Why'd you even come if you were so violently opposed to the idea of a ten-year memorial?"

"I'm not 'violently opposed.' I'm tired I guess. I'm just really, really tired."

"Well, then I'd suggest you go home and get some rest, Mads. Get some beauty sleep."

I couldn't remember when or why things had got so bad between me and Nate. One day he was the person I called when I couldn't call anyone else, and the next—well, I couldn't even tell you. He'd simply stopped returning my calls and eventually I'd stopped making them. But he'd never spoken to me like that, with such open hostility I could feel it pounding off him, such shortness that his words threw me so much I literally stepped backwards and onto Leo's foot.

But Nate didn't stick around to hear my response, even if I'd been able to somehow stumble across one; he simply slipped past me and into the crowd, joining his mother in the kitchen.

It could have been a concerned comment, I suppose, something sincere and almost loving, "go home, get some sleep." But it wasn't and the sudden realization of how little he thought of me then roared in my ears, drowning out everything else.

It took me a while to realize Leo was talking to me, saying something soothing but ultimately meaningless: How difficult this was for Nate, how he'd been having a hard time, how difficult today was for everyone. I didn't need Leo to tell me any of that; I knew it all already, implicitly. It was in evidence everywhere you looked in that room, and it lived inside me that day just as it did every day, but casual cruelty had never been a part of my relationship with Nate, had never formed an integral part of our language. If our silences had no give to them anymore, then neither did our words. They were brittle, ready to break at the slightest of touches.

I tried to think back to when Nate was the person I rang in the middle of the night, to when his voice was the only thing I could bear to listen to. Just like everything else then it felt so long ago, a lifetime ago. It had been years since I'd seen his name flash across the screen of my phone and, just as with Nora, my relationship to him had gradually been reduced to snowy memorials, stuffy rooms, and stilted small talk.

I took a sip of coffee, while Leo talked at me, and balked at its temperature. Depositing the mug on the coffee table I made my excuses to Leo and headed towards Ange, who was standing on the edge of a conversation between a variety of parents, not joining in. Her eyes were glazed as she drank her coffee and she failed to notice me as I approached.

"Hey," I said, shaking her out of her reverie, "when are you heading off?"

Ange looked at me and shrugged. "Probably in twenty minutes or so, I guess?"

"No, I mean when are you heading back home to Madison?"

"Oh, not till tomorrow morning. I'm meant to be having dinner with my parents tonight."

"I can still drive back with you, right?"

"Yeah, of course. So, have you talked to Nate yet? How's he doing?"

"He told me I should go home to catch up on my beauty sleep," I said while reaching for Ange's coffee cup and taking a sip.

"Wow. How caring of him. When did you guys last speak?"

"Last year's memorial, I guess? Definitely haven't heard from him since then. I'm trying to work out what I did to offend him so badly, but I think it might just be my very presence." I tried to make my voice sound light, indifferent, but failed. The truth was, I really was trying to figure out what I'd done, where it had all gone so horribly wrong.

Ange made a face at me, grabbing back her coffee. "You know that's not it."

"Do I? We're not exactly friends anymore. If we ever were."

"You're friends. Don't overanalyze this, it's just a weird day."

"Yeah, I know. I'd say something trite, like 'can you believe it's been ten years?' but mostly I just feel old. And tired."

"You know what I keep doing? I keep looking at Noah and thinking that he was a baby when she went missing. That's what I can't believe. That his entire life has been the same length of time as Nora being gone."

I looked around for Noah, unable to find him, and wondered if he'd gone upstairs to join his sister. He'd been almost a year old when Nora disappeared. He had no memory of her except the one we'd built for him in her absence, and I wondered what that looked like. What that could possibly look like. We'd spent the past ten years of our lives at events like this, memorializing someone we loved, someone we missed, but for Noah this had effectively become his life. He had no memories that weren't connected to, and hijacked by, Nora's disappearance. At the very least I could look back to when she wasn't gone, but for Noah, it was all he'd ever known. I thought back to the day he was born, and realized his birthday was coming up. February 14th.

***

Nora's pissed because the birth of her baby brother is ruining her Valentine's Day plans, so we're lying on the couch in her parents' living room, illegally eating marshmallows. "I don't know what they think they're doing," she says, widening her eyes at me, "having a baby at their age. It's gross. Plus, you just know this is a save-the-marriage baby. It's so obvious."

"That's not fair, your parents always seem pretty happy to me. And your mom's not that old," I say, but Nora's eyes just get wider.

"Oh, really? You know the doctor said Mom had a geriatric womb?"

Nora starts laughing, and I can't help joining her, throwing a marshmallow at her head at the same time. But she catches it easily, popping it in her mouth and starting to chew while saying: "She said she almost stabbed him with a scalpel or whatever."

"That sounds about right."

"Yeah, as soon as I reach, like, fifty, I'm gonna start carrying a knife around to threaten people who call me 'old' with. No one will be able to arrest me though. I'll just be the eccentric, kinda scary old lady."

"It's the perfect plan."

"Right? I'll get away with so much."

Elle comes into the room then, complaining about being hungry, and Nora holds out her arms to her, beckoning her to the couch. She hops up to join us, snuggling up in between us, and Nora starts to feed her marshmallows, daring Elle to keep her mouth open while she attempts to toss them in there. "You excited to meet your baby brother, smelly head?" she asks, and Elle scowls, her face a picture of cartoonish displeasure. She is not excited to meet her younger brother. Nora pulls her onto her lap, squeezing tight and says: "You know I wasn't excited to meet you either," which makes Elle turn her head towards her older sister in shock. "Yeah, I thought you were going to ruin everything for me because I loved being the baby and I loved being the center of attention. But then I met you, and you were just the coolest, even though you cried, like, all the time, plus you thought I was awesome, which made me feel awesome, and now you're my best friend."

"I thought Maddie was your best friend," Elle says, looking over at me suspiciously.

"Well, sure. But you're my other best friend."

Elle doesn't look all that convinced, but I smile at her and she slowly takes another marshmallow from the bag and begins to chew thoughtfully on it.

Their parents hadn't arrived back with Noah until much later, and Katherine had wanted to let Elle stay sleeping, but Nora had crept into her room and woken her. I could still see the look of sleepy awe she had on her face when she gazed down at the baby. I wondered if Elle remembered that day at all; she'd been six, so it was plausible that she did, but I knew that I'd had to fight so hard to remember Nora any other way than being gone that sometimes those memories of her being here felt too far out of reach even for me.

"Have you spoken to Louden yet?" Ange asked, cutting through my memories.

I shook my head. Louden Winters was Nora's ex and the brother of one of our high school friends, Hale, who hadn't made

16

it to the memorial but had sent a vast bunch of lilies in her place. We'd all been friends at one point, more than friends really. A group of mismatched friends and siblings who'd grown up together from scraped knees and training wheels right through to tequila shots and heads hanging over the toilet bowl. I'd once been as close to Hale as I was to Ange; but then Louden had been named as a suspect in Nora's disappearance and for some reason Hale hadn't taken too well to me accusing him of killing our friend. I'd been trying to ignore Louden's presence altogether, pretending he wasn't there, but he was six foot three, taller than most everyone else there and it had been getting harder and harder to ignore the fact that I hadn't even said hello.

"When did you last see him?" Ange asked.

"A couple of years ago at Christmas I think. At the bar. You were there."

Ange nodded. "Right, yeah. You really haven't seen him since?"

"No. Have you?" I asked, unable to keep the trace of suspicion that licked through me then out of my voice.

Ange swallowed a mouthful of coffee and nodded. "Yeah, I was in Chicago for a couple of days last year, remember? I went for a drink with him and Hale."

I raised my eyebrows, looking between Ange and Louden. "Why?"

Ange shrugged. "Why not?"

I stayed staring at Louden for longer than I meant to, trying to arrange my thoughts in a way that made sense, jigsaw pieces scrambling to find their mate and failing. I knew what I wanted to say: *because he might have killed our best friend*, and it was almost there, rising higher and higher in my chest until I pushed it down, away, saving it for myself. I wasn't allowed to say such things anymore.

It had been okay for a while, at least, the wild accusations and rampant theories. Louden's arrest had come just days after Nora went missing, one of the main suspects, but he'd provided an

17

alibi and been released without charge. It hadn't stopped my own suspicions of course, and neither had it stalled the small-town gossip, but all these years later there was something childish about those words, an intense naiveté that I wasn't allowed to indulge in anymore. They were words from another life, another lifetime, the one right after she went missing. Nevertheless, cold sweat pricked at my skin all of a sudden, the airless room stuffy with bodies, my own body still cold from the world outside as Louden turned towards me, feeling my stare, liquid brown eyes catching light. He lifted his chin in my direction and I let out a heavy breath before turning back to Ange.

"What did he have to say for himself?" I asked, my attempt at small talk still managing to sound like an accusation.

"The usual. He'd just started seeing someone, but I don't know if it stuck."

"Lucky her."

"Mads," Ange said, warning lacing her voice.

"What? All I'm saying is he's a bad boyfriend, that's all."

"That was over ten years ago. People change."

It was something I wanted to believe, desperately, that people change. And maybe I did believe it, just with certain caveats; that change was glacial, imperceptible, and when it did come it didn't necessarily mean anyone had changed for the better. It seemed to me as though it was the world that kept changing, often with a loud, deafening crack as life tore itself apart, and we were all left struggling to keep up. Not all of us managed to. I was testament to that; I was still struggling to keep up with the thundercrack that had torn through our lives ten years earlier and led us all there, to that room on a snowy day.

As I stood there, just waiting for the day to end, waiting for that heavy, empty feeling to lessen just slightly, even though I knew it wouldn't, that it probably never would, I couldn't possibly have known that another crack was coming, waiting to tear us all apart yet again. That less than twenty-four hours later, Noelle would be dead, and I would be left once again, breathless, desperate, trying to make sense of a world that seemed determined to leave me behind, too broken and battered to even try and catch up.

CHAPTER THREE

I woke the next morning to the same shattering glass and a feeling in my chest like I couldn't breathe, the same way I'd woken up the day before, the same way I'd been waking up for the past ten years. The weight of the memorial the day before still hadn't lifted on top of which I had a slight hangover. I wished it felt different, I wished I felt different, but whatever I did, whatever I tried, nothing ever seemed to change. Or maybe I wasn't trying hard enough; there were definitely people out there who would prescribe to that theory. As if she knew I was thinking of her, my phone began to buzz insistently on my bedside table, the illuminated screen telling me Serena was calling.

"Hey," I said, pushing myself to sit up in bed as I spoke.

"Hey," she said, her voice sounding a little breathless down the line. She was on her way to work. "How are you? How did yesterday go? Are you doing okay?" The questions came short and sharp; rat-a-tat-tat, like incredibly efficient gunfire.

I closed my eyes and took a deep breath, trying to keep my voice steady. "It was fine, I guess. It was … the same as it ever is. Hard. Cold. Strange."

"I can't believe it's been ten years, Mads. It's insane. I really wish I could have been there for you. For Nora too." Serena had modulated her voice, gentle, gentle, but there was wind whipping around her as she walked down the street, traffic noise practically drowning her out, so I had to strain to hear her.

"I know, it's fine. It was all fine. Ange was there, we stuck together."

"Mom said you guys went out for a drink after?"

I rolled my eyes up towards the ceiling. My mom and sister sharing notes about me wasn't breaking news however, so I let it slide.

"Was Nate there?" Serena continued.

"At the memorial, yeah; he didn't come for a drink."

There was a little beat, the briefest of pauses before: "How was he? How was that?"

I held my breath before answering, one, two, three, four, before remembering that what you were actually meant to do was count to ten while breathing to calm yourself down, not cut off the supply of oxygen for ten seconds. When I finally let the breath out, the sigh that emanated from me seemed to fill my entire bedroom.

"It was about as awkward as I thought it would be," I said at last, "actually, you know what, it was worse than I thought it would be. He seems to actively dislike me now. I don't know what it is I'm meant to have done, but there it is."

Serena made a sound I had a little difficulty translating and then said: "He needs to get over himself. You'd think after everything that's happened he could at least be nice to you."

"It was the tenth anniversary of his sister going missing, Serena. I think we could cut him some slack," I said, allowing Nate more sympathy than I'd given him the day before, always on the defensive when it came to him.

"Yeah, and it was the tenth anniversary of *your* best friend going missing! He could cut you some slack."

I couldn't argue with her there and she soon arrived at her L stop, so we hung up, Serena promising to call me later, and

21

getting me to promise to call our younger sister, Cordy, even though we both knew I wouldn't. The room felt colder, and I felt older the moment her voice left it. As I started to think about what the day actually meant—about Nora having been gone for ten years, about ten years of limbo, living in purgatory, not knowing where she was or whether she was alive—I also felt the old familiar weight begin to grow. It started in my chest, always, a boulder I couldn't budge, a wall I couldn't climb over or knock down. Trying to ignore it, and my phone still in my hand, I did what I did most mornings and began trawling through Instagram, anaesthetizing myself with photos of coffee, home décor tips and puppies. Should I have been doing something more profound on the morning of the official anniversary of my best friend going missing? Maybe.

It wasn't enough though, not nearly a big enough distraction, and so I started to wonder what Nora's family were doing, whether they would mark the day in some way, or if they felt the day before had been enough. There was no grave to visit, not for Nora. Without a body Nora had never been buried but she still left her mark. She was their mark and she was my mark. Maybe we all have them, I don't know. Maybe I just got mine a little earlier in life than usual. But she was. She was my mark. Indelible. Permanent. Ineradicable. In some ways I was thankful for the constancy of it; I knew she'd never be fully gone as long as I was still here. Maybe that was why the pane of glass I dreamt of every night and could feel slipping from my hands almost every morning kept haunting me; because, in some ways, I didn't want to wake up to anything else because the moment I did I'd know she was truly gone.

So, I lay in bed and imagined the Altmans slowly waking up, getting dressed and gathering for breakfast. I could see them walking down the staircase that was still gazed down upon by dozens of photos of Nora; I could see them settling down at the large table in the kitchen, coffee smells trailing through the house, snow falling outside the window just as it was falling outside mine. More likely, Noelle and Noah were getting themselves ready for school while Nate packed up to head home to Texas. Jonathan had probably already left for work, and Katherine would still be in bed, staring as blankly up at her ceiling as I had when I first woke up.

I couldn't have known that Noelle wasn't there, that Nate was the first to realize, that he tapped gently at his mother's bedroom door, had to shake her to get her attention and ask where his younger sister was. That when he rang Elle's phone it went straight to voicemail and a bubble of panic began to build somewhere near his duodenum, and Noah looked on, his wide brown eyes taking everything in. That Nate rang his dad next who was on his way to his law practice in Madison, where he spent most of the week, and that Jonathan couldn't pick up because he hadn't set up his hands free that morning because he didn't want to speak to anyone that day at least not yet. That eventually Nate rang Elle's girlfriend, Jenna, who said she hadn't seen her since Saturday, and then finally he rang his buddy, Leo, who was already at the scene and suddenly that bubble of panic popped except it turned into a tidal wave rather than disappearing into air and he had to struggle to keep up with what Leo was saying because it couldn't possibly be true.

It might have been around that time that my own phone rang again, Ange's name popping up on my screen. She told me she'd be over to pick me up in an hour to take me back to Madison, and I pushed my covers off, body aching, limbs too heavy, preparing myself for a shower.

I suddenly couldn't wait to get back to Madison, not because there was anything waiting for me there, but because waking up in that house, in the exact same spot I'd woken up ten years before, only to hear the news that Nora was missing, had too much poetic symmetry for me to handle at any one moment. My teenage bedroom rang with her memory, every inch of that room simply sang with her presence, low and clear, piercing; there was nowhere I could look that didn't bear some trace of her. Perhaps I should have relished that. Especially on that morning. But really all I wanted was to get away from it all. I didn't need to have the memory of Nora screaming at me from every wall and every corner to remember her any better, to miss her anymore than I already did. I wanted to hide somewhere deep and dark where Nora had never been, and do my very best to leapfrog over that day. But that was never going to be a possibility. Not that day.

I showered and dressed in the same clothes I'd been wearing the day before for no reason other than when I'd packed to go home I hadn't been able to think beyond the memorial. Mom had already left for work by the time I made it down to the kitchen, and my dad, who was a retired school principal—my high school principal, in fact—was sat in the breakfast nook drinking coffee. The familiarity of my family home, the sight of Dad reading the newspaper, the muffled light of the kitchen as snow crowded the window pane, crouched over me as it always did when I was back there: Here was my home, a reluctant sanctuary, and yet I did not feel safe. I never did.

"Morning, Mads," Dad said, glancing up from the paper as I wandered past to help myself to coffee and maybe even a bowl of cereal.

"Morning."

"When are you heading back?"

"Soon. Ange will be over to pick me up in an hour or so."

Dad nodded, sipping at his coffee as I leaned back against the kitchen counter and took a long drag from my mug.

"When are you planning to take your car in to get fixed?"

"I can't afford it," I said shrugging, "not right now anyway."

"We can lend you the money."

"It's fine, Dad. I just need to save a little money and I'll get it done."

24

"But how will you get around until then?"

"I can just get the bus, it's not the end of the world."

Dad looked out the window at the snow and then back at me, an eyebrow raised in skepticism. "You can borrow the Explorer if you want? I don't use it so much anymore anyway."

I shook my head. "Dad, if I left you without a car you'd basically be stranded whenever Mom left the house. It's fine, don't worry about it."

"But the bus—"

"Is a perfectly legitimate form of public transportation."

"Okay, okay, I get it. I'll back off."

"Thank you."

There was a slight pause while Dad weighed out his words and said: "You know your mom and I are always happy to—" his voice trailed off but his words still managed to fill the room, unspoken yet heard loud and clear.

I'd lost count of the number of times we'd had this conversation. It wasn't always that exact conversation, of course; it wasn't always about my broken-down, practically worthless VW. Sometimes it was about rent or my meds, occasionally about the cost of therapy and health insurance. It was always there, the helping hand, perennially extended out towards me along with the tendrils of guilt that inevitably accompanied it whenever I took it. But guilt pounded its way through my life, relentless and as all-encompassing as rain in a summer storm, regardless of whether I accepted the help that was offered me.

"I know, Dad." I said at last.

"Okay, I just thought it needed to be said. Because you've been doing really well recently, but if you need a little help with money, then that's okay. And I know yesterday must have been hard for you, not to mention today, but we just want you to stay on the right track." He said it all in a slight rush, even though he normally spoke slowly, thoughtfully. He'd obviously worked up to this a bit, not wanting to spook me, as if I was a highly

25

strung racehorse. I wondered if he and Mom had discussed it before she left for work that morning, or maybe even the previous night when I stumbled in through the front door, a little worse for wear.

I thought about every bitten back word I'd never spoken to my parents, and every catapult line I'd thrown out at them and wished I'd pulled back on. It had been a long ten years, and I couldn't help feeling that I'd made it even longer. The guilt I felt over losing Nora had seeped out, into, and over everything, and eventually evolved into a guilt about feeling guilty; hell, it might even have been guilt over having any feelings at all. There's no manual for grief, and there certainly isn't one for being someone a missing person leaves behind; but however you were meant to act in the face of the impossible, I was pretty sure that I'd failed. Everything I did was filtered through that failure, grimy with that guilt, and as much as I hated asking for help, I seemed to be in need of it, all the time. I wanted, desperately, to get to a place where that helping hand didn't immediately feel like a punch to the gut, but I had no idea how to get there, no idea if I ever would.

I nodded, staring into my coffee cup. I could feel the grief building in me. The small round rock of loss that lived somewhere around my abdomen and rose through my stomach and lungs, and up through my esophagus until it stayed somewhere right at the back of my throat, threatening tears and an inability to breathe. Sometimes it rose even further and lived for days inside my head, growing moss, clouding my thoughts and vision. Those were the days my limbs felt too heavy to get out of bed. Those were the days that had taught me that sometimes it was easier to say nothing at all. I had to be careful here, to maneuver myself around all the ways I might trip up, or fall down, or however you want to put it, because if I didn't, if I didn't look for the signs and pay attention, that rock would get bigger and bigger and heavier and heavier and I wouldn't make it out of the house, let alone back to Madison.

"You want me to make you breakfast?" Dad added gently once it became obvious I didn't have it in me to reply.

I shook my head again, this time a little more forcefully and said: "I'll just have cereal."

I was sitting in the breakfast nook eating my cereal when Ange called me again.

"Hey, I'm just finishing up my breakfast," I said on picking up, assuming she was parked outside somewhere waiting for me to come out, "you want to come inside and wait for me here?"

"Maddie," she said, her voice a breathless straight line.

"Yeah?" I said, suddenly sitting up a little straighter. There was something about the shape of her voice that instantly shook me, old memories rattling around in my ribcage making my heartbeat pick up.

"I … I—"

"Ange, what's going on? What's happened? Are you okay?" My voice was snappy and sharp, but I couldn't help it, I knew where conversations like that went and my fear translated to frustration all too easily.

"I was just driving through town to come get you and all these police cars passed me."

There was no way I could have possibly known, so of course I thought of Nora, blindly following my memory back, racing those cop cars as fast as they could go to a morning so vivid it could have happened yesterday.

***

I wake up slowly, one side of my face still smashed into the cool blue of my pillow case. When my eyes open the room is an even, cold grey. Ange is already up, the bed empty and the curtains opened halfway, not that it's made much difference. Outside the world is one single color. White.

27

I reach for my phone, checking to see if there are any calls or texts from Nora, but there aren't any. There's one from Nate but I don't read it, not yet anyway. I can smell hot butter and coffee, and I pull on my bathrobe and slippers before heading downstairs to the kitchen. Cordy is sat in the breakfast nook, her back to the window, feet on the bench and knees pulled to her chest while she texts someone feverishly and almost completely ignores me as I walk into the room. Instead of my mom at the stove, Ange hovers over the skillet, spatula in her right hand, waiting to turn the French toast over. She's still dressed in her pajamas, one of my hoodies pulled over her T-shirt to keep her warm. Mom walks in through the garage door, waving a bottle of maple syrup triumphantly in one hand.

"I knew we had more somewhere," she says, closing the door behind her, "disaster averted."

"Since when do we put guests to work?" I ask, waving my hand towards Ange, and then staring pointedly at my sisters.

"Ange isn't a guest, honey," Mom says, squeezing Ange to her side, and kissing her on the side of her head, "she's family."

"Yeah, she's family. And family makes family breakfast," Cordy says.

"You're all disgusting. And Ange, I apologize."

Ange laughs and flips over four slices of bread in the huge cast iron pan, one by one.

"Have you heard from Nora?" I say to her, helping myself to a cup of coffee from the machine.

She shakes her head. "No, nothing. Have you?"

"Not since before I left work last night. You think we should be worried?"

"I dunno. It's not like her, but maybe she went up to the lake house and forgot to take her charger or something?"

"Yeah, maybe."

Just then I hear the sound of the front door opening, and my dad's low chatter as he welcomes whoever it is that's just appeared.

They walk into the kitchen together, Dad hanging back in the doorway as Bright enters the room. He's running the rim of his hat through his fingers as Mom smiles at him.

"Michael, what are you doing here? You know Serena's back in Chicago, right?"

Bright nods his head but doesn't answer my mom, instead looking from me to Ange who's still studying the progress of her French toast.

"Maddie, Angela, have either of you heard from Nora today?"

We look at one another, Ange's face suddenly slack, and I shake my head at Bright. "No, we were just talking about her. Neither of us have heard from her since last night. Why?"

"When last night?" *Bright asks.*

"Um, she left a voicemail on my phone." *I pull out my phone from the pocket of my bathrobe and head to recent calls.* "At about 7:30. 7:27 to be exact."

"What's this about, Bright?" *Ange asks.*

"Nora took her dad's car last night, and it was found earlier this morning, unlocked, keys in the ignition, just off Old Highway 51."

"Yeah, so?" *I ask.* "Where's Nora?"

"We don't know."

I could feel the same grip of panic and loss that had folded and tightened itself around me ten years before when I said to Ange: "Where were the police cars going?"

"They were headed towards the old highway, so I turned round and followed them because—" Because that was where Nora's car had been found, and Ange was a reporter and certain habits are hard to break.

"Are you there now? What's going on? Is it Nora?"

"Mads, it's not Nora. It's not Nora, but there's a body and I think … I think it's Noelle."

All the air I had in my body was pulled out of me and replaced with lead, or granite, or concrete, or something heavy and immovable that dragged me down, down, down. My vision swam, images of Elle rising to the surface. She'd looked so young at the memorial and yet so weary, the weight of the world crowding her shoulders. How could this be happening again? A little over a week earlier I'd met her at CJ's, treating her to a hot chocolate which had always been her favorite. She'd been filled with a razor-edge energy, cracking jokes and telling me stories about her girlfriend, Jenna, but then something had shifted in her and she'd started asking me questions about Nora. I'd put it down to the anniversary coming up so soon and had been happy to answer them. Normally when anyone talked about Nora I clenched up, went into lockdown, but it was different with Elle. I didn't have to guess what her motives were when she brought Nora up, unlike with so many other people who just wanted to indulge in their morbid curiosity, to gossip about a missing girl as though she were a celebrity spiraling out of control.

I closed my eyes and tried to keep that picture of her in my mind: sitting in a booth at CJ's, skimming the edge of her mug with her forefinger so that a pile of whipped cream and mini marshmallows appeared there before she stuck it in her mouth, while I groaned in faux disapproval and she grinned wickedly at me. I wanted to hold it there forever, but I knew how quickly that memory, that moment, would be eroded, degraded, twisted and turned into something else. I knew how quickly she'd go from Elle—the girl I'd helped teach how to ice skate and roller-blade and who'd hated to lose at Scrabble but still tried her best to win every time—to yet another person I'd be forced to mourn.

I was struggling to keep my head above the water when Ange said: "Mads, are you there?"

"Yeah," I gasped. "I'm here."

She talked me through what she was looking at: two cop cars and an ambulance. She recognized most everyone at the scene, including Bright and Leo and Leo's father, Chief Moody. She knew better than to ask me if I was okay, and I knew better than to ask her. She spoke slowly, taking her time, but each word was weighed, freighted down and heavy. She'd spent a couple of years on the crime desk of a Milwaukee paper when she first graduated, but had since moved to the news desk, where if a grisly or interesting crime came up, it was invariably scooped up by one of her colleagues still working on crime. Every time she'd had to cover the death or murder of a woman or girl I saw Nora was all she had said to me at the time; it was all she needed to say. But she was clearly trying to pick up the pieces of her training there, still a reporter at heart, even as she tried to make sense of something that would never make any sense.

"And you're sure it's Elle?" I asked eventually, my voice small and young-sounding in the enveloping warmth of my parents' kitchen.

"I don't know for sure obviously, but I overheard the cops talking. They all know her, Mads, they know what she looks like. It must be her."

I nodded, even though she couldn't see. There wasn't a single officer on our police force who wouldn't know who Noelle Altman was.

"I have to go, Leo's coming over. I think he's going to ask me to leave."

"Okay," I said.

There was a small beat and then, "Should I still come over?"

"Yes," I said, even though both of us knew we wouldn't be leaving Forest View anytime soon.

I sat there for a long time, the morning seeping away from me until Ange arrived and told me what had happened after we'd hung up. Leo had been very proper, apparently. Refused to give her any details, saying they couldn't confirm anything until the forensics team arrived from Wausau. When she'd asked him if it was really Elle, he'd glanced back towards the body—*the body*—and said he couldn't say, but she said she knew.

31

I was having trouble getting to grips with what she was saying though, and although I could barely trust myself to speak, I said: "You're sure? You're really sure it's Elle?"

Ange took a deep breath and seemed to steady herself. "I can't be 100 per cent sure, but I heard them say her name. Why would they do that if it wasn't Elle?"

I didn't have an answer for her but my mind was a storm of other possibilities, other reasons, any other reason but that one which was so impossible I just couldn't contemplate it. After everything that had happened, after ten years of missing Nora, of Nora being missing, how could it possibly be happening again? As we sat there I felt the past ten years diminish, shrink down to nothing so that we could have been seventeen again, Ange and I, stood in this very same room, as Bright explained to us that Nora was missing and we had to tell him anything and everything—every last detail—of the last time we'd seen or spoken to her, because every little thing mattered now. I thought about Elle's pale face the day before, her quiet voice. She'd looked sick, or sickened by something, and I hated myself for not having pushed her more, dug deeper, delved further and figured out what—beyond the obvious—was wrong. And I realized then that I'd already accepted it, that I was already thinking of her in the past tense, and the steady pounding of guilt and grief began to build and build until it filled up the whole room.

Eventually, Ange looked down at her phone, which she'd been passing from hand to hand, twirling it distractedly between her fingers. "I need to call work," she said, her voice strained, and I realized I needed to do the same.

"To tell them you won't be coming in?"

"To tell them … to tell them about this."

I don't know why I was so shocked. She was a reporter after all, but still I could feel my eyes involuntarily widen, and watched as Ange bit down on her lower lip, maintaining my gaze.

"This is big, Mads. This is going to be really, really big."

"You mean for your career?" I said, wishing as soon as the words had come out that I could take them back.

Ange slammed her phone down onto the table. "You know that's not what I meant. Jesus Christ, Mads, could you at least give me some credit?"

"I know, I'm sorry. I didn't mean it."

Ange looked at me warily. "You meant it a little."

"No. I didn't. I think after everything that happened with Nora with the press, my natural instincts kicked in, that's all."

Ange took a deep breath, and sighed heavily, weighing down the air between us. "If I don't call in about this, I'll be made to look like just about the worst, most inefficient reporter of all time. We're talking about the younger sister of Nora Altman being found dead ten years to the day, and in the same spot that Nora's car was abandoned."

"I know, Ange," I said nodding, really trying to mean it.

"And if *I'm* writing about it, then maybe it could be just that little bit better this time?" she said, although it came out sounding like a question, as if she herself didn't quite believe it.

"It's possible," I said slowly, although I too didn't believe it. When Ange first told me she was going to major in journalism I couldn't help but see it as a kind of reaction to everything that happened when Nora went missing.

The first time a reporter knocked on my door Nora had been missing for just under a week. The local paper had been covering the disappearance since the beginning, but it took a while for a bigger paper to take notice. But once they did, they didn't let go. Not for a long time. She'd been a reporter for a Madison daily— Ange worked for its rival now—and she'd tried to get out of me whatever it was the Altmans had refused to give her. When I too had refused to talk, she'd described me as "pained and pale" and had questioned why it was that Nora's best friends weren't willing to talk about her disappearance. What were we hiding? What did we know? Didn't we want to help spread the word about our missing friend?

It would be worse this time: I already knew that much. Ten years was a long time and not only would there be reporters and well-meaning chat show hosts pondering over this sad, tragic mystery, but now anyone with an internet connection could join in the fun too.

I wondered if Elle's family knew yet, if their day of remembrance had been interrupted by something so familiar the remnants of it were still strewn around their lives. I didn't even have to imagine their faces as they were told the worst; I'd seen it before. The image of Nate with red-rimmed, sleepless eyes, his shoulders shaking uncontrollably reared up at me and I looked down at my phone, almost convinced that, despite everything, there would be a message from him, but there was nothing. I could hear the hollow knock at their front door as the Chief stood outside in the gently falling snow and could see as Nate answered, already knowing the worst from Leo and yet still unable to quite believe it. Katherine would be in her bathrobe still, knuckles white as she gripped the hallway bannister, refusing to break down, unable to speak, her wide brown eyes drowned in exhaustion, all color drained. The only one I couldn't see in all of it was Noah. It was only in his mind that the memory of Nora's disappearance wouldn't be playing in full technicolor, reliving the same moments again and again, trying to make sense of how it was all happening again.

My heart clenched, a cold, iron fist squeezing tight, the shock of it no less bright, no less big because I'd felt it before. We'd all been there before and yet familiarity doesn't always mean comfort. Sometimes what we fear the most is the unknown. But other times, knowing what's coming, the shape of it, the taste, the smell, is so much worse. How it sets the world on edge, blurs the edges of your vision, peels back layers of skin only to reveal more and more of the same damn thing. Sometimes, knowing what's coming doesn't save you, it just sets your heart pounding as you teeter on the edge, waiting for that rush of air before the earth rises up to greet you.

CHAPTER FOUR

I didn't make it back to Madison of course. I went to bed early, not because I thought I'd be able to sleep the day away but because retreat has always been my first and last form of defense. I chose something on Netflix that I'd watched a thousand times before and didn't have to think about at all, so that when my phone gently buzzed beside me I was only dimly aware of what Lorelai and Rory Gilmore were saying to one another. You would have thought that upon seeing it was Nate texting me I would have read and replied to the message immediately, but instead it stilled me, froze me even, and I had to wait a few minutes before shoring up enough courage to read it in full.

You awake?

he wrote.

My thumb hovered over the keyboard for a few seconds before I replied:

Yeah.

A few more seconds passed and then my phone started ringing in my hand. I didn't answer immediately, I couldn't. I just stared as his name lit up my phone screen and desperately tried to think of something to say when I picked up.

"Maddie?" Nate said, as soon as I answered, not waiting for me to say anything.

"Hi, Nate." There was a pause and I looked around at my room, squeezing my eyes shut in an attempt to block everything out. I got the feeling, even from down a phone line, that Nate was figuring out what to say too, how to speak. I took a deep breath and did the decent thing and spoke for him.

"I heard about Elle," I said, practically whispering in the dim bedroom light. "I'm so sorry."

I could hear his breath catch, words getting caught in his throat. Words were always getting caught, trapped, in my world. There were just some things that couldn't be said, couldn't be heard out loud, not because that would make them more real but because sometimes sharing certain pieces of you makes them less real. Or maybe it was a combination of the two, I don't know. I just know that there are times when language is made impotent.

"Nate," I said, "is there anything I can do? To help?"

I heard that catch of his breath again and then the release. "Yeah. Yes, thanks. We have to go down to the station tomorrow, to the police station, but Mom doesn't want Noah to come with us. Could you come round to sit with him?"

"Of course."

"Thanks … thank you, Maddie." There was another short pause before he added a little stiffly, "I know my mom will appreciate it."

If I hadn't already been stunned into submission by Elle's death, I would have been heartbroken over the formality of Nate's request. It was better, although only marginally, than the outright hostility I'd gotten from him the day before; but Nate talking to me as if he barely knew me, as if I barely knew him, was a special kind of heartbreak. The kind that had already begun to heal years before. It was like brushing your fingers over the remnant of a scar; your skin was raised, changed, marked and when you took the time to remind yourself of it the ache was still there, but only just. But

Elle was an open wound, blood still pumping to the site of the injury, demanding all my attention just to keep it from hemorrhaging. Hearing Nate's voice, however briefly, however stilted and formal, made that stupid old scar throb with pain though, however much I didn't want it to. The last time I'd spoken to Nate over the phone, the last time I had called him, I'd still been living in New York. I was twenty-three, over a year out of college and finding it increasingly difficult to get out of bed every morning.

***

It happens the way it always happens; shutters screaming shut over everyday life. I pull on my running shoes because they're the first pair of shoes I find, even though I haven't run in months—since I got to New York, really—and even then it was only ever something I did because my therapist and all my doctors told me I should. Exercise, they all say, as if it's some kind of magic word. Abracadabra. I grab my keys and my cell and as I'm slamming the door behind me I pull the hood of my gray sweatshirt over my head. I have to walk up the basement steps just to get to street level and when I do I can smell it, despite the city smell: the engine exhaust and the trash cans, the Chinese takeout and the pizza place a couple doors away, the dog shit and probably the human shit too. Snow. Not yet. It's not snowing yet, but it will. I shiver, from anticipation mostly but also regretting not putting on a coat warmer than my leather jacket. I start walking, hands stuffed into my jacket pockets, not even looking where I'm going, but still feeling the too-huge feeling in my chest. It's grown in the last couple days to the point that I can barely breathe. Even now, with the cold stinging my eyes, they're already smarting from almost crying anyway. I try not to cry, I really do, but I do it anyway.

The brick wall keeps rising up no matter how hard I try to knock it down, or stop it from building up in the first place, and I haven't left the apartment in days. It has taken me the last fifteen hours just to force myself out now, and the only reason I've been able to do so is because it's night, the middle of the fucking night, and no one will care who I am or where I'm going, or why I'm doing what I'm doing, or why I am the way I am. Every time I think about seeing anyone, or speaking to anyone, or having to stand at an ATM, or in line at a coffee shop, or make eye contact, or purchase milk, the scratching feeling starts up at the back of my eyes and it's as if I can actually feel my retinas. The block of granite gets bigger and bigger inside my chest, and the brick wall builds itself up again, as if I never managed to knock it down in the first place.

I take a deep breath to steady myself, and even stop, my hand resting on a black iron railing in front of a brownstone. I almost lean over, head between my legs, about-to-faint-style, but I just keep a hold of the freezing iron and let that reassure me. After a couple of seconds, or maybe even minutes, I'm able to look around me somewhat and I notice that there's a guy on the other side of the street walking in my direction. He's wearing what looks like a magenta shell-suit jacket, and corduroy trousers and shoes without socks and he kind of looks right at me, but not as if he's seen me. Just as if he were watching a movie and I was a secondary character he wasn't really all that interested in. Blank look, then move on. I feel warm relief spread through me, as though I've just done a killer pee, and begin to walk on again. I don't stop until I get to the East River.

I hunker down in my sweatshirt and jacket, trying to make myself as small as possible, hoping that it'll also make me feel warm as well. The snow smell is even stronger here, the wind whipping it up along the river and mixing with that almost-salty metallic smell you get from the water as well. I sit down on a bench and it takes me a while to realize that there are people lying under some of the other benches, presumably because it's got too cold to lie on the actual benches. One, two, three, four flakes of snow hurl themselves at my face, but if you ask me, they're not trying hard enough. I lean back on the bench and, suddenly, my hands still stuffed in my pockets, my right hand curls around my cell and then, as if it's not *four o'clock in the morning, or damn close, I'm calling Nate.*

He picks up on the seventh ring when I'm about to give in and hang up.

"'Lo."

"Nate?"

I can practically hear him sit up in bed, even across half—more than half—the country, across one time zone, thousands and thousands of miles of night, and black sky, and farmland, and mountains, and rivers, and road, and motels, and tollbooths.

"Mads?"

"Yeah."

"Are you okay?"

"I dunno, Nate." I'm sitting looking at the Manhattan skyline but it's not even like I'm looking at it at all. The slick blackness of the river looks nice though.

"Where are you?" he asks, as if we're back in Madison, back when this used to happen all the time, and I'd call, and he'd ask where I was and he'd come meet me, and sit with me, until the too-huge feeling went away or at least lessened slightly. Sometimes, he'd even spot me walking across campus and he'd come after me, without me even having to call him. I never asked if he was watching for me, or just sitting up, late at night, unable to sleep, and looking out of his window. I never asked.

"I'm looking at Manhattan. I'm in Brooklyn. Where are you?"

"I'm in bed." Oh, of course. I wonder for a second if he's lying down, or sat up next to Emmaline. I wonder if she's there, asleep next to him, dreaming. Probably not even dreaming yet. Pre-REM.

I don't say anything for a while and it feels like a full minute goes by until I hear Nate cough softly and then say: "You should go home, Maddie. Go back to bed."

But I can't tell him about how I haven't left the apartment in almost three days, and how every time I even think about doing so, my vision swims and black, black, black seems to rise up in front of my eyes.

40

"I need to ask you a favor," I say instead.

"Yeah, of course."

"Can you read it out to me? Do you have it?"

I hear him suck in his breath, even across those thousands and thousands of miles, because of course he already knows, instantly, that I'm asking him to read to me the last words Nora ever said to me. It's the last voicemail she left me—the last voicemail she left anyone—and I transcribed it years ago, worried I would lose it one day, which of course I did when I finally upgraded my cell phone. Nate's the only other person in the world who has that transcript, and this isn't the first time I've asked him to read it out to me.

"Mads."

"Please, Nate."

There's a pause before he says: "Okay. Just give me a second."

I wait while he turns on his computer I guess, and I can hear him moving about, and moving furniture around, and the sound of a Mac starting up. It takes a while of tapping and typing and then he says, with a catch in his throat: "Mads, it's me. Where—oh God, Maddie I can't do this. I'm sorry. I can't read this out."

I can hear in his voice that he's about to cry, about to break down, and I wonder to myself if I've done this purely to know that someone else is crying at the same thing, and at the same time, as me, to know that someone other than me feels the same pain. I squeeze my eyes shut.

"I'm sorry," I croak, "I should never have asked. I shouldn't have called—"

"No, that's—"

But I cut him off before he can finish his sentence and I say, "I love you, Nate," and then I hang up before he can reply, if he even replies at all.

Back in my childhood bedroom, almost four years later, I managed to ask him what time I should be round the next day to look after Noah before crawling out of bed to root around in my bag for a bottle of diazepam I hadn't had to use in months.

Ange and I met for breakfast at CJ's the next morning. It had taken me a little while to get out of bed; my limbs heavy, my brain sticky. I'd almost given up and texted Ange to cancel, but I didn't want to do that to Elle. I lost so much time, so much of myself after Nora went missing. Days, weeks, months had slipped by, sometimes with me barely even noticing, at other times with a heaviness and a slowness so thick it spread itself all over everything, smothering me. I couldn't be sure that wouldn't happen again; I never could be, but I wanted to do my best, my very, very best to ward it off for as long as possible. I felt as though I owed Elle that. At the very least.

The door stuck a little as I pushed it open, making a gentle sucking sound as it finally gave way and I walked into the overheated diner. The windows were temporarily frosted with condensation and I immediately started to unwind my scarf as I looked around the room, trying to find Ange. CJ's wasn't a chrome 'n' leather kind of diner. Just a wooden box by the side of the road with vinyl booths and a slightly off-putting plaid and taxidermy theme. The sloped roof met in a point in the middle of the building, atop which spun a slowly revolving sign that just said "waffles." Ange was sitting in the booth furthest away from the door by a window overlooking the road rather than the parking lot, and she already had a cup of coffee in front of her when I sat down. The diner was quiet despite the hour; it was just before nine in the morning and normally it would have been busy, but there were only three other booths full of people and there was a general hush over the place that pricked at my skin.

"Morning," I said to Ange.

"Hey. You sleep okay?"

"Once I popped a couple of pills, sure."

Ange's lips pursed just as she was raising her mug to her

lips and she put the mug down before even taking a sip.

"How about you?" I asked.

"Not great. I spent most of the night emailing my editor and trying to write up an article about Elle's death that he deemed printable." She stared down into her coffee. "This is my fourth cup of coffee this morning."

I raised my eyebrows and said: "I should probably catch up then," while signaling to a dyed-blonde waitress I didn't recognize that I was ready to order. "Is the paper sending anyone else up to help you?"

"No, I managed to convince them that I could handle it myself. They wanted to send up Elise who works for the crime desk but, in the end, I told them just to send up a photographer and I'd handle the rest."

"Are you sure that's such a good idea?" I asked.

"What do you mean?"

"Well, this isn't just some random crime. This is Elle. You knew her. We were there when Katherine and Jonathan brought her home from the hospital, Ange. Are you really going to be okay writing in detail about her murder? Not to mention writing about Nora."

"I'll be fine," she said shortly, looking up to smile at the waitress who'd just appeared at our table.

"Can I get you girls anything?" the waitress asked.

"Coffee," I said before looking down at the plastic-encased menu, although God knows why I did; I already knew what I wanted. "Plus waffles, side of bacon, two eggs over easy. Bacon extra crispy though. Like, carcinogenic."

The waitress kind of chuckled but Ange gave me an edgy look.

"Sure thing. And for you, Ange?"

"Just more coffee, waffles and a fruit cup, please."

"Should I know who that is?" I asked Ange once the waitress had gone to place our order.

Ange shrugged. "She's been here about a year. Ruby. She's nice. Never charges for maple syrup."

Before Nora disappeared CJ's decision to start charging for maple syrup was one of the most controversial things to ever happen there. Ruby returned with a mug for me and poured me a cup of coffee before topping up Ange's.

"Your food will be right out," she said before leaving us be.

"I went by to see Willard Knowles before coming here," Ange said. "Do you remember him?"

"Yeah, of course I remember him." Willard Knowles was the editor of the local newspaper, and both Ange and I had done work experience with him while we were still in high school. "Is the paper still going?" I asked, unable to keep the surprise out of my voice. It had always been on the edge of collapse, even ten, eleven years ago.

"Yes and no. He's gone online and he's working out of his basement but the *Forest View Examiner* still lives. I went over to see if he knew anything about what happened to Elle. I'd been hoping to work out of his office, but when I saw his new setup I thought better of it."

"Depressing?"

Ange shrugged. "Just a little weird. His photocopier is on top of his tiki bar."

I let out a short snort of laughter despite myself, and reached for my coffee.

"He didn't know much more than me; the police are keeping pretty quiet on this one. Willard thinks they're waiting on the state police before they officially announce anything. But he did have some photos."

"Photos?" I asked, barely able to get the word out. I wanted to press pause, to catch my breath; everything was moving so fast, too fast. Two days before I'd stood in front of Elle, talking to her, watching her, worrying over her, and now Ange was talking about crime scenes and photos and I couldn't quite figure how we'd got here.

"Yeah. He went up to the scene as soon as he heard about it. I must have just missed him yesterday when I was there. They wouldn't let him take any until the scene had been cleared and the body—"

There were those words again. *The body*.

The color drained from the room around me and I was drowning in silence.

It was impossible for me to reconcile those two words with Elle. I didn't want to slip into such anonymity so quickly and so easily. I wanted to hold onto her, as I knew her, for as long as possible, because I knew, so very well, and so very, very painfully, how quickly and easily that whole person would soon turn into an image, an idea, a talking point, and finally, just a memory.

One of the strangest things about when Nora disappeared— around the time of the media furor, anyway—was how present and not-present she was. She was everywhere. In every article, on every TV news show, she even made it into *Us Weekly* for Christ's sake. But she was nowhere as well. There were no photos of a crime scene because there wasn't one. The photo that got circulated to the media was the one taken in junior year for the school yearbook. She was just simply—gone. But Elle was being referred to as "the body" now. Stripped down to her most basic function. When I thought of Elle I thought of her either laughing while sucking on a milkshake aged sixteen, or staring me down hard-eyed while playing board games aged six. I didn't want to replace that with this new image that was coalescing in my mind, based on scraps of information and an overworked imagination.

"Maddie?" Ange was saying, reaching over to lay her hand over my forearm. "You okay?"

"Yeah," I said, swallowing, "I'll be fine."

"So, Willard managed to get a picture of something that was left at the scene."

"What was it?" I asked, suddenly sharp.

"It was this kind of symbol. In the snow."

"Do you have a photo of it?" I asked.

45

"Not a good one, but Willard emailed it to me so that my paper could use it."

"Can I see it?"

"Are you sure you want to?"

I swallowed, not sure if I could answer, not sure if I really did want to see the photo. I realized that it hadn't quite sunk in yet; that I'd been skating over the surface of this loss, waiting for the ice to break under my weight and for me to fall through the frigid water below. I still couldn't believe it, that all this was happening again, that Elle was gone, that Elle had been murdered. It felt ripped from the pages of a horror movie script, and yet I knew it had to be real because it all felt so familiar. I hated how used to grief Nora's disappearance had made me, but I still wasn't sure I was ready to confront the reality of Elle's death, because doing so would chip away at my memories of her that were already starting to dim and distort.

The body.

The words echoed in my head and I shivered involuntarily as Ange said: "Mads, you want to see the photo?"

I could have said no, of course, but I didn't want to give up so easily. Elle—a lot like Nora—had often demanded attention, and if there was any time she deserved it, it was now. So, I nodded yes, and Ange flipped her iPhone towards me after scrolling through her photos. I stared down at the screen.

"Does this mean anything to you? The symbol?" she asked.

The photo was taken at a strange angle, Willard obviously having tried his best to get the clearest shot, but all I could really make out was a symbol drawn into the snow the way a child does. It was the image of what looked like a compass, except that where the four points should have read N, S, E, W, every single one pointed to an "N." I stayed looking down at it for what must have been a long time because after a while Ange had to clear her throat just to get my attention.

"You all right, Mads?" she asked.

46

"Yeah—" my voice caught on the word and I took a gulp of coffee. "Yeah." I passed the phone back towards Ange. "It's that compass thing the Altmans have at their lake house. Their granddad made it when Noah was born, remember?"

"What?"

"The symbol. It's a copy of the 'N' compass at their lake house. You don't recognize it? All of the 'Ns' represent one of the kids, right?" I traced my finger around the outside of the circle. "See? Nate, Nora, Noelle, Noah."

"Shit, I didn't even think of that. And we were just at the lake house on Sunday."

She shrank down into her booth with a heavy sigh as Ruby the waitress deposited our breakfasts in front of us. I smiled up in thanks and noticed her glancing quizzically down at the phone in Ange's hand. Ange quickly made the screen go dark and said: "Thanks, Ruby."

"You girls need anythin' else?" Ruby asked.

"Just more coffee, please."

"Sure, you want me to keep it coming?"

We both nodded and with that Ruby went off to get us more coffee. Ange deposited the contents of her fruit cup over her waffles and then poured over at least three quarters of her jug of maple syrup. I watched as she began cutting up the waffles, adding blueberries and sliced strawberry to the forkful and then swirling it around in a pool of syrup.

"What do you think the significance is?" she asked as her dangerously loaded fork wavered towards her mouth.

I looked down to focus on my own plate, breaking off a piece of crispy bacon with my fingers and distractedly dipping it into my jug of syrup. I couldn't get the words "the body" out of my mind. It was ricocheting off everything else I heard or thought, tainting everything, draining the world of meaning.

"I don't know," I said softly, wishing that I did. We were both quiet for a while until I asked: "So, did you get your article finished?"

She looked up sharply, her brown eyes coming into focus on me before she swallowed her mouthful of waffle and said: "Well, it's my job, right?"

"I'm not judging you, Ange. Just wanted to know if you met your deadline."

Ange flattened her lips into a straight line, picking up her phone again and looking for something on it. "It should be up by now," she said. "Yeah, here we go. You want to read it?"

I nodded, reaching for her phone again and leaning back in the booth to read her article. As I did so a white noise roar screamed inside my head, drowning out the rest of the diner.

48

CHAPTER FIVE

Madison Journal

Teen Girl Murdered in Small Town

By Angela Cairney

January 9, 2018

The body of a 17-year-old girl, Noelle Altman, was found just outside Forest View close to the side of the road just off Old Highway 51 in the early hours of yesterday morning, January 8th. She is believed to have died between the hours of 8 p.m. on January 7th when she was last seen and 7 a.m. on January 8th when she was found by a local woman who drove past and noticed an abandoned car.

Noelle was the sister of Nora Altman who has been missing from Forest View since January 8th, 2008 when her car was found abandoned in the same spot by a local police officer. As with the disappearance of Nora Altman, the police currently have no leads as to the murder of Noelle Altman, and are asking that anyone with any pertinent information to please step forward. They do not think the two incidents are connected and a spokesperson has revealed that the possibility of suicide has been completely ruled out.

The Altman family have requested peace and understanding at this time, and our condolences and heartfelt thoughts go out to them as they deal with this tragedy.

It was a short article, and I read it quickly, drinking in the few facts Ange had managed to glean from somewhere. What time Elle was found, when she was believed to have died, the exact location she was found. It was all relevant, pertinent, and yet it didn't feel real. How could I be reading about Elle?

"The same spot," I said, lingering over that detail. "How close was it exactly to where Nora's car was found?"

Ange raised her eyebrows. "Really close. Willard said her body was a little ways off in the woods, but you could see the road still. The car was right by where the ribbon is."

I reached for my coffee, as if going to drink some, but couldn't lift it to my lips. Sometimes, when I closed my eyes, I could still see the headlines and photographs that filled the newspapers in the days and months after Nora's disappearance. But that little patch of land where her car had been found existed somewhere inside me, desolate and snowy, even in the summer when the sun managed to warm my skin and my mind managed to crawl its way out of a perpetual winter. For Elle to have been found there—to have been left, abandoned there, as if she were nothing but a scrap to be discarded and forgotten—gave shape to her death in a way I hadn't anticipated. Whoever had done this may as well have placed Elle within the chalk outline of the body Nora had never left behind.

CHAPTER SIX

Wisconsin Daily News

Family Fears for Missing Teen

By Gloria Lewis

January 15, 2008

It's been seven days since Wisconsin teenager Nora Altman went missing from the small town of Forest View, and her family is concerned. "This isn't like Nora," her father, attorney Jonathan Altman, said at a press conference held in nearby Waterstone last night. "She has never left home without telling either her family or friends where she is going, and we are very, very worried that something terrible has happened to our wonderful girl. We remain hopeful that she is somewhere, healthy and alive, and if that is the case then Nora, please come back to us. Please get in touch. With anyone. To anyone who may have taken her, may have hurt her … I beg you, please come forward. Please bring our girl back."

An emotional Mr Altman was unable to finish his statement and plea to the wider public to be on the lookout for the tall 17-year-old girl who went missing over the course of the night of January 7. Her car was found abandoned by the side of the road, on a lonely and unpopulated stretch of Old Highway 51 the next morning, January 8, by local policeman and friend of the missing teen, Officer Leo Moody. It was Moody's father, Chief of Police Patrick Moody who took over from Mr Altman at the press conference, issuing the description of the brunette and asking the public to report any sightings, and for any witnesses who may have seen her as she exited her vehicle or later on that night to come forward.

In a separate statement, the police department made it clear that despite the family's fears they do not yet suspect foul play. Nora is a popular, smart, and tenacious young woman by all accounts, and there is no evidence yet that she left the area under anything other than her own steam. Nora Altman is described as being roughly five foot nine with dark brown, almost black hair and blue eyes. Anyone with any information regarding her whereabouts is asked to call the number below.

CHAPTER SEVEN

When we were about six or seven Nora decided that the only popsicles she would eat were the red ones. They didn't seem to have a flavor; they were just red the same way red M&Ms are just red too. Anyway, from then on she only ever ate the red popsicles. Even when we were seventeen. I didn't care what color I had; as long as I had one, I was cool. Nora was like that about a lot of things. Single-minded, determined. Tunnel vision, I guess is what you'd call it. I used to laugh at her refusal to try any other flavors because it meant she often went without one, even when there were other colors available and I was happy sucking down on a blue one, or whatever else was available, but she was so sure of herself, so intent on the right-ness of her choice that her lack of desire to try something else seemed almost admirable.

By the time it came round to picking out colleges, Nora already knew where she was going to go. She'd known since our freshman year for Christ's sake. It was absurd to me that she would limit her choices so much by only applying to Carnegie Mellon, but she was just so damn sure of herself. Of her choices. She'd been singing forever, and had appeared, more often than not as the main character, in every single musical theater production our high school had ever put on. It was pretty exhausting being her friend, to be honest. Me, I had about a thousand different ideas of where I wanted to go. I wanted Northwestern and NYU, Columbia and Stanford, Berkeley and Vanderbilt. By which I mean I didn't know what the fuck I wanted. I was just as big a mess back then as I am now, I just used to have more options available to me. I laughed at Nora's certainty about Carnegie Mellon just as I'd laughed at her red popsicle decree. She didn't need any backup. She didn't need options or choices—she knew exactly what she wanted, even before the rest of us realized we were expected to have formed some sort of opinion on our future selves. That is, of course, until she had all her options taken from her. Until her future went from certain to nonexistent.

I can't untangle lost-Nora from alive-Nora; they've become the same person so much that every memory I have of her is blighted, dimmed by the fact of her being gone. Sometimes I can see her as bright and clear as a summer's day. She stands in my mind in full technicolor, a riot of color saturation. But most of the time the way I think of her is the way I think about the time when we lost her. They've become one and the same, and in a way it's like losing her all over again. Just as I was robbed of my best friend, I was robbed of my memories of her too.

She got in of course. The letter came, in all its cream-colored glory, heavy with anticipation and congratulations, Carnegie Mellon somehow the only people in the country who didn't realize what had happened to Nora. Nate showed it to me and Ange, his face grim but somehow determined, and I tried so hard to work out what he was feeling; did he think she was still out there, desperate to be found? Or maybe desperate to remain lost? It took me a couple days to realize that he'd just come to the same conclusion I had. Because in that moment, when I saw those words, "*Congratulations, Nora Altman, and welcome to Carnegie Mellon!*" I just knew. I knew she was gone for good and not because she didn't want to be found.

It's exhausting coming up with synonyms and euphemisms

for dead. We had to use so many in those first few months when she was simply gone. Missing. But that was the first time I let the word enter my vocabulary. It was the first time I realized she wasn't just a space in my life. Someone hadn't simply thrown their hand into the ring and snatched her out of our lives. Someone had killed her.

The impotence I felt in that moment and in the months, years, that followed doesn't even bear describing. It was all-consuming. It's one thing to realize your best friend has been murdered; it's a completely different thing to watch, from the sidelines, as those in power, those with control, fail at almost every turn to find or apprehend the killer. To refuse even to admit that she has been murdered. It is, apparently, very hard to find a killer when you can't even find the body.

So, it was that impotence, that dreaded powerlessness that I was thinking about when I parted ways with Ange at the diner, and instead of going home to crawl back into bed as I probably would have done ten years before, I got into my dad's car and drove out to where Noelle's body had been found and Nora's car had been abandoned all those years ago. My hands gripped the steering wheel ever tighter the closer I got and by the time the flickering yellow police tape came into view a low buzzing hum had taken up residence throughout my entire body.

I tried to breathe deeply, pulling over to the side of the road and staring out at the desolate scene. There was nothing much to see, but just a few yards away I could make out the ribbon tied to one of the nearby trees. It must have been replaced a thousand times, but there had been one there ever since Nora went missing. I could still remember the discussion of what color ribbon to choose; the mundane back and forth between yellow and blue barely cutting through the cloud I'd been drifting through since she disappeared. Finally, I'd had to shout, yell, my voice catching on the words, that it should be purple. I was the only one who remembered it was her favorite color.

I got out of the car and walked towards the police tape before looking around me and slipping underneath it. There was nothing to see, really. I followed a very small path into the woods, but the recent snow meant everything had been covered over. Willard must have been quick to get even his low-quality photo. I stopped walking after a while, aware that I was just getting ever deeper into the woods, and with no real reason. Whatever it was I was looking for, I thought, I wouldn't find it here.

I heard the crunch of the snow coming from behind me before I heard his voice.

"You shouldn't be here, Fielder."

I turned around to see Leo standing at the edge of the clearing. He was with Bright, both of them dressed in their blue police uniforms.

"Didn't you notice the big yellow 'do not cross' line down at the road?"

"I didn't come from the road. I was just taking a walk and came across it."

Leo rolled his eyes at me. "Don't lie to us, Mads. I recognize your dad's car. I saw it every day in the high school parking lot, remember? Just like everybody else." Just one of the many downsides to having a parent as your high school principal.

I grimaced. "Oh, right."

"What are you doing here, Maddie?" Bright asked gruffly. Bright and Serena had been together for almost all of high school and even into college before they broke up, and I like to think he held a certain amount of affection towards us Fielder girls. He never really said much to me, but then he never really said much to anyone, so I didn't take it too personally.

"I just wanted to see it. I'm sorry."

"How'd you even know where to come? I didn't think details had been released yet." Leo's chest was puffed up in indignation, his face a caricature of concern.

"Ange," I said simply. I didn't add that an article detailing the

56

existence and nature of the crime had already gone live on the *Madison Journal*'s website.

Leo groaned and turned away from me as if disgusted, kicking at a small drift of snow. Bright and I caught one another's eye, but I looked away quickly. He just stood there, arms crossed against his broad chest, jaw set firmly against the cold and the crime scene, determined to remain as stoic as ever. I'd seen him like this countless times before: impassive as a rock in the face of grief, loss, anger, frustration. He was perfect for police work really, never giving anything away, but it sure did make for cold comfort.

"Well, I'd better get going," I said, suddenly deflated. I'd hoped going out there would help me understand what was happening, what had happened to Elle, but all I felt was a mixture of disappointment and dread that I couldn't quite decipher.

I walked back the way I'd come, squeezing between the two men, knocking Leo's arm with my shoulder. His head turned sharply towards me but I just stared at him, daring him to say something. Instead, his face dropped and he gave me a soft little smile, mouthing "I'm sorry," at me. Just so I knew he wasn't a total asshole. Just so I knew he was only doing his job. I shrugged at him and carried on walking.

I got a few strides away from them before I heard Bright speak up again. "You heard from Nate?"

I turned back to check he was talking to me and not Leo and nodded. "I'm going round there later to watch Noah."

Bright gave a single nod and then turned back to the clearing.

There was someone else down by my dad's car when I got back to it, waiting, but I didn't think for me. Hidden beneath a bright red bobble hat and matching padded jacket—whoever it was was so small that I'd been taken aback to see they were probably about Elle's age—when they turned around at the sound of my approach, and not a child as I'd wrongly assumed. The girl had been staring silently at the purple ribbon when I arrived, but now I could see her face and there was something about the terrifying blankness of her eyes that I recognized. Not from a picture or photo I'd seen, but from the reflection of my own face whenever I'd managed to look in the mirror ten years earlier when Nora had first gone missing. It was that, more than anything else, that made me say: "Jenna?"

The girl took a step back initially, and then moved towards me, shoes crunching on snow. "Do I know you?"

"I'm Maddie Fielder," I said. "I … was Nora's friend. I knew Elle, too. You are Jenna, right? Elle's girlfriend?"

Jenna nodded eventually, swallowing hard, and taking a quick look back at the purple ribbon, fluttering a little in the wind. "You're Maddie? Elle spoke about you a lot." Her words were stilted, hard come by, almost lost in all that cold air, and I felt bad even forcing her to say Elle's name, although it's unlikely there was anyone or anything else on earth currently taking up her mind and time. I looked back up the way I had just come, aware that Leo and Bright were probably going to come crashing down through the woods at any moment. I thought I could just hear the low rumble of their voices, getting louder and closer, but I may have been imagining it.

Before I really knew what I was doing I asked Jenna if she wanted to go someplace warm and chat, and she surprised me yet again by agreeing to, so we both got into our own cars and drove off back towards CJ's in convoy.

Somehow I ended up getting to CJ's a little before Jenna and watched as she pushed open the heavy door, letting a puff of cold air into the warm diner. Her short reddish hair was cut into a pixie cut and she fluffed it up with her right hand as she walked towards me, having just pulled the bright red bobble hat off her head. Underneath her red coat she was wearing jeans and a massive sweatshirt that completely dwarfed her slight frame.

Jenna slipped into the booth, Ruby silently depositing two cups of coffee and two menus on the table in front of us as she did so. I smiled my thanks and she left us to it. Jenna wrapped her hands around the mug of coffee nearest her and stared into the brown liquid. She wasn't wearing any make-up, but her skin was clear except for one spot by the corner of her mouth. Up close, her eyes, which I'd thought looked so horrifyingly blank, were hazel, and upon closer inspection looked puffy but not red. From crying but not too recently.

I probably should have said something first, I was the grown up after all—I had suggested we come here, and on top of everything I wasn't the one who had so recently lost their girlfriend—but for some reason I simply couldn't speak. Couldn't think of a single thing to say. So, silence settled all around us until finally Jenna looked up and said: "I can't believe she's gone. I was on Facebook last night and that was all anyone seemed able to say, you know? 'I can't believe you're gone.' It doesn't feel real. Even with all … the other stuff." She looked up at me then. "Did it feel real with Nora?"

It took me a little while to answer. For some reason I hadn't expected Jenna to ask me about Nora, but she had every reason to, of course.

"At first it was like I was watching it all happen to someone else," I said slowly, watching her face, "but then, finally, I don't know, something snapped and I realized it was real. That she was gone."

I didn't normally talk so easily about Nora, especially with someone I'd never met before, but I felt as though Jenna deserved it. The truth. Or my truth at least. I also couldn't help but notice that we'd completely dispensed with and skipped over the small talk. There wasn't any place for it there, not then.

"Do you ever think that she might still be alive?" she asked, her words whispered, her eyes lowered again. Like she was asking me something embarrassing.

When I said "No," very firmly she looked a little taken aback by my conviction. "If she were alive I'd know. There would have been something. She would have let us know, somehow." It always surprised me how shocked people were by my belief that Nora was dead rather than still missing. They thought I should still have hope that she was out there somewhere, alive, but hope had given up on me long ago. I wasn't willing to indulge in it for the sake of people finding me easier to deal with; when I told people I thought Nora was dead it was as if I had killed her. And maybe I had, up to a point. I'd killed the idea of her being alive, and if I didn't believe it, then who were they to? What they don't understand is that hope is relentless, unforgiving, and living within its grip isn't like living at all. So, I chose to believe in something that let me live, even if only a little, even if only just.

To her credit, Jenna simply nodded, taking a sip from her mug of coffee and then, as if she'd suddenly just summoned the courage to do so, she looked at me, her jaw set, her chin raised slightly in an image of determination. Her eyes looked steely somehow, something metallic catching amid the green and brown. I could see how she might present quite a formidable opponent on the ice, despite her small size.

"I want to know what happened to her. To Noelle. I deserve to know."

"Of course."

"No, you don't get it. No one's telling me anything. Not the police, not her family." Her eyes looked a little wild then; so wide they seemed to jump out of her face. Her resolve from just seconds before had left her completely and she was having trouble looking at me, or anything, for more than a split second. Her gaze flicked from one thing to the next, to the next and I wondered if she'd taken something. "I mean, I get it," she continued, after taking a deep breath and trying to calm herself, "there's not much to tell yet, but I'm her girlfriend." Her chin dipped ever so slightly and the firm, set line of her mouth turned down somewhat. "Was. Was her girlfriend."

"Can I ask why you weren't at the memorial on Sunday? For Nora?"

Jenna wiped a hand across her face, exhaustion written all over it. "It was my grandmother's eightieth birthday. I couldn't miss it; my mom would have killed me." She stilled suddenly, her eyes catching mine, her face pale. "I mean … I didn't mean that, I didn't mean to say that."

"It's okay, Jenna."

"No, no, no. You don't understand—"

"I do understand. And it's okay."

Jenna slumped forward, her arms resting on the table, showing me the crown of her head. I thought perhaps that she was crying, but when I said: "Had Elle been acting any differently recently?" she jerked her face up and it was clear of tears.

Taking a deep breath she turned her gaze to the window, which was a little steamed up, snow drifting lazily past it. Calmer by then, she said: "A little, I guess, yeah. She'd been more withdrawn than usual."

Elle had been particularly quiet on Sunday when I had last seen her, and although I wasn't used to seeing her like that, I hadn't thought much of it at the time; it was the ten-year anniversary of her sister going missing after all. If she had a right to be withdrawn at any time, it was then. I wanted specifics though, so I asked: "What do you mean by 'withdrawn'?"

Jenna sighed, pushing back her hair so that it stood on end. "Quiet, distracted. She kept cancelling stuff at the last minute. Like, we'd arrange to go to the movies, or just to hang out, but then she'd cancel right before we were supposed to meet. I thought … I actually thought she was going to break up with me." She looked back at me, her eyes once again wide and a little wild, filling with tears.

"Do you know why she wasn't home on Sunday night?" This

was a question that had been bothering me; why had Elle not been at home and why hadn't anyone noticed that she was missing earlier?

"She … she was supposed to come over to my house, to hang out, but then she texted to say she wasn't feeling up to it, so I figured she was just going to stay home with her family. I texted and called a couple times but when she didn't answer I thought maybe she'd just gone to bed early or something."

There was a shot of silence while I swallowed a mouthful of coffee. "Do you think she went out anyway? To meet someone else?" I asked at last.

Jenna nodded, blinking rapidly at me as a way to stave off tears. "Maybe. It's the only reason why her parents wouldn't have known where she was. If they thought she was at mine, then they wouldn't have been worried, right? But what if she told them she was with me but she was actually somewhere else?" Her voice broke as she was speaking, tears falling silently down her cheeks, and I reached for a napkin from the stainless-steel dispenser and handed one to her. She took it silently, wiping away at her face.

"Had she ever done that before?"

"I don't know," Jenna said, shrugging her shoulders helplessly. "Maybe, I guess."

"Do you think she could have been seeing someone else?"

"You mean cheating on me?"

I drew in a breath, watching Jenna's face fall ever further. "Yeah."

Jenna swallowed, shaking her head. "I didn't ever think she'd do that. But I don't know now. Maybe she would?"

I felt awful asking Jenna all these questions, making it so much harder, so much worse. It was like I was digging through the rubble of a ruined building and kept uncovering body parts; I wanted to stop, but there was a chance there was a live one down there, and I needed to know. "Is there anyone you can think of

62

who she might have been seeing? Anyone at school she was flirty with? Anything like that?"

"No," Jenna replied, just looking at me.

"Are you sure? What about if I put it this way instead: Was there anyone who seemed interested in her? Even if she wasn't interested back?"

Jenna put down the mug of coffee she'd been drinking from and licked her lips. "Yeah, there were a few."

"A few?"

"There were some guys at school who were constantly hitting on her. As if we were just some sort of act. Like we were there just to turn them on or something, and because everyone knew Elle was bi, they'd always hit on her, super creepy, all like, 'let me know when you want a man' or whatever. As if because she was attracted to men and women she'd be attracted to a complete asshole."

"Who were they?"

Jenna thought for a second. "Johnny Phillips, Mike Stiles, Adrian Turney. I don't think she was seeing any of them though. She thought they were assholes."

"Are you sure?"

She shrugged, and leaned back in the booth. "I guess I don't know."

"Did the police ask about these guys?"

"No, they just wanted to know where I'd been and if Elle had seemed different at all recently. They asked if she'd been seeing anyone else, like you did. If we had an open relationship." She raised her eyebrows at me.

"So, there's no reason these guys—Johnny, Mick and whoever—would be questioned by the police?"

"Mike. And no, I don't think so. Unless they decided to question the whole school."

"Okay. Do you have any of these guys' numbers? So I could get in touch with them if I need to?"

Jenna shook her head. "No, I don't think so. But they're all on Facebook. You could just message them there."

"Right, of course."

Jenna gave me a thin smile and shifted in her seat, looking down into what I assumed was her nearly empty coffee mug. I could tell she wanted to leave.

"Hey, have you ever been up to the Altmans' lake house?" I asked, and Jenna nodded.

"Yeah, plenty of times," she said.

"What about those guys? Would they have been there too?" I was thinking about that compass drawn in the snow next to Elle's body, all four points leading to an "N."

"Maybe, but I don't think so. Mike might have been to a party there once or twice. Why?"

I told her about the compass, which she didn't seem to have read about yet, and watched as her face drained even further of any color.

"Anyone could have seen that compass though," she said after a pause. "Elle had a tattoo of it on her ankle."

"She did?" I asked, but as soon as she had said it, it all came flooding back.

I'd sat there, in that very diner, sometime at the end of the last summer, catching up with Elle and she'd told me all about it. I hadn't seen her in months, not since the beginning of the year probably, and we'd had a lot to talk about. She'd spent a few weeks of the summer in Austin with Nate and then they'd driven back together so that she could take possession of his old Land Cruiser.

***

"You got a new tattoo," she says excitedly, reaching for my arm and turning it over so that she can better see the arrow pointing

down towards my palm, its tail just scraping the inner crook of my elbow. "Why an arrow?" she asks.

I look down at my arm, her warm hand still wrapped around my wrist, and it feels as though I'm looking at someone else's. I'm used to the tattoo by now—I've had it since January—but for some reason I feel unhooked from my body, let loose from its rigid confines. "I got it for Nora," I say eventually, my voice sticky, constricted, and raise my eyes to meet Elle's, watching as they widen a little. "She always seemed to know exactly where she was going. I could use a little of that in my life I guess."

Elle grins at me and she seems to be bubbling over with something. "It's like we match," she says animatedly, pulling her leg up onto the diner bench and twisting her ankle towards me so I can see it: an inky black compass with all points ending in "N." It's still a little red, sore. "Nate got one too," she says, "on his arm though. Guess we'll have to force Noah to get one at some point too. But look," her finger traces the compass on her ankle gently as she speaks, "it's like your little arrow matches the pointers on the compass. Part of the family."

Something heavy fills my stomach and even though I find it difficult I manage to smile at her. "Don't you have to be eighteen to get a tattoo?"

Elle makes a face as if she's disappointed I'd ask her such a question, and proceeds to roll her eyes. "Yeah, and Mom absolutely flipped. It was ridiculous. As if she doesn't have more important things to worry about than me getting an effin tattoo."

I can't help but really smile at her then; there is nothing more endearing to me than Elle's quiet refusal to curse. We move onto talking about her parents, who, Elle believes, are in the process of getting a divorce, although neither one of them will talk about it with her.

"As if our family needs any more skeletons we're not allowed to talk about," she says, all her previous enthusiasm drained.

"Shit, I can't believe I forgot about the tattoo," I said to Jenna, feeling deflated. I'd been assuming that whoever had drawn that compass had been to the lake house, which might have narrowed down the suspects a little, but if anyone could have seen it on Elle's ankle, then it was far less significant.

After paying for our coffees I walked Jenna to her car, an enormous dark blue Dodge truck that looked far too big for her, and watched as she climbed into it. Before she drove off I asked her if she was heading back home.

She was staring out through the windscreen as she shook her head and said: "I can't stand being in my room anymore. It's so full of her. I can't stop thinking ... I just can't stop thinking. About her. About it. I need to be distracted. By anything."

"So, what are you going to do?"

She shrugged, looking lost, looking so much younger than seventeen—far too young for any of this—I thought. "I guess I'll just go to school. Nowhere else to go."

I had tried going to school as normal when Nora first went missing. Those in-between days when we all assumed she'd be found quickly and be back home soon took on a strange, vague quality to them, as if I wasn't even there. It's as though someone has told me about them and I'm remembering their telling of it. I remember sitting in the school gym on the Monday after she'd been reported missing, in an assembly for Nora, an assembly called by my own father, who was obviously having trouble getting the tone right. Were we grieving the loss of a fellow student and friend? Were we telling one another that there was still hope, that we could still find her? Were we being warned about the dangers of being a young woman out late at night? Were we blaming drugs? When we got to the drugs part I got up and walked out, Ange close behind me, and we spent the rest of the day crying in the backseat of her car. No one came to get us and force us back to class, and I ended up missing weeks of school.

I'd raged at my dad that night, stormed at him as soon as he got through the door, face like a distant thunderstorm. He didn't understand, I screamed, couldn't possibly understand; Nora hadn't run away, she wasn't some messed-up kid on drugs trying to find her way out. Nora was always on her way up, always, and I couldn't understand how everyone could have suddenly forgotten that and recast her in this new role of troubled teen. He'd answered in a low voice, quiet, levelheaded, sympathetic even, telling me he knew, he knew, he knew, that he knew Nora as well as I did, but he had professional obligations, he'd been briefed by the police on what to say. I can still feel the hot tears that stained my face that whole evening as I realized my father had loyalties that extended beyond me, beyond Nora.

When I finally went back to school, every glance cast at me and every scrap of gossip thrown my way implying that I'd been given special treatment because my dad was also the principal, it was to a different place entirely. What had once been safe, innocuous, boring, was now unbearable. It was on one of these first interminably long days back at school that I found my first note.

***

It flutters to the floor as soon I open my locker, and I pick it up idly, expecting it to be from Ange.

It's written in Sharpie, stark black against the clean, perfect white of the printer paper.

Your friend probably killed herself why don't you do the same

I stare down at it, not taking it in. All I can see for a second or two is the black and white, the curve of the writing, the slope of the sentence. It starts to tremble gently in my hand, but the reaction seems completely divorced from me. I lean my shoulder against the locker next to mine, creating a shield with my open locker door, and read the note again. I almost want to laugh in some way; as if anyone could hurt me now. As if any number of notes stuffed into my locker could make me feel the way Nora being gone makes me feel. I fold the note over carefully, once, twice and then slide it into the back pocket of my jeans.

I slam my locker door shut, forgetting what it is I went there for in the first place, and walk out of school. The metallic noise of the doors banging into the wall sings in my ears as I step out into the dazzle of sun and snow. I squeeze my eyes shut and feel that familiar anvil pressing me down into the earth, the weight of life suddenly a burden too heavy to bear. I walk home through the snow slowly, slowly and crawl into bed, knowing I won't leave for over a week. I don't tell anyone about the note—it doesn't even occur to me—until Serena comes home a few days later.

"You're not asleep," she says, coming into my room without knocking.

"No." I don't bother telling her that I'm never actually asleep. Just exhausted.

"Cool. I just wanted to come say hi." She walks over to the window and stares out at the evening, which is a perfect dusky purple. "How are you doing?"

"Fine."

"Mom and Dad are really worried." She turns to look at me finally, staring me down, which I can tell she's been wanting to do the entire time. Serena isn't a stareoutthewindowattheevening kind of girl. That's me. Or at a push Cordy, but definitely not Serena. "I'm worried too. I thought you'd gone back to school. I thought things were better."

"They got worse again."

"Can you tell me why?"

I have no idea how to tell her, so I just stay silent. She sighs, padding over to the bookshelf.

"Have you read anything recently? Maybe that would help you feel better."

Several words, hell an entire sentence even, rise up inside me but end up getting trapped somewhere in my chest, so again I say nothing. Serena's eyes drift along the bank of books, taking them all in until something stops her in her perusing. I stuffed the note in between two books rather than tearing it up and throwing it away, which I'm now regretting. She pulls it out from between The Return of the King *and* The Silmarillion *and stares down at it before turning to look at me. My face is stuck to the pillow. I haven't moved since she walked into the room.*

"What is this, Mads?"

"An anonymous missive from a concerned classmate."

"Maddie." *She's staring down at it again, her eyes drawing in on themselves.* "Have you told anyone about this? Shown it to anyone?"

"No."

"Why the hell not?"

I finally push myself up, leaning my head back against the head-board and closing my eyes. "Because it doesn't matter. That's not the problem, Serena, just a symptom."

"This is really fucking serious," *she says,* "this is aggressive. Horrible. They're telling you to kill yourself."

My eyes snap open, and Serena is staring right at me, her grey-blue eyes headlights in the near-dark of my bedroom. "It's nothing," *I say, my voice a rubber band suddenly stretched too far.* "Just some sick, psycho jock trying to hurt me."

"Has this happened to Angela too?"

"I don't know." *I wonder suddenly what Ange might be keeping from me in light of what I'm keeping from her.*

"So, you literally haven't told anyone?"

"No."

"Well, I'm sorry but I have to tell Mom and Dad."

I don't say anything as she walks out of the room, evidence in hand. I rearrange my pillows and slide back down the bed. The world isn't any less demanding from this position but at least when

*it asks its impossible questions I'm not forced to come up with an
answer.*

I close my eyes.

After leaving Jenna, I headed over to the Altmans'. Katherine was
a small woman, with none of the height and strength I always
associated with Nora. Noelle looked more like her although she
was much taller. The same fine features, with Katherine's dark
brown eyes and chestnut hair, rather than Nora's deep-blue eyes
and almost raven hair. We hugged silently and when she released
me about a thousand different words remained stuck in my throat
and all I could manage was: "I'm so sorry."

Katherine nodded and folded her arms across her chest. Her
face was a strained white, with no make-up and purplish, bruised-
like bags under her eyes.

"Nate asked me to come sit with Noah. I think-I think he
thought you guys might appreciate the help." I inwardly cringed
at the inadequacy of my words. Of all words.

"Of course. Thank you, Maddie. We have to … we have to
go to the police station. For questioning."

I raised my eyebrows and followed her into the house. "For
questioning?"

Katherine sighed heavily as she pushed through the door to
the kitchen at the back of the house. Beyond the kitchen island
there was a vast window that overlooked the snow-filled garden.
It was quiet and white, with a cold, icy beauty. Completely
untouched. Most backyards would bear some trace of the
human—childish—touch. Piled up drifts of snow where snowmen
have melted, dislodged snow on the climbing frame or swing set,
the disintegrating outline of a playful snow angel. A trail of
footprints at the very least. But there was none of that in the
Altmans' garden. I guess Noah wasn't much for playing, despite
being only ten years old.

Katherine scraped a chair back along the tiled floor of the

kitchen and sat down. She pointed towards the coffee maker to indicate that I could help myself, and I set about making us a pot.

"They let us have the evening but they want us to come in and answer questions about when we last saw Elle. We're not suspects," she added, before saying even more quietly, "yet."

I turned to look at her, both of us clearly thinking about her eldest son, who had been arrested, although never charged, when Nora first went missing. He hadn't been able to produce a solid enough alibi, or so the cops had claimed, but when no other evidence turned up, and no body either, he was released without charge.

"Is Nate here?" I asked.

"Downstairs, I think. He's … we're … we have to leave in a few minutes," she said, finally finishing her sentence. Her mouth was straight and taut, pulled thinly against the pale skin of her face. "Thank you for coming, Maddie," she said quietly, "it really means a lot."

I looked around the kitchen and noticed how bare, almost barren, it was. There were no bouquets of flowers, no letters or notes of condolence. When Nora went missing, someone inexplicably sent the family an enormous brown-furred teddy bear with a bright red bow tie proudly fixed around its chunky neck. It sat in the corner of the living room for a few days before migrating down to the kids' basement rec room, its cuddly, warm presence too much of an incongruence for the family room. Maybe there simply hadn't been enough time for the flowers and the cards and the inappropriate plush toys to begin to flood in. Or maybe they never would. Maybe no one knew how to react, how to express comfort and sympathy, compassion and condolence to a family that had already lost so much. Or maybe it was something else entirely. Maybe people had already started talking, hushed tones hiding dark thoughts and malicious accusations. Either way, I suddenly felt extremely empty-handed. When the aroma of fresh coffee began to fill the desolate kitchen I sighed with perceptible relief. It wasn't much, but at least I could make Katherine a cup of her own coffee.

"Thanks," Katherine said as I handed her the mug. "Noah's upstairs. I think he might still be asleep to be honest."

I raised my eyebrows at that; it was already well past noon.

"You'll be okay here with him?" she asked, hesitantly.

I nodded. "Of course. We'll be fine."

A door shut with emphasis somewhere in the house, and Katherine looked over at me quickly before leaving her chair and walking out of the kitchen, mug in hand. She squeezed my shoulder before leaving the kitchen, and I heard her call out Jonathan's name, the shuffle of feet and rumble of voices and undercurrent of a murmured, urgent conversation. Before I knew it, Nate was standing in the doorway of the kitchen, looking in at me.

"Mads," he said, his voice hollow in that large room.

I stared at him as though it was the first time I'd seen him in years, when in fact I'd seen him just two days before. Something burning began to build behind my eyes; something scratchy and insistent and all too familiar and all I managed to say was simply "Nate," before his dad also called his name and he shrugged and made a face at me and left to join his parents at the door.

I followed him, standing where he'd just been in the doorway, and said goodbye, watching as all three of them left and the front door slammed solidly behind them. I hadn't been to the house in a while, so I let the quiet of it sink down into my bones before heading upstairs to say hi to Noah.

That house was as deeply entrenched in my memories, as much a part of my childhood and adolescence as my own home, but ever since Nora went missing I hadn't spent much time there other than for memorials. Then, just like my memories of Nora herself, my memories of the house were warped and tainted by time, and filled with all the spaces that she should have been in and instead was missing from. There were plenty of vigils held in her name when she first went missing, but it wasn't until she'd been gone for a year that her family held their first memorial.

***

Nobody knows what to say but everybody's talking. It's like a white noise machine, the sound turned way up, and then suddenly on mute as I drift in and out of conversations, as the crowd teems and seethes around me, and then suddenly I'm all alone in an aching well of silence. Every time I walk through the hall I see Nora's face, and either I can't help but stare even though all I want to do is look away, to forget, or I turn away, unable to take it anymore and feel guilt coil through me, even though all I want is to see her face.

It's been a year. A whole year.

I've never seen the Altmans' house so full of people, and I've spent half my life here, at the kind of parties where balloons are attached to the gate and you're sent home with a party bag, and at the kind of parties where only the adults are really having any fun and you sit around in too-formal dresses, drinking luridly colored fizzy drinks and watching boys playing video games, and then at the kind of parties where vodka and rum are sneaked out of parents' liquor cabinets and into empty water bottles, and used to spike cups full of diet Coke as you sit on the edge of the kitchen countertop and wonder how it is everyone seems to be having more fun than you.

I push through the crowd even though all I want to do is go home, or at the very least go up to the bathroom on the top floor of the house, where no one else would dare go, and sit on the closed lid of the toilet and sit and wait until I'm allowed to leave. I don't though, because I know what people would think, what people already think, and because Serena has already warned me against this, and because, really, I couldn't do that to Nora's parents, or to Nate and Noelle and Noah who all must be trying even harder than I am just to get through this day.

73

I spot Ange sitting on one of the living room couches, her hands resting primly on the black wool of her skirt, the hot pink of her nail polish flashing against the deep brown of her fingers. She's looking straight ahead, dead-eyed, her mouth pulled taut, eyes rimmed red, but as soon as Leo starts speaking to her, his head tilted down towards her on the couch so that she can hear, she lifts her chin, manages to smile, and even her eyes seem to enliven, although she can't do anything about how bloodshot they are. I wonder how she can do it: how she can flick the switch from genuine grief to inane small talk. She sees me watching her and pushes herself up from the couch, making her excuses to Leo, and comes towards me.

"You okay?" she asks, and I nod. She looks around, taking it all in, her gaze resting on one of the photos of Nora that line the downstairs hallway. "She'd hate this," she says finally.

"Of course she'd hate this, Ange. It's her fucking memorial. It's basically a funeral."

"I know, I know. I just can't help thinking—do you think she'd want us to give up like this? To stop looking? This feels so final."

I close my eyes for what feels like forever, and when I open them all I can think to say is: "It's been a year, Ange."

She shakes her head, leaning back against the wall. "I just always thought we'd know something by now. Anything."

A burning feeling starts up behind my eyes, and I want to close them again, to close them against all this, and to lie down and to be in bed, and not be surrounded by people who want so much. Who want to know where Nora is, and what happened to her. Who want to not hurt so much anymore, and not think about her anymore. Who want, more than anything, to lay this all to rest and to finally move on. I can't figure out if they just haven't figured it out yet, or if I'm the slow one, if I'm the one playing catch-up, because there is no moving on. There is no closure. Nora's disappearance will hurt us and haunt us for the rest of our lives, and there is no funeral, or memorial, or vigil that will

74

make that better. I just shake my head and whisper through the
thickness in my throat and mouth which is building up as I try
not to cry.

"Maybe we'll never know."

The hallway and staircase wall were still full of photos of Nora even then. Nora staring out moodily from wooden frames, her blue eyes the color of summer's late-evening sky … in another, Elle grinned up from an ice cream cone, her nose freckled and sunburned, gap-toothed and happy. I squeezed my eyes shut for a second before climbing the stairs, suddenly desperate to ignore the clamor and the clang of memories.

I knocked on Noah's door and pushed it open quietly. "Noah?" The bed appeared to be empty, so I pushed the door open further and walked into the room. "Noah? It's Maddie."

He was standing at the window, looking out over the snowed-in backyard. He made no move to greet me, so I went over to stand next to him by the window. He was tall for a tenyearold, I guess.

I knocked his shoulder with my elbow and said: "Hey, bud. You okay?"

He looked right up at me, his eyes hard but clear and answered simply: "No."

I blinked, taken aback for a second by the bluntness of his answer and then just nodded. "Me either."

Noah seemed to deflate at that. Maybe he was relieved that I offered him no platitude of condolence. He slumped forward and leaned his forehead against the cold glass of the window.

"Hey, have you eaten? You want some lunch?" I asked.

He shrugged noncommittally but led the way downstairs none-theless. The kitchen still smelt of coffee, and as I moved around, opening cupboards and searching the fridge for something to eat, I tried to make as much noise as possible. To fill that empty house with something other than ghosts. I ended up making us grilled cheese, and canned tomato soup.

"They won't tell me what's going on." His eyes remained focused on the velvety orange liquid that filled his bowl.

"Oh," I said, almost choking on my own spoonful of soup.

"I know she's dead. Elle. But they won't tell me why."

There were so many dead spaces in that house that no one knew how to fill them up again. What did he even know of Nora? How did they explain her pictures on the wall? Who even spoke her name on a regular basis anymore? I placed my spoon back in the bowl and carefully pushed it towards the center of the table.

"They think she was murdered, Noah."

He looked up, his brown eyes meeting mine and then flicking back towards the tabletop. "Like on television."

I let myself think for a second that I wished Nate or either of his parents was still here to deal with this and then said: "Yes."

"Was it the same person who took Nora?"

"I don't know, Noah. I wish I had more answers for you."

And then he said with a grim determination, his face fierce and angry, his eyes lit up with a kind of righteous clarity that only children can carry off with conviction: "I just want to know. No one lets me know anything."

I nodded and answered quietly: "I want to know too, Noah."

"Will you tell me? If you find out? Will you tell me?"

"I'll tell you."

"Promise?"

"I promise."

"And will you promise you'll find out? I want to know, Maddie."

"I promise, Noah. I promise I'll find out."

It probably wasn't even my promise to make. I certainly wasn't sure I could keep it, and presumably his parents had their reasons for keeping things from him. For trying to protect him from the pain that the world had already inflicted on him at such a young age. But I had to. For some inexplicable reason Noah trusted me enough to do it, and even though I didn't have the same level of trust in myself as he did, I knew that I needed it as desperately as he did. That I needed to find out who had killed Elle, and to finally find out what had happened to Nora, and that I wasn't leaving Forest View until I did.

The doorbell rang then, and Noah and I looked at each other, he just shrugging at me before picking up his spoon and continuing to plough away at his soup; it was my job to deal with a ringing doorbell, not his. It rang again, too soon after the first ring for it to be described as anything other than insistent. I checked my phone quickly to see if maybe Ange had texted to say she was coming over, but there was nothing. The doorbell rang again.

Pushing back my chair I told Noah I'd only be a minute and for him to stay where he was. By now I was pretty sure I knew who, or what, was at the door.

"You've got to be kidding me," I said when I finally pulled the door open to reveal who was standing there. I would have recognized Gloria Lewis immediately, even if she hadn't made the transition from print to TV journalism. She had been first on the scene when Nora had disappeared, the first reporter to break the story at a regional rather than local level and hadn't dropped the subject even when all the other media outlets sloped off home. A few steps behind her stood a tall man wearing a grey fleece and navy puffy vest with a backwards ball cap on even though it was snowing. He also had a large video camera stretched across his left shoulder.

"Maddie … Madeline Fielder. I wasn't expecting to find you here," Gloria proclaimed. It had been ten years but she still recognized me. I shuddered a little.

"What are you doing here?" I demanded.

"I was looking for the Altmans. They haven't released a statement yet and I was hoping they might want to do so to me.

Talking to someone with a recognizable face might make it easier for them."

I actually laughed, the situation was so preposterous. Gloria raised an eyebrow and took one very slight step back from the doorway as I did so.

"Are you fucking kidding me, Gloria? Why on earth would anyone in their right mind think that the Altmans would want to talk about any of this to you of all people? You almost destroyed them."

"The world's a different place than it was ten years ago, Maddie. It's not just rolling news now. It's Twitter and Reddit and podcasts and a million armchair detectives. The Altmans need to get their official narrative out there as quickly as possible. I can help them do that. I want to help them do that."

"'Official narrative'? Will you just listen to yourself? This is their life. Their daughter just died. Please just give them some space and some peace."

"What about you then? You seem a little more willing to talk than you were ten years ago. You've certainly become more strident. Care to share what you know? Or some memories of Noelle? When did you last see her? Were you close at all after Nora's disappearance? And what about the rumors about the Altmans' divorce? I hear they're having some issues; do you think that might have played a part here?"

I shook my head, nausea rolling through me, unable to believe the gall of it, her audacity, her confidence in showing up there, but my venom surprised even me when I said: "Go fuck yourself, Gloria," my voice scratched and ropey, about to break.

I slammed the door shut, the bang reverberating through me, echoing the heavy thud of my heart. I stood there with my back against the front door for a while, my skin like static, my teeth on edge. I could feel every single vein inside my body desperately pumping blood to and from my heart. There was this feeling right underneath my skin like a razor's edge; like any minute it was all going to be peeled off from my bones. I heard Noah's chair scrape and the soft pad of his feet on the tiled floor before he appeared in the kitchen doorway.

"Are you okay?" he said, watching me. I think he probably heard every single thing Gloria Lewis and I had said to each other.

"Yeah, yeah. I'm okay. Just give me a second." My voice was a pant. I could barely even breathe.

"Do you want some water?" he asked and before I could answer he turned back into the kitchen to retrieve my glass of water while I, for some godforsaken reason, burst into tears. Taking the glass of water Noah proffered me, I let the familiar slip of it running down my throat refresh me. *One thing at a time*, I thought. One goddamn thing at a time.

CHAPTER EIGHT

It took me a long time to build up the courage to go up to the top floor of the house. Gloria Lewis's visit had shaken me more than I would have liked it to, and Noah and I sat in the living room watching TV to recover from it before I made the excuse of needing the bathroom and left him down there alone. Nora and Elle had shared the top floor of the house, their rooms divided by a bathroom, and I wasn't sure what I'd find once I got up there. I didn't know if Katherine and Jonathan had emptied Nora's room of her touch, if they'd redecorated and transformed it into a guest room, but I had a feeling they probably hadn't.

The door was ajar and when I pushed, it opened silently, stealthy. The day had dimmed, light leaking from the sky, and I turned on the overhead light, illuminating Nora's bedroom, a room I hadn't stepped foot in for over ten years. It reverberated with her: from every wall, on every surface, there she was, bellowing her name at me. It was appropriate really; Nora had always been shouting at me about something, why not now? There was a musty smell though, and dust lined the bookshelves where her favorite books still sat. When I opened her wardrobe I was surprised to find it mostly empty; evidently Katherine had donated a lot of her clothes to charity, even while she couldn't bear to part with Nora's other possessions.

Nora had been a prolific photo collage maker and my own face looked out at me from the walls, pressed up against photos of Ange and Louden, Leo, Hale, and whoever else. I ran my finger along the spines of her books, stopping when I found a comic I'd made her for her sixteenth birthday. I drew it out carefully, the paper crisp with age, the whole thing bound together amateurishly with string. It was from a series I'd once drawn called "the Forest View Furies" that featured animal versions of me, Ange, Hale, and Nora. I used to draw stuff like that all the time. Nora was a wolf known as Wolfora; I was a fox called Foxeline; Hale a doe called Haloe; and Ange was Squirange, the squirrel. It was a way to pass time at school, and I managed to involve all of us in it by intentionally leaving the speech bubbles blank so that either one of the other three could fill them in. I had difficulty getting words out even then. Sometimes it had just been an extremely elaborate way to pass notes, but other times there was a theme or a narrative running through them.

I hadn't drawn anything since graduating high school. I hadn't ever been good or anything, just enthusiastic. Or to put it another way; I could have been good if I tried, but I stopped trying. This was one of the few comics I'd actually drawn outside of school. Nora had loved "the Forest View Furies," or at least she'd loved the superpowered, hyperactive, wolf version of her I'd created, so for her sixteenth birthday I'd drawn a whole comic centered on Wolfora coming of age and receiving her final superpower; a super-strength howl that allowed her to destroy her enemies with her voice.

I flicked through the comic, that strange teenage relic, and listened as the shouts of remembrance got louder and louder. So loud I couldn't drown them out any longer. I hadn't been surrounded by so much Nora-ness for years. Normally she was a whisper rather than a shout. A persistent, permanent, very, very present whisper, but a whisper nonetheless.

I didn't miss Nora then any less than I had done when she first went missing. If anything, it was worse. The conviction that she was more than simply gone had embedded itself firmly within me but that wasn't the worst of it. It was the way in which her being gone—her being, as I believed, dead—had become an accepted part of my daily life that I hated.

The normalcy of it was what I railed and raved over; the fact that this person whom I loved could be gone, and that could be normal, routine, everyday. It nauseated me. I missed her face, and her hair and her teeth, her mouth and her smile, her body and her fingers, her long, wide legs, and her surprisingly small feet, and the second toe that was longer than her big toe. I missed all of it. Her brain and her heart, and her words. I missed her words. All those words she had said to me, but most of all the ones we missed out on. So many fucking words. The phone calls and the Skype calls, the texts and the emails, the flick of a grin as she teased me, the downturn of her eyes as I said something overly curt. Too far, Mads. Too far. The accumulation of words and a post-adolescent college life. A life lived apart and yet still together. So many words she'd never say to me, and I'd never get to hear.

How was it even possible to miss something I never had? And now there she was, shouting at me from every wall, every corner, every crack of her ancient bedroom and I had no idea what she was trying to tell me.

***

"What are you doing out here?" I ask, closing the door to the lake house quietly behind me and joining her down on the grass. Her face is looking straight up into the clear sky which pulses and streams with starlight.

"I'm just trying to find all those constellations you pointed out to me that time, but I can't remember a single one." She turns to me suddenly, her face deadly serious in the milky moonlight. "What's your favorite thing about life?"

"About life?"

"Yeah."

"You mean what's my favorite thing in the world?"

"Sure, if you wanna put it like that."

"A cold night and a sky full of stars," I say without even stopping to think for once.

"That's a good one," Nora says. She raises an eyebrow. "Very apposite."

I laugh. "What's yours?"

"Something sweet on my tongue. A good tune on the radio. The sound of a friend laughing." She pokes me in the arm then but I don't laugh this time; she seems far too solemn to laugh. "The smell of grass and earth and the lake."

"Those are good ones too," I say. "Summer."

"Yeah, yeah. Summer. But more than that. Us summer. Our summers."

"Us summers are good."

"I'm scared this was our last. That we'll never have a summer like this again."

I make a face at her, my nose burrowing into my forehead. "We'll have as many of these summers as we goddamn please, Altman. There's no contract you have to sign on enrolling into college that says you never get a great summer again. In fact, I'm pretty sure it's the opposite."

She sighs and sucks in a breath and then laughs, shrugging and turning her face toward the sky again. "What are you doing up anyway? I thought you fell asleep already."

I hunch my shoulders up to my ears and fold my arms across my chest to keep warm. It's late September and it's cold already, the frigid air seeping through the ineffective material of my sweatshirt and pajama pants. "Something must've woken me up."

"Me too," Nora says, her eyes staring off into the dark. "I thought I heard a car coming up the road, but I guess I must have imagined it."

We look at each other and I feel nervous but also kind of hysterical suddenly, a tightness knotting up my chest and heart, even though we've sat out here until dawn a hundred, a thousand times. Even though the Altmans' lake house is as familiar to me as my own home, even though there are three more girls sleeping peacefully in the house as we speak.

"Let's get inside," Nora mutters, trying to dispel the unease that's suddenly come over the two of us.

Once inside, Nora turns the lock in the door for what must be the first time since the beginning of the summer. The metal cries out from lack of use, and Nora has to jiggle the door a couple times, sighing with annoyance as she does so, before finally we hear that comforting click as the lock slides home.

A loud noise tore me from my reverie and I ran downstairs, my feet slipping on the stairs as I rushed to see if Noah was okay.

"Everything all right?" I asked as I got to the hallway and looked in on the den where I'd left him. He was sitting up on the back of the couch, staring out the window and just turned to look at me and then back outside in answer. I joined him on the couch and watched as Gloria Lewis and her team set up their cameras and lights next to their bright blue van emblazoned with the WISNews 3 logo.

"What do they want?" Noah asked.

"They want to know what happened to Elle," I said.

"Then why aren't they at the police station like my parents? We don't know what happened to her."

But Noah's logic meant little in the face of a tragic rolling news story, and I wondered how long it would be before Gloria was joined by other news channels determined to get to the bottom of another mystery that now surrounded the Altman family.

I ignored Gloria Lewis and her colleagues as I left the Altman house just as Jonathan and Katherine had done when they returned, Nate still being interviewed down at the station. Noah and I had still been watching TV, but the sound of Jonathan's SUV in the driveway made us sit up and peer through the window again, watching as Katherine's already pale face blanched as Gloria Lewis shoved a microphone in her face.

I walked quickly over to Cool's, the local bar, where I had arranged to meet Ange for a drink, not just ready to get in out of the cold, but very, very ready for a drink. Ange's paper had sent up a photographer to cover the case with her, and it was Jack, a friend of both of ours who had never been to Forest View but had heard a lot about it. It was relatively early still and the bar was quiet, so spotting them sitting in a corner booth wasn't hard.

"Hey," I said, removing my coat and scarf and gloves.

"Hey, Maddie," Jack said, raising his hand half-heartedly and smiling thinly.

I smiled back, throwing my stuff down in the furthest corner of the booth, and offered them both a drink, which, already having them, they declined.

"Can I buy you a drink?" someone asked me as I stood waiting for the bartender to return with my beer at the bar.

I squinted at him through the barroom lighting, trying to take him in. "Why?"

I was wearing the same sweater I'd been wearing for the past two days, and jeans I hadn't washed in … well, I couldn't remember the last time I'd washed them.

He laughed in response, but it wasn't real. His right hand was wrapped around the halffinished bottle of beer he was clutching and I watched as his index finger tapped out a silent, nervous rhythm on the bottle neck. He wasn't very good at this.

He coughed. "I just wanted to—well, buy you a drink."

"Why?" I said again. People rarely have an answer to that question. Regardless of context, the question of "why" hardly ever gets answered.

I didn't recognize him, but I'd noticed him alone in one of the smaller booths when I walked in to meet Ange. He'd been trying to subtly scour the room, gauge the atmosphere or whatever, but his subtlety left a little to be desired. There weren't enough of him around yet to lend him invisibility. But they'd come. I was sure of it. Hell, he was sure of it. That's why he was there *now*. Trying to get in early, get an exclusive.

The bartender brought me my beer, finally, and I didn't let the stranger pay despite his insistence.

"Can I give you a little advice?" is what I ended up saying after taking an initial sip.

He swallowed. "Sure."

"Don't act like you're hitting on someone when actually you want to interview them. It's creepy and ineffective."

"Oh, right. Yeah. Sure." His eyes boggled a bit, and I wondered how old he was, who he worked for, what he was doing here. "You are Madeline Fielder though, right? I thought I recognized you."

I didn't have to answer him, I could have just returned to the booth with Ange and Jack but, instead I said: "Yeah. I'm Maddie."

"And you knew Noelle? The girl who just got murdered?"

"I know who Noelle is. You don't need to clarify."

"Right, right. So, do you think I could ask you a few questions?"

"You just did."

"No, I mean a few more."

"I don't think so, buddy." I said, leaving him standing at the bar. I already knew what questions he wanted answering, and either I didn't have them or I wasn't prepared to give them.

"Who was that?" Ange asked as soon as I sat back down.

I glanced back over to the bar, but the guy had already slunk back to his own booth. "I'm thinking independent blogger trying to make a name for himself."

"Interesting. My first guess was BuzzFeed."

"He was a little too sweaty. And too young."

Ange let out a huff of unconvincing laughter. "I guess we should have expected this. They'll be slithering in from all over the country soon enough."

"You're taking a rather dim view of your fellow journalists there, Angie."

She sighed, expertly twirled her beer bottle between her hands and took a long drag from it. "We already know what to expect. No point sugarcoating it."

"I've already seen Lewis," I said.

"What? You didn't say."

"There wasn't time; she came by the Altmans' this afternoon while I was with Noah. She's still camped outside there with her camera crew."

"Jesus, she is such a snake."

"A snake who managed to secure a nice little TV job after capitalizing on Nora's disappearance."

"She's a terrible person, Mads," Ange said in a quiet voice, "we all know that."

I shrugged, as if it was all the same to me; water off a duck's back, no skin off my nose. But I don't know why I even bothered. If anyone had known how much all this meant, it was Angie.

"How you doing, Jack?" I asked, changing the subject.

"Been better."

"I'll bet. Ange given you a tour of our beautiful little town here yet?"

"Well, I've been to CJ's and now here, so I guess I'm hitting up all the major spots."

"You forgot the Walgreens."

"I'll make sure to stop by before I leave."

"Have you found out anything more about Elle?" I asked Ange.

She didn't answer immediately, her mind presumably else-where, her head tilted to the right and, at first, I thought perhaps she was lost in thought over Elle. It was easy sometimes to fall into pockets of everyday life, to find yourself laughing and talking, perhaps even enjoying yourself, only to then suddenly be dragged back out of it, and brought back to a reality you barely recognized. But she wasn't lost in thought and her eyes were focused on someone or something that was coming up behind me.

As I shifted in my seat to turn around I saw Leo and Bright walking towards our booth. Leo dumped himself down into the empty space next to me without even a "hello," while Bright remained standing.

"You contaminated anymore crime scenes recently, Fielder?" Leo asked, grinning as a way to tell me that he was only joking, only teasing. The sight of his white teeth flashing against the dim of the dark bar jarred me, and my hand gripped a little too tightly around my nearempty bottle of beer.

"Nope," I said, practically through gritted teeth, "just the one for me so far."

"Good. That's good." He waved a finger between me and Ange. "You two need to be careful."

"Why?" Ange asked, her eyes flashing.

Leo sighed, looking between us, his shoulders slumped a little. "Come on, Angela. Don't be stupid about this. Someone's been killed. Just be careful, okay?"

"I'm a reporter, Leo, reporting the news is kind of my job," Ange pointed out to him.

"And that's great; there's just no need to go all Erin Brockovich on me. Just try and be careful, is all I'm saying." He cut his eyes to me, they looked glacial in this light, and said: "Don't go tramping around in the woods, maybe, that's all I'm asking."

"You mean because we're helpless little women?" Ange said.

Leo rolled his eyes. "Jesus, do I really need to spell this out

88

for you? Yes, you're women. Whoever killed Noelle—killed a woman. Ergo, you need to be careful." He said this all extra slowly, as if talking to children. "If it makes you feel any better, I'm going to be extra careful too. So's Bright. And whoever your friend here is, too, I'd also advise him to be careful."

"I'm Jack," Jack said, belatedly introducing himself while reaching across to shake Leo's hand, who did so casually. "I'm a photographer, working with Ange."

"Good for you, man. Nice to meet you. Sorry it's not under better circumstances," Leo said.

Jack nodded and tipped his beer bottle towards Leo in agreement before taking a sip.

"Was there evidence that Elle was sexually assaulted?" I asked suddenly, the words running together as my heart turned to an overworked jackhammer inside my chest. I shifted in my seat a little so that I could see Leo better, but it wasn't Leo who answered.

"We can't answer that." I looked up at Bright, and he was staring right at me.

"Because you don't know?"

"Because we can't answer that."

"It'll get out, Bright," I said, thinking of Gloria Lewis while looking over at Ange.

"If it gets out, it gets out. But it won't be because of either me or Leo. Not that we know. Or can say."

"Sorry, champ. Looks like that's all you're getting." Leo clapped his hand around my shoulder and got up to leave, looking over towards Ange. "You'll have to find yourselves another source. See you guys around."

Bright didn't make a move as Leo wandered away and we stayed staring at one another for a couple of beats before I said: "Bright, come on, this is us, just try and pretend you're not a cop for a second, and Ange isn't a reporter. Isn't there anything else you can tell us?"

Bright looked behind him, at Leo's retreating back. His eyes flashed in the dim light of the bar, but his resolve didn't flicker, not an inch. "You know I can't do that, Maddie. Even if we did know anything. Which we don't."

"Does that mean the state police have been called in already?" Ange asked.

"Yeah, we've been benched," Bright said stiffly. "Not that I'm complaining, rather them than me."

"Seriously?" I asked. "You don't want to help with the case?"

"Sure, I want to help. But there's only so much you can stomach, you know? I've known Elle her whole life. I'm not sure I could deal with photos of her dead body coming across my desk."

His candor surprised me. I couldn't quite align this confession with the perennially stoic Bright that I knew, but I was relieved to hear that the state police were investigating already. When Nora first went missing there'd been a flurry of police activity and interest until all their leads dried up, all the search parties returned home with nothing, and all their suspects, including Louden and Nate, came to nothing. Nora had vanished, and it may as well have been in a puff of smoke for all the good our police department did in trying to find her or find out what had happened to her.

It was normal for cops to keep things close to their chest, of course. I wasn't stupid enough to think that if Bright and Leo actually knew anything they were going to tell us over beers and a soundtrack of AOR but that didn't make any of it any easier. Back at the Altmans' I'd promised Noah that I'd find out what had happened to Elle, and I realized now that I'd meant it: It wasn't just the police who had to redeem themselves here; I had to, too. I'd let myself disappear when Nora went missing, but if the last ten years had taught me anything it was that I hadn't managed to stay any closer to her by keeping myself away from everybody else.

Even Elle I'd kept at arm's length, only calling when it suited me, answering emails after months had gone by when I should have been putting her at the top of my list. I liked to think we'd remained close, or at least as close as possible with me away from home, but the truth was I hadn't done nearly enough. She was a kid, barely even seventeen, and she'd already seen so much, been through the worst when she'd found out one snowy night in January that however bad it gets, there's always worse to come.

Maybe that had been my biggest mistake, of thinking that just because I'd lived through one nightmare, that another one couldn't possibly come along and wake us all again screaming. Words like resolution, redemption—revenge even—have such a solid, sincere certainty to them that they're easily mocked and discarded. But sometimes you have to grab hold of something solid to keep yourself afloat, and I grabbed hold of them as if they were my one last lifeline.

I couldn't wait and see what happened this time, not with Elle. If anyone should have made it out of this town alive, it was her, but we—*I*—had let Nora hang like a question mark, a mystery over everything and now she'd been the one to pay the price.

My phone buzzed on the table next to me, and I looked down, surprised to find a message from Nate. He hadn't been with his parents when they returned earlier in the afternoon, so we still hadn't really talked. I stared down at my phone where the words

Where are you?

had appeared. I replied, telling him I was at the bar, and was even more surprised when he wrote back:

I'll be there in 5.

In the end it took him much longer to reach us at our corner booth. I'd watched him work his way through the crowd that had built up while we'd been sitting there, trying as hard as he could to keep his dark head down, eyes to the floor, praying not be noticed or recognized. But of course he was. He stopped to have his shoulder clapped and his hand grabbed, his arm squeezed

91

in futile attempts at solidarity and sympathy. But there were also sidelong glances and whispered conversations that stopped as he passed, only to start up again once he was presumed to be out of earshot. It was all so skin-crawlingly familiar from ten years before, I had to grit my teeth against it.

***

"Oh my God," someone says and soon I can hear it everywhere, the gathered crowd of students all collectively saying, "Oh my God," as they turn as one towards whatever has caught their attention.

I'm staring down at the turned earth, waiting for this to be over, for the damn maple tree to be planted, for some kind words to be spoken by someone—probably by my dad—so that I can just go home. But the ripple of whispers continue, rolling through the assembled crowd, and Ange nudges me, hissing, "Mads, it's Nate."

I look up instinctively, my eyes locking on Nate's almost automatically. He's standing at the edge of the crowd, his shoulders rigid, a makeshift, futile shield against the buzz of whispers and staring faces.

"I can't believe he's here," someone says behind me.

"Chill out," another voice says, "it's not like he actually killed her. He wasn't ever charged, remember?"

"Still. Can you imagine having the balls to show up here, like this?"

"She's his fucking sister," I spit out, turning around to face them. "Where else do you expect him to be?"

It's two juniors I recognize from the hockey team, one square-jawed and thick-necked, the other tall, thin, fast. They would've been playing with Nate just last year, but all that's forgotten now as they speculate on his guilt.

Ange tugs on my arm, turning me away as she says in a low voice: "Come on, Mads, they're not worth it."

But the moment's ruined, if there ever was a moment to save, and when I look back towards Nate, he's gone.

Eventually, Nate found his way over to us and sat down next to me, two bottles of beer in hand. He placed one next to my almost-empty one and smiled, a small, almost-empty smile, at Jack and Ange.

"Hey, Nate," Ange said softly, her voice almost lost in the now-fevered energy of the bar. "How you doing?"

He gave two curt nods, his eyes lost in the crowd and then turned back to the table. "I don't know, Ange. I don't know how I'm doing."

"I'm really sorry for your loss," Jack said.

Nate's face pinched slightly as he peered at Jack. "I'm sorry, I don't—?"

"This is Jack," Ange interjected quickly, "we work together."

"Well, thanks, Jack," Nate intoned, giving me a sidelong glance as he drank from his beer bottle. "I need to talk to you," he said in a low voice as Jack got up from the booth to get a couple more beers for him and Ange.

"Okay," I said.

"Not here."

I took a sip of my beer, not looking at him. "You just got here," I said.

"I know, I just wasn't sure if you'd come meet me or not."

"Why?"

Nate sighed. "I don't know, Mads, maybe because we haven't really talked in about five years?"

I didn't know what to say to that, so I just continued drinking. "Can I at least finish my beer?" I asked eventually.

"Sure. I'll walk you home when you're ready to leave."

But we didn't leave for a while. The bar was busy by then and our booth was attracting its fair share of attention, but it was easy enough to ignore with the benefit of a few beers down me.

93

It was only when I got up to go to the bathroom that I really noticed just how much of a spectacle we were as friends and relatives of Nora and Noelle Altman. Working my way through the crowd I swear I could feel people staring at me, voices lowering as I passed and then rising again, just as they had done with Nate; but in all honesty I could have been imagining it.

It wasn't until I was on my way back to the table that someone actually shouted "Hey," at me, while simultaneously grabbing at my arm.

I pulled back just out of habit and turned to see who it was. The overly young blogger.

"I don't want to answer your questions. I'm sorry," I said. It wasn't as if I owed him an apology, but he really did look so young and out of place. I wondered for a second if he was even old enough to drink. He shifted a little from foot to foot and tried to smile.

"I think we got off on the wrong foot." He stuck his hand out as if to shake mine. "I'm Keegan Ellis."

"So?"

"I … I went to school with you. I was in the same class as your sister. You don't recognize me?"

"With Cordy?" There was no way this kid was the same age as Serena.

"Yeah. We did a load of the same classes together senior year."

"Sorry, Keegan. I don't remember. And it still wouldn't change anything. I don't want to answer any questions. Not from you or anyone."

"Okay. Yeah, I'm sorry. I get that."

I turned to leave but before I could go he grabbed my arm again. "I'm sorry," he said again, and to be honest he did look a little terrified, "I'm really sorry to bother you like this, but I have this blog. It's-it's about Nora. Altman."

"What?"

"I write a blog about Nora. About her disappearance. It's

investigatory. I just wanted you to know. I'm not here to pry into your life or anything. Or Noelle's. I just really, genuinely, want to know what happened to Nora."

Something fizzed in my ears like static and for whatever reason I couldn't think of anything to say.

"Don't you?" Keegan said when he realized I wasn't about to say anything. "Don't you want to know what happened to her?"

"Of course I fucking do," I said, the words jumping out of me, ready to attack.

"Then, will you help me?"

"I can't … I can't talk to you." I said, the static getting louder and beginning to crawl through me.

"You okay?" someone said to me once I'd reached our table, but I couldn't tell if it was Ange, Jack, or even Nate. I shook my head, trying to shake it off, as someone stood up from the table to grab my arm. I pulled away as I had done with Keegan, alarmed, but it was just Nate.

"We should leave," he said, looking around, his face hardening as he did so. "We shouldn't be here anyway."

I nodded in agreement and began to put my coat on.

We said our goodbyes to Ange and Jack, Nate raised a hand to Bright and Moody, still stood at their table on the other side of the bar, and we walked through the door and out into the cold dark. Our boots crunched through snow that was swiftly filling up the parking lot of the bar with a fresh fall. It was soft and heavy, and once the door swung shut behind us, immeasurably quiet.

"Did you walk here?" Nate asked, turning his face to the sky, letting a few snowflakes fall there silently.

"Yeah."

"Come on then, I'll walk you home."

We were both quiet on the walk, heads bowed against the snow. The town was blanketed, soft and silent, but I thought I could sense something underneath it. Maybe I was imagining it, probably I was, but I couldn't let go of the sense of something sharp and bitter beneath all that snow, struggling to come to the surface. A car rolled past us, going way too slowly, even for such a snowy night, the headlights glancing off us in the dark. I thought I could see whoever it was in the driving seat leaning forward, trying to make out who we were just as I was trying to make out who they were. I shivered, even though I wasn't especially cold.

"You okay?" Nate asked, his voice coming at me as if from a great distance.

I nodded and then really thought about it and shook my head. I most certainly was not okay. I took a deep breath, steeling myself. "What was it you wanted to talk to me about?" I asked.

There was a long pause, long enough for me to turn to Nate in the dark, check that he'd heard me. He looked nauseous in the light almost, sick with grief and heartbreak. Finally, he just said: "Gloria Lewis."

"Is she still hanging out around your house?" I asked.

"Yeah, her and her little cameraman. She wants to film an interview, all four of us. Remembering Noelle or something. She thinks it will help stop people throwing their own theories out there, as if anything could ever do that, let alone a fucking TV interview."

"She said the same thing to me too."

"You spoke to her?"

"Not officially. She knocked on the door, and we spoke, but I'd never do an interview with her. You know that."

"I just wanted to check."

I slowed my pace, cold and tired, but not quite ready to leave Nate just yet. "So that's all you wanted? To tell me not to talk to Gloria Lewis?" I asked eventually.

Nate didn't say anything, and I wondered if that was really why we were there, or if there was something else going on, something he wanted to say but didn't quite know how. Long gone were the days when I could figure him out with just a look, so I said: "Because you didn't need to tell me that."

"I know."

There was a long pause before I got up the courage to ask: "Did you see her?"

Feeling terrible, I watched the blood drain from Nate's face, as he realized I meant Elle's body. The sleepless bruises under his eyes appeared to grow even as we walked together side by side, but he managed to answer me.

"No. Mom and Dad identified her. I-I couldn't go in there."

We were nearing my parents' house; I could see that the lights from the kitchen and den were still on, their amber glow warming up the cold night air. "Do they know how she died?" I asked quietly, watching Nate carefully.

He swallowed and nodded at the same time, unable to answer at first before saying: "She was suffocated. But the killer stabbed her as well."

The world drained away to nothing but the two of us. I wished I hadn't asked and yet was also glad I knew. The loss of Elle, the shock of it, the vastness of it was being obscured by the horror of it.

I tried to think of Elle before it all happened and couldn't quite reach her. She was being edged out by all the horror, and it was still only two days since she'd been found. What would become of her in the coming years? She'd be yet another story for people to pass around and claim ownership over, just as with Nora. Or maybe, eventually, she would find her way back to us. Her memory whole and real, rather than fractured and broken. As much as I wanted that to be true, I couldn't quite believe it; it still hadn't happened with Nora after all, and it had been ten years.

"And did he ... do they know—had she been assaulted? Raped?" I could barely get the words out, they got stuck in my chest, my throat, my mouth, but for some reason I felt as though I had to know.

"No. She hadn't been. Thank God," Nate replied, although he sounded like he was biting down on something.

I felt something wash through me then, something like relief but not quite, and I had to stop myself from crying. I could have said something then about small mercies, but nothing about it felt either small or merciful, so I said goodnight, even though I wasn't quite sure I wanted to, and left him out there alone in the night as I closed the door behind me.

CHAPTER NINE

My parents were still up when I got in, sitting in the den watching the news, but I said hi and goodnight, making my excuses and heading straight up to my room.

"Maddie," someone said from the bottom of the stairs, and I turned to see my mom standing there staring up at me. She made her way slowly up to meet me on the landing before saying: "Where does your work think you are right now?"

"Right now?" I asked archly.

"You know what I mean. You've missed two days of work already."

"I called in sick."

Her hands were on her hips as she spoke and I watched as she pursed her lips, rolling them into a flat line and then stared down at the floor in disappointment. "You can't afford to lose this job, Mads," she said at last.

"I know that."

"We'd all understand if you went back to Madison. You don't have to deal with this and you shouldn't feel like you have to."

"Noelle has been murdered, Mom," I said, watching as her face paled a little, even in the soft glow of the landing light. "What on earth makes you think that I'd be able to just drive on back to Madison and carry on as usual?"

"You don't have to carry on as usual, honey. Just look after yourself. This can't be good for you, any of it."

My heart beat slower, heavier, the sound of waves crashing filling my ears.

"Maddie?" Mom said.

"I'm fine," I said.

"If you were fine, wouldn't you be going back to work?"

"I mean, I'm fine being here. I'm not about to fall off a cliff."

She took a step towards me, her hand reaching to tuck a strand of hair behind my ear and then letting it rest on my shoulder. She looked tired, lines of worry stretched across her forehead, her mouth downturned, and her light blue eyes smeary with almost-tears. "You don't have to do this," she said, her voice quiet but strong, "you don't have to take this on."

I wanted, more than anything, to melt but instead my body stiffened, reflexively, and her hand dropped from my shoulder.

"I'm fine," I said again. "I just need to go to bed."

"Okay," she said after a long pause. "Okay, Maddie, you go to bed."

I didn't go to sleep though. I had enough diazepam left that meant I could have slept for the next twelve hours, but instead I turned on my laptop after crawling into bed and looked up Gloria Lewis. Even though she'd since been hired by a TV news channel, the *Wisconsin Daily News* seemed to have hired her back to cover Noelle's case, and I started reading her most recent article, her insinuating, insidious words bringing it all back to me.

It took me a lot longer to shore up the courage needed in order to go back and read over the highlights of her work from ten years before. I didn't need to be doing this, I kept reminding myself; I already knew the shape of her words and the sting of them. I'd never forgotten them, even as everyone begged me not to read the articles, told me to ignore her, reminded me of how little Gloria Lewis's words meant. But they meant something; they still did then. Even if all they meant was that in the midst of a storm not only could you get wrecked but there was always someone willing to go through that wreckage, pick it over and use it any way they wanted.

After a while I had to stop. Everything suddenly too much. Elle and Nora had begun to merge in my mind, until the particulars of Nora's disappearance traced over the current reality of Elle's murder. History wasn't so much repeating itself as it was being rewritten. It was the same story with a different ending and yet I was still trying to figure out how it had all got started. *How had we got here?*

I wanted to throw my laptop across the room, the white noise of the hard-working fan suddenly making me feel sick, but instead I thought about the young blogger from Cool's who claimed to be classmates with Cordy. Searching for him on Facebook I saw that he hadn't been lying and he and Cordy were Facebook friends, albeit with very few, if any, interactions. Grabbing my phone, I called Cordy.

"Hey," she said on picking up, "what's going on? Is everything okay?" Her words were a rush of concern, sending a jolt of warmth through me that quickly turned to guilt. I was the older sister here, but I was so used to being the one in constant need of comfort that sometimes I forgot Cordy was still just twenty-two.

"Hey, I'm okay. Hanging in there."

"I can't believe it, Mads," she said, hushed now, reverent, "how can this have happened?"

Cordy was just twelve when Nora disappeared, those five years' difference in our ages shielding her from the worst of it; and yet she, too, like Elle, like Noah, had grown up in the long, long shadow cast by Nora.

"I don't know," I said, wanting to elaborate, wishing I had something to tell her, but coming up empty-handed.

"Do they have any idea who did it yet?"

"I don't think so. At least, not that they're telling us."

"What about Nate? Have you seen him, what does he say? He must know something."

"Like what?" I said, suddenly sharp.

"Just that they would've been all together that night, right? On Sunday? He'd know if she was acting strange or ..."

"I don't know, Cordy," I said with a sigh, suddenly exhausted, "I really don't know anything. I wanted to ask you about Keegan Ellis though, do you know him?"

"Keegan? Sure, I know him. Why?"

"He stopped me in the bar, said he wanted to talk to me for some blog?"

"Oh, the blog. Yeah, that makes sense, I guess."

"So, you knew about it?" I don't know why this annoyed me so much, but it did. Why hadn't she told me about it before?

"Sure. He's been writing it for ages. I didn't realize he was still going with it, to be honest, but I guess now ... with Elle."

"Yeah, he's back with a vengeance," I said, spitting the words out.

"You don't have to worry about him, seriously. He's a nice enough guy; he'll leave you alone if you ask him."

"I just don't get it," I said. "Why's he so interested? So obsessed? He didn't even know Nora."

There was a pause and I could hear Cordy's breathing coming down the line.

Eventually she said, ever so gently: "I think maybe you don't understand how much it affected everyone. Not just you. Yeah, Keegan and I are a lot younger than you but Nora's disappearance was still a big deal. He just wants to know what happened to her. You can understand that, right?"

I think Cordy meant her words to reassure me but, for whatever reason, they didn't. Of course, I understood wanting to know what had happened to Nora; that was all I'd ever wanted myself, but I didn't want to know because her life was an interesting mystery to be resolved. I wanted to know because I owed it to her to find out, and because if I didn't then I might end up just as lost as she was.

Maybe that was why I hadn't ever entered this parallel online universe, where everyone had something to say about Nora but no one seemed to know anymore than I did. The internet meant a certain degree of safety and comfort for me. Mostly it was just my Netflix watch list and episodes of television I already knew the endings of and films I'd watched a million times before. It certainly wasn't somewhere I went in order to figure out what had happened to Nora.

I was in the minority, apparently, because when I finally put Nora's name into the search bar there were way more hits than I'd been counting on. I took a look at Keegan Ellis's blog first, trawling through his introduction as a native of Forest View who'd lived through Nora's disappearance and wanted to see her found. I rolled my eyes as he overstated his connection to both the Altmans and the case. As a classmate of Cordy's that made him all of twenty-two, meaning he fell right between Nate and Nora on the one hand, and Elle on the other, who was five years younger than him. He hadn't even been in high school at the same time as any of them. But that hadn't stopped his curiosity or borderline obsession by the looks of things.

The density of his research made my head spin, but the blog hadn't been updated in a while and there was nothing written about Elle so far despite his presence in town. So, instead I went back to my initial search for Nora and found a Reddit thread about her that had been updated in the past twenty-four hours:

/r/noraaltman
Anyone see the news about Nora's sister being found dead?
Submitted 17 hours ago by NeverGoesOut
Nora's younger sister Noelle has been found dead at pretty

much the exact spot that Nora's car was found ten years ago. Looks like it's murder.

27 comments

Sorted by: best

skeletonkey

Fuck man it's the anniversary isn't it? She was found on the 8th – that makes it ten years to the day since Nora went missing. Insane

WHOKiLLedLAURaPalMEr

You're right it's the anniversary. And her sister was 17 as well—same as Nora when she went missing. God that poor family.

DeathsDoor

Poor family? Starting to think something might be pretty rotten in that family. Both their daughters dead or missing by 17? That's fucked up. Someone should take their little kid away from them before he ends up dead too

hellomarshmallows

Jesus that is horrible why would you say that?

DeathsDoor

Because it's obvious! What's the common denominator here? The Altmans. I reckon it's the mom. Can't cope with her daughters being young and beautiful still so goes full fairytale and kills them

hellomarshmallows

You can't just go around saying that kind of shit

DeathsDoor

This is the internet it was built for saying that kind of shit

skeletonkey

/u/NeverGoesOut bud, you there? What the hell's going on?

NeverGoesOut

I'm here. As in literally in Forest View. Got here last night. Can't believe it.

104

skeletonkey

Good to hear you're up there on the front lines again man. Any news? Any info? Been looking online but there's not a lot to go on so far

NeverGoesOut

Pretty much how it is up here too tbh. Police haven't released any statements yet so it's just me sitting in the bar trying to overhear any interesting conversations

It didn't take a detective to figure out that **NeverGoesOut** and Keegan Ellis were one and the same, and although it didn't surprise me to find him virtually hanging out here too, I was shocked by how all this commentary made me feel.

It was one thing to be aware that all this kind of stuff existed, but another to actually be confronted by it. Maybe I should have been comforted by it, but I felt carved out, hollow instead. I remembered Gloria Lewis's words when she knocked on the Altmans' door that afternoon; it was going to be so much worse this time round. And not just because of Reddit, Twitter, Facebook and whatever else. Here were two sisters, one dead, one long missing, both gone; it was the kind of thing that drove people to talk about family curses—at best—and at worst to grimly gossip about the rest of the family.

From a place of objectivity, I knew this scrutiny was warranted and in some ways right: most murders are committed by someone the victim knows. But there was no place for objectivity, not here, not now, not for me. I didn't get that luxury.

If I'd been paying closer attention, I might have been able to see what was coming. I could have traced the events directly over those that happened when Nora disappeared and prepared myself. But grief and shock, and horror and fear weigh you down and cloud your vision, even when you've been there before, even when you know the journey and the destination by heart. So, even though I'd promised myself that I'd find out who killed

Elle, it wasn't as if the resolution banished those clouds from my eyes and enabled me to see clearly at last. I wanted to do right by her, but finding the right way was difficult when you didn't know which way was up.

I should have gone to sleep then of course. Should have shut down my laptop and shut my eyes, but instead I wandered back over to Facebook and added Keegan Ellis as a friend. If he was keeping tabs on me, I wanted to be able to keep tabs on him too.

My News Feed was full of people writing on Elle's wall, and I clicked through to see her profile. It was already full of messages of condolence, shock, horror, sadness. No one had mentioned the way in which she had died; it was as if she'd simply been carried off out of our lives forever on the wings of some ill-timed but benevolent angel. The messages were all "I can't believe you're gone," and "We'll remember you forever," and "I'll think of you whenever I go ice skating." Pretty but empty.

I remembered the barren kitchen at the Altmans' house and wondered where everyone's condolences were when it came round to actually doing something.

I scrolled though the whole thing, right down to the last thing Elle herself had posted, which was an ancient photo of her and Nora. She must have scanned it in, or maybe it was a photo of a photo from her phone; the picture was grainy and a little blurred but I recognized it immediately. An eleven- or twelve-year-old Nora sat on the long-gone couch from the Altmans' TV room, leaning forward around an almost-toddler Elle who looked like she was about to cry and was nestled against Nora's chest. Nora was grinning for the camera, ecstatic to be left in charge of her baby sister by whoever had taken the photo. Elle had posted the photo on Sunday, the day of the ten-year memorial, and had simply written "Nora" underneath it. It had been liked 312 times.

One of the likes had come from Jenna who, upon scrolling back up Elle's page, I realized hadn't left any message of shock or condolence like her peers. I went to her profile page, her picture a close-up of her own last name on a forest green hockey jersey: FAIRFAX.

A few people had written on her wall too, sharing in her grief but she hadn't replied to any of them, nor updated her status to a blanket expression of either thanks or grief. I didn't read too much into it though; if you went on my Facebook page you'd probably assume I'd gone into hiding, it was so sparse and irregularly updated. In fact, adding Keegan Ellis as a "friend" was the most activity on my profile in years. Thinking of this, I added Jenna as a friend too and was surprised when she accepted almost immediately, the green dot by her name indicating she was online and free to chat.

I have a weird question

I wrote to her

> *OK*
> Do you know what Elle's password was? For Facebook, I mean
> *Yeah. She had the same password for everything.*

I breathed out, relieved: This was what I'd been hoping for; that Elle had been as lax about online security as her sister had been.

How would you feel about letting me know what it was?

It took a little longer for Jenna to reply this time, but eventually she wrote:

> *Why?*
> I want to log into her account and see if she was messaging anyone out of the ordinary
> *You mean like any of those guys I mentioned from school?*

107

Maybe yeah

You really think one of them might have killed her?

I honestly don't know. I just want to try and see what was going on with her in the last few weeks. Or months

OK

she wrote back,

Her password is Noelle1998. She used it for everything. I used to tease her about it because anyone could guess it.

I took a shaky breath and laughed. Jenna was right—I probably could have guessed that password if I'd tried hard enough. I wanted to ask Jenna if I was a terrible person to even ask her this favor, to even think about doing it, but I didn't want to place that burden on her. If I was doing a terrible thing, I was doing it, in that moment, for the right reasons. So instead I just thanked her and logged out of my own account before logging back in as Elle. A surge of nausea rolled through me, forming a pulsing, ragged, ropey knot in my abdomen as I typed in Elle's email address and then the password Jenna had given me.

She had well over a hundred notifications, all friends who had written on her wall since she'd died. I quickly turned off chat so that Elle wouldn't appear online to anyone else and freak them out, and went to her message inbox. There was a message from Jenna sent on the day of Nora's memorial, mere hours before Elle would have been killed. Just seeing it there made me think about the unforgivable breach I'd made. I was betraying Elle's trust, and invading her privacy, but even as my hands, which were hovering over the keyboard of my laptop, began to tremor and shake, I took a deep breath and clicked on the message:

Hey babe, just tried calling but guess you're still up at the cabin with no reception so thought I'd try here. So sorry I

wasn't there for you, lmk when you're heading over to mine?
Or can come to you, don't mind. Love you xox

I stayed looking at that message for a long time, my heart turning to a crater inside my chest. It had been sent at 8:34 p.m. on Sunday night. Elle had never even read it.

I thought about turning back, about logging off and shutting down my laptop and not taking this any further. What exactly was I trying to achieve, trying to prove by reading Elle's private messages? But I couldn't bring myself to log off, not yet. I'd come this far after all; the painful, soft vulnerability of that final message was going to be hard to beat.

So, instead I checked her inbox for messages from any of the guys Jenna had mentioned at the diner—Johnny, Mike, and Adrian—making a sound of frustration when I came up with nothing. Thinking that perhaps she might not have been friends with them online, I checked the "message request" part of her inbox, where messages from non-friends are filed. My eyes widened a little when I saw how many there were. Some had appeared since Elle's murder; people she didn't know or did know but wasn't friends with on Facebook, sending fruitless messages of sympathy that would never be read. So, I scrolled further down, looking for something, anything from just before she was killed.

And there, after a few seconds of scrolling, although it felt like many long minutes, I found someone calling themselves "John Smith" who had been messaging Elle since her last birthday:

From: John Smith 08/13/2017 06:45
Happy Birthday Noelle. You're 17 now right?
From: John Smith 09/21/2017 18:26
I saw you in the diner yesterday. You look so much like your sister
From: John Smith 09/21/2017 18:34

109

Why won't you answer me? I'm a good person I promise. Just telling you happy birthday and how much you remind me of your sister

From: John Smith 09/22/2017 00:13

Do you remember her? Your sister? I can spend hours just looking at her profile. Sometimes I think about where she'd be now if it hadn't all gone so wrong. Do you?

From: John Smith 09/22/2017 17:56

Sorry if these messages freak you out. I don't mean to I just want you to reply?

From: John Smith 09/30/2017 18:22

You look so much like her

From: John Smith 10/17/2017 18:54

I was watching you at the diner again earlier. Did you see me?

From: John Smith 10/21/2017 02:42

I thought maybe we could be friends? All I want is to talk to you Noelle that's it. It's not much to ask is it?

From: John Smith 10/23/2017 23:16

You're a selfish bitch you know that? I've never met anyone so fucking self-involved. I was watching you today laughing with your friends having fun. What about your sister Noelle? Have you forgotten about Nora?

From: John Smith 10/24/2017 01:01

I used to think you looked just like her that you were just as beautiful as her but your not. Your nothing compared to your sister

From: John Smith 11/01/2017 16:13

I'd be worried that what happened to Nora will happen to you if I was you

From: John Smith 11/22/2017 20:37

I saw you fall over in the parking lot today. I was going to come over and help but then someone else got there first. Are you ok?

From: John Smith 11/23/2017 01:31
I DON'T UNDERSTAND WHY YOU WON'T JUST FUCKING ANSWER ME
From: Noelle Alexandra Altman 11/23/2017 18:11
I'm going to report you to Facebook. Please stop messaging me
From: John Smith 11//23/2017 18:15
You little fucking bitch you make me fucking sick

I felt nauseous and sweaty, angry heat crawling through my body, and even went to reach for my trash can, but nothing came out. The last few messages had been sent on Thanksgiving. I looked at the time stamp and realized that I might even have been with Elle when she got them. I'd been home for the holiday and went round to the Altmans' for pie as I'd always done when Nora was still here.

***

Elle is sitting at the far end of the table, surrounded by cousins and her aunt and uncle, pushing her pie around her plate, not talking, not listening, her shoulders slumped. Altman family gatherings have been quieter ever since Nora disappeared, but this feels different. There's noise, and chatter, and clattering of knives and forks, glasses accidentally chiming other glasses as they're placed back down on the overcrowded table, but all that noise and action, all that purpose and activity comes from the extraneous members of the family Altman. Katherine is in the kitchen, quietly clearing up, even though everyone else is still eating, and her three children are all staring down at their plates in uniform, while Jonathan is nowhere to be seen.

I watch as the iPhone sat next to Elle's hand flashes silently and she grabs it, suddenly hurried. She doesn't look up from it as she

x

111

pushes her chair back and leaves the room. I take a few more bites of the pie Katherine cut for me when I got there before getting up to follow her. She's in the living room, sat precariously on the arm of one of their sofas, one leg crossed over the other, still engrossed in her phone. She hasn't heard me walk down the hallway and come into the room, and there's a pained look on her face like she can't quite figure out what it is she's reading and is mad at herself because of it.

"Hey, are you okay?" I ask.

Her head flips up at the same time as she shoves her phone into the pocket of her jeans.

"Mads, hey. Yeah, everything's fine."

"You sure? Everything okay with you and Jenna?" I haven't met Jenna yet, but Elle's told me all about her in the long emails which she sends me, even though I'm terrible and only ever manage to reply to about one in three of them and, even then, only with a few sentences.

She smiles, easy now. "Yeah, Jenna's fine. We're all good."

"What about your parents?" I ask. "Where's your dad?"

Something flashes across her face—anger, hurt, frustration—I can't quite tell, but her shoulders slump and she looks smaller, younger all of a sudden. "He's not here. They're-they're getting a divorce. They told us last weekend. Finally."

"They're getting a divorce?" I ask, taken aback. The Altmans have been on the precipice of divorce for at least ten years, but for some reason it still comes as a shock. Maybe I just thought they'd never actually go through with it—as far as I know from Mom, they basically live apart anyway, only really staying together for the sake of the kids. But maybe Jonathan met someone after all those months, hell, years, spent alone in Madison, or maybe, for all I know, Katherine has. Or maybe they've just reached the end of the line. After all these years, after everything they've been through, maybe they just need it all to be over. I can't help thinking of Nora, not of how she would've reacted, because she probably would've just

112

*turned to me, a righteous look on her face and said, "told you so."
No, I can't help thinking that this is yet another final nail in her
nonexistent coffin.*

*"Yup, they're getting a divorce, and Nate knew the whole time.
Isn't that hilarious? Even my own brother's been lying to me, been
in on the joke the whole time." She looks up at me, brown eyes
catching the light, flashing amber almost. Her face has hardened,
and there are red patches on her cheeks, but she's smiling, somehow,
as if she too were in on the joke. She stands up, so we're eye to eye,
and continues to smile, but now it looks stretched, strained. I can
feel myself about to ask her again if she's okay, really, but I can't.
Her smile's fake, but she's trying, so hard, and what can I possibly
say in the face of all that effort?*

I'd known the Altmans when they were so full of life it spilled
out and all over everything. They were infectious; their laughter,
their energy, their noise. I'd watched from the sidelines over the
last ten years as all of them, together and apart, had been dimin-
ished, waned. I'd stopped myself time and again from being
brought back into their orbit because I knew what lived there,
at the heart of them, because it lived in me too: that giant, cata-
clysmic black hole that Nora had left behind. I thought I'd done
just enough, a few emails here, a knock on the door there, but
all I'd been doing was the bare minimum, to make myself feel
just that tiny scrap better and just a jot less guilty. I hadn't even
stopped to think about Elle in all that mess. There she'd sat,
crying out for help, on the arm of their couch, and all I'd been
able to think about was Nora.

I wondered then if I'd ever let Elle out from underneath Nora's
shadow, and the answer was, of course, no. I should have pressed
on, pried her out from behind that forced smile, to talk to me,
tell me the truth. Because, sure, she was angry and in pain about
the divorce, but it was now abundantly clear that there was
something else going on as well. I read over the messages again,

paying attention to the dates and times they were sent, trying, too little, too late, to figure out who this "John Smith" could be.

But as the night went on all I could think about was that forced, stretched smile, Elle hidden behind it, just out of reach. I logged out of Elle's Facebook and back into mine, messaging Jenna, who was now offline, to ask if Elle had ever mentioned getting any threatening messages on Facebook. Then, after thinking about whether or not I should text Nate—my phone in my hand the whole time as I stared at his name on the screen of my iPhone—I instead texted Leo and asked him if we could meet up "tomorrow."

Finally, I swallowed down a diazepam and turned my computer off, waiting, desperate to fall asleep. Elle's face, grim, taut and faking a smile, greeted me as soon as I closed my eyes.

CHAPTER TEN

I was back in CJ's by 8 a.m. the next morning, having woken up to a text message from Leo telling me when and where to meet him. He was already there when I arrived, hunched in a booth, cradling a cup of coffee.

"Hey," he said, looking up at me, and then "Jesus," flinching slightly.

"What?" I said.

"Nothing—you just … you don't look great, Mads."

I sighed, sitting myself down in the booth and pushing hair back out of my face. "I'd only just woken up when I got your text. Didn't have time to shower."

"Well, did you have time to wash your face?"

"Did you ask me here to discuss personal hygiene?"

"No, but maybe we should," he said, smiling slightly, "seems like you might need a refresher course."

Ruby suddenly appeared with menus, and a cup of coffee for me, which I took gratefully. "It's too early for this," I said once she was gone, "can we just talk about what we came here to talk about?"

"Well, you're the one who texted me. What's this all about?"

I took out my phone and showed him the screenshot of the

messages on Elle's Facebook account I'd found the night before. His forehead creased as he scrolled through the photos, looking up at me occasionally.

"I don't get it, what exactly am I looking at?" he said finally.

"Those were all sent to Elle in the few months leading up to her death. Going all the way back to her birthday in August."

Leo sighed and put the phone down, taking a sip from his coffee. "How did you get these?"

I explained about signing in as Elle to Facebook, Leo emitting several low groans as I did so.

"Look at those last few ones, they were sent on Thanksgiving. I was *there*, Leo, I was right there when she was getting them. And she was scared. I didn't realize it at the time, I thought she was upset and angry about what was going on with her parents, but I think she was really freaked out by these."

Leo's face had cleared as I spoke, and now he reached across the table towards me. I thought he was reaching for the phone, to take a closer look at the messages, but instead he took hold of my right hand. It felt warm and a little clammy in his, but he squeezed tight. "You're feeling guilty, Maddie. That's all this is. You feel bad that you couldn't help Elle, that you couldn't stop this from happening, but this isn't the way to help now."

He was right, of course—I did feel guilty. But that wasn't all it was. "So you don't think those messages mean anything? You think they're just some random creep, completely unrelated."

Leo leaned back in his seat, shrugging. "Honestly, I don't know. I can pass this all on though if it makes you feel better."

"You can?"

"Sure. I'm not involved in the investigation—I'm just a lowly police officer—but if you think it's important, I'll get it to where it needs to be."

I let out a deep breath. "Okay. Thanks."

"Make you feel better?"

"A little, yeah."

"There's nothing you could have done, Mads," he said after a short pause. "What happened to Elle … it's awful, should never have happened, but it wasn't your fault, it wasn't any of ours."

"You really think that?" I asked.

"Yeah, of course."

"I guess I just can't help thinking that if we'd done more when Nora went missing, if we'd found her, or found the person who hurt her, none of this would have happened."

"What could you have done? You were seventeen, a kid. There's nothing you could have done."

I stared at him, his blue eyes turned gray in the flat light. Outside, the world was a blank witness, a field of gray. It seemed to have infested the room and everyone in it. I didn't believe him, I couldn't; maybe there was nothing I could have done, but I still hadn't done enough. And now we were all paying for it, although it was Elle who had ended up paying the highest price of all. I could still see her, in that overly warm cabin on Sunday, when I'd interpreted her drawn face, and tired eyes, her blank looks as grief, but maybe what they had really been was fear. Fear of what, or who, I still wasn't sure, but I knew I couldn't be convinced of my innocence in all of it. There was no getting out from underneath all the guilt, at least not without a fight.

They were waiting for me when I got home. Dad was chatting to them easily in the den when I walked in, and he called out my name.

"You've got visitors," he said, as I took my coat and boots off in the hallway, catching my reflection in the mirror that had always hung there. My eyes were rimmed dark purple and full of sleep, and I suddenly realized what Leo had been talking about back at the diner. But I followed Dad reluctantly through to the den, where they were both drinking coffee and sitting on the couch in the wintry sunshine.

"Meet Detectives Lee and Gutierrez," Dad said.

117

"Actually," the man said, standing to shake my hand, "it's Agents Lee," he pointed to himself, "and Gutierrez." He pointed at the woman who had stayed sitting, but now stood, smoothing down the fabric of her pants, and also shook my hand.

"Maddie," I said.

"Take a seat, Maddie," Agent Gutierrez said, "we just have a few questions to ask you about Noelle Altman."

I looked back at Dad, who nodded at me before leaving the room. As I sat down on the other couch both agents proceeded to take their own seats, Lee making himself comfortable, leaning right back against the couch cushions. He smiled at me, dark eyes catching the low winter sun, and crossed one leg over the other, while Gutierrez sat forward in her seat, her knees angled towards me, hands clasped in her lap as she leaned forward.

"When did you last see Noelle?" she asked.

"On Sunday. For Nora's anniversary memorial."

"And that was at the Altmans' family lake house?" Gutierrez asked, looking down at the notepad that was also in her lap.

"Yes."

"What time did you leave the event?"

"It was about four, I guess. Ange—Angela Cairney—and I went to the bar after."

"Cool's?" Lee asked, and I nodded. "Little early to start drinking," he noted, and I turned my attention from Gutierrez to him.

"We'd just marked the tenth anniversary of our friend's disappearance."

Lee pursed his lips and raised his eyebrows, an expression that could have been apologetic or accusatory, I couldn't tell.

"What time did you make it home? After the bar?" Gutierrez prompted me.

"It was probably a little after seven. Ange was having dinner with her parents, so I came home too. My dad might be more sure of what time it was exactly."

Gutierrez nodded. "We'll be talking to him too. How much do you think you'd had to drink at that point?"

I stared at her for a second or two before answering. "A couple bottles of wine maybe."

"Between the two of you?"

"Yes."

"Did you drive home?"

"No, I walked. It's not far."

"It was cold though."

"I'm used to it," I said, shrugging. "Plus, I'd had all that wine, right?" My voice grated the air and I looked between the two agents.

"You certainly had," Lee said.

"Did you talk to Noelle or any other member of the Altman family in that time?" Gutierrez asked.

"You mean on the phone?"

"Or in the bar."

"No."

"You didn't see or speak to Nathan Altman?"

"Nate? No. He was still at the lake house when Ange and I left. They all were. The whole family. At least I think so." A buzzing had begun in my head, one I was very familiar with. The palms of my hands itched but I was too scared to look down at them in case I would see them trembling. Instead, I buried them under my thighs, feeling like a kid being told off by the school principal.

"So, you don't know at what time he left the lake house?"

"No, I don't know when any of them left."

"Before Sunday, what was the last contact you had with Noelle?" Lee asked.

I had to think for a second, to be sure of my answer before I said: "I saw her the day after Christmas. We met at CJ's and I bought her a hot chocolate."

"Did you meet often?"

119

"I tried to see her whenever I was in town. And we emailed each other semi-regularly. Text, WhatsApp, you know."

"How did she seem in these interactions?"

"She seemed okay, I guess. Not great. She was really quiet on Sunday but that made sense to me at the time. I remember she went upstairs to lie down; she said she wasn't feeling well."

"What about when you saw her at Christmas?"

"She was pretty upbeat to be honest. She was happy Nate and her dad were both home. I mean, her parents were in the process of getting a divorce, but her dad spent the day with them, and that seemed to make her pretty happy," I explained.

"We know that, thanks, Maddie," Lee said, smiling again.

Then why bother asking, I thought mutinously.

I tried to take a deep breath without revealing I was doing so and focused once again on Gutierrez. She was older than Lee, probably in her forties. Her eyes crinkled at their edges in a kind way. It made it look like she smiled a lot, but in her line of work that was hard to believe. She wore a black blazer, with a grey shirt underneath that was made of a silky looking material and she had black wool cigarette pants on that were tucked into black Sorels. She looked like a woman who might spend a decent amount of her paycheck on clothes; but what did I know really? At that moment I was wearing an old sweater with the words "Sunnydale High" stretched across my chest, and jeans I'd long been meaning to give to Goodwill.

"So, she seemed happy?" Gutierrez said.

"It was the day after Christmas. Her family was as whole as it ever got, she'd got a new computer from her parents, and she was drinking hot chocolate. In that moment, yes, she seemed pretty happy."

"And did that appear genuine to you, or did she seem preoccupied in some other way?"

"It seemed genuine, I guess, but I didn't have any reason to think it wasn't. I do think you can have a lot of shit going on in your life and still find moments that make you feel good though."

"And that's what you think was going on?"

I didn't say anything.

"Maddie?" Gutierrez prompted me.

"Look, I don't know. Jenna said she'd seemed distracted, Elle, I mean, over the past few weeks, but she seemed okay when I saw her."

"We've already spoken to Miss Fairfax, thanks," Lee said.

"I know," I said, and he raised his eyebrows.

Gutierrez drew something from her notepad and passed it to me. Her card. "Would you give us a call if you think of anything else that might help our investigation?"

I took the card and looked down at it:

Stephanie Gutierrez
Wisconsin Department of Justice, Special Agent,
Wausau Office.

"Of course. But can I ask you something?"

"Yes," Gutierrez said, giving her partner a little look before staring back at me.

"Will you be reopening Nora's case?"

"There's nothing to indicate, at this moment in time, that the two cases are related," Lee said, as if on autopilot.

"They're sisters," I said, my voice urgent all of a sudden, too sharp. "Not to mention she was found right where Nora's car was abandoned, *on the anniversary of her disappearance.* You can't seriously be telling me you think this is all coincidence? And what about the compass, huh? The one left in the snow?" I was rambling now, my voice jittery and jerky, giving myself away. I could practically hear them back at the precinct, their clinical, objective judgements sketching out an image of me I'd barely recognize. I drew a deep breath, and I was about to tell them about the messages I'd found on Elle's Facebook, the ones I'd taken to Leo that morning, but there was something about the way they looked at me, their shared glances, that made me think twice about it. I could so easily imagine the look they'd give one another that I dreaded witnessing it in real life. I'd be just another paranoid bystander to them, someone to laugh at and roll their eyes over when the day was too long and they were looking at spending yet another night in a lonely, seedy motel room, so I just stayed silent.

After a short, loaded pause Gutierrez said: "It's an ongoing investigation, Maddie. As you know. We can't comment on it. But if anything comes up you can be sure that we will do all we can to solve both cases."

CHAPTER ELEVEN

Wisconsin Daily News

Their Silence is Deafening: Why won't Nora's friends speak out?

By Gloria Lewis

February 9, 2008

It's been just over a month since Nora Altman disappeared from her home in Forest View one snowy night in January. As fears mount as to the teenager's whereabouts, the town has held almost nightly vigils for the girl once voted "most likely to make it to Broadway." Notably absent from these evenings of cold comfort and candlelit sympathy are some of Nora's closest friends. While many of her classmates camp out by the side of the road where her car was found unmarked and locked up tight, but with no gas in the tank, it has been said that her two best friends feel themselves too superior to visit the memorial.

"I've only seen her here once," one of Nora's classmates, Eliza Clarke, remarked regarding Nora's best friend Madeline Fielder. "And she was basically only here to take Nora's little sister away as far as I could tell. What's wrong with the kid wanting to come and be with other people who are worried about her sister as well? I don't get it."

Another thing these Waterstone High Schoolers don't get is Fielder's prolonged absence from school. "I understand she's upset," fellow senior, Ben Ludgate, opined, "but she's clearly getting special treatment because her dad's the principal. It's not fair. Loads of us are worried about Nora but we're still making it to class. Even Angela is, so why can't Maddie?"

"People think maybe she knows more than she's letting on," Eliza continued, "Maddie and Nora have been friends forever. If anyone knows where Nora is, it's Maddie."

Insights from the two girls could certainly aid the investigation into Altman's disappearance at this crucial juncture. As Ludgate pointed out, "Nora's family thought she had spent the night at Maddie's that night with Angela. So why didn't they raise the alarm when she didn't turn up? Maybe she would have been found by now if they'd known a little earlier that she was missing."

Ludgate raises a good point, one that hasn't gone unremarked upon in preceding weeks; why didn't anyone realize the 17-year-old was missing for a full twelve hours?

A spokesperson from the local police department informed the *Daily News* that both Miss Cairney and Miss Fielder have been interviewed by the police regarding Nora's disappearance and have been cooperative throughout. The investigation into the teenager's disappearance is ongoing and anyone with any information is urged to contact the police at the number below.

CHAPTER TWELVE

The doorbell rang a little after seven that night. Nate was standing as far away from the front door as possible when I opened it, staring out into the whitewashed front yard. It was as if he hadn't rung the doorbell at all, or perhaps as if he'd rung it and then forgotten why he was there.

"Nate?" I called, my voice ringing in the cold air. "What are you doing here?"

He turned towards me, his face a pale smudge between the double black of his ribbed beanie and North Face coat. "You wanna come for a drive?" he asked.

I folded my arms across my chest, and glanced back inside to see if there was anyone else around. "A drive? Why?"

"I don't know. I just couldn't stay in that house any longer, and this was the first place I thought of coming."

I swallowed, my face starting to go numb in the cold, while my heartbeat picked up. "Why don't you come inside and we can talk?"

"Not here. I'm sorry, Mads, I just can't. I don't want to have to see your parents, and talk to them about all this. Will you please just come with me?" He hadn't moved any closer, he was still at the other end of the porch from me, but his voice

125

was stretched thin and high. He sounded childlike almost, so young.

"Yeah, okay. I'll come for a drive. Just let me put on some shoes and grab a coat."

He drove straight to the lake house, though, as if that was where he'd been planning to go all along, the headlights of his Land Cruiser cutting through the dark, touching on the purple ribbon tied around Nora's tree. More bunches of flowers had appeared, a few soft toys, and there were even some candles, still lit, their fragile light guttering in the wind. I didn't say anything as we approached the house, still so uncertain around him. I'd seen and spoken to Nate more in the past three days than I had in the past three years but that really wasn't saying much. The silence felt taut still, stretched, but there was a chance it was relaxing slightly, maybe just a little. I looked over at him as he pulled the car to a stop.

"Are we getting out?" I asked.

"Yeah."

"So, that's it. Drive over?"

Nate lifted his eyes to mine. "You can stay in the car if you want, but I'm going inside."

"Nate, what are we doing here?"

"I just needed to be alone," he said, and I couldn't help letting out a shot of laughter.

"But you're not alone. I'm here."

"You don't count." A rock the size of a fist lodged itself inside my stomach. Seven or eight years ago that statement—*you don't count*—wouldn't have dislodged me quite so violently. I probably barely would have noticed it. Back then, Nate was one of the only people, more so than either of my sisters or even Ange, who I could be around without wanting to curl up and disappear. "You don't count" had been a linguistic token between us, exchanged in moments when neither one of us could bear to be

126

alone but, at the same time, couldn't face anyone else. I hadn't heard it in a long time; he hadn't invoked it, and neither had I, and while I understood that with Elle gone these were different times, as much as I had wanted to accept that token, I wasn't sure if I could just yet.

I watched as he got out of the car and went around to the trunk to get some bags out before unbuckling my own seat belt and following him inside. Snow started to fall just as I got to the front door and I thought of those guttering candles by the side of the road, flickering bravely, about to be snuffed out.

Nate was moving around the kitchen when I walked in, looking right at home as he removed groceries from shopping bags and put stuff away in cupboards, opening and closing the fridge, his coat, hat, and scarf discarded on the living room sofa. I took mine off too, throwing them on top of his and then watched him, wary, confused.

"What are you doing? Moving in?"

"I'm making us dinner." He suddenly turned towards me. "You haven't eaten yet, have you?"

"No."

"Okay, good."

"Nate," I said, taking a few steps towards him, "what are you doing? Why are you making us dinner?"

"We have to eat, don't we?"

"Yes …"

"So, that's what we're going to do."

He'd gone back to unpacking his goods, moving around the kitchen and I had to grab him to hold him still and make him look at me.

"Nate. This … this isn't a normal evening. You can't just come and pick me up and bring me here and pretend like everything's normal and making dinner is just a regular thing to do. Elle died three days ago."

"I know she did, Mads, do you think I've forgotten that?"

"I don't know, I can't tell."

"I can't believe you of all people would say that to me; do you really think I've forgotten what happened to Elle? You really think I could do that? She's my fucking sister. *My* sister."

I took a step backwards, blood pumping extra hard in my veins, my breath shallow, my mouth dry. "You can't talk to me like that, Nate, it's not fair. Not when you dragged me out here to supposedly make me dinner after months, *years* of no contact. I'm just trying to figure out what the fuck's going on. You could barely look at me on Sunday, and now what, we're best buds again? Just try and help me make sense of this."

Nate took a deep breath, eyes trained on the ceiling. "I'm just making dinner, okay, Maddie? That's all. I'm not doing cartwheels in front of the fucking police station. Please don't try and make me feel guilty for needing and wanting to eat."

He hadn't answered my main question of why, exactly, I was there too, but I decided to back off, at least for now, and said: "Okay, okay. I'm sorry."

"Because I've been there before. I've done all that before, and I can't do it again. I thought you'd understand." He was looking at me then, finally, eyes blazing, his voice a little loud, too much for the small cabin.

"I do understand," I said, slowly, carefully, even though I didn't. But there was a large enough part of me, a part I wasn't particularly proud of, that was just happy Nate was talking to me at all. That on his way out there, he'd stopped to pick me up. Or perhaps happy isn't the right word at all. Perhaps "relieved" would be better, or whatever German word exists to explain the feeling of finally being back home again, even when that home is haunted.

Nate passed a hand over his face, all the energy in his body suddenly drained away. He pulled his phone out of a pocket and after messing around on it for a few seconds passed it over to me. "I'm guessing you haven't read this yet?"

The phone was open on a newspaper article:

Wisconsin Daily News

Tension Mounts in Unsolved Murder Case

By Gloria Lewis

January 10, 2018

Tension mounts and nerves are frayed in frozen Forest View this week, where local teenager Noelle Altman was found murdered just two days ago. The case is very closely related to that of missing girl Nora Altman, who is the deceased's older sister. Waterstone Chief of Police Patrick Moody, who is overseeing the investigation into the 17-year-old's death alongside Special Agents from the Department of Justice, released a statement today confirming that the girl had indeed been murdered. While they have yet to name any suspects in the case, Chief Moody did reveal that forensics investigators in Wausau were helping with the investigation and that they hoped to have important results from an object found near the body verified soon. He declined to comment on whether or not the object was the murder weapon or possible murder weapon.

Although it is still not yet two full days since Miss Altman's body was found, the lack of information regarding her demise feels overly familiar and is frustrating for her family and community alike. Jennifer Childs, a teacher at the elementary school Noelle Altman attended said: "this is like a nightmare. None of us can believe this is happening again. How can someone have murdered Noelle? We need to know who did this and bring them to justice." Another local, Jim Bent, declared that the town was "being terrorized. First Nora and now her sister. We don't deserve this."

While the case of missing Nora Altman has long fueled a lot of local mysteries in the town of Forest View, not everyone has always believed foul play was involved. However, with her younger sister now found murdered at the site where her car was abandoned, it is looking increasingly likely. Town members are clamoring for Nora Altman's case to be reopened and long-held private suspicions are beginning to be aired in public. "You have to wonder what's going on with that family, for this to happen again," said one local who wished to not be named.

The Altman family has so far declined to comment or release a statement regarding the death of their daughter and sister, but that didn't stop older brother Nate from hanging out at the local bar last night. One has to wonder, indeed.

"Jesus, Nate."

"Yeah, so. Now you know. You're having dinner with a potential sister killer. A *serial* sister killer."

"Fuck, please don't say that." My hands had begun to tremble and I had to put the phone down on the kitchen table. I took a deep breath and stared hard at the air in front of me, at nothing. Nate's arrest after Nora went missing meant that any time Nora's name was mentioned in this town, Nate's wasn't all that far behind.

***

I hear the phone ringing, somewhere in the distance, but leave it for someone else to pick up. No good ever came from a ringing phone anyway. I'm in bed, staring at my ceiling, unable to sleep, just as unable to get up, but when Mom calls my name I hear the urgency in it, and somehow summon the energy to get out of bed.

"That was Katherine," she says when I walk into the kitchen. It's a thick, gray day, the sky heavy with snow, and the light is low.

Mom is standing by the kitchen island, the cordless phone dangling from her right hand, as she rhythmically bangs it against her thigh, a nervous tic.

"What's going on?" I ask, and my voice feels thick and heavy too. From disuse maybe.

"Honey," she says, walking towards me, pained concern written across her face, but also something else. Something far more worrying: confusion, shock. She takes a breath, swallowing it down before continuing, "Nate's just been arrested."

"For what?" I ask, momentarily stupid, because what else could it be for?

"On suspicion of kidnap."

"Of Nora?"

"Yes. Of Nora."

"Why?" I ask, voice cracking in two. "On what grounds?"

"I don't know the specifics, sweetie. Katherine didn't really know herself, but Jonathan's gone with Nate to the station, so hopefully they'll know more soon."

I stumble over to the breakfast nook, sitting down with a thump. "He'd never …" but I can barely get the words out, and have to start again. "Nate would never hurt Nora. Never."

"You can't know that for sure, Mads. They didn't always get along," Mom says.

I turn to look at her, but I don't see her, don't recognize her. If even my mother thinks that, what hope is there that anyone else will believe in Nate?

"They came to see me earlier. The Special Agents," I said, puncturing the silence that had fallen over us.

Nate's face whitened a little. "What did they want?"

"Just to know where I was Sunday night, if I'd seen Elle at all, that kind of thing."

Nate was nodding although I couldn't be sure if he was taking anything in.

131

"Can we just talk about something else?" he said suddenly, as if he hadn't been the one to show me the article, to come to my house, to cook me dinner, to bring it all up. As if there was anything else we could possibly have talked about.

"Okay," I said slowly, "if that's what you want."

"That's what I want."

"Okay."

I poured us both some wine, settling into the uncomfortable wooden dining chair as best I could. Nate started chopping vegetables, his back to me. It was easier that way. I turned to look out of the windows that looked out over the porch and towards the lake. It was dark and snow was falling, slow and lazy, glinting like gold dust in the buttery light that flowed out from the living room windows. Beyond that there was nothing, nothing I could make out at least. Just a dark, cold night.

"Mads?" Nate said softly, and I realized I hadn't been listening to him.

"Yeah?" I said, as if coming out of a daze.

"Could you pass me that can of beans?" He was pointing to an area right next to my elbow on the kitchen table.

I nodded and passed the can to him, not daring to look at him. The lake house felt small suddenly, as small as it had done for Nora's memorial on Sunday, just three short but incredibly long days ago. My hand gripped my glass of wine a little tighter, raising it to my lips. When I put it back down on the table I realized it was empty. I poured myself some more, almost spilling it when Nate said suddenly: "Emmaline and I broke up."

"Oh," I said around a mouthful of wine, "I'm sorry."

He sighed, stirring slowly. "Yeah. Thanks."

"Why?"

"It was before all this, don't worry. Before Elle."

"I … okay. So, when was it? When did you guys break up?"

"The office Christmas party if you can believe that." He let

132

out a bark of laughter and something about it made me cringe.

It was the same as when he'd said "you don't count." It had been too long since we'd talked like this for me to just slip right back into it. I wanted to, but there was something about the whole situation that made me feel trapped and a little wild, as if Nate was trying to transport us back to a time that simply couldn't be revisited. I wanted to scream at him that we weren't that anymore, that it wasn't that simple and it never would be. That relationships, friendships were hard and required effort and you didn't get to slip them back on like an old sweater you'd previously discarded because you needed comfort and familiarity.

But then there was Elle, still haunting the corners of that cabin, her fingerprints lingering over every item I touched, the image of her perched on the arm of the living room couch on Sunday afternoon burned on my mind. And then there was me, who wanted to sink down softly into the comfort Nate used to be able to give me too, but couldn't. So, I didn't say what I wanted to say which was *why are you telling me this?* and instead just drank some more wine.

It continued on like that while he cooked. We talked, a little about Emmaline but mostly about small, inane things and I held back everything I wanted to say while wondering what it was he was holding back. I tried to read between the lines to decipher what it was he was really saying, but I lost my ability to translate for Nate years ago and was left making small talk with someone I'd known for most of my life. Maybe he wasn't saying anything else at all. Maybe he had nothing else to say to me. Or maybe he just needed distraction.

At one point I tried to raise the subject of the messages I'd found on Elle's Facebook—although I wasn't exactly looking forward to admitting to him that I'd hacked into his younger sister's private account—but just the mere mention of her name caused Nate's face to visibly blanche. His fork clattered onto his plate, food abandoned as he looked at me sternly, reminding me that he didn't want to talk about Elle, didn't want to talk about any of that.

"What made you leave New York?" he asked me instead. I'd just taken a mouthful of chili, the shock of its heat making me reach for my wine again. Nate looked up at me, raising an eyebrow. "Too spicy for you?"

I shook my head. "Just hot."

"So … New York? Why'd you leave?"

I hadn't lived in New York for years, hadn't even really thought about my time there for years, but it had been the last time Nate and I were in anything that approximated regular contact, so I guess it made sense for him to ask. It still took me a while to answer though, muddling my way through the intervening years to try and remember exactly what had happened and why I'd left.

Like anything, there wasn't exactly a simple answer, but I tried to find one anyway. "I couldn't control anything, or I didn't have a handle on anything or something like that. I don't know. Sometimes it comes out of nowhere, you know? That drop. I was doing okay and then I just wasn't doing anything anymore." I still ended up talking in roundabouts though, using euphemisms and a shorthand I hoped he still understood so I didn't have to say the word out loud: depression.

"Like in college?"

"Yes. Except it wasn't guidance counselors and the dean telling me I had to get my shit together or get out, it was being fired via email because I hadn't made it into the office for over a week."

"They fired you just like that?"

"It was an internship," I said, sighing heavily, "they didn't even really have to fire me. They just told me not to bother coming in again."

***

134

It's Serena who comes to get me. It's always Serena. She appears in her perfect brushed camel coat, subtle checked cashmere scarf, black leather gloves, and oatmeal-colored beanie on the doorstep to my dingy basement apartment, and she is, most emphatically, despite my having been living in New York for almost eighteen months, the most glamorous person to appear there, ever.

"Thanks for coming," is all I say and she kind of tips her head at me.

"Of course." She looks around the room, making the very short walk from doorway, to kitchen, to bed. "Well, at least you don't have a lot of stuff. It's messy but we can just throw most of it out." She glances at my unmade bed, where, curled up amidst an unfurled duvet is my laptop, yet another episode of Gilmore Girls paused mid-scene and mid-sentence. "Turn Lorelai back on and we'll get started."

"So, is everything okay?" Serena asks, once all the packing is done. "I promised I wasn't going to say anything until we each had a Bloody Mary in us, but what are you doing, Mads? Why are you moving back home?"

I shrug. "It's just not working out," I say.

"What isn't working out?"

"Do the specifics really matter, Serena?"

"Of course they do! If you're leaving because you haven't found your perfect job yet, then I'd tell you to grow up and no one ever gets their ideal job when they're twenty-three; if you're leaving because you need money then I'll offer to lend you some; if you're leaving because you realized New York just isn't the place for you and you're finding it hard to meet people and make friends, I'll say fine then, come live with me in Chicago and we'll go from there; if you're leaving because you've stopped taking your meds and haven't been to a therapy session in months then I'll say, don't be an idiot about your own well-being; and if you're leaving because of some other unknown, vaguely quantifiable reason that I'll probably never be able to understand then I'll say please, please don't move home, because I'm scared of what will happen to you there."

"You're scared of what will happen to me there? Jesus Christ, you make it sound like we escaped from a cult. I'm just moving back in with Mom and Dad. It's not exactly the end of the world."

"I'm scared you'll backslide. You were doing so well."

"No, Serena," I say quietly, *"I was not doing so well. I am not doing well. At all."*

She takes a deep breath, expelling it loudly. "Okay. I just want to be sure that this is something you want. That you haven't just backed yourself into a corner," she says.

"This is what I want, Serena. Just because you don't understand it, doesn't mean it's inherently wrong."

She furrows her brow which always makes her look like she's pouting. "I didn't say it was wrong. I just want to be sure that you're sure."

"I'm sure."

"Okay then."

It was also Serena who made me apply for my master's that winter, convincing me that it wasn't a terrible idea, that I could go back to school, that I could handle it. Ange had already made her move to Madison, so she'd be close by, and maybe the familiarity would do me good. Maybe New York had been too much, too soon. Who knows. Most of the time everything felt like too much, too soon. But Serena could be pretty convincing, and, in the end, I got in and then spent the rest of that year working at the local movie theatre before heading back to college. I still think that was my best job. The safety of a dark room. The gentle drone of whatever movie was showing filling my head with noise. The buttery warmth of the popcorn smell that met me every day.

"So, you just left?" Nate asked, bringing me back to the lake house, the chili, the glass of wine in my hand.

"It wasn't the place for me," I said. "Or maybe I wasn't for it. It doesn't matter anyway. Worse things have happened." We were both quiet, the silence heavy, loaded. I drained my wine glass, emboldening myself. "Nate, come on, what are we doing? We haven't spoken in years, you could barely look at me on Sunday and now you want to hear about everything I've been doing since I last saw you?"

Nate leaned forward, his elbows on the table. The kitchen was dimly lit, half the lightbulbs blown out long ago, and the orangey light made his eyes glow amber. "Who else would I want to talk to?"

I felt as drained as my wine glass. I was too tired. I poured myself another glass, uncertain at this point of how many I'd had, but pretty sure I'd drunk most of the bottle we'd just polished off. I tried to think of the last time I'd got drunk with Nate and couldn't remember. He'd been a big drinker when we were in college but I had no idea if he'd toned it down at all in his twenties. Something told me he probably had. I wanted to ask him questions, to listen to him talk about Emmaline, his work, to maybe even talk a little about his parents' divorce, but I just couldn't quite bring myself to claim that space between us that had grown so wide.

So, instead I said: "You could talk to Leo, or Bright, or anyone, really."

Nate looked at me, his head tilted to the side. "Come on, Mads. You know I've never really talked to them. Not about this stuff anyway."

"What 'stuff,' Nate? We're not talking about anything, not really. You're just asking questions and I'm answering."

"So, you ask some questions."

My tongue and lips had gone fuzzy from red wine and I licked them to try to rectify it, failing miserably. "What do you think happened to Elle?" I asked.

Nate's shoulders slumped, his eyes drawn away from mine. "Not that. Don't ask me that."

"You don't think it's worth talking about?"

137

"Of course I do. I just don't want to talk about it right now."

"Then when?"

"I'll let you know, shall I?" he spat out, his eyes flashing as he squared his shoulders and stared me down.

It was hard to believe we'd ever been anything more, words like daggers flying past one another's heads. Even before Nora went missing, Nate and I had been able to communicate in the kind of shorthand you spend a lifetime building. But we'd traveled so far from that time, and now that easy lexicon was like a dead language: untranslatable and incomprehensible to me. Maybe once I would've known instinctively what to say to bridge this unpassable gap, but not at that time. So, I didn't say anything, just looked right back at him, my back a little straighter than usual, my hand curled into a fist.

Nate passed a hand over his face and shook his head at me. "I'm sorry. We've had reporters calling all day, photographers outside the house. It's bringing back bad memories. All these questions. And then that fucking article."

"You said I could ask you questions, Nate."

"I know, I know. I meant about ... I just didn't mean Elle. I thought maybe we could pretend for a little while, you know? That none of this had happened. That it was just us again."

"Even if it was just us again there'd still be Nora."

"Yeah," he said and took a long drag from his wine glass, "I guess you're right."

CHAPTER THIRTEEN

After dinner, Nate fell asleep on the couch and I watched him for a while, uncertain. Did he expect me to stay the night? Eventually I shook him awake, kneeling down beside him, my hand clenched around his arm.

"Hey," he said, sleepy, "what's going on?"

"I'm heading out. I just wanted to say goodbye," I whispered.

"You're leaving?" Nate went to sit up, his eyes only half open but his voice suddenly loud.

"Yeah."

"But you don't have a car."

"It's fine. Ange came to get me. She's waiting outside."

"You rang Ange?"

"Yeah. I need to get home. I'm tired." I'd had to use the ancient landline because the cell reception was so shitty out there. Luckily the number for Ange's parents' house was one of the only phone numbers I still knew by heart, and her dad had picked up with a cheery "hello."

"So, stay here." He was lying beneath an ancient wool blanket, the fabric worn and torn, and from beneath it his hands reached for and then wrapped themselves around mine so that they were pressed against his chest.

"I can't."

"Sure, you can. It's fine. There are plenty of beds."

"I mean I don't want to, Nate."

I watched his face clear of sleepiness, the drowsiness wiped away by realization. "I didn't mean that we—"

"I know." I felt like taking a deep breath, like taking a few deep breaths, but there didn't seem to be enough air in the room, not for the two of us, so I said very quietly: "I can't do this. I can't be your buddy. It's not fair, Nate. There's too much … too much of everything for me to just hang out with you like this and have it not mean anything."

"Maddie." Nate's hands tightened around mine, but I shook my head and disentangled myself from him. He let me go.

"If you need me to look after Noah or something like that, then I will. But I can't do this. Whatever it is."

"You mean you can't just be my friend?"

It was horrible to hear him say it like that, so bluntly. Because that was what I was saying, effectively, I just wouldn't have phrased it that way: If I couldn't—or wouldn't—be his friend now, then when could I be? All I knew was that if I stayed there even a minute longer, I'd be wandering down a path I couldn't find my way back from. "I have to go," is all I said in response.

"Fine. Don't forget about the high school memorial happening on Friday night." I'd got the Facebook invite earlier that day; the school was going to hold a small memorial for Elle just before the hockey game on Friday. "You know, if you can be bothered to make it," Nate said as I closed the door behind me.

Ange didn't say anything as I slammed the door of her Jeep shut and she continued not to say anything until we'd pulled out onto the old highway and had passed the purple ribbon tied around the tree trunk. All of the candles lit for Elle had gone out.

"So, what was all that about?" Ange asked finally.

"I wish I knew."

Ange turned to look at me and then quickly back at the road. It was snowing still, and she was going slow, careful. "He just made you dinner out of the blue? Why?"

"I think he wanted to be distracted."

Ange nodded, her face dimly lit by the lights from the dashboard. "You know there's already rumors that it was Nate, right? That Nate killed Elle."

"I read Lewis's most recent article if that's what you mean."

"Well, that is what I mean, but I also mean in town. People are already talking about him as if he did it. As if it's a foregone conclusion."

"All because he was arrested when Nora went missing? That doesn't mean anything; he was released almost immediately."

There was a short pause as Ange turned the car slowly onto my street. "Yes, but then he moved away and nothing happened for ten years until the night of Nora's memorial when her younger sister was killed and Nate happened to be in town."

Her words were clear and efficient, cutting through the soft dark of the car; a bloodless litany of why Nate should be suspect number one, and suddenly I hated her professionalism at a time like this. She was Nate's friend too, had known him almost as long as I had, and here she was accusing him of murder alongside everyone else in town.

"But Nate's been in town plenty of times since Nora disappeared and no one was killed or went missing."

"I'm not saying the logic isn't severely flawed, but that's the theory everyone's running away with."

"What about Louden? He was here that night too. And he was arrested when Nora went missing."

Ange pulled to a stop outside my house where the porch light was still on, emitting a dusty circle of light. "I don't know, Mads. He was arrested for Nora, sure, but he doesn't have any connection to Elle. Before Sunday, the last time he probably saw her was when she was ten. Why would he kill her? What would his motive be?"

"What would Nate's motive be? Why would he kill Elle? Or Nora?"

Ange switched off the engine and turned to look at me in her seat. "I don't know, okay? I don't know anything. I just thought you should know what everyone's been saying."

I stared out the windshield, the world turned a menacing monochrome. Ange had left the headlights to the Liberty on and snowflakes danced there, two small beams of light in the dark night. "What do you think?" I asked quietly. "Do you think he killed her? Do you think Nate killed Elle?"

"I think it's way too early to say. But my editor likes him for it."

I pulled my gaze from the spotlit dancing snow and made a face at her. "What does that mean?"

"Just that if nothing comes to light soon, if no one's arrested, then the media is going to come up with a perpetrator and that person is probably going to be Nate."

Nate. The image of him asleep on the couch mere minutes before flashed through my mind. I had never once suspected Nate during Nora's disappearance, but plenty of others had, and it wasn't as though I was surprised by most of the town thinking he might be involved in Elle's murder too. I still couldn't get there though. Nate was difficult, a forest I couldn't see my way through, and yet I knew the path so well, knew it almost by heart, I felt sure my feet would lead me to the other side eventually.

Or at least that used to be the case. I wasn't sure of anything anymore. Not Nate, not how I felt about him, and certainly not what had happened to Elle. I was worried the need to know, the call for resolution and even revenge, would become too strong though, and would maybe, possibly, probably, lead us down the wrong path altogether.

"Do you really want to be doing this, Ange? Raking over the

142

loss of your best friend's family? Is that really what's best for you?"

"I can handle it, okay? I can do my job and deal with Elle and Nora at once. I'm not you."

Her words hung in the air, stranded between us. When I'd woken up that morning I'd had three missed calls from my manager at work, as well as an inbox full of emails I was hoping would go away simply by my not opening any of them. I knew I'd already stayed there too long. And not just because if I wasn't careful, I was going to get fired, but because if I wasn't careful then that metaphorical freefall I'd been trying to describe to Nate earlier might decide it was ready for me again, and I wasn't so sure I'd survive the landing this time.

Ange had always managed to hold things together a little more securely than I had, even before Nora went missing. It wasn't as if I didn't know she was hurting when Nora disappeared, I guess maybe she was just better at living with that hurt than I was. I could count the number of times on one hand I'd been the one to comfort her. She'd called me in tears once when we were still in college, and I could still remember my surprise when I realized I could hear the breathy, jagged edges of her voice. She'd just broken up with her girlfriend, the story choked out in between sobs, her mood oscillating between anger and despair. I wasn't used to her like that and I wondered if she'd been hiding this part of herself from me, out of some kind of misguided protection. People were always lowering their voices around me, shielding me from the more knotty and thorny parts of life back then, as if I wasn't well acquainted with all those parts already. But the thought of Ange doing that too, side-stepping around certain subjects, walking on eggshells around me, made me realize that when we'd lost Nora we'd lost so much more than just her.

"I know you can handle it," I said at last. "It's just whether or not you *should*."

Ange let out a bark of mirthless laughter. "Are you serious, Mads? Imagine if I'd said that to you."

She was right, of course; in fact, I was practically parroting what my mom had been telling me the night before, and it wasn't as if I'd paid her any mind. "Okay, fine." I said finally. "Just ... just don't write anything you don't believe, okay?"

Ange took her time, staring out the window at the snow. "I don't know what I believe right now, Mads."

"Yeah," I said, "me neither."

My sisters came home on Friday evening, Serena having taken the afternoon off work and Cordy having missed her last lectures of the day. I was scrolling through Adrian Turney's Facebook— one of the boys Jenna had told me was always hitting on Elle—when they arrived, their voices chasing their footsteps up the stairs and along the hallway towards my room. Cordy tumbled in first, followed by Serena, who, because of the way she carried herself, always appeared to be gliding somehow.

"Hey," Cordy said, immediately pulling back my bed covers and crawling in beside me while rearranging the pillows to better suit her comfort. She tucked herself up neatly next to me, her head on my shoulder. "I can't believe it, Mads. What the hell happened?"

Serena sat at the end of the bed, looking at us both. "You okay?" Serena asked in a low voice when I didn't answer Cordy's question.

"Yeah ... I mean, no."

"How's Nate doing?" Cordy asked.

"Not great. No one's doing great, let's be honest."

Serena raised her eyebrows. "Have you been over there? We need to send them something. Flowers maybe."

I nodded, thinking about the bare kitchen I'd made Noah lunch in days before and almost began to cry. All three of us looked at each other for a while. I knew their faces so well, the

144

sound of their breathing. I could feel Cordy's feet begin to twitch next to mine; she was terrible at sitting still for too long, whereas Serena was perfectly named; perfectly serene, practically sphinx-like.

It was Cordy who broke the silence, hating any one thing to go on too long. "Who … who do you think did it?" she said, her eyes wide, teeth biting down on her bottom lip. "Who would kill Elle?"

But I didn't have an answer for her. I was beginning to think that, just like Nora, maybe we never would.

Serena looked at her watch. "We should leave soon for the memorial if we want to get a parking space. Maybe you should shower, Mads?"

My high school class had planted a tree in Nora's honor upon graduating. It was a maple. I have no idea who chose a maple, or indeed why. I always thought that if Nora had to be memorialized in arboreal form it should have been one of those trees that grew really tall and wide and was covered in spikes. A monkey puzzle tree. I'd watched while they planted it, that little sapling. It would be over ten feet tall now, I thought.

I closed my eyes, wished that I could stay in bed and then pushed back the covers. "Fine," I said, "I'll shower."

"Good girl," Serena said. She even managed to sound sincere.

We met Ange at the school, after struggling to find somewhere to park. I had never seen the arena so full of people. Ice hockey was a big draw in the town and whenever there were games at home the place would fill up, but I'd never seen it like it was that night. I wondered how many of them were reporters, how many of them were rubberneckers, here to get a glimpse of genuine grief before going home to expound their theories about Elle and Nora on the internet.

The crush of bodies built up a crushing feeling inside my chest, and I tried to take a big breath to steady myself, just to get some oxygen to my brain, but the air was heavy and almost wet with life. Ange turned to me, raising both her eyebrows, and breathed out the word "wow" before pressing on through the crowd.

"Can you see Nate?" I asked the others once we'd pushed our way through the crowd to find the best available spot. After the way he and I had left things the night before last I wasn't sure why I was so concerned to see him; maybe I just wanted him to know that I was there. That I had bothered to show up.

"No," Serena answered before placing her hands on both my shoulders and slowly pivoting me around, "but I have seen Louden Winters."

Louden Winters. He must have come back especially for the memorial, because the last I'd heard, he'd left town the night of Nora's memorial on Sunday. Stood next to him, and only a few inches shorter, was his sister Hale. I hadn't seen her in years; their family still lived in Waterstone but as far as I knew both Louden and Hale were living in Chicago, meaning we never really crossed paths. I'd been a little surprised not to see her on Sunday but here she was, turning up for Elle. I turned back to Ange who was standing on her toes, craning her neck through the crowd trying to keep an eye on the Winters, which was difficult considering she was all of five foot five.

"Everyone here knows about the memorial the family is holding tomorrow as well though, right?" she asked, catching my eye.

I'd got a call from Katherine's sister, Rebecca, earlier in the day, explaining that although a small funeral would be held at a later date, the Altmans wanted to hold "a larger memorial for Elle tomorrow." I'd been taken aback, at first, but I think after Nora, after all the waiting and the hoping, the wondering, the all-night vigils, the uncertainty, maybe the Altmans needed a certain level of finality when it came to Noelle.

Cordy just shrugged, her eyes darting around the room, but Serena put a hand on Ange's shoulder and said in a low voice:

"I'm sure plenty of people know about tomorrow, Ange, but the Altmans wouldn't want this many people showing up anyway. This is for the school, you know? So everyone gets to grieve."

There were vigils held for days after Nora disappeared, with hundreds of people standing around in snowdrifts close to where her car was found, clutching at flickering candles until they burned down to stubs and the wax papered over their skin. As her best friend I suppose I should have been there every night, burning every candle I could lay my hands on down to the wick, but I couldn't go.

In fact, the first time I went to the roadside vigil was also the last.

***

The car is gone of course. Long gone. Taken for evidence, never to be seen again. But for some reason—because there's no body, which means there's been no funeral, which means there's no grave, which means there's no place to go and mourn—everyone has taken to gathering by the side of the road where Nora's dad's ancient Volvo was found. It's like one of those crash sites you see next to highways, moldering bunches of flowers bought in gas station forecourts tied to lampposts or tree trunks to mark the spot someone left this world forever, except there aren't even any bunches of flowers.

People I barely know have gathered here, have been gathering here for days, and even though I hate spectacle in general, and the spectacle of grief even more, I have to admit, there's something pretty about it. Tealights guttering in the cold air, protected from the wind in used jelly or mason jars, making the snow glow in an eerie fairytale-like way. Real fairytales always have tragic endings, of course, is what I'm thinking. It's not all glass slippers, true love's kiss, or marrying a handsome prince. It's getting lost in the woods only to realize you're not lost, just trapped.

I hear footsteps crunch behind me, and I'm surprised when they stop just to my left. Everyone else has been walking past me, standing on the edge of the gathering, heads down, a tight grim smile or terse nod of the head sent my way as they continue towards the gathered crowd. I turn my head and see Hale's gold-amber eyes glowing out at me from beneath a fake fur-trimmed hood. She doesn't smile, just reaches out to grab my hand, refusing to let go.

"What are you doing here?" I ask.

Her eyebrows pull together. "Same thing as you, Mads. Paying my respects."

"To who? The manufacturers of Yankee Candle?"

Her look reminds me so much of Nora I have to look away.

"You're not the only one who's scared, Mads. You're not the only one who's sad."

"But your brother ..." I can't finish the sentence but, luckily, I don't have to. She knows what I'm trying to say.

"Don't you dare," she hisses, and her hand holds on even tighter to mine, so much so that it hurts when I pull it free. "You know he didn't do this. He has an alibi."

"I don't know anything, Hale. Not anymore."

Just then, through the shadowy silhouette of people I barely recognize, I spot one I'd know anywhere. Elle. She's looking around her with an unreadable expression on her face, her hood pulled forward, gloved hands holding a jar with a flickering candle inside it. The girl standing next to her leans forward to say something, and Elle just grimly nods in response, her baby face made suddenly old, mature.

I make my way towards them, knowing they aren't meant to be there.

"Elle," I say quietly, only just managing to keep the quiver of fear and anger that stabbed through me when I first saw her out of my voice, "what are you doing here?"

She shares a look with her friend, shifting her weight from foot to foot, not meeting my eye until I grab her shoulder, turning her to face me.

148

"Leia's sister brought us here," she whines. "It's fine, Maddie, I promise."

"And do your parents know you're here?" I ask, already knowing the answer. There's no way in hell the Altmans have let their youngest daughter come here unattended. I look to Leia, recognizing her from innumerable visits to the Altmans'.

"Where's your sister? Point her out to me," I demand.

Leia looks shifty, her eyes anywhere but on me, and points towards a group of girls who have gathered together to gossip in hushed tones, their eyes wide in fear and delight at the ready-made drama they've managed to find themselves living through.

I recognize them in a vague way, figuring them to be freshmen. I shake my head, but mostly to myself, and say to Elle: "Come on, I'm taking you home. You shouldn't be here."

"This isn't fair, Maddie," Elle protests, "she was my sister." She looks around at the crowd, eyes welling with tears, her mouth a twist of scorn. "If anyone should be here, it's me," she says obstinately, finally sounding her age again.

"I know, but you're way too young to be here without your parents, Elle. You both are."

Elle closes her eyes against the tears that are now falling silently down her pale cheeks, and I meet Leia's gaze in the flickering dark. She looks terrified, but I don't know if it's of being out here, where Nora went missing just days before, or of this new, scared, grieving Noelle. Gently I take Elle's hand and she allows herself to be led away, towards my father's car, Leia following on behind us. Hale watches as we all clamber into the Explorer, and it's only when my headlights scrape over her as I turn the car around that I realize she's crying too.

CHAPTER FOURTEEN

Something drew my attention to the main doors as a small group of guys walked in. One of them I quickly recognized although it took me a couple of seconds to realize why. I'd been staring at his photos and his Facebook posts all day. "Hey," I said into Ange's ear, "try and keep an eye on that guy."

"Why?"

"I think he's Adrian Turney. One of the guys Jenna told me was always hitting on Elle. I want to talk to him."

Ange glanced at me, her brow a little furrowed. "Okay ... although I don't really see why you want to talk to him."

"I think there might have been something going on with Elle."

"Like what? You think she was seeing this dude?"

"I'm not sure," I said, thinking about that stream of messages in Elle's inbox from John Smith, "but I want to find out."

Ange shook her head almost imperceptibly, and just then all the lights in the arena went out, an eerie hush descending over the assembled crowd. A beat started up over the loudspeaker and it only took a couple of seconds for me to realize it was the beginning of "Firework," by Katy Perry, which had been one of Elle's favorite songs growing up.

Then, instead of the team of burly hockey players I was imagining were about to invade the ice, the slight silhouettes of three girls glided onto the rink, their blades slicing through ice, their bodies performing torturous-looking moves, and their feet twisting, turning, twirling them through the air, as they, all three of them, performed the routine Elle had created and taken to the state championships. Flashes of green, red, blue, and white lights filled the arena, until at the very last moment, when each girl threw herself into a Y-Spin and the whole room erupted in gold, flashing lights. I felt Serena's arms go round me, and I leaned against her shoulder as Katy Perry's vocals ended and a deep silence filled the room before the applause began.

Standing across the rink from us, with her face slightly warped by the protective glass that surrounded the ice, I spotted Jenna. I swear our eyes caught for a second but I doubt she could see or recognize me through her wall of tears. There was another girl, much taller than Jenna, with her arm around her shoulder, and she was also crying.

It soon became apparent that the memorial was over and the hockey game had, in fact, been cancelled as people started drifting and then pushing themselves towards the exit.

"Keep an eye on Adrian," I said to Ange, but she just gave me a sideways look and let out a derisive laugh.

"Okay, okay," I said as I raised myself up onto my toes and scanned the tops of heads, looking for curly black hair, but the only people I could pick out were Louden and Bright, both of whom were tall enough to tower over everyone in the room. Bright caught my eye and gave a little nod before turning to his left and talking to someone slightly shorter than him. A second later, Leo popped up next to Bright and sent me something halfway between a wave and a salute. I waved back and continued my scan for Adrian. He was about a hundred people back from the entrance, so I leaned down to Ange again and said: "Okay, so he's way behind us. We'll just wait outside for him to appear and ambush him there."

"You're not supposed to use words like 'ambush' at a memorial service, Mads," Ange said.

But I'd never been good at figuring out how I was supposed to behave at those things, so I just shrugged and continued to slowly push my way out through the crowded arena.

"Hey, Adrian!" I called, when we finally got out to the carpark and I could see him through the crowd, my voice sounding stiff in the cold, dark air. The boy stopped and turned towards the sound of my voice, his face peering through the light streaming out through the open door to the hockey arena. I raised my hand and he ambled over to me and Ange.

"Do I know you?" he asked, looking us both up and down.

"Not yet," Ange replied.

"I'm Maddie Fielder. I was friends with Noelle."

"Oh right. You were Nora's friends." He looked between the two of us. "What can I do for you two ladies?" A sly smile whipped across his face, and I wanted to peel it right off him.

"Jenna mentioned to me that you might have some information about Noelle. Where she was before …" I let my sentence trail off, not quite being able to bring myself to say "killed" or "murdered" yet.

A crease formed in between Adrian's dark eyebrows and he looked back out towards the dispersing crowd, as if he could maybe spot tiny Jenna and her comically red hat in it.

"Jenna said that, huh? Well, no offense, but Jenna doesn't know shit. I barely knew Noelle. I mean it's sad and everything, but we didn't exactly move in the same circles."

"But you wanted to?" I asked.

"I wanted to what? What does that mean?"

"Jenna said you were always hitting on Elle."

Adrian rolled his eyes and looked backed towards the crowd again, this time probably trying to spot his buddies in the melee, bored of us. "Yeah, she was hot, okay? Noelle Altman was hot and everyone knew she was bi and yeah, okay, I hit on her a few times."

"A lot. You hit on her a lot."

"What's a lot, man?"

"Jenna said you were pretty persistent," Ange interjected. "That Elle told her she found you threatening."

I raised my eyebrows at her.

"Threatening? Jesus. No. No, I wasn't threatening."

"My guess is that Elle was probably a better judge of whether you were threatening or not than you. No offense," I said.

"Well, then I didn't mean to be."

"Did you mean to kill her?" I asked, and Ange kind of took a step back, and shook her head.

Adrian let out a shocked bark of laughter before saying: "Fuck you, man. I didn't kill anybody, let alone Noelle Altman. You're fucking crazy though." He pointed both his hands, gun-like at me. "No offense."

"Offense taken, asshole," I called out to his retreating back, unable to think of a better retort in the blur of anger.

"Well," Ange said after Adrian had disappeared into the crowd, "we pretty much blew that."

"You mean I blew it," I said.

"I was trying to be nice," Ange said.

"I don't think he did it anyway. He's not smart enough for one thing."

"Yeah, but if you hadn't accused him of doing so, we could have got a little more out of him, Mads. Maybe got a better idea of how other people felt about Elle, or whether anyone else thought she was seeing someone other than Jenna. Besides, you don't exactly have to be smart to kill people."

Serena and Cordy caught up with us then, having hung back while we struggled after Adrian in the crowd. Cordy was looking down at her phone as she said: "I'm going to head to the bar to meet Keegan. Do you want to come, Mads?"

"Keegan? Blogger Keegan?"

"Yeah, I texted to let him know I was here, but we thought it would probably be easier to find each other at the bar. You should come; he'd really like to talk to you."

"I already know that, Cordy."

"So, you'll come?"

Keegan could be helpful, of course I realized that. He'd also be willing, happy even, to talk to me, unlike Adrian had been.

"I overheard Adrian talking to a couple of his friends," Ange said, "they're all going to CJ's now. I was going to head over there to get some interviews and quotes for the paper, but if you came with me we could ask around about Elle as well if you wanted?"

I agreed that that was a good idea and arranged to catch up with my sisters at the bar later, before the four of us parted ways.

CJ's was full of high school kids, the booths stuffed full with brightly colored coats and scarfs, the air hot and almost syrupy with the sound of spitting bacon and the smell of coffee. I spotted Jenna stuck over in the corner with a few friends gathered round, by far the most subdued group in the place. One girl with a waterfall of strawberry blonde hair kept scanning the room with bright brown eyes, but none of them were talking. The blonde seemed to be surveying the scene, perhaps deciding when an appropriate amount of time had passed and they could all leave without being too heavily judged and go grieve somewhere a little less boisterous.

"Hey, there's Jenna, maybe she can point out the other guys she mentioned to me," I said to Ange in a low voice. As the only non-high school aged people in the place other than the waitress, the two of us were drawing some looks. Jenna, who had been staring down at the plate of food in front of her, listlessly pushing something around with her fork, looked up suddenly and caught my eye, nodding ever so slightly in recognition. I looked at Ange and she just shrugged as if to say "okay then" and we headed over to where Jenna was sat with her friends.

154

"Hey, Jenna," I said when we reached them, and all five of their strained faces turned towards me.

Jenna shifted in her seat so she was sitting up straighter. "Hey. Guys, this is Maddie. She's friends with Elle's brother," she said to the group of teenagers hunched in her booth. "And sister," she added after a brief pause.

"And this is Angela," I said, jerking my thumb towards her. "She's friends with Nate as well. And Nora."

"We both knew Noelle pretty well. We're really sorry for your loss," Ange said to the group.

The girl with strawberry blonde hair, who I now saw bore a striking resemblance to Jenna, had cocked her head and was staring at us both with interest.

"Jenna, do you think you could point out those guys you were telling me about? Are they here?" I asked. I explained that we'd already spoken to Adrian Turney, but I either didn't recognize the other two from my internet stalking, or hadn't yet spotted them.

"Sure," she said, her voice dull, trying to peer around the room, "can you guys see Johnny or any of those guys?" she directed at her friends.

A tall black girl twisted in her seat, her eyes directed to a booth across the room from us, and I realized suddenly that it was Leia, one of Elle's oldest friends. Her hands were covered in stacked, silver rings, and were wrapped around a mug, bangles and bracelets clinking and twinkling against the ceramic, while in front of her was a plate of halfheartedly eaten waffles. "Johnny and Mike are over there," she said, her mouth twisting in barely disguised disgust. "Johnny's the one laughing too loudly, and Mike is … pouring out all the sugar onto his plate."

Ange and I shared a look but before heading off to the offending booth I pulled Jenna aside and asked about the messages from John Smith I'd found on Elle's Facebook.

"Who?" she asked, clearly unaware of what I was talking about.

"John Smith. It looks like a fake account, but he was messaging

155

Elle before she died. I was wondering if she mentioned any of this to you? I messaged you about it."

She looked at me a little blankly and gave a small, defeated shrug. "Sorry, I haven't been on Facebook much at the moment. It all just feels so … fake. What were the messages about?"

"They were creepy. Stalker-y, I guess. They mentioned Nora, and how Elle was the same age as her now, how they looked alike, stuff like that."

Jenna's face came alert then, a shot of surprise blowing through her grief, but she still shook her head. "She didn't mention any of that to me." Her voice croaked with an extra layer of sadness, another wave of loss to deal with.

"Okay, well it was worth a shot. Sorry for bringing it up," I added, because I hated seeing her look so lost and broken. "I just wanted to be sure."

"It's fine," Jenna said, swallowing, lifting her chin in that same act of defiance and determination I'd noticed when we first met. "I'll be fine."

She didn't quite convince me, but I left her to her friends and followed Ange over to the boys in question, who were both blonde, although of wildly varying shades. Mike, the sugar pourer, had a coppery, almost gold quality to his, while Johnny was ash blonde, with pale blue eyes that looked like they held absolutely no depth. He was the first to speak.

"Hey, I know you," he said, his finger jabbing its way towards us. "You guys were friends with Noelle's sister, right? The one who went missing."

It surprised me a little that he'd recognize us as Nora's friends. Her disappearance was the biggest thing to ever happen there, of course, but still—ten years was a long time for a face to ding his memory so instantly like that. Or maybe he'd been looking into Nora's disappearance recently too, in light of Elle's murder, and recognized me from his research.

Ange gave me the subtlest of glances and introduced herself.

"Angela Cairney. I work for the *Journal*, and we're writing a kind of editorial piece about Noelle Altman, trying to get a better picture of who she was, what she liked, who she hung out with, that kind of thing. This is Maddie Fielder." She tipped her head towards me, and the group of young men eyed me with interest.

"I'm right though, right?" Johnny continued. "You knew Noelle's sister?"

"Yeah, we knew her," Ange said reluctantly. "We're just trying to learn a little more about Elle though."

"Well, you were better off where you were, man. That booth over there is full of all her friends. And her girlfriend. Jenna Fairfax. You know that was her girlfriend, right?"

"Yeah, we know, thanks. We're just trying to get as wide a view of Noelle as possible."

Johnny shrugged and looked around at his friends. "Well, I didn't really know her, man. She seemed nice though. I knew her mostly from seeing her at the rink before practice—because of her figure skating, you know? And from parties and stuff, but we only ever had a few classes together. We didn't hang out."

"She was smart," Mike said, then, with the forefinger of his right hand swirling through the pile of sugar in front of him.

"She was smart?" Ange asked.

"Yeah, I had a bunch of classes with her freshman and sophomore year. She was pretty much all AP these days though. I can't touch that shit."

"What classes did you have together?"

"Um, Spanish, biology. She was really good at Spanish. I think she wanted to do it at college."

"Really?" I was surprised by this information but mostly because I knew it was true. I hadn't expected any of these guys to actually know Noelle.

"Yeah. She liked it."

"Were you and Elle friends?" Ange asked.

"Not like friends friends, but we'd stop and talk in the hall."

"Did you have a crush on her?"

"Did I have a crush on her? Jesus, what are we, twelve? Fuck, I mean I thought she was hot. Everyone thought Noelle Altman was hot. But her and Jenna had been together since like forever, so there wasn't any point." Jenna and Elle had in fact been together for less than a year, but I guess that could be seen as "forever" if you were seventeen.

I waited for Ange to take the lead again, not wanting to be the reason this little interview went downhill again, and just as I knew she would, she stepped up.

"Jenna says you guys would try to hit on Elle. At parties, after games. That you two," she waved a finger between Mike and Johnny, "were trying to hit on her all the time."

Johnny scowled. "Yeah, I mean maybe, but we weren't assholes about it. Just, you know, wanted to make sure she knew she had options," he said, finishing his testimony with a smirk.

A small "ugh" sound escaped from the back of my throat, and Mike jerked his head up towards me, so I decided to change tack a little. "Do you know of anyone who would want to hurt her in any way?"

All four of the boys at the table looked at one another then and began shifting in their seats. Mike's eyes returned to his pile of sugar, but instead of messing around with it as he had been doing earlier, he simply stared down at it. "I don't think so," he said eventually, and looked back up at me and Ange.

"There wasn't any sense that she was resented due to her relationship with Jenna?"

"Are you asking if we're homophobes?"

"No, I'm asking if you think anyone at your school might have hurt Noelle due to the fact that she wasn't straight."

"No way," Johnny answered.

"No way?" Ange asked, looking from Mike to him. "You know that a kid who identifies as LGBT is, like, twice as likely as a straight kid to be attacked in some way, right?"

"Yeah, I mean, no I didn't know that, but I don't think that's what happened here," Mike said.

"It was some sicko, man," one of the unknown boys said, his gray eyes turned to me. "This was proper psycho level shit. Like movie shit. How could someone we know have done that?"

"Yeah, man. It wasn't anyone from school. It couldn't have been anyone we know," Johnny said.

I looked between Johnny and Mike, their faces equal parts defiant and surly. "What about someone called John Smith; you know anyone with that name?"

The two of them shared a look, eyes blank. "Wasn't that one of the founding fathers?" Johnny asked, his voice serious, no trace of a joke to be heard.

"That was John Adams," Ange offered, and Johnny's face cleared.

"Oh, right, yeah. Then no. No one called John Smith at school, is there?"

Mike and the rest of the table all shook their heads, agreeing with Johnny. I'd thought, for a second, that John Smith could have been a pseudonym of Johnny's—the first name almost matched after all, and he'd immediately recognized me as Nora's friend—but either he was a very good actor or he genuinely didn't know anything about it, and I was inclined to believe it was the latter. Because as much as I wanted to find out who had killed Elle, I also wanted to find out what had happened to Nora, and the longer I stayed, the more convinced I became that the two were related. I'd known, from the moment Ange had called to tell me she'd been found dead, that it had something to do with Nora too. Even if the police weren't willing to reopen Nora's case, I would. However long it took, whatever lengths I had to go to, however it may hurt me, I was going to find her finally.

The bar was busy by the time we got there, and it took me a while to spot Serena and Cordy through the crowd. They were

159

sat with a guy I immediately recognized as Keegan Ellis and, to my great surprise, Hale Winters. I looked around the bar to see if Louden was there as well, but couldn't see him anywhere. Ange and I waited at the bar for a while, each buying a pitcher of beer and taking it over to my sisters' booth.

"Hey," I said, dropping the pitcher on the table and pouring out a few glasses of beer. Serena and Hale moved up on their side of the booth so I could squeeze in.

"Hey, Mads," Hale said quietly, "it's been a while."

"Yeah, it has. How are you?"

"I'm—"

"That was a stupid question. I don't know why I keep asking people it. Obviously, you're not great."

"Yeah," Hale said, "not great. I guess I'm just trying to wrap my head around everything. I can't believe it. I can't believe anyone would kill Noelle. She was so sweet."

I took a long sip of my beer and gave Hale a sidelong look. She was wearing a black turtleneck and large gold hoop earrings almost hidden by her waterfall of black hair. Her make-up was perfect; winged eyeliner, dewy bronzed cheeks and dark plum lipstick. I couldn't remember the last time I'd looked that well put together. Probably never.

"When was the last time you saw her?" I asked.

"It was a while ago but I tried to stay in touch with her a little. Especially recently. She reached out to me because she was thinking of attending Northwestern."

"Really?" I asked. I hadn't realized Elle was in touch with Hale at all. I wondered who had first reached out to who, and felt that quick kick of guilt roll through me again, wishing I'd kept in better contact with Elle, wishing I could have known what she was going through, wishing I'd done my job, and just looked out for her better.

"Yeah," Hale said, "were the two of you close at all?"

"A little. We emailed pretty regularly," I said, glossing over all the emails Elle had sent and I'd never answered.

160

"And what about you and Nate? Are you guys still close?"

I drew my eyes from her, taking a look once again around the bar. After Gloria Lewis's article it seemed unlikely that Nate would turn up here tonight, I thought, but I wanted to be sure. "No," I said.

"That's a shame," Hale said, giving me a small smile once I'd turned back to her.

It was strange to think how close I'd been to Hale at one point. How well we'd all known each other, how much time we'd spent together, how we'd spend all day at school together only to go home and call one another on the phone to talk about who knows what, and yet, then I was struggling to fill even that short time with something to say. It was partly that too much time had passed, too much had happened, too many things had been said, but I also wondered if I'd lost something as I'd got older, that elastic ability to spend time with people, to enjoy their company, and for it to not necessarily mean anything. Everything felt loaded to me now, weighed down. I wanted to crawl out from underneath it, to lighten up, but I had no idea how.

"So, Keegan," I said, catching his eye, "did Cordy tell you that I changed my mind?"

Keegan's eyes lit up as he looked at me over the rim of his glass and it looked like he might choke on his beer. "Really? You'll talk to me?"

"I don't want anything I say to end up on your little blog, okay?"

"Um," Keegan looked towards Cordy, who shrugged, and then back at me again, "so, what do you want to talk about exactly?"

The bar was loud, music booming over the sweat of bodies who were all wearing too many layers of clothing. There were several baskets of food in the middle of the table, most of them demolished, but there were some fries remaining and I picked at one, tearing it apart before popping it in my mouth. It was cold. "About Nora," I said.

"But not for the blog?" Keegan clarified.

"No, not for your blog. I'm not giving you an interview, there are just some things I want to get clear on and I think you might be able to help me."

"About Nora?" Keegan said, his face furrowed. "But you knew her better than anyone?"

"I wanted to get your thoughts on what happened the night she went missing."

"Oh," Keegan's face cleared a little and he leaned forward in his seat, taking a draught of beer before continuing to talk, "well, there are a bunch of theories, but the most common one is that when she ran out of gas someone came along pretty quickly and offered her a ride. There's a chance she might have been followed, either by someone random or by the person she was on her way to meet in the first place and so she just got in their car with them. She can't have stayed out there too long though because she would have frozen."

"That would account for why she didn't call anyone to come help her as well. If someone came along right after her," Ange said.

"Right, right. But do we know for sure that she even had a cell phone? They never found one, did they?" Keegan said.

"She had one," I said.

"Okay but what would the cell reception have been like? I've been up there recently and it's not great now; I can't imagine it would have been any good in 2008."

Ange, sat beside Keegan who was squashed in between her and Cordy, nodded. "Yeah, you're right, it was always terrible at the lake house, remember?"

"It still is," I said.

"And where her car was found is right between there and town. Maybe if you got stuck there you'd consider walking back to get help, but in winter? I don't know," Keegan said. "Do you think she was headed to their lake house?" he said, looking directly at me.

I shrugged. "That's what I've always assumed. I don't know for sure though."

The conversation was starting to make my blood thicken. My limbs felt too heavy to move and yet I wanted nothing more than to get out of there, even though I was the one who'd initiated it. I took a deep breath, swallowed down some beer and scoped out the bar for the hundredth time. It was packed with people, their faces indiscernible to me. Someone let out a bark of laughter that rang like a shot over the music and the constant buzz of conversation. I looked to where it had come from and spotted a middle-aged man, his head clear of hair, waving his bottle of beer around in wild gesticulation as he entertained his watching crowd. My stomach began to punch at the wall of my abdomen and I took another sip of beer, turning back to my booth.

"You okay?" Hale said in a low voice right next to me. "You look like you might throw up."

Before I had a chance to answer, Keegan turned to Hale and said just a bit too loudly: "You're Louden Winters's sister, right?"

"Right," she said, stiffening a little next to me.

"Do you think Nora was on her way to meet up with him that night? They were dating, right?"

"He had an alibi," Hale said almost robotically, before adding, "and they were broken up by then." She started pulling on her coat, awkwardly elbowing me and Serena as she did so. "I have to go. I'll see you all tomorrow," she said as I got up to let her out of the booth.

"Bye," I said, looking at her back as she disappeared into the crowd.

Keegan sighed as I sat back down. "Man, I'm sorry, do you think I offended her? I didn't mean to make her feel uncomfortable."

I raised an eyebrow. "Really?"

"Sometimes I forget we're talking about real people, you know?" His confession dislodged me, the sound sucked from the room, the whole world slowed down to a sluggish drag before the roar of the bar came back to me and everything sped up once again. I'd never been able to forget we were talking about real people.

I thought of Elle lying among the snow, her body lifeless and alone, her eyes unseeing, her skin so pale it bled into the ground next to her. Blood roared in my ears and I had to close my eyes to clear the image from my mind. I had to hold onto her, but she was slipping away so fast. *Her eyes were brown*, I thought to myself desperately; her favorite ice cream flavor was mint choc chip, although she'd recently developed a liking for salted caramel. She'd read *A Wrinkle in Time* six times and *Fangirl* four. She loved *Jane Eyre* but thought Jane deserved better. She'd listened to the *Serial* podcast despite her mother's protestations. Her favorite color was green. Her favorite character on TV was Captain Holt although Joan Watson from *Elementary* ran a close second.

She didn't yet know what she wanted to do when she grew up.

We never would.

CHAPTER FIFTEEN

WHERE IS NORA ALTMAN?

whereisnoraaltman.blogspot.com/2013/2/what-happened-to-nora-altman-timeline/2.html

It's five years since Nora Altman went missing from Forest View, WI in January 2008 and we still have no idea where she is, or what happened to her. As a concerned citizen of the town (not going to reveal my name, sorry), I want to see if a little internet sleuthing can turn anything up that the (incompetent) local police department missed or overlooked in those crucial first few days.

What Happened to Nora Altman: A timeline

This is the second post in my "timeline" series in which I try to stitch together the timeline of Nora's disappearance on January 8, 2008. If you haven't read the first instalment, then please do so here.

Days 4–6

It was a few days before the police really started to investigate Nora Altman's disappearance. Aged 17, she was still a minor, but the general consensus with missing persons who disappear around that age is that they've taken off on their own. This was their first mistake.

There are still people out there who think this theory possible. To them I would ask: have you ever been to Wisconsin in January? If Nora was planning on leaving town she would have decided to do so another day when her car hadn't run out of gas by the side of the road. By all accounts she was a smart girl, knew her own mind, and definitely, definitely knew that she wouldn't be getting anywhere any time soon without some wheels. So to me, at least, that's that out. And if you're still not convinced, then I say: come up here one winter and see how long you'd last.

The town started to get antsy around day four. By this point the police had spoken to Nora's friends and family, but only in a casual manner: they still didn't think she'd been kidnapped, or worse, killed. It had fallen to her friends and family to search the area around where the car had been abandoned, which is densely wooded and, at the time, very snowy. Without the help of trained professionals or sniffer dogs, they came up empty and walked away disappointed.

Following significant pressure from Nora's dad, and in particular from the media who were starting to take an interest in the case, the chief of police announced that they were opening an official investigation into the disappearance of Nora Altman and treating the circumstances surrounding it as "suspicious." Louden Winters was arrested two days later.

There are a lot of people who like Louden for Nora's disappearance and possible (probable) murder. I'm just going to state right here for the record: I am one of them. To me it seems obvious partly because it *is* obvious. It may be boring but it's true: it's always the boyfriend, and I don't think this case is any different.

Here are some facts for you: Louden was the last person Nora spoke to on the phone, which means he might also have been the last person she spoke to *period*. She left her final voicemail on her best friend's phone, but twenty minutes before that she had a four-minute conversation with Louden that none of us know the content of. Were they planning to meet? It seems more than likely. Of course, he's denied this repeatedly and provided the police with an alibi that let him walk away from the arrest without charges, but the fact that his alibi was a police officer in the Waterstone Police Department has always struck me as a little suspicious.

Here's another thing to think about: If he did do anything to Nora, he had plenty of time to cover it up and plan his alibi. How much easier would that have been with friends in the police department? Even if his friend didn't actively help him, Louden would have been able to pick up on what was going on pretty easily, and known he had time to cover his tracks.

I probably don't need to say this but this is all conjecture of course (don't sue me for libel!).

CHAPTER SIXTEEN

In those first few weeks after Nora went missing everyone went over and over and over again the various different reasons why and how she had disappeared. Did she just up and leave? Was there any reason she would have run away from home? That was a question they asked me, sat in a freezing interrogation room in Waterstone that actually seemed to be shivering.

Is there any reason you can think of that Miss Altman would leave home, Miss Fielder?

No.

There really was no reason that I could think of. I answered that question every which way to Sunday, but they kept asking it.

***

Is she on anything? She has a lot of commitments, doesn't she? She's a member of several different clubs and organizations at school. And early admission; she's applying to college early, isn't she? And not just any school. A prestigious, competitive school. She put a lot of pressure on herself; her brother won a hockey scholarship to the

University of Wisconsin. Did her family put a lot of pressure on her too?

Well, they have four kids, sir. I'm sure any scholarship or financial aid Nate and Nora get will help them out.

Don't get smart.

Is Nora on any drugs? Adderall? Ritalin?

She's on the pill.

My sad joke is met by silence.

Is it possible she was taking anything other than … the pill?

Is it possible? Sure. Is it likely? No.

I spent a lot of time with Nora. Both Ange and I did, in the way that close friends in high school invariably spend a lot of time together, and I could account for most of her time when school was in session, but over the holidays it was a little harder. I'd been working at the local movie theater since the summer, and took on as many shifts over Christmas as possible, saving for college.

Ange had a job too, but Nora hadn't wanted to take anything on over the Christmas break because she was so busy with the musical theater production she was in. They were doing *Rent*. This was something I tried, in vain mostly, to get across to the officers or detectives or whatever who were asking me these questions. Yes, Nora took on a lot, but she was so focused, so determined, she was always able to loosen the knot in exactly the right spot, because she knew exactly what she had to do to get what she wanted, and where she wanted.

They didn't get it. They didn't get that yes, Nora was under a lot of pressure, just like most high-achieving and ambitious kids at that point in their lives, but that Nora was the one person in the world who almost never cracked under pressure. If anyone could cope, it was her.

The last few texts and the very last voicemail she had sent me were of course pored over for days and days. Not just by the police, but by me too. I was the last person she contacted before going missing and the police wanted to know everything about our final, virtual interaction. There was very little I could tell them, though. Other than what Nora revealed in her own words:

***

"Maaaaaaaaaaads, it's me. Where are you? What are you doing? Why are you ignoring my calls?? God, I think I'm losing my mind. I can't stop thinking about Louden fucking Winters, even though I, like, totally don't care. Ughhhhhhh. I don't actually care, do I? That's not what this is, is it? Because if so, it fucking sucks and I was right all along about feelings and emotions and how we should avoid them at all costs because I. Do. Not. Like. This. Anyway, call me back you monster. Think I might go for a drive and clear my head, or whatever it is you sensitive types do. Love you, loser."

Is it normal for her to decide to go out for a drive in the evenings?
    Not really, no, but she's been pretty upset recently, so who knows?
    What is she upset about?
    Her boyfriend's been cheating on her.
    Is this a recent thing?
    It's … an ongoing thing. She found out in November. He's in college, and someone sent a picture to Ange of him hooking up with someone else in a bar somewhere.
    This was in November?
    Yeah. But, they got back together again, kind of over Christmas. He came home, like around the twentieth, I think, and they hooked up, and they were trying to figure things out over the break.
    You sound like you don't approve.
    I don't. He's an asshole. He cheated on her. Multiple times. She deserves better than that.
    Did you tell her that?
    Yeah, of course.

170

Did they seem happy together? You say she was upset over the past couple of weeks, but if they were back together shouldn't she have been happy?

Yeah, I guess. But how happy would you be if you were with someone you couldn't trust?

You don't trust Louden Winters?

I didn't trust him not to cheat on Nora again. Which he did.

When was this?

New Year's Eve. At a party we were all at. Nora was in, like, the next room and he was having sex with Natalie Carmichael. They broke up officially after that.

Even less believable to me than the idea that Nora had simply walked away from Forest View, abandoning her car just because she had a faulty fuel gauge and had unwittingly run out of gas by the side of the road, was the idea that she had killed herself. The question was only raised a couple of times before being discarded; there was no body, no note, and no history of depression or mental illness. Ange and I talked about it once one evening when we were hiding together up in her room, her voice hushed with the impossibility of the subject. It had been over a month since Nora had disappeared and by then we'd been forced by the police and the media and our parents to think about every possible scenario a thousand times already. Neither of us believed it really. We couldn't believe that she was just gone—nowhere—but neither could we believe that she would, or could, have killed herself. Not without one of us sensing something was wrong, not without her leaving a note, or some evidence, somewhere, that that was what she was doing. But if Nora was anything, she was meticulous. If she didn't want someone to find her, they didn't. If she wanted to disappear, she was gone. If there was anyone, out of everyone I have ever known, who could have somehow disappeared herself, or killed herself without leaving any kind of clue behind, it was her.

I was still stuck over the reason why, though. There are oceans, rivers, mountains, swirling constellations inside all of us, of course. I know this as well as anyone but I was still stuck there, on why. She wasn't torn up over Louden, she was mad. Mad as hell. Her last message to me wasn't "I can't believe he's broken my heart," but "why do I care so much?" That was Nora, always, not so much giving in to her own feelings as fending them off with a large stick.

Maybe that was why she managed to stay so clear, so focused and resolute the whole time. In the end it was all for nothing, all those questions.

But Keegan's questions the previous night had reminded me of all those hours spent in that freezing interrogation room, my mom sat in the corner chewing the bottom of her lip as she watched her daughter be turned inside out. To the detectives asking all those questions, Nora had become a riddle, a puzzle to be solved. She'd lost her distinctness, her shape, whatever it was that made her real, rather than just a face on a poster. It was at that point I knew that although we may never know if she were dead, she was already a ghost.

Noelle's memorial was held in the church, even though there wasn't going to be a burial because her body hadn't been released to the family yet. I shivered in the church pew after shrugging off my coat and watched as Ange and her parents filed in before coming over to join me and my family.

"Hey," Ange whispered as she sat down next to me and grabbed my hand.

"Hi."

"Have you spoken to Nate?"

I shook my head and returned to watching the back of Nate's neck as I'd been doing before she arrived. I could feel my mom's arm as it stretched round me to squeeze Ange's shoulder, and she whispered, "Hi, sweetheart. You doing okay?" Out of the corner of my eye I could see Ange's grim, taut smile and the slight blurriness to her eyes that meant she was about to cry. I held on tight to her hand.

Katherine and Jonathan Altman were sitting in the first pew with Noah in between them, and Nate sat next to his father, furthest from the aisle. Next to him, tiny as usual, was Jenna, and the strawberry blonde, who by now I'd figured out was her sister and then Leia, Elle's best friend.

Nate, tall and broad, looked strange and all alone, but I realized that Bright and Leo, along with Louden and Hale were sitting almost directly behind him. At that moment, as if feeling my gaze, Leo turned around and noticed me watching. He nodded at me and I tried to smile but failed. His gaze moved along my pew, to Ange and her family and back to me and my mom and my sisters who were all sat between me and Dad. Leo shook his head a little, sadly, and suddenly I felt myself about to cry. He turned back around and leaned forward to say something in Nate's ear, who twisted around then and mouthed "You okay?" right at me. I almost laughed. I shook my head instead. No, I was not okay.

At the one-year anniversary memorial of Nora's disappearance "Seasons of Love" from *Rent*, the last musical she performed in, was played towards the end, which is a little like throwing a hand grenade into a crowded room and hoping it won't go off. Everyone fell apart, of course. There should be a law against playing "Seasons of Love" at funerals or memorials, but it was as good a way as any to say goodbye, I guess. If you have to say goodbye at all, why not do it with one of the most operatically sad songs ever written in human history? Nora would have liked it. She was dramatic, and to the point, and way more sentimental than she would ever have admitted and she would have loved it.

Nate told a story about how, when they were younger, when he was eight, and Nora just seven, he'd lost her at the grocery store. It was a little distasteful to be perfectly honest, considering

173

the circumstances, but Nate told it so well, with a kind of strange, off-kilter robustness that made me think at the time that maybe he didn't truly believe his sister was gone.

He spoke about how when Nora was five she wore his old Superman costume every day for two weeks, and that after the first time she watched *The Lion King*, she sang "Circle of Life" so many times he stuffed her into a cupboard and didn't let her out for forty-five minutes.

He told us all about how if you didn't let her win at Monopoly she'd throw the board across the room and not speak to anyone for the rest of the day.

Nora had still been alive in those stories he'd told, and there'd still been this tiny sliver, this taunting, tempting chance that she was still alive, and still herself and not just in the stories we were set to tell one another for the rest of our lives.

This time was different. This time Nate was barely controlled, barely contained. I'd never seen him like that, and I'd watched him over the past ten years, as we both followed the same path that grief leads you down. None of the parts of his face seemed to match up, and when he looked out into the assembled crowd, which he did just once, and very quickly, I could have sworn there was fear in his eyes.

"No one should die aged seventeen. I think we can all agree on that." He spread out a sheet of paper on the lectern, and shook his head almost imperceptibly, just to himself. "I've lost both my sisters now. Both seventeen. Both vibrant, and bright, and big, and beautiful. Noelle was ... Nora and I always called her 'stringy.' Because she grew so quickly and there always seemed to be parts of her that were just trying so hard to keep up, and for some reason it made her arms and legs look like pieces of string. To us, anyway. But she was strong too. You don't become a figure skater without being strong, and you don't come out to all your friends and family aged fifteen without being even stronger than that. When we were growing up she was kind of

174

like this little mascot to us. Long and loose, and always dancing, always twirling, and spinning, but only around us.

"When we were with company she became this smaller, more contained person. Happy, but quiet. She'd tuck herself into a corner, and watch everything, everyone with bright eyes and then snap back alive again when everyone had gone and it was just us. She made us laugh. She made me laugh, a lot. I think she probably made a lot of you laugh too. The thing about Noelle, and this is something she had in common with Nora, was that she seemed so sure of who she was. You don't meet a lot of people with the kind of certainty and self-assurance both my sisters had at such a young age.

"I don't have any wise words for you. I tried, and failed, to find an appropriate quote, even from one of her favorite books, because there's nothing I can say to make any sense of this. Which means there's nothing anyone can say, no matter how good a writer, or poet, or philosopher they are, that can make sense of Noelle being gone.

"When I think of Elle I think of how her hair used to reach down almost to her knees when she was seven, or I think of her skating over the frozen lake up by my grandparents' old cabin, this huge, enormous smile on her face. And I think of her driving all the way back from Texas with me last summer, forcing me to listen to Taylor Swift, and Katy Perry, and Ariana Grande even, making me sing along, teasing that I basically knew all the words anyway. I think of her whole, and alive, and wholly alive. I'd like you to do the same."

They played one of Elle's favorite songs, "No Goodbyes," by Dua Lipa, as we left the church.

Outside the church, news station vans dotted the street, parked between the cars of mourners, family and friends. There was a knot of reporters and photographers hanging out round the entrance to the churchyard; I'd already spotted Gloria Lewis as

175

we arrived. She'd looked like she was about to say something, her microphone with its WISNews 3 emblem on it about to be thrust towards me, but Dad had put his arm around my shoulders and hurried me towards the church.

They were still there, and I watched, unable to look away as the photographers moved closer, snapping pictures as more and more mourners filed out and into the whitewashed graveyard. It all happened in mere minutes. The family came last, their faces pale, drawn. Noah's hand was buried deep inside of one of Nate's as the two brothers wordlessly left the church together and someone shouted "Noah!"

Noah was shivering as he raised his face from where he'd been staring at the ground and looked towards whoever had called his name. The flash went off instantaneously, his eyes huge and wide, and someone else shouted: "What the fuck do you think you're doing?"

Jonathan Altman had launched himself at the photographer, grabbing at the camera, wrenching it from the man's grasp and, in one easy move, brought it back to make contact with the photographer's head. It made a huge noise in the quiet church-yard, and I looked towards Nate, who didn't seem to know what to do other than grab his brother and move him away from the scene that was unfolding.

Ange made a noise of surprise as her own dad strode towards the two men, calling out Jonathan's name, telling him to stop. The photographer had stumbled backwards when Jonathan initially hit him, but obviously felt very strongly about his camera, as his first move was to reach towards it in an attempt to pull it free of Jonathan's grasp.

We all watched as Ange's dad pulled Jonathan away from the photographer, talking to him in a low voice neither of us could hear. It all happened very quickly but it didn't lessen the shock, the wrongness of it. Inside the church we'd been allowed to remember Noelle, at least for a little while, exactly as she was.

176

Out here the world interfered, inflicted even more distress and pain.

Out of the corner of my eye I watched as the small figure of Jenna wandered over to the edge of the church's graveyard and proceeded to sink down into a crouch amid the snow. She looked so small in her violently red coat, shivering against the cold, the tops of her boots just showing beneath a landslide of snow. She was staring down into the ground, a blank look on her face, her skin streaked red and white with tears.

I went over to join her, saying: "I'm so sorry, Jenna," as I crouched down next to her.

She made no move to indicate that she'd even heard me, but instead drew a long, rattling breath deep inside her and hiccupped through her next words. "It didn't seem real for a while, I was, like, sleepwalking through it like a dream but now it's so real. So fucking real."

"I know."

"Did you love her? Nora?" she asked suddenly, her face pressed against her folded-up knees.

"Of course I loved her. I still do."

Jenna moved her head an inch until one watery eye was looking up at me. "But not like …?"

"No, not like you loved Noelle. But I still loved her. I don't know if it's … less, it's just different, you know? I still see her everywhere. I still think about how she'd think about things. Does that make sense? She always thought things through so differently to me. I think about what she'd say every time I make a huge mistake, or say something really stupid. Or cruel."

"But how did you cope?"

"I guess I didn't really."

"And it never stops?" She was crying then, really crying, as if not only the loss of Elle, but the fact of having to live with it for the rest of her life had suddenly hit her like a freight train. I remembered that feeling from ten years before and seeing it written all over Jenna's face stole every breath I had right out of me.

I shook my head. "I don't know about never, but it hasn't stopped yet. So maybe never. I think maybe I'm getting better at living with it, but I probably shouldn't be anyone's blueprint for coping with grief."

"You're okay, Maddie."

I looked at her, with her red-ringed hazel eyes wide with misery, and wondered how okay it was that we were only ever going to get to be "okay." Jenna deserved so much more. We all did.

But I didn't know what to say to her, so I just placed my hand on her back and finally let myself cry with her, our tears dripping off our faces and pockmarking the snow beneath us.

"Jenna?" I heard a voice say behind us, and the two of us stood up to turn around. It was Leia, Elle's best friend. She kind of half nodded at me and said to Jenna: "We're heading over to the Altmans' now. You wanna ride with us?"

Jenna nodded and stood up, brushing snow from her black jeans. She said goodbye to me quietly and walked off to join a group of sad-looking teenagers who were all waiting for her. Leia moved as if to follow her, but then stopped and turned back to me.

"It's Maddie, right?"

"Right."

"I'm Leia. I didn't properly introduce myself yesterday. I don't know if you remember me," she said a little shyly as she reached out her right hand and I went to shake it, a little surprised by her formality.

"Of course I remember you," I said.

"Did you get anything out of those guys, yesterday? Mike and Johnny?"

"Not really."

"Do you think one of them hurt Elle?"

178

I noted that she said hurt rather than killed; dancing around the reality of it still. "I don't think so to be honest."

She nodded her head and stamped her feet against the cold a little, small bits of snow falling from her shoes onto the ground. "Yeah, I don't think they did it either. I kinda-I kinda think it might have been the same person who killed Nora."

I jerked my head back in surprise. "Really?"

"Yeah. Do you … do you think so too?"

"Yeah, I do."

Leia cleared her throat, finally meeting my eye. "Back when Nora disappeared, she-she couldn't really understand what was going on, you know? Elle, I mean. Neither of us could, I guess. But she was sad for so long. I know that sounds really stupid, like of course she was sad. It was just all so weird but then she seemed so much better, so much more like Elle, and now this."

"How did she seem before she died? Did she seem any different to you? Jenna said she seemed distracted somehow."

Leia brushed some tears from her eyes and took a deep breath. "Yeah, she'd been quieter than usual, I think, but that's not all that weird."

"Do you think she might have been seeing someone else?"

Leia's eyebrows pinched together. "Other than Jenna?" I nodded, and Leia shook her head "No. I don't think so. She wouldn't … I think I would have known."

"Are you sure?"

"As sure as I can be, I guess. She wasn't secretive. And I genuinely don't know who it would have been."

"When did you notice her getting quieter?"

Leia shrugged. "It happened gradually. To be honest I put it down to a couple of things. College applications, her birthday back in August. And Christmas and New Years were always hard, with the lead up to the anniversary."

"By her birthday do you mean because she was turning

seventeen?" I said, thinking about those messages from John Smith that had started on her seventeenth birthday.

"Yeah. We talked about it a couple times. About the fact that she was now as old as Nora when she … went missing."

I'd sent Elle a text the day she turned seventeen telling her "Happy Birthday" but it had been almost midnight by the time I remembered and Elle had clearly been drunk, or rapidly heading towards it when she texted back:

Thanks, Mads. Made it to 17. Now just gotta hope I make it 18.

Thinking about it now sent a river of cold sweat down my back, but even then the text had taken me aback, not because we never talked about Nora, because we did, but because it sounded so bitter, so angry. I'd never seen or heard Elle talk that way about Nora, but maybe she had actually been scared, scared of never making it past seventeen, scared of turning into her sister and ending up exactly where Nora had: lost and gone to us one snowy January day.

180

CHAPTER SEVENTEEN

The house was crowded but strangely quiet by the time Ange and I arrived at the Altmans'. Almost everyone who had been invited was there already, and although the crowd was significantly smaller than the congregation at the church earlier, there were still a few more people present than the house could comfortably hold.

I looked around for Noah, peering around people's bodies and into crevices and corners for his bright, brown hair but couldn't spot him anywhere. I was worried that, in it all, he was going to get lost. *I* felt lost.

Nate was stood in the corner of the living room. His Aunt Rebecca, who was talking to Louden and Bright, stood next to him, but Nate's eyes were focused, unseeing, on a spot straight ahead of him. He wasn't hearing anything anyone had to say, and his eyes didn't even flicker as I tried in vain to catch his gaze.

There was a heavy knot of déjà vu growing in my stomach as I stared around the room. Everyone looked older and significantly more tired but this could have been ten years earlier. I looked down the hallway to the big open-plan kitchen and spotted Serena, Cordy, and Leo laying out food, plastic plates and napkins

181

on the trestle table that had been set up next to the Altmans' wooden kitchen table.

Ange took her coat off, and sort of pulled at the arm of mine as a reminder for me to take it off. I gave it to her and stepped through the crowd, stopping to say hi to my parents, kissing Nate's aunt on the cheek when I arrived at their group.

When Nate seemed to finally realize I was there, he looked as though he'd just woken up from a dream. He blinked once or twice at me and then said in a hoarse voice: "Hey Mads."

"Hey, you okay? You need anything to drink?" I hadn't spoken to him since I'd left him at his parents' lake house but that didn't matter. At least not today, I thought.

He shook his head but Rebecca reached over to him, patting his shoulder. "I think maybe you could do with some coffee, young man. I need to check on the food anyway."

She stroked his cheek as she left, something I recognized as a very Katherine Altman thing to do. Nora used to do it too.

"Nice to see you, Mads," Louden said, "it's been a while."

"I saw you on Sunday," I said.

"Yeah, but I didn't get a chance to say hi. I hear you've been catching up with Hale though." Louden's posture was rigid; his eyes, which were almost identical to his sister's, stared down at me, not giving me the option to ignore him.

"Yeah, we went for a drink."

Louden made a sound at the back of his throat, and Bright kind of elbowed him and gave him a look that said *not here*. Nate remained silent. He'd gone back to staring into the middle distance; he could have been anywhere. I had a feeling he'd rather have been anywhere but there.

"I was actually wondering if we could talk sometime." I looked around the room, faces of people I'd known my whole life blurring together. "Maybe not here, but sometime soon."

"Talk to me?" Louden said, as if he hadn't heard me.

"Yeah."

182

"Why?"

"I just want to ask you a couple of questions."

"About what?"

"Just about Nora, and what you can remember from—back then."

Louden's eyebrows shot right up and his eyes widened in surprise, but it was Nate, suddenly roused from his silence, who said: "Mads, are you kidding?"

"No."

"You're talking about this here? Now?"

"I'm sorry, I just wanted to be sure I caught Louden before he went back to … Chicago. You're still in Chicago, right?"

Louden looked at me through narrowed eyes, his mouth set in a rigid line and his jawbone pulsing rhythmically. "Yeah."

"Right, so, will you still be around tomorrow?"

"Mads, seriously. Why don't you just Facebook him or something?" Nate said, sounding exasperated.

"Because he'd just ignore me, obviously." No one disagreed with me, so I raised my eyebrows as if to prove my point. "Could we meet for a coffee or something?" I asked.

Louden didn't get a chance to reply, although he looked like he might be about to actually guffaw, before Nate grabbed my arm and steered me out through the living room, down into the kitchen, and out the back door.

"What are you doing, Maddie?" he asked through gritted teeth.

"I want to get a sense of what was going on right before Nora disappeared. See if I can find out anything that might link it to Elle."

"Louden didn't kill Nora. Or Elle." I didn't say anything, and Nate threw his arms up as if despairing of me. "Are you serious? You're back on Louden?"

"What are the alternatives, Nate? Have you got any idea what people are saying?"

"Of course I do, I'm fucking living it. That doesn't mean you

183

can start pointing the finger at just anyone. You're doing the exact same thing as Gloria Lewis and everyone else is doing to me, you ever think of it like that?"

I sighed, my breath frosting the air between us. It was freezing and neither of us was wearing a coat, so I crossed my arms in front of me, burying my hands beneath my armpits, trying to keep them warm. I started bouncing up and down on the balls of my feet, the jaunty movement completely at odds with the situation. "You're not worried?"

"About what?"

"About everything, Nate. About fucking everything. Elle was killed almost a week ago and they haven't named a single suspect. Doesn't that make you wonder?"

"Wonder about what? They're just doing their job as best they can."

"They're doing it badly." I shivered, gluing my jaw shut to stop my teeth from chattering.

"Don't involve yourself in this, Mads, it's not your place. You don't have to figure out who killed Elle, or what happened to Nora and whatever else is bothering you. Just let the police do their jobs, and let everyone else get on with their lives."

"*Get on with their lives*? And how exactly do you suggest we all do that? I'd really like some tips, actually, because I don't know about you, but I've been trying to do just that for an entire decade, and nothing's seemed to take. I'm just so tired, Nate, aren't you? Tired of being in the same place, and feeling the same thing for so long. Like nothing's ever going to change. And now here we are." I threw my arms up into the cold, cold air, taking the entire situation in, not saying Elle's name even though the whole day, and this conversation, were about her. But Nate just stayed stoically looking at me, as if he had no idea what I was talking about, and suddenly all my energy was gone, and I sighed. "I'm just so tired of not knowing anything, Nate. How can you not get that?"

"I do get it," he said, and his face pinched a little, a frown

184

beginning to form and I wondered what he was stopping himself from allowing himself to feel, or think.

I shook my head, so unsure of him after all those years, hating that I had to try and decipher him like that when, at one point, he'd been the one person I never had to puzzle over. "I don't think you do, otherwise you wouldn't be so fucking sanguine about everything."

"*Sanguine*? You think I'm being sanguine? You have no idea what you're talking about, not now. You don't know me, Madeline. Not anymore."

The words hurt, even as I'd already admitted them to myself, even as I knew they were true, and it was all I could do to watch as he left me out there in the cold, the air burning my ears, gasping for breath.

Hours later, back home, my phone rang. It was Nate.

"Come downstairs," he said. "I'm outside."

He was sitting on the steps up to our front porch. When I opened the door, the slice of warm, buttery light turned him from shadow to silhouette, but when I shut it behind me, the world was darkness, cut through only by the light of the moon, and the great tangle of stars above us.

"Hey," I said, sitting down next to him.

"I wanted to apologize. For being such an asshole earlier."

"Okay."

"This week's been …"

"Yeah. I know."

He shifted towards me, turning so that I could see his face a little better, even in the dark. "And I wanted to say sorry for Wednesday night. I shouldn't have just assumed you'd be up for hanging out. Not after so long."

"It's okay," I said after a pause, "like you said, it's been a week. I shouldn't have made such a big deal out of it. I want to be there for you, you know? I'm just trying to figure out what that looks like now."

Nate nodded, and the movement made his coat make a rustling sound next to my ear. "I'm sorry I … pulled away. It wasn't about you," he said.

I stared up into the great swathe of stars above us. Eventually all I could think of to say was, "It wasn't?" the words cracking in my throat.

Nate sighed, the sound of it almost animalistic in the dark. The night wrapped itself around us, a velvet darkness sharp with snow and secrets still barely covered, words left unspoken for so many years. It was early January, deep midwinter and the snow wouldn't melt for months, but those secrets were all coming to the surface whether we wanted them to or not. I turned to him, but he wasn't looking at me, his familiar face in shadow, still hiding, still hidden.

***

"Settling in okay?" Nate asks, walking into the small room and looking around.

"It's fine," I shrug, shutting the door behind him and going to sit down on my twin bed. It's the beginning of my senior year of college and I'm living off campus in a house full of quiet oddballs and introverted misfits. People who barely say hello when you see them in the kitchen, who get back from class or the library and head straight to their rooms, doors closed, headphones in. Not that I'm complaining. As far as I'm concerned it's right where I belong, I'm right there with them. It's the last place Nate would end up though, the last place I expect to see him, which is why I was so surprised when he texted to say he was in the area, could he drop by?

"Feels kinda sad in here, Mads," he says, kicking a box I have yet to unpack with the toe of his sneakers.

"Yeah, I'll get to it eventually," I say, sitting back on my bed, getting comfortable.

186

Nate's eyes flick to my face, taking me in. "When did classes start?"

"Couple of weeks ago," I say.

He lets out a gruff "huh," and I know what he's thinking: that it's high time I got my act together and unpacked some fucking boxes. He pulls the chair out from underneath the desk and swivels it around, sitting down without me offering him a seat.

"So, I came to invite you to a housewarming," he says, rubbing his palms together like a cartoon villain. "It's this weekend. Think you can carve some time out of your busy schedule for it?"

"Ha ha. Come on, Nate, you know I hate parties."

"You didn't used to," he points out gently, "maybe it's time to be getting out there a bit more. Get the old Maddie back."

I look at him, sitting innocently in my desk chair, eyes bright, face open. Is that what he's done, got the old Nate back?

"What d'you say? I'll even buy you your own special bottle of vodka. Put your name on it and everything."

"I'll think about it," I say eventually, the best I can offer him.

But it's not good enough, apparently, because Nate puts his head in his hands, shaking it back and forth, saying, his voice partially muffled: "It's been almost four years, Mads. We have to move on, we have to move past this."

"We?" I ask, my voice almost breaking on those two letters.

He gets up suddenly, moving to sit on the bed beside me, his hands resting right by my feet. "I stayed in Madison for you, you do know that, right?"

His demeanor has changed entirely, no easy jokes, no good-natured cajoling. He is all seriousness, eyes dark, jaw set, face turned toward me. I want to ease into him, to fall into the soft landing stage he's holding open for me, but I can't. What he wants from me, what he wants from—and for—us, I can't give him. I've thought about it, thought about him, thought about us every day for four years, longer even, but I just can't let myself walk down that road. At least not yet.

187

"I didn't ask you to do that," I say, my voice not much louder than a whisper. I meet Nate's eyes, and there's such disappointment there, but frustration too. It seems like I can't help letting people down.

Nate ended up leaving Madison and moving to Austin not long after that. He told me at the time it was because he'd got a job offer he couldn't refuse, but I'd always wondered. As much as I'd always wanted him close, I'd continually pushed him away, until finally he took it upon himself to move thousands of miles away from me.

"Well," Nate said at last, "maybe it was a little about you. You didn't want me the way I wanted you, so I thought it was better for both of us if I just took myself out of the equation."

Even then, so many years later, I couldn't quite bring myself to tell him that I did want him the same way, I just didn't think I could.

"It doesn't matter though," he continued, "I shouldn't have treated you the way I did. Should've answered your phone calls and emails. It wasn't fair."

I shook my head, still staring up at the sky, closing my eyes against the tears. "Hey, if anyone can understand feeling like you have to drop out of everything it's me, right? There are a couple of people in my life I've done the exact same thing to. So, I get it, okay? I get it. But you should never have been the person I called or wrote to in the first place. It wasn't fair. You were going through your own thing, and just because it looked a lot like what I was going through, doesn't mean I should have used you as some sort of security blanket. I should never have thought I could put you in that position."

"'Security blanket'?"

"You know what I mean. After Nora disappeared you were always the first person I wanted to call. Even when most of the time I couldn't even bear to talk to anyone. But, you shouldn't have been."

188

"I liked that I was," he said, his voice low, and I turned back to look at him. Then, he was facing me, finally, and my eyes had adjusted to the dark so I could see his face clearly, still in shadow maybe, but no longer hidden. The moonlight made the scar on his jaw gleam, pearlescent almost, and the one that cut deep into his right eyebrow and skated past his eye glowed also. Nathan Altman had been a clumsy kid.

Without stopping to think, I stretched out my hand and ran the pad of my thumb down over the scar by his eye, and as I did so he closed his eyes, and I listened as he slowly breathed in and out. It felt like everything I'd ever felt before was blooming in my chest, pushing out at my breastbone; it was painful, like a deep ache but also like being let loose, and as I drew his face down towards mine I couldn't stop the tears from falling. I was thinking for a second about how many times I'd already cried today, but then I was kissing him and nothing I thought mattered much anymore. It had been years since we'd last done this, and it felt familiar and strange at the same time. His lips were so cold they tasted like snow. Like air.

I pulled away first, waiting for my senses to catch up with reality. "I'm sorry," I said, "I shouldn't have done that."

"No, I—"

"I wasn't thinking, I'm sorry."

"Jesus Christ, will you stop apologizing? You'll give me a complex."

I let out a laugh, hollow and dark. "Nora would hate this, you know that, right? She absolutely hated the idea of us getting together."

***

I wake to a mouth coated in grime, my head a solid brick enveloped in cotton wool. Groaning, I roll onto my side, and as I reach out

189

for the glass of water I say a silent prayer of thanks to myself for pouring it when we got back to Nora's last night. But before I can take a sip, Nora's face is in mine, hot breath rolling across my skin.

"Jesus, Nora," I say, blanching, "what's the problem?"

Because clearly there is one. Her blue eyes are lit like righteous lanterns, piercing the dimly lit room.

"How drunk were you last night?" she demands.

"Pretty drunk," I say, running my tongue over my fuzzy teeth as if to confirm it.

"So, do you or don't you remember making out with my brother?"

Groaning again, I cover my eyes with my hand, and manage to mutter, "Yes, I remember."

"And was it a so-drunk-he-could've-been-anyone make out, or was it a youwerefinallydrunkenoughto-make-the-first-move make out?"

"Does it really matter?" I ask, still hiding behind my hand.

"No. Because as far as I'm concerned, it's never going to happen again."

"What?" I say, voice strangled as I drop my hand from my eyes and sit up in bed to look at her properly. "You're kidding, right?"

She shakes her head, her hair—still thick with the half a can of hairspray she used last night—remaining stoically still. "It's too weird, Mads. It's like my sister and brother suddenly dating."

"It's not like that at all," I say slowly, turning to look as the door opens and Ange and Hale walk in, both bearing two cups of coffee. Ange holds one out to me, and I take it gratefully, gulping down a burning hot mouthful before saying: "I'm not your sister, and I'm certainly not Nate's."

"Uh oh," Hale says, sitting at the foot of the bed, "I see Nora's already raised the main issue of today's meeting."

I point my arm in Hale's direction, but I'm talking to Nora when I say: "How can you even have a problem with me and Nate when you're dating Louden? It's so fucking hypocritical."

"I've never claimed not to be a hypocrite," Nora states.

190

"Well, that's true," Hale mutters, as I catch her eye.

"Nora, come on, you can't be serious?" I say, but I can already see that she is. Nora doesn't say anything she doesn't mean; in fact she's so straightforward sometimes she doesn't even get sarcasm. But this feels different, petty, selfish even. I never thought she'd put her own feelings over mine, but it's clear now that that's exactly what she intends to do. Me and Nate makes her feel uncomfortable, and so it simply can't happen.

"I am serious, Mads. How would you feel if Ange all of a sudden started dating Serena?"

I look over at Ange, who just shrugs at me. "A little weird at first, I guess, but then I'd get over it."

Nora makes a scoffing sound and stands up, bored of the discussion now. "You're just saying that because you don't want to sound like a shitty person."

"So, you admit you're being a shitty person?" I ask.

"Sure, but apparently you're a much more understanding person than me, so I know you'll do the right thing."

For a second, I'm not sure what the right thing here even is. Nora is being irrational, hypocritical, selfish, but if I ignore her and go right ahead with what I want, does that make me any less selfish? But then she turns around and our eyes lock. And I realize she's right; I may not actually be Nate's sister, but she is mine.

"Is that why …?" Nate coughed, clearing his throat. "Is that why nothing ever really happened, between us? Because you thought Nora wouldn't approve?"

The night seemed to deepen then, the cold seeping into my bones as I turned away from him and stared out into the dark. I almost suggested going inside but couldn't quite bring myself to. I could barely breathe, let alone speak. "Maybe," I said, finally. "I think I thought it would be like betraying her. But I think I maybe also used that as an excuse a little bit."

"So, you do regret it?" Nate asked.

"What?"

"Us sleeping together. After Nora's memorial."

"No … no, I don't regret it."

"Oh. I always thought you did," he said quietly.

"Why would you think that?"

"Because it never happened again?" he said, letting out a puff of laughter.

"That doesn't mean I regretted it, just that it never happened again."

"You know I needed you too, right? Seems like maybe you think it was just you needing me, but I needed you too, so don't worry about all the security blanket stuff." He smiled. "I guess you were mine too."

"So then why'd you leave?" I asked, when what I really wanted to ask was: *why did you leave me all alone up here?*

"Because I didn't want to need you anymore."

It was a punch to the gut when he said it like that. But I understood; I didn't want to need him anymore either. I leaned back against the steps so that I could look up at the sky better without having to strain my neck. There were so many stars in the cold, black sky they entirely filled my field of vision. I wanted to drink them in the way you can take in big, huge, gulping breaths of fresh air and have it never feel enough. Even when the air burns your throat and scorches your lungs.

"It's so easy to forget they're there," I said after a while.

Out of the corner of my eye I could see Nate as he turned to look at me and then slid down so that he was lying next to me, his face turned up to the sky also. "You mean the stars?"

I kept my eyes on the sky. "Yeah. When you're in the city, you know? It's so easy to look up every night and think that an almost-black sky and one or two stars is how it's meant to look, but it's not. This is how it should look. And they're there, the whole time, they're just hiding. Hiding in the light. All those streetlights and headlamps, and neon signs. Hiding this. Seems kind of impossible, really. How could anything man-made blot all this out?"

Nate turned his face from the sky and I could feel him looking at me. "Someone's feeling very pensive."

"I just missed it, I guess. Don't you?"

"We get stars in Texas."

"Just the one though, right?"

"You know you're not half as funny as you think you are."

"I'm exactly as funny as I think I am," I said, but I wasn't done thinking about those cold, stony stars painting a silent riot above us. "They're so much colder here than anywhere else. Unforgiving. Don't you love it?"

Nate laughed and it was soft and warm and breathy and right by my face, filling the gap of cold air between us, however briefly. "I'll leave the unforgiving stuff to you and the stars, I think."

"What does that mean?" I said, suddenly sitting up.

Nate sighed, shifting away from me slightly, looking back up at the sky.

"No, really, Nate, what do you mean by that? Is this about me talking to Louden earlier?"

"I just think that you need to drop it. It's dangerous for one thing, and for another I'm not sure it's good for you."

"*Good for me*?"

"You know what I mean."

"Oh, I know exactly what you mean."

"I'm just worried," Nate continued, slowly, slowly, "that if you keep tugging on this thread the whole world could unravel."

"The whole world *has* unraveled, Nate. That's already happened. I'm just trying to stitch together a picture of what actually happened. Of how it unraveled."

His jaw twitched and although he still refused to look at me I knew he was trying not to cry. His eyes looked like they were set even deeper and his whole face had paled. I could feel him wanting to say something, the words coming and then going but never quite reaching me; but whatever it was I didn't want to hear it.

I made myself breathe in, out, turning sharp frantic breaths to something deeper and calmer. "You should go home," I said, and he turned to look at me at last, "it's been a long day."

"Yeah. It's been a long day."

I was the first to stand, my feet numb from the cold, and I held out a hand to help Nate up. He took it, and his hand was somehow still warm as it pressed against mine. I wanted to hold on, but holding on felt harder than letting go, so I let go.

I spent the next morning battling with my parents and Serena about going back to Madison. Serena had gone as far as to offer me her couch in Chicago, just in case I simply didn't want to be alone, my parents exchanging an anxious glance as they knew this would hardly help my case at work. I'd finally called my boss earlier that morning, caving in to the emails and voicemails and the dense pressure system that had built up inside my chest. I'd missed a whole week already, produced no doctor's note, and generally behaved in a way that usually led to a firing. Carla liked me though, had been privy to the thinnest wedge of what I'd been through over the years, and she spent most of the phone call sighing heavily.

"You're incredibly lucky, Madeline," my dad said, "anyone else would surely have fired you by now."

Serena snorted. "I missed a morning of work once—a morning—because someone had literally run over my foot with their fucking scooter, and I still almost got fired. For one morning! And I had a note from the ER doc."

"I know, Serena," I said trying to keep the groan out of my voice, "you've only told me that story a dozen times."

Serena shrugged, raising her coffee mug to her lips. "I just think it bears repeating. My foot was in a cast and they still barely believed me."

"I know," I said again, this time not bothering to keep the frustration from showing. "I still have the photo you sent me on my phone. You're incredibly impressive and have an unmatched work ethic, is that what you want me to say?"

"No, that's—" Serena started to say before Cordy, wisely, interrupted her.

"Okay, can we just stop this, please? If Maddie feels like she needs to be here then that's what she needs to do."

I gave her a grateful look; even though I was the middle child, she'd always had to act as peacekeeper.

"Well, that's all very well," Mom said, training her eyes—identical to Serena's—on me, "but she also needs to keep her job." Her voice was gentle, but there was grit there too. She was tired, I could tell. Tired of having to constantly help me pick up the pieces every time I let my life fall down around me. I wanted to tell her that this was it, the last time, just one last time, and it might all, finally, be over, but the words couldn't quite make it out and suddenly my phone started to ring.

I looked down, surprised to see Jenna's name illuminated on the screen.

"Hi," I said on picking up, "everything okay?"

"Yeah. I mean no, not really." Her voice was breathy and light, as if she'd just come in from running.

"What's up?"

"I just went on Facebook and I've got these weird messages. They're about Elle."

I sat up a little straighter in my seat. "Elle?"

"Yeah. It made me think of those messages you found on her Facebook?"

"Are they from someone called John Smith?"

"No, it says 'A Friend.' But I tried to go to their profile and it was private. And they don't have a profile picture. I think it's a fake account."

"Have you told the police?"

"No, I … I didn't know what to do, so I called you."

"Oh," I said, letting that sink in. I think it might have been the first time anyone had ever called me for advice. "Well, you should probably head down to the police station, show them the messages. Even if they turn out to be pranks."

"Have you shown them the ones from John Smith? The ones you found on Elle's account?"

"Yeah, I showed them to Leo as soon as I found them."

Jenna didn't say anything for a moment, and all I could hear was her breathing. "Okay, okay I'll take them down. But will you come with me?" she said eventually.

"Sure, okay." I said, blinking away my surprise. "See you at the station in thirty minutes?"

Jenna was standing on the steps to the police department when I arrived, looking around her and pulling nervously at the sleeves of her coat. She looked incredibly small, incredibly young standing there as giant snowflakes began to drift down silently. "Hey," she said, sounding relieved as I walked towards her. "You're here."

"Of course. Have you been inside yet?"

She shook her head. "I was waiting for you."

"Okay. I texted Leo, but he's not around, so he said to find Bright instead."

Jenna nodded her head rhythmically, seemingly unable to stop, but didn't say anything, so I put my hand against her back and gave her a little push inside. The woman at the front desk was called Iris and had worked there for years. She recognized me almost immediately, cocking her head to the side and saying what a shame it was about that Altman girl. I agreed with her, glancing towards Jenna who once again didn't seem able to look at any one thing for more than a second, and asked if Bright—or rather, Officer Brightman—was in.

Bright's desk was in the furthest corner, easily the tidiest and least adorned in the entire room. He stood up as we approached, his eyebrows drawing together as we did so.

"Everything okay?" he asked.

Jenna looked towards me, not speaking, so I explained about the Facebook messages and watched as Bright began to frown. "Can I take a look?" he asked Jenna, who nodded and silently pulled out her phone to show us both the messages.

"It's not anyone I know. I found them in that filter bit where messages from people you don't know go," she said as she handed the phone over to Bright. It looked comically small in his hands.

Once he was done reading the messages, Bright passed me the phone, cold nausea rolling through me as I scrolled through them. The messages had started the day Noelle's body had been found:

From: A Friend 01/08/ 2018 20:46
You're next bitch
From: A Friend 01/09/2018 00:14
Your gna be next bitch just you wait
From: A Friend 01/10/2018 07:32
Whores and lesbians are fair game imo so guess your gonna be next
From: A Friend 01/10/2018 17:11
Your girlfriend deserved to die
She wanted it. She got wat was coming
From: A Friend 01/11/2018 10:04
Y don't you reply bitch. Too scared? Little pussy girl too scared to reply? Good I'm glad your scared you fckin should be

"You only found them today?" Bright was asking Jenna.

"Yeah. I've had a ton of messages, so I didn't see it until this morning. I was … well, I was looking for anything weird, like the ones Maddie found on Elle's account."

Bright raised his eyebrows; he was looking intently at Jenna,

197

and his expression was as unreadable as ever but that had clearly surprised him. Looking between me and Jenna, he said: "What messages on Elle's account?"

I explained about John Smith again, about how I'd logged in as Elle a few days before and found messages going back months from him, but Bright's expression of confusion didn't change. "Leo didn't tell you?" I asked.

"No, I guess he forgot. He probably just told the agents about it and left it at that. I wouldn't worry about it." He turned back to Jenna, and said: "The agents aren't actually here at the moment, but I think you should wait and show them this. You okay with that?"

Jenna's gaze flickered towards me. "You can't just deal with it?" she asked Bright.

"It's not my case. It's not even the department's case. The state got involved as soon as her body was ID'd." Jenna swallowed, her face paling visibly and Bright said quietly: "Sorry. Didn't mean to put it so bluntly. They're going to want to ask you some questions though. More questions." Jenna nodded, resigned, and Bright placed a hand on my shoulder. "I'll take her to the break room to wait. It's warmer in there," he said to me, "but stick around, okay? I want to talk to you."

I shrugged my assent. It's not like I had anything else to do.

"I heard you had a bit of a run-in with Nate at his parents' place," Bright said once he'd returned.

"We're fine now," I said, although I wasn't really sure that was true.

"You know you're the only person he ever really fights with."

"Well, I guess that makes me the bad guy, then," I said.

"I didn't mean it like that."

I sighed. "Whatever, Bright. I'm too tired to talk about this with you."

Bright sat down in his chair then, motioning me to do the

same by pulling a chair out from underneath someone else's desk. "Did you ever find out who was sending you those notes?"

"What notes?" I asked quickly.

"The notes you got when Nora first disappeared."

"How did you know about that?" I asked.

"Serena," he said smoothly. Of course, Serena. He cleared his throat, looking nervous suddenly as he leaned forward in his chair. I thought he was about to reach out and take one of my hands, or maybe even lay one of his over my knee, but he looked like he thought better of it, and just clasped them between his two knees. "She called me earlier. Your sister," he said, clarifying unnecessarily. "She's worried about you. What are you still doing here, Mads? It can't be healthy for you."

"Not you too," I said with a groan. "I thought you'd understand at least, as a cop."

He shook his head. "Believe me, if I didn't have to be here, I wouldn't. It's all way too close to home for my liking."

"You seriously don't wish you could be in the room with the Special Agents right now, even just as a fly on the wall?"

"If it was anyone else, maybe. But Elle ..."

"I didn't realize you were close at all," I said, shifting in my seat. Bright's gaze had left mine, and he was now staring blankly at the air just to the left of my face.

"We weren't, but there's just something about this whole thing. Ten years after Nora. It's personal. How could it not be? I hate watching Nate go through it all again too. You must get that," he finished, finally meeting my eyes again.

"Yeah," I croaked, heat suddenly rising up my neck. "Do you think Jenna's messages will lead to anything?" I asked, changing the subject.

"Probably not. They're probably just from some kid messing around. Like your notes probably were too. Maybe even those ones you found on Noelle's account."

"What will they do with them? The Special Agents?"

"I don't know to be honest. Maybe monitor her account? Don't know how it all works at that level."

"Do they have any idea of who killed her?" I asked, blood starting to beat heavily in my ears.

"We're doing everything we can," Bright said, almost robotically, before adding, his voice suddenly low and insistent, "I know you think we're not, but we are."

I made a noise that sounded a lot like a scoff. "It's been ten years since Nora disappeared; a week since Noelle was killed. And what do you have so far? Nothing."

"Not nothing, Mads." He looked around the room then and dropped his voice even lower, his head tilted dramatically towards mine. "We found a knife. Near the body."

"Near Noelle?

"Close, yeah. It was—covered in blood. They're just waiting for the results to see if there's a match and then they'll make a statement. Maybe even an arrest. Look, I shouldn't be telling you this; they don't want it getting out until there's something concrete to report, so please don't mention this to anyone."

"What kind of knife was it?" I asked, unable to keep my voice from trembling. Even my hands began to shake and I placed them under my legs, as I always did when I was worried someone would notice.

Bright pressed his lips together and closed his eyes for a second. "Hunting knife."

"But that's not … that's not how she died, right? She was strangled?" I said, struggling a little to get the words out.

"She was asphyxiated. Suffocated. But at some point, she was stabbed as well, and it seems as though we've got the weapon that did it."

"Do the family know all this?" I asked, cold sweat pricking at my skin, saliva thickening my throat.

He nodded again and then suddenly his head jerked up in

response to something and when I turned around I came face to face with Chief Moody.

"Madeline," he said, "I hear you're responsible for bringing Miss Fairfax's messages to our attention. Thank you for that."

"Sure," I said, although my voice didn't sound like my voice at all and all I could think of was Elle.

"She's going to be here a while longer, so it's probably best if you head on home."

I nodded dumbly, not realizing until he spoke that Bright was walking me out of the station.

"Are you going to be okay?" he asked, staring down at me as we reached the front doors.

"I'm fine," I said, but I could tell neither of us really believed that. "Why didn't Leo tell you about the messages I found?" I asked, confused.

Bright shrugged and stared down at me, face immobile. "It probably just slipped his mind. There's been a lot going on, Mads."

I nodded, suddenly unable to speak and set off towards my car without saying goodbye.

Once inside I locked the doors and gripped the steering wheel, watching as the skin along my knuckles turned whiter and whiter. I tried to focus on them, on watching my stretched, pale skin, but all I could see was Elle, lying suffocated in the white snow, a knife's sharp blade glinting somewhere nearby, trembling with violence. My breathing was sharp, shallow and I tried desperately to even it out, but nothing worked, so eventually I stopped trying and just gave in, the cries that escaped from my chest and throat barely even recognizable as being human.

CHAPTER EIGHTEEN

I was still sat there in my dad's car when a sleek black car pulled up in front of the steps of the police station, closely followed by at least half a dozen cars and vans stamped with the insignia of various news channels and media outlets screeching to a halt just behind.

I opened my car door with shaking hands, pushing through the crowd that had built up almost instantly. It was impossible to get to the front, and soon I couldn't see the black car at all, my view completely blocked by reporters wielding giant microphones and photographers pressing on towards the front.

I looked around, heart pounding in my chest, trying to find Ange, who surely must've been there, before someone shouted, "There he is!" and the crowd surged forward as the back door of the car opened and out got Nate.

Suddenly there was a chorus of reporters chanting his name, out of sync with one another, but loud enough to drown out even the thoughts inside my head. Nate walked up the steps of the police station, head bowed, sandwiched between two Special Agents, and I tried to weave through the crowd.

As I edged closer to the front, I heard a familiar voice call: "Don't say anything, son. Don't say a word," and turned to see Jonathan getting out of another car, accompanied by Leo.

Jonathan was already following his son up the steps, taking them two at a time, but I was able to get Leo's attention.

"What's going on?" I asked, breathless.

He looked down at me, doing a double-take, before following Jonathan and saying: "What are you doing here, Mads?"

"I was here already … I'd been to see Bright about Jenna's messages."

"Oh, right," he said, clearly distracted.

"What's going on? What's happening?"

He stopped walking then and pulled me to the side, trying to get as far away from the crowd of reporters as possible.

"Nate's just been arrested for Elle's murder."

I heard his words, but couldn't make sense of them—even with that chaos surrounding me, confirming it, I couldn't quite take it in. It was as if what he was telling me was coming at me through a snowstorm, the growing, silent static of fear, incomprehension drowning out even the noise of the amassed media. I realized that even as I'd worried what might happen, I'd never actually believed Nate would be arrested.

Leo was still talking but all I could see was his mouth moving, his lips forming strange shapes I could hardly recognize. He stepped towards me, hands wrapping around my arms, holding me in place, and I watched as his mouth made the shape of my name, *Maddie*, but I couldn't hear or say anything. My body dripped with cold and my heart and lungs, stomach, pancreas and whatever else turned to granite inside my chest. I was so, so heavy.

Before I knew what was happening, Leo had walked me up the stairs and into the police station waiting room, pushing through that churning, desperate crowd with seeming ease. He gently pushed me down into a chair, telling Iris to keep an eye on me and came back a couple of minutes later with a mug of something.

"Maddie?" he said again and this time I looked up at him. He was proffering me the mug, "Take this, drink."

"What is it?"

"Just coffee."

"You don't have anything stronger?"

"Maddie."

I took the mug and swallowed down a few mouthfuls, the coffee thin and bitter, made hours earlier. Leo sat down in the chair next to me and turned to me slightly, his knees gently knocking mine. "They found Nate's fingerprints and DNA on the knife," he said slow and quiet, and when I didn't—couldn't—say anything, he placed a hand on my knee adding, "his DNA's all over it, Mads."

"How could that be?" I asked eventually.

"Maddie. How do you think?"

The heat was slowly draining from my mug of coffee. There hadn't been much there to begin with, but instead of listening to Leo it was as if all my attention was directed at the mug being held between my two hands. My senses had funneled themselves to one point; all I could feel were my hands and the lukewarm ceramic pressed against them. The world went in and out of focus, at one moment screaming at me, and then just as quickly reducing to the still surface of the black coffee, not even a ripple disturbing it. Leo was saying something important, I could tell by the tone of his voice, but my brain refused to listen. The snowstorm roared in my ears again, so loud I felt sure other people could hear it. How could they not hear it?

This had happened before, of course, but not for a while. My freshman year of college it happened almost daily.

***

There's a girl sitting in the second row from the front of the lecture hall who looks like Nora. I've seen her a couple of times before, I think, from further away, but as I walked in late, I got a better look of her and realized how striking the similarity is. Not identical of course, nothing like that. If Nora was still around maybe I wouldn't even have noticed this girl, but her absence makes her presence—even the whisper of it, a ghost of it—more pronounced.

I'm staring at the back of her head. Her hair catches the wintry light that falls as shafts through the tall windows. It must be more auburn than it looks at first glance because it gleams black and copper as she leans forward to make a note of something the professor has just said, sun catching as it does on a bird's wing. I'm not taking notes. I haven't even got a notebook out on the desk, let alone my laptop. I haven't taken a single thing out of my bag to be honest.

It's a film theory class. One of the few classes I'm still bothering to turn up to. Even when I get to the lectures, it's all I can do to stay in the seat amidst all those people. All those faces. The professor has this long iron-gray hair she wears loose down her back. She has an interesting sense of style; one lecture she even turned up wearing a cape. She's talking now, hands gesticulating; everyone's drinking it in. She's not just a theorist, she's made movies. They've been shown at film festivals. Won awards. This class is almost impossible to get into, which is why I'm still here, showing up.

She asks a question, or at least I know she must have asked a question because the entire room has fallen completely silent; the kind of silence where you know everyone thinks they're being cloaked in some kind of invisibility by not making a move or a sound. She casts around the room, amused, exasperated. She genuinely wants one of us to venture an answer. To try. She's interested. That's the worst part of it.

She doesn't call my name. How in the hell would she know my name? Any of our names? Instead she says: "You, with the green hair," pointing up towards where I'm sitting, right on the end of an aisle, my legs stretched out onto the stairs. My eyes are still on not-Nora's hair as she turns around to see who the professor has picked on, and widens her eyes at me. Me, with the green hair dye still clinging to the tips of my hair. Her eyes are brown, not blue,

205

but she has the same thick eyebrows, and a similar mouth and jawline. I realize that she looks more like Noelle than Nora, really, but they always looked so similar, the mistake is justified.

"Hmm?" The professor tries again. "Sorry, I don't know your name. But would you like to try answering the question?"

The world comes crashing into focus and out of it again in a matter of seconds. Split seconds. I pull my eyes from not-Nora's gaze; she looks concerned somehow. For some reason. And suddenly I'm looking at an entire lecture hall looking at me. My heart turns to granite in my chest, and my ears fill with buzzing. I struggle with my bag and my legs as I unfold from my chair and try to leave the lecture hall as quickly as possible. My limbs feel like lead, like I'm trying to walk through water, and yet the lecture hall itself is in the process of dissolving in front of my eyes in some kind of fierce fury.

I rush through the doors, blood pumping, and out into the hallway but there are people everywhere, crowds of strangers and students everywhere. Something stings at the back of my eyes. I have to get out of here.

I walk quickly, almost running, but barely even aware of myself, to the nearest bathroom, which happens to be in a campus Starbucks. I stay in there for minutes on end. First five, then ten. Fifteen, twenty. But I can't leave. People knock at the door, calling for whoever is in there to get the hell out, but I can't. Fear lies thick at my throat, it fills my mouth, fogs my brain. I can't leave.

Eventually I scramble with my bag, finding my phone. Breathing heavily, in, out, in, out, like they tell you to. I pull up Ange's name and call her, but it goes straight to voicemail. The same with Serena. Eventually I call Nate, and he picks up on the fourth ring.

"Mads? What's up?"

I tell him where I am, my voice heavy, staccato. I can barely breathe. I cringe at every word I say, every chip in my armor revealed to him. But he isn't far away, he says, the noise in the background telling me he's somewhere busy, somewhere on campus.

I stay there, in my bathroom fortress, trying not to be sick, telling *myself to be calm, be calm, be calm. I've never been good at listening to myself though. Or at least, not when I have anything useful to say.*

And then he's here, his knock on the door strong and direct, his voice calling my name. It still takes me a while to open the door though, and when I eventually do—for one second, less than a second really—instead of Nate's face, it's Nora's that greets me. I shut my eyes, no longer able to trust them, and Nate pulls me into a hug, his breath warm against my neck.

"You're okay," he says, and as I stand there, allowing myself to be held, I try my hardest to believe him.

"Maddie?" someone said, but this time it wasn't Leo and it certainly wasn't Nate. My brain came into focus, dragging me back to the police station, back to reality. My dad was standing over me, his face white, drawn, lines around his mouth but not from smiling. "Maddie, honey, let's go home."

The coffee mug Leo had given me was still in my hands and I looked down at it and then up at my dad again. "When did you get here?"

"Just now. Leo called me; he didn't think you should drive home."

I listened to the two of them have a murmured conversation while I got myself together. Dad was thanking Leo for looking after me, before asking about Nate.

"He's being questioned at the moment," Leo said.

"Has he been charged yet?" Dad asked.

"They've got seventy-two hours to charge him, but with the hunting knife it's looking pretty open and shut," Leo said.

I could hear Dad sucking in his breath, it sounded like a low whistle, but it was the sound he made when he was most in distress. "And is Jonathan in there with him?"

"Yes, sir, but I think they're going to try to get him a different lawyer."

207

Dad was nodding, staring at Leo as he spoke, until he noticed that I was standing now, ready to go. "Okay, well thank you, officer," he said a little wryly, before putting his hand on my back and walking me out of the station.

They were still there. The reporters, cameramen, photographers, and I heard someone call my name, my eyes blinking at the flash of a camera when I turned to see who had called my name. Dad rushed me down the steps, my eyes now trained on my feet, looking down, down, down.

Once we were through the crowd I spotted Mom waiting in her truck, the wipers going to keep her windshield clear of snow. She waved as we walked towards the Explorer, and started her engine. Dad took the car keys from me, and I got into the passenger seat, the muffled quiet of the car protecting me from the outside world offering little relief.

We were silent on the drive home, the only sound the clicker as Dad signaled left. Through the lightly falling snow I could see the red lights at every crosswalk leading out of town and towards Old Highway 51. Everything blurred together, the white of the snow, the changing color of the stop lights, the turquoise neon as we passed the movie theater.

"It's going to be okay, Mads," Dad said eventually, his voice echoing strangely in the car.

I pressed my forehead against the cold glass of the passenger window. It is just as heartbreaking at twenty-seven as it is at seventeen to realize your parents are as helpless as you are.

CHAPTER NINETEEN

Wisconsin Daily News

Ugly Twist as Brother of Victim Arrested for Murder

By Gloria Lewis

January 15, 2018

A suspect has been arrested in the tragic case of the murder of Noelle Altman which occurred in Forest View, WI on January 8. The suspect in question is no stranger to the case, nor to the family in question. In fact, it is the brother of the Wisconsin teenager, Nathan Altman.

Mr Altman was also a suspect in the disappearance of his other sister, Nora Altman, who went missing from the area ten years ago. However, with no evidence to go on, the police were forced to release him with no charge, and this oversight appears to have had tragic consequences.

In a statement to the press, the local chief of police

revealed that a knife, believed to be the murder weapon, had been found buried in the snow some distance from where Noelle Altman's body was found. Forensic examination has revealed that not only was the blood on the knife found to be Noelle Altman's, but that her older brother's fingerprints were also present.

The 28-year-old, who was back in Forest View on the night in question for the tenth anniversary of Nora Altman's disappearance, has also been unable to provide the authorities with an alibi.

Friends describe Nathan Altman as good-natured and friendly, but have noticed a marked change in his behavior and attitude since the disappearance of his sister Nora. One even went as far as to remark that he seemed "troubled."

Could there be something darker underlying Nathan Altman's boynextdoor demeanor? It certainly seems strange that just two days after the body of his youngest sister was found the young man still found time to share a couple of drinks with friends at a local bar.

The Altman family could not be reached for comment.

CHAPTER TWENTY

"*He seemed troubled?*" I said as soon as Ange picked up. "Is she fucking kidding? Of course he was troubled, his sister had gone missing!"

I could hear Ange sigh before she said: "You read Gloria Lewis's article."

"Yes."

"She's just doing her job, Mads, you do get that, right? He's been arrested, this is what happens."

"Oh, so that's it, someone gets arrested and the case is closed?"

"Pretty much, yeah."

My heart was beating inside my chest as if I'd just run a mile in the snow, despite still lying in bed. I could feel it cracking against my ribcage, trying to break free, knocking again and again at that fragile wall of bones.

"Look, I'm working today, but how about meeting me later? Try not to focus too much on this though, okay?"

"You mean on Nate being arrested for murder?"

"Yeah," she said, but even down the phone I could hear how little she believed that to be possible.

Instead of heeding Ange's advice, I continued to scroll through newspaper articles about Nate's arrest, before eventually ending up back on Reddit. I was interested in seeing what Keegan Ellis had to say on the matter.

/r/noraaltman
Nora's brother has been arrested for the murder of their younger sister, Noelle Altman
Submitted 14 hours ago by NeverGoesOut
Police have taken Nathan Altman into custody for the murder of his sister. A knife was found buried under a pile of snow close to where Noelle's body was found. The blood has been identified as matching Noelle and the fingerprints are Nate's.
31 comments
Sorted by: new
DeathsDoor
I knew it. Fuck man I knew it. Knew it was gna be someone in the family. Had to be
WHOKiLLedLAURaPalMEr
Shut up man, you never once claimed it was the brother
DeathsDoor
OH DIDN'T I???????? PRETTY SURE HE WAS THE FIRST PERSON I POINTED THE FINGER AT
WHOKiLLedLAURaPalMEr
Whatever man you'd probably claim you were first person who landed on the moon if Buzz Aldrin wasn't still around to dispute it
I just wanna know what happened to nora altman
Have they reopened her case? Or mentioned if they're gonna look at a possible connection?
skeletonkey
yeah that's what I wanna know too. No mention of it in the press release from the police though
/u/NeverGoesOut what's going on? You reckon the brother did it?
NeverGoesOut

It fits I guess

Fingerprints are hard to deny

My main issue with it is why? Why does someone kill both their sisters?

WHOKiLLedLAURaPalMEr

So if it's the brother that killed them both are we assuming that he also killed Annalise Rigby from 5 years ago? Anyone remember that?

Kinda sad to be giving up on the theory that NA is still alive though. Always hoped she'd pulled a Gone Girl and run away

The name Annalise Rigby came out of nowhere; I hadn't seen her mentioned in any of my previous Reddit perusing, but it still snagged at me, so I put it into the search bar, hoping to jog my memory.

She had gone missing from Stokely, which was less than a forty-five-minute drive north from here, five years before. Aged twenty-two when she went missing, she was born the same year as Nora and I were but the only mention of Nora's disappearance in articles about Annalise were vague and perfunctory. There was nothing to indicate anyone thought seriously that they were related, so I headed back to Reddit, to the "Unresolved Mysteries" thread about Nora, and scrolled down to the very first mention of Annalise Rigby.

/r/UnresolvedMysteries

This is an archived post. You won't be able to vote or comment.

What Happened to Nora Altman?

hellomarshmallows 5 years ago

Hey new to the thread and just read pretty much everything you guys have posted. Have you heard anything about the girl from Stokely who went missing recently? It reminded me of the Nora Altman case so I started searching everything I could online and found you guys. Anyone think they're connected?

DeathsDoor

Why would they be connected?

WHOKiLLedLAURaPalMEr

Cos Stokely's like a 45-minute drive from Forest View!

DeathsDoor

Oh right didn't realize. The Rigby girl just left though right? That seems pretty clear to me. She wanted to leave town anyway and she'd had a fight with her boyfriend so she left. She was like 21 she can do what she wants.

hellomarshmallows

Stokely's actually even closer to where Nora went missing (or at least where her car was found) than Forest View is. It's more like 30 minutes away. Seems insane two girls would just disappear like that and it not be connected

DeathsDoor

Been 5 years since Nora went missing now though

WHOKiLLedLAURaPalMEr

So?

DeathsDoor

So that's quite a lot of time to pass

WHOKiLLedLAURaPalMEr

Not really dude. Does anyone know if Nora and Annalise Rigby knew each other? Went to school together or anything?

hellomarshmallows

No they didn't. Annalise had only been living here (I'm from the area but not from Stokely) for like 7 months so they never would have crossed paths. She was living with her boyfriend while his dad was sick and helping out his mom at their bar.

SimoneDeBoobsPhwoar

Oh man that's so sad

LLCoolJake

Anyone else think maybe the boyfriend did it?

skeletonkey

Why does everyone always suspect the boyfriend?!

SimoneDeBoobsPhwoar

Cos it normally is the boyfriend! Or an ex obv

skeletonkey

Where's /u/NeverGoesOut in all this? Wanna hear your take man

NeverGoesOut

I'm here.

Not sure what to make of the Rigby case but does seem like too big of a coincidence if I'm honest.

DeathsDoor

Even 5 years later?

NeverGoesOut

Well if you subscribe to the foul play theory (which I do) that Nora was abducted and probably murdered then the most likely scenario is that she was killed by someone she knew. Not just because statistically most people are (especially female victims) but because of the context. She ran out of gas by the side of the road and was presumably picked up by someone pretty quickly after that because she didn't even call anyone when she realized she was out of gas. In which case it had to be someone she knew because most people would prefer to call a friend/parent/sibling and wait to be picked up than get in a car with a stranger wouldn't they?

All this to say that if it was someone she knew then there's a strong possibility they still live in the area—or at least visit regularly (going back to see family etc) and could therefore have pretty easily either run into Annalise or got to know her over the past few months.

On top of which Annalise went missing over the weekend of a popular festival that Stokely holds this time of year so the town would have been busier than usual (it's pretty quiet in the winter otherwise).

If it was the ex who killed Nora—which as I say, I think it probably was—then I know that he doesn't live in the area anymore, but because of the festival that weekend, there's a chance he might have come back for that. Just postulating tho, nothing concrete here at all.

hellomarshmallows
This
I agree with all of this

A little more enlightened, but still ultimately unsatisfied by the lack of information, I sent Keegan a Facebook message to ask if he wanted to meet for a drink later.

CHAPTER TWENTY-ONE

Keegan was already at the bar when I arrived, sitting alone in the same booth we'd sat in the night of Elle's memorial. He was most of the way through a beer, his laptop open in front of him, making the most of how quiet it still was, as well as Cool's free but intermittent Wi-Fi. I got myself a drink and joined him. He was clearly concentrating hard though, because he looked up, startled, as I sat down, and it took him a beat for the cloud of confusion to pass and for him to recognize me.

"Maddie, hi," he said, "sorry, I'm just trying to get this thing written up, will you give me a minute?"

"Sure," I said, taking a sip of beer and letting my gaze wander around the bar. It was a little after four and there were only a few other people in the room. Everything is made of wood in there, and the already low ceiling is strung with strange tchotchkes and memorabilia, so that it feels cozy but a little claustrophobic at times too.

"Okay," Keegan said after a while, "I'm as done with that as I can be," and shut the lid of his MacBook.

"What were you doing? Writing a blog post?"

"Well, kind of. It's for the *Huffington Post*."

"Oh."

217

"Yeah, just kind of a little atmospheric piece about what it's like here at the moment, with the specter of Nora, and Nate being arrested for Noelle's murder. How it's affected the town, its mood and morale, that kind of thing."

"'The specter of Nora,'" I said.

"Yeah,"

I took a drink and looked at him. "Right, well on that note. What can you tell me about Annalise Rigby?"

"Annalise Rigby? That girl from Stokely?" he asked, his forehead creasing a little.

"Yes, the missing girl from Stokely."

"I can't tell you much, to be honest. I just … I don't think she's connected to this necessarily."

"That's not what you said on Reddit."

He looked down into his glass, which was almost empty now, and drained it before speaking. "Well, that was a while ago. Before Nate."

"You said that if Nora was killed or kidnapped by someone she knew—which you thought was the most likely scenario—then the chances were that that same person could feasibly have kidnapped or killed Annalise, considering Stokely is less than forty-five minutes from here. That's what you said."

"Yeah, so?"

"Well, Nate was in Texas when Annalise went missing, so it doesn't match up," I said.

"So maybe Annalise's disappearance isn't related. All that's just speculation, anyway. If Nate wasn't here when Annalise went missing, then they're probably not related."

"And what if it's not Nate? What if Nate didn't kill Elle, or Nora, or Annalise? And what if the fact he wasn't anywhere near Forest View or Stokely when Annalise went missing proves that?" I asked desperately, my voice catching and falling on my own words.

"Look, I guess it's still possible all three of them are connected, but with Nate's fingerprints on that knife, and if, as you say, he wasn't actually here when Annalise went missing, then it's beginning to look highly doubtful."

"Will you just tell me what you know about Annalise?" I said, frustration leaking out of me.

"There's not much to tell," he said with a shrug. "You probably know as much as I do just from searching for her online."

"So you've never researched her disappearance the way you did with Nora's?"

Keegan shook his head. "No, there's just not as much information around about her. Do you want another drink? I think I want another."

I stared at him, annoyed by his change of subject, and said: "I'm fine."

Keegan went up to the bar and, as he did so, the door opened, and I felt the kick of cold air even in our corner booth. I looked over to see who had come in and was surprised to see Agent Lee, completely unaccompanied. He peered around the bar, getting a good look at the whole room and shot me a halogen-bright smile when he spotted me.

"Mind if I join you?" he said after I'd watched him saunter over.

"I'm with someone," I said.

"Who? The child at the bar?"

"He's twenty-two," I pointed out.

Lee held up his hands. "I wasn't planning on carding him, I promise. You think he'll mind if I sit with you guys for a while?"

"Shouldn't you be working?" I asked.

He smiled again, once more showing off his teeth. "Who says I'm not?" I made a sound at the back of my throat, and he laughed. "Look, why don't you let me buy you a drink?"

"I thought you didn't approve of drinking before five."

"I have been known to make exceptions."

"Fine. I'll have the same again," I said, shaking my glass at him.

I wasn't even nearly finished with my beer, but for some reason having this guy buy me a drink I didn't even need felt like a victory. A bitter, petty victory, but a victory nonetheless. He smiled, this time keeping his teeth to himself and wandered off to the bar, where he held out his hand to shake Keegan's and the two of them started talking. They returned a few minutes later with a pitcher of beer and sat down on the bench opposite me, so it looked and felt as though I was being interviewed.

"So, what should I call you, is it 'Agent Lee,' or do you prefer the more informal 'Agent'?" I asked.

"You can call me Steven," he said, not bothering to tilt the glasses, and pouring out three very frothy beers.

"Steve and Steph," I said, referencing his partner Gutierrez, "that's cute. Where is Steph tonight anyway? Have you two had a fight?"

"Oh, we fight all the time, but we always make up. She's Skyping her daughter," he said, passing me a glass and then taking a drink from his own.

"Keegan and I were talking about Annalise Rigby before you got here, but hadn't got very far. Maybe you could help us out a little."

"Annalise Rigby?" he said, "I'm not sure I recognize the name if I'm being honest."

"You're not very good at playing dumb, Steven."

He grinned over his beer glass at me. "Ah, maybe I'm just too smart for my own good."

"If you were actually smart you'd be able to fool people all the time."

"You make a good point, Madeline. A very good point. Why were you talking about Annalise Rigby?"

"She went missing from Stokely five years ago."

"I'm aware. Hey, would you guys go in on a basket of fries if I ordered some? I'm starving."

"The waffle fries are really great here," Keegan said.

"Good to know, man, good to know. Waffle fries it is. Maddie? You have any recommendations for me?"

"No."

"Fair enough."

"Can we get back to Annalise for a second?"

"Sure, but I don't know what I can tell you, really. It wasn't a DOJ case. The county sheriff would have been in charge of that one."

"Who was that?" I asked.

"I don't know; I don't have total recall when it comes to every single county sheriff in the state, somewhat surprisingly. You could find out for yourself pretty easily though. Now, back to those waffle fries, should I get one basket or two?"

Lee got his fries in the end and I spent much of the evening watching as he and Keegan chatted away. I expected Keegan to grill him more—here was someone who had inside knowledge of Noelle's case, after all, but he was too deferential, a little too deer in the headlights for that. I tried as best I could to steer the conversation back to either Annalise, Elle, or Nora, but Lee was a conversational expert when it came to changing subjects and misdirection apparently. He never appeared rude or disrespectful when he did, but instead a few seconds would have gone by and we'd be back to talking about something random and inconsequential like the weather—which was particularly bad—or *Mindhunter*—which was particularly good—and I wouldn't even have noticed that he'd steered me off topic again.

"So, you're based in Wausau?" I asked, trying at least to get him to talk about his work in some form.

"Yeah. I'm from Milwaukee though originally. You went to college there, right?"

"Madison."

"Oh right, it's Angela who was in Milwaukee."

I took a sip of beer and looked at him. We'd eaten our way

221

through the two baskets of waffle fries he'd ordered and were onto another pitcher. "That's right," I said slowly.

"How did you become an Agent?" Keegan asked, sitting forward a little in his seat.

"The usual way: I applied. Why? You think of joining me?"

"He's a writer," I said.

"For now, sure. But he's twenty-two. He could change his mind, right, Keegan?"

"Oh, um. I don't know. Not really. I still need to graduate, right?"

"That's the spirit," Lee said, slapping him on the back. He turned his gaze back on me. "You've changed your mind a few times on what you want to do, right, Maddie?"

"What's that supposed to mean?" I asked, stiffening.

Lee shrugged, eyes on me while he swirled the last few gulps of beer he had left in his glass around and around. "Just that people change. Their minds, their majors. It's pretty normal."

"Did you always want to be a cop?" Keegan said.

"Sure. My parents wanted me to be a lawyer, but by the time I finished law school I knew it wasn't for me and went the other way. Luckily they didn't stay mad at me for too long."

Just then Ange appeared at my side. The bar had filled up by this point and she'd managed to work her way through the crowd towards us without me even noticing. "Hey," she said, looking between the three of us in the booth, "what's going on?"

"Miss Cairney," Lee said, smiling delightedly at her, "how lovely to see you."

"Right, you too. I guess." She scooted in next to me on the bench, giving me a look that silently asked what I was doing with these two.

I'd been about to leave at that point. All I wanted was to go home and try and find out who'd been in charge of Annalise Rigby's investigation, but I'd felt stuck there for some reason, unable to just get up and go. As the bar had got busier and busier, I'd felt less and less like I wanted to be there, and yet more and

222

more like I was trapped there. There was no reason for it of course; I could have left whenever I wanted, but my legs were lead, stuck hard to the wooden bench.

Jack, Ange's colleague, joined us a few minutes later, carrying drinks for them both, and was introduced to Keegan and Lee.

"So," Ange said, when there was a lull in the conversation, looking directly at Lee, "how's Nate doing?"

"Ah, I was wondering when that would come up. I was actually betting you'd bring it up, Maddie."

I shrugged, feigning indifference and Ange spared me a look before turning back to Lee. "Well? What's going on?"

"You know I can't answer that. It's an ongoing investigation, plus you're a member of the press, et cetera et etcetera."

Ange sighed and leaned back in her seat. Suddenly, all her energy seemed to have been pulled out of her, and I noticed her lips were chapped, red raw and downturned. I wanted to tell her that she didn't have to be here, that we could go, leave town, get the hell out of there, but I couldn't even get myself to believe that, let alone Ange. Instead, I took a long drag of beer and watched as she did the same with her gin and tonic.

Lee's phone vibrated on the table next to him, and he said after checking it: "Well, I guess that's my cue. I'll be seeing you all soon." He finished off his beer, wiped his mouth with the back of his hand and took off.

"I hope he's not driving," Keegan said, watching him leave, "he's had like four beers."

For some reason I looked at Ange just as she looked at me and we both started to laugh—hard, hysterical, lost laughter that was already fraying at the edges. The type of laughter that feels like a lifeline rather than a celebration; like you're desperately trying to capture something, even as it catches you.

That night I dreamt of a thousand different faces. They scrolled past me as if I was scrolling through a slideshow online, and every time I tried to stop one before it moved on it changed into Nora. If you didn't count the pane of glass dream that had been torturing me ever since she'd disappeared, it was the first time I'd dreamt of Nora in years, however abstractly.

Before Nora disappeared I used to have a recurring dream in which my sister died. It was never Cordy, which you might expect, her being younger, but always, always Serena. And it was never the same either. There were house fires and drownings, car crashes and airplanes that simply fell from the sky. One night I woke up shaking having dreamt my mom was kneeling before me in the very bed I was sleeping in, telling me in a shaky whisper that the doctors had tried, but they hadn't been able to save Serena. I didn't sleep for three nights after that one.

But once Nora was gone those vivid, wake up crying nightmares were gone too. It was as if the worst thing I could possibly imagine had happened and even my subconscious simply couldn't beat it. So, it simply tormented me with the same feeling asleep as I had during the day: that the world was too much to carry; that everything was slipping through my fingers; that there was nothing I could do to stop it.

So, to wake up with a gnawing, growling pit in my stomach, ready to be filled up with something made for something of a change. Usually the feeling that filled me to the brim was of being too much. There was something inside me that was too big, too heavy, too much and I was too stitched up and stitched over for it to get out. No matter how hard I tried I couldn't unpick all the messy scars I'd left all over my body.

Wanting something, needing something, this feeling of desperation was new to me. I needed to find out what had happened to Nora, and to Elle, and maybe even to Annalise as well. More than anything, I was worried that if I didn't find out what had happened to them, the brick wall would build itself back up again, the silvery shutters would come down, and I'd be walking around in a black hole for the rest of my life.

224

I found Dad in the kitchen, staring grimly down at the front page of the newspaper. For the second day in a row there was a picture of Nate splashed across it. "Maddie," he said, looking up quickly and turning the newspaper over so it was face down on the table in one smooth movement, "you want some eggs?"

I was torn because I did want eggs, but I was also frustrated by the fact that he thought he could hide the outside world from me. Then again, I'd been hiding from the outside world for so long who could blame him? I accepted his offer of eggs and sat down in his vacated seat, turning the paper the right way up and looking down into Nate's averted eyes. The picture had been taken as he'd been hustled into the police station a couple of days before. Dad passed me a cup of coffee and I said: "Have you spoken to Katherine or Jonathan?"

"Mom talked to Katherine last night."

"And?"

"They're not doing great, as you might expect. There's a small army of reporters and photographers camped right outside their house pretty much day and night. Her sister's taken Noah back to Madison with her, but he's not really talking to anyone."

"You mean he's not talking about what's going on or he's literally not talking?"

"Apparently, he's barely said a word since Nate was arrested. All the media attention can't be helping either. Your mom said he had a mini breakdown after the memorial on Saturday. Can't imagine it's unconnected to that awful photographer trying to get a picture of him outside the church." Dad was stirring a pan of scrambled eggs as he relayed all this to me, the wooden spoon making gentle figures of eight in the sunshine yellow mixture. I watched, mesmerized, until he turned the heat off and began to load up a plate with the eggs.

I should have gone to see them as soon as I heard Nate had been arrested. Should have gone to Noah after the memorial. Should have gone in all my inarticulateness, and attempted to help in some way, any way. Noah wasn't speaking? How many other ways could that family be damaged, tortured, devastated? And then there was Nate. I took the fork Dad handed me and set about eating the plate of scrambled eggs and toast, but it all just disintegrated in my mouth like ash.

I drove up to Stokely in Dad's car after taking a pass at the Altmans' house. He'd been right about the media encampment. Despite the fact Nate was currently sat in the county jail, there were vans parked up and down the street, the logos of their TV channels splashed along their sides, while a small group of photographers and journalists were gathered at the bottom of their driveway. I looked for Ange again, dreading seeing her there like that, relieved beyond measure when I couldn't spot her.

The house looked blank. There were no lights on, but a car sat in the driveway, a thin layer of snow scattering the roof and the hood, meaning someone was home. I didn't pull to a stop, nerves clutching at my heart and my stomach, as one of the photographers turned away from the house and appeared to recognize me. Before I knew it, both she and another reporter were striding towards my car. Without even thinking I put my foot on the gas and sped off. I had to keep checking my rearview mirror to make sure no one had decided to follow, but, apparently, I wasn't worth the trouble.

One of the posters on Reddit had mentioned that Annalise had been working at a bar in Stokely when she went missing, and as it was a bit of a one-horse town, I was pretty sure I knew the place. Stokely was more of a seasonal town than Forest View, and there was a lost resort feel to it when I got out the car and blinked into the watery sunshine.

When I thought about how much of an impact Nora's disappearance had had on Forest View I couldn't believe that Annalise could have gone missing from there and barely left a mark. But there was something about it, its transience, its

226

end-of-the-road-ness, that made me think you could quite easily slip in and out of Stokely and no one would know the difference. She'd been a recent addition, according to Reddit, just passing through, so maybe that was what everyone had assumed; she'd passed through and passed on and that was that.

The bar was on the main street, down towards the lake, and my eyes took a little while to get used to the gloom when I walked in. There was a guy sitting at the bar with his back to me, hunched over a paper and a beer. He was the only person in the place apart from me and the bartender. She looked to be in her late forties maybe, with dyed-blonde hair that looked more yellow than anything else. There was a noticeboard right by the entrance and suddenly I found myself looking right at Annalise Rigby.

I took a step to inspect it more closely, taking in her name, her age, height, and weight and the number to call should I know anything. The color was faded of course, five years on, but from the photo you could tell she also had dyed-blonde hair, dark showing at the roots. She had blue eyes.

"Hey there," the woman behind the bar said as I walked over, "can I get you anything?"

"Coffee? If you have it."

"Sure do."

I looked back at the noticeboard as she turned away to the coffee machine and poured me a cup. As she placed it in front of me I pointed at the aged flyer and said: "Did you know her?"

"Annalise? Yeah. She worked here."

I didn't want to let on that I already knew she'd worked there, so I just said: "She did?"

"Mmhm. Came for the summer to be with a boy, ended up staying for the winter. You probably know the story."

"A little bit," I said. I took a sip of coffee. It was strong and hot and burned a little as it went down, warming me through. The man sitting four stools down seemed to peer at me round his shoulder. I nodded at him, and he gruffly returned to his paper. He was doing the crossword. "I'm from Forest View," I said by way of introduction to the bartender.

The woman blinked at me. "I thought you might be."

"Really? Why?"

"You have your own missing girl, don't you? The high school girl?"

"Yeah."

The woman nodded as if to herself, confirming her suspicions. "And the girl who just died down there. It was her sister."

"Yeah."

The woman nodded again, not saying anything more.

"I'm sorry, I don't really understand. Why did you just assume that was why I was here?"

The woman shrugged. "This type of thing brings it all back up again. Everyone's been stopping to look at Annalise again since that girl was murdered. She was never found you know, just like your girl." She shook her head. "That type of thing shouldn't happen here. And yet here we are."

"Nora—the girl who went missing in Forest View. She was a friend of mine. My best friend."

"So, you knew her sister as well."

"I did."

"I'm sorry for your loss." Her gaze turned towards the noticeboard again. "I don't know a lot, but I know Annalise should be here."

"Do you remember what happened around the time she went missing? I know it was a long time ago—"

"Oh no, I remember. I got a good memory, and you don't forget that kind of thing easily anyway."

"Who was the boy? The one you said she came to be here with?"

She pushed herself off from the bar she was leaning against and topped up my cup of coffee. "Ben, you want anything?" she said to the man and his paper. Ben shook his head, and she turned her attention back to me. "I'm Regina, by the way."

228

"Maddie," I said, pointing at my chest with my thumb.

"Well, Maddie. The boy was my son."

I raised both my eyebrows and glugged down some coffee, wishing it was something stronger. Regina had been holding out on me. Regina told me the story, how Annalise and her son, Kyle, had met in college, how the two of them had moved up here the summer after graduation to live with them and work in the bar while his dad recovered from surgery.

They hadn't broken up, as I'd thought, or at least not according to Regina, but there had been some problems. By winter, Kyle's dad had been up and about, meaning Regina didn't need their help in the bar or at home so much. But Kyle had been reluctant to leave despite Annalise's worry that there weren't enough opportunities there. I looked around the practically empty bar as Regina said this and had to agree with Annalise.

When she went missing, Regina admitted to thinking at first that Annalise had simply left. It was only Kyle's insistence that she wouldn't do that—along with the fact that none of her belongings, including her car, had been missing—that alerted the police to any wrongdoing or foul play. And then they went and arrested Kyle. He was released, but Regina told me that he'd never been the same again.

"He loved her," she said simply, "and she's gone."

"Did you or Kyle ever have any suspicions about who could have done this?"

Regina shook her head. "There are so few people to suspect here. You kind of have to look outside the town."

I took a good long look at Regina. She was drying some glasses with a dish towel and looked right back at me.

"And do you think it might be connected to Nora going missing?"

"Look, to me, it's always been pretty obvious. Two girls going missing like that so close to one another?" She shook her head. "Has to be connected."

"But you have no idea who could be responsible?"

"I don't know what to tell you, hon. I just don't know. Wish I did."

"But you remember that night? The night she went missing?"

"Pretty well."

She was going back on herself a little but I decided to press on. "Was she working here that night?"

"Uh huh," Regina said, nodding. "Behind the bar. It was actually pretty busy because it was the Friday before our big Star Light Festival in February. It's kind of a winter festival thing we do every year."

I knew the festival. I'd been plenty of times.

"So, you wouldn't be able to say who was in the bar that night? Who Annalise spoke to in particular? Nothing like that?" I wanted to pull out my phone and show her a photo of Louden Winters right then and there, anything to prove that someone other than Nate had done all this. That was why I was there, after all, clutching at Annalise's life, like it was my one last straw that might stop this nightmare from coming true. Because despite everything, I'd never once contemplated that Nate might have killed Nora.

"No, hon. Nothing like that. The place was full to the rafters with out-of-towners. You ever been to the Star Light Festival?"

I nodded. "When did you file the report? That she was missing?"

"Well, she didn't show up for work on Saturday and I thought that was a little strange, I remember. I called Kyle—they were staying out in a rented cabin by that point. They needed their space from us parents, I think. I thought maybe she was just sick or something, but he said she hadn't been home that night. He was worried already by that point, but the police weren't bothered. You have to wait forty-eight hours, you know." She pierced me with a look. "You probably do know that. Anyway, it wasn't till the Monday that they started paying us any attention. Kyle was beside himself by that point."

"Did the police ever mention Nora's case in relation to Annalise?"

"Uh huh, but nothing ever came of it."

I made a vague sound of disgust, and Regina looked at me sadly.

"Do you remember who was investigating her disappearance? The sheriff in charge?"

"Sure, it was Sheriff Lundgren. Based out of Eagleton."

I took out my phone and noted down the name, planning to track him down.

As I was doing so Regina said: "You know, they look a little similar, don't you think? I always thought so."

"Who?"

"Annalise and Nora. If Annalise hadn't dyed her hair. It was pretty dark naturally; you only have to take a look at her eyebrows to see that."

I turned and looked back at the faded poster. She had a big smile, a grin. Nora had rarely smiled in photos, preferring something else instead that you could really only describe as a pout.

"Yeah, I guess they look kind of similar," I said. The resemblance certainly wasn't striking, but I could see Regina's point.

"Would I be able to talk to Kyle, Regina? See if he remembers anything more from that night?"

Ben looked over at me again, this time not even pretending to need to rub his chin against the wool of his sweatered shoulder. Regina continued rubbing at the beer glass she was drying, as if she were trying to get the genie to unwind itself from inside the glass and offer her three wishes.

"Kyle's not around anymore," she said carefully.

There was no sound for me to hear in that quiet, dark bar, only the three of us breathing. In, out. I couldn't work out what she meant, not exactly. She'd chosen her words so carefully, but I knew what it meant to choose certain words when others would or wouldn't suffice. To weigh them up in your mind before deploying each and every one. Or to feel them rising up in your throat before they died in your mouth. Right at the tip of your tongue.

Regina didn't offer up anything else, so I finished my coffee, left a big tip, saying thank you as I did so and left her and Ben to their quiet, shuttered morning.

Outside, the day burned with winter sun, the air so cold it was like sandpaper against my skin. I walked down to the lake, just to reassure myself it was there. I wondered where Kyle was and what had happened to him, and then I wondered where Annalise was and what had happened to her. I thought about Elle lying in the snow, waiting to be found and, finally, inevitably, I thought about Nora.

CHAPTER TWENTY-TWO

Despite having gone missing years apart, and despite being several years apart in age at the time of their disappearances, Nora and Annalise did have a few things in common other than geographical proximity. They were both in relationships that were experiencing problems, and they were both living in a small town they wanted to leave. They wanted something more. They wanted something bigger. I had no way of knowing what it was exactly that Annalise had wanted, or where it was she wanted to go, but Nora had been clear on what she'd wanted pretty much since we started high school, probably even before then. She had never imagined herself failing. She had never imagined herself falling.

I'd spent years thinking about those last few days leading up to Nora's disappearance. She'd been in a weird mood, dealing with doubts and fears she'd never really confronted before. She'd been like that ever since Thanksgiving when she'd first found out about Louden's cheating.

***

Nora is sat at the far end of the long wooden table when I walk into the Altmans' kitchen for my annual Thanksgiving pie visit. She's slumped down in her chair staring dolefully at her plate, dressed in a pallid outfit of oatmeal-colored pajamas. I have literally never seen Nora wearing pajamas outside of the hours of 9 p.m. and 9 a.m. so an obligatory alarm goes off in my head as I catch Nate's eye and he gives me a questioning look. Sitting down next to Nora, she finally looks up to register my appearance.

"Hey," I say.

"Hi, Mads," she intones blandly, her voice hollow. Up close her dark, pitch-black hair looks dull, lighter in color almost, and her skin is red-and-white blotchy, her eyes puffy pouches. I have never seen Nora cry. I've known her almost fifteen years but never seen her cry. Not even at The fucking Notebook.

There's general chatter and clatter from the rest of the table, the family generally ignoring Nora's forlorn demeanor, which seems strange to me because in general she's the sun around which the rest of the family merely orbits when it comes to social gatherings and occasions. Only Nate seems in the least bit perturbed, and I meet his gaze again. His face is as inscrutable as my own, however, and I can't tell whether he knows about Louden yet. Nora wouldn't have told him of course. The pair of them barely communicate these days. Nora's pushing her fork around the cake plate in front of her, the blueberry pie half-demolished, and yet barely touched.

"Um, are you okay?" I ask in a hushed undertone. The question is redundant though, as she very clearly is not okay. She looks out at me from under a thatch of uncharacteristically unwashed hair. Her eyes say it all: of course I'm not fucking okay.

"Let's go upstairs," she says suddenly, grabbing the arm of my dark burgundy sweater. "You can bring your pie." I risk a look at Nate, who's still watching us, and follow Nora out the kitchen and up the stairs to her room.

With the door shut Nora collapses onto her bed, her eyes open, staring straight up at the white ceiling.

"What's going on?" I ask, pulling the chair from out beneath her desk and wheeling it closer to her white iron bedstead. Leaning back in the chair I rest my feet on the side of the bed and look down at Nora as if I were the psychiatrist and she were my patient.

"I saw Louden. Last night."

"And?"

She doesn't say anything for a while, which throws me. In fact, the whole thing is throwing me. Nora doesn't wallow. Nora doesn't contemplate and ruminate. She doesn't fret and agonize. And she always has an answer. To everything.

"And he was ... Louden."

"What does that mean?"

"I mean, he opened the door and, I don't know, I was expecting guilt or something. A look of shame, anything. Just ... something. But he opened the door and he just—he was just Louden. He looked pleased to see me, Mads. Pleased to fucking see me."

"So, what are you saying—you guys didn't break up?"

"Yes. No. I don't know."

This was possibly the first time I'd ever heard Nora say: "I don't know." I shift in my seat and stare down at her, willing her to talk.

"It was just so weird, Mads. I don't know what I was expecting: him to just open the door and immediately admit to having slept with someone else in Chicago? Everything was just so freakishly normal. We went into the living room to say hi to his parents—even though, like, I've literally seen them more often in the past three months than he has—and then we went up to his room and he started kissing me and saying how much he missed me and ... Oh my God, Mads, I just kissed him back and said how much I'd missed him!" Nora sits up straight suddenly and stares at me with rounded, wild eyes.

"So what are you saying? It just never came up ...?"

"No, no. I-I eventually said something."

"Well, what did you say?"

She slumps back onto the bed, her eyes back to staring at the ceiling. Just then my cell beeps and I slip it out of my pocket to read the text message. It's from Nate.

Mads, what's going on? Nora says she has flu, but she doesn't have a single symptom. What the hell has happened? She's acting pretty fuckin weird.

"Who is it?" Nora asks, suddenly suspicious, and for some reason I lie.

"Cordy. Checking I know I've gotta be back for family Thanksgiving charades." I roll my eyes at Nora even though I love charades and am excellent at it.

Nora puffs out her cheeks and sighs as I rattle off a quick reply to Nate.

Well, she's not got flu but don't wanna say much more.

He texts back almost instantly.

Come back downstairs.

I frown at my phone and stick it back in my pocket.

"So, what did you say to Louden?" I prod Nora with the toe of my shoe, and she kind of just shakes her head at me.

"It was so awful, Mads. I just suddenly blurted out 'how many girls have you hooked up with since moving to Chicago?' and he just—He looked like I'd accused him of murder. But also like he'd committed murder, you know?"

"What happened after that? Did you dump him?"

"I don't know. I don't really know what happened, it's kind of a blur. He said I don't know what you're talking about and then I said don't be stupid, I've seen a photo, and he kind of looked like I'd accused him of another murder, and then I said how many again, and he said just one, and I said I didn't believe him, and then I left. It was so weird though. I really thought I'd go over there, and he'd sit me down and say college was different to what he expected and he couldn't carry on having a relationship and it was stupid to think that he could, and that would be it, you know? Like, I could accept that. I could respect that. But he just wanted to carry on as if he wasn't a conniving, cheating, unrepentant asshole."

236

"Wait, you went round there hoping he'd break up with you?"

"Not hoping. Just expecting. I really didn't think he'd cheat on me for the sake of it. I didn't think he'd do it just to carry on going out with me. I thought that would be it—he'd gone to college, realized he wanted to fuck loads of other girls and was gonna break up with me. Fine. I can cope with that. I could cope with that. I'm reasonable."

"Sure."

"I am! I'm not some hopeless … high school girl sitting at home imagining how my wedding to Louden fucking Winters is gonna look."

"Right. You're Nora fucking Altman."

"Exactly! I'm Nora fucking Altman and I'm not sure if I've actually broken up with my cheating boyfriend yet, or if it's just implied I have."

"Have you heard from him?"

Nora listlessly passes me her phone and it has sixteen missed calls and a ton of messages. All from Louden Winters.

"Have you answered any of these?"

"No."

"Okay."

"Is that a positive or a negative okay?"

"It's completely neutral."

"You're not allowed to be neutral."

"Well no, obviously I'm not neutral neutral, you know how I feel about neutrality in general."

"It's best left to the Swiss."

"If that, the sneaky, neutrality loving bastards. No, I am 100 per cent on your side, but maybe you need to speak to him? To make sure he actually knows you guys are over? I mean, he's not the brightest crayon in the box."

"He's not stupid, Mads."

"Well, he's not smart either. He cheated on you for one thing."

Nora doesn't move a muscle, and my phone beeps again, but

237

this time it really is Cordy, and it really is time for me to go home. I have a championship title to defend, after all.

Nora catches one of my feet before I can swing them both down off the bed and onto the ground and says quietly into the gloom that has descended in her room: "I thought I'd want to kill him when I saw him, but I didn't. What does that mean?"

"It just means that you're not homicidal, Nora, not that you shouldn't break up with him."

I don't think she ever really expected to be hurt by Louden. Or at least not as much she was. Not because she didn't expect Louden to hurt her, but because she didn't think she could be hurt. By him or by anyone. It was part of her entire attitude towards life: that it was something to be grabbed and molded into a shape or figure of her own making. I often wondered how long it would have taken her to realize that life wasn't something we got to shape, but instead it was what shaped us. Not all that long probably; life had a way of announcing itself as the architect rather than whatever it was you were trying to build. It could knock things down just as easily—*more* easily—than build things up. Destruction takes seconds. Creation takes years.

By the time I got to Eagleton the day was slipping away from me, the winter sunlight was being leached from the sky, trees turning black as the air turned indigo. The waiting room was empty when I wandered in, small and stuffy from overworked radiators, and a young man in a brown uniform was sitting behind the reception desk looking bored.

"Hi, is Sheriff Lundgren around?" I asked, disturbing the receptionist from whatever it was he was looking at on his phone.

"Lundgren?" he said, looking up sharply. "Sure, who's asking?"

"Maddie Fielder," I said. The deputy just looked at me, his face blank, so I continued, "I just have a few questions."

"About what?"

"I'd really rather ask him."

238

"Her."

"What?"

The deputy offered me a smirk and said: "The sheriff's a her."

He pointed at a room to my left, where a woman had just appeared in the doorway, and I grimaced internally at my mistake.

Sheriff Lundgren had brown-gray hair and wide, high cheekbones that made her face look expansive and welcoming even as she frowned at me. She was in the same brown uniform as her deputy, hands on hips, feet placed wide apart.

"What can we do for you, Miss?" she said, her voice pleasant, almost soothing.

"It's Maddie," I said, "and I wanted to ask you about Annalise. Annalise Rigby."

"Annalise, huh? Well, what do you want to know about her? And why?" The deputy was looking between Lundgren and me, riveted, and I glanced at him momentarily before Lundgren said: "Would you prefer to do this in my office?" and I nodded.

Her office was colder than the waiting room—clearly the deputy had the radiator cranked up high—and messier. She went to sit behind her desk and waved her hand at one of the spare chairs in front of it for me to sit in.

"So, you wanted to ask me about Annalise? What exactly about her?"

I stared at her. I wasn't sure what I wanted to ask her about Annalise exactly, except that I wanted to know every detail about her disappearance and investigation. I had a feeling that wasn't really on the table, so instead of asking a question, I said: "I was friends with Nora Altman. And I knew Noelle too, obviously."

The sheriff nodded curtly, and I knew immediately there was no need to clarify any further. "Okay, and now you're here asking me about Annalise? Just as their brother has been arrested. Should I assume you know him too?"

"I do."

Lundgren narrowed her eyes and shifted in her chair, getting comfortable. "What do you remember about Annalise's disappearance?" she asked.

"To be honest, nothing. I only came across her name yesterday. I can't believe I've never heard of her."

Lundgren nodded. "Well, she didn't get as much media coverage as Nora, that's true. Nora had the benefit of being a few years younger in that case, although obviously there are no benefits here. Annalise also wasn't from Stokely so that inevitably made people assume she'd simply left."

"You don't believe that?"

"I'd only been sheriff for a few months when Annalise went missing. Ever since I've always worked from the assumption of worst-case scenario."

"What does that mean?"

Lundgren sighed, looking around her office for the words she needed. "I made a lot of assumptions with Annalise at the beginning. Based on the fact that she was an adult, and, from the lack of any pertinent evidence, I thought she was probably okay. That she'd simply upped and left. I made a lot of mistakes and even though I realized that fairly early on, it was too late to rectify any of them."

"Did you ever look into Annalise's disappearance being connected to Nora's?"

"Well, there were some pretty clear similarities to Nora's case, or at least I always thought so, but unfortunately most of those similarities were due to how inconclusive both cases were."

"How do you mean?"

"The suddenness of the disappearance, the lack of evidence, the way there were no real personal effects missing at all apart from what they had on them." Lundgren ticked off each item on her fingers as she listed these similarities, as if they were items on her grocery list. "I requested the file from Nora's disappearance, for comparison, but we never got it. By then Nora's case had already gone cold, and the department claimed it was in the process of being transferred to a new facility and couldn't be located."

"So, you never actually saw the file?" I asked.

"No, I did not."

"Would that have been the Waterstone Police Department you requested the file from?"

"Sure was. I asked the Chief a couple times, but it was 'no can do' every time."

"Do you think he was lying to you?" I asked, sensing a little more resentment from her than simply being annoyed at Waterstone for having lost the file.

Lundgren sighed and twirled a pen around in her hand. "I'm not accusing him of that. Probably they just mislaid it because it had been so long by that point, but it did strike me as a little odd that they weren't more willing to help with Annalise considering everything that had happened with Nora Altman. Look Maddie, I'm guessing you're here because you think all this—Nora, Annalise—has something to do with Noelle's death. Am I right?"

"Yes."

Lundgren nodded and directed her gaze straight at me. Her eyes were the same faded blue as stonewash jeans. "Do you think Nathan Altman is guilty?" she asked.

"I don't know," I said, answering as truthfully as I could.

"I don't think you'd be here if you really believed it." She was looking at me still, so steadily I had to look away. I'd spent the last ten years being looked at the way she was looking at me then: like she couldn't decide if I should be wrapped up safe and put away, or picked up, brushed off, and set on my way again.

"I don't think I can believe it," I said slowly, trying to articulate something I hadn't quite wrapped my heart and my head around. If Nate was guilty, then I had lost him too. And I wasn't sure I was prepared to lose anyone else; I wasn't sure I'd survive that too. But that fear—that he really was guilty, and I was just too scared to see it—was there already, at the edge of everything, like frost on a windowpane. It had been there for a long time I suppose, sketching itself over that pane of glass that still loved to taunt me at night, but it felt different now, more urgent; maybe now it wasn't just at the edges of the windowpane, but had frosted over the whole thing. Shadows moved beyond it, but the frost was too thick to see through. I wanted to smash it, to break through, to watch those cracks break and shatter and finally see through to the other side. I just didn't know how. Maybe I wasn't strong enough yet. Maybe I never would be.

"I think you need to start getting used to the idea that Nate Altman might well be guilty," the sheriff said quietly but firmly. "Sometimes the solution's just staring us right in the face, as much as we don't want to look at it."

By the time I left the Eagleton police station the world had gone completely dark. I looked up, expecting stars, but clouds must have rolled in at some point in the evening because there was nothing. I breathed in the sharp, clean air, grateful for the way it scraped my throat and lungs.

There was a time when the only way I could face the world was like that, air burning my lungs, darkness protecting me. I used to wait out the days, which were full of people and expectations, in my room until night fell and I could breathe in fresh air again. I would leave my dorm room at two, three in the morning, the hallway quiet or close to it, but strip lighting removing any sense of nighttime eeriness.

I wouldn't breathe easily until I got outside, the cold washing over me as I took off at speed, long strides, my head down, hood up, still hidden but looking for all the world as if I knew where I was going. I liked to feel the build-up of breath in my chest, air clinging to my throat and lungs, the feeling familiar and something close to comfort. When I breathed, in, out, in, out it was like I was trying to push something away but also like I was taking something back too.

There were nights when I'd return from a walk like that to find Nate waiting for me. The first time it was February, just a month or so after the one-year anniversary of Nora's disappearance.

***

He's sitting on the floor with his back against the door, head tipped back, eyes closed. I kick the soles of his shoes.

"Hey. What are you doing here?"

He opens one eye, grins, and pops up to standing. "Hey. Where you been?"

"Out."

"It's half three in the morning."

"Exactly. What are you doing here?"

"Just came to see you ... you gonna open the door?"

I open the door even though I really don't want to. I wish there was somewhere else we could go but it's late and everything on campus is closed. The door swings open and I look at the room through Nate's eyes. My laptop sits, still open, the screen a serene blank black, within the swirl of my duvet and blankets. The bedside table is crowded with dirty glasses and mugs, books I haven't yet opened piled high next to the lamp which has been shunted in between the bed and the table and is about to fall to the floor at any moment. My garbage can overflows, an extra plastic bag filled with trash sitting next to it. Clothes scatter the floor, draping themselves over a small chair that's hiding in the corner. It smells of stale yoghurt.

"Sorry it's so ... gross."

"I live with five other guys, Mads. This is nothing. Seriously."

I choose to believe him, if only because I'm too tired all of a sudden not to, and sit down on the edge of the bed. "What are you doing here?" I ask again.

"Was in the area. Thought I'd stop by."

"It's late, Nate."

"Yeah but I knew you'd be up. It's not like I woke you, right?"

I'm struggling to talk, to make conversation, even with this person I've known most of my life. I want to crawl into bed and stare at the screen of my laptop while whatever DVD is already loaded plays out.

"You okay?" he asks eventually after I don't say anything.

"Yeah. Fine."

"I get worried about you sitting all alone up here. You need to get out more."

My throat constricts, my chest contracting. I want to say I get worried about him out there, even with other people all around him, but I can't. "I was just out."

"Yeah, for one of your weird nighttime walks. Can't believe you're still doing those."

"I like it at night. I like the dark."

"Well, you need to get out in the light more, Mads. Seriously."

I don't bother trying to explain it to him: that he is the light. That it spills out from him, without him even realizing. That I'm over here, lost in the dark, just trying to find the switch and he's over there, glowing, phosphorescent. I wonder what he'd say, what he'd do, if I said that to him. If I ever said that to him. But of course, I don't. I don't say anything at all.

Nate looks at me kind of sadly, and I let myself see him for a second before looking away. "Well, I guess I better go," he says, "turns out this was a doomed mission."

I want to ask him to stay. I want to be brave enough to ask him to stay. But a much, much larger part of me can barely even stand to let him look at me. My insides grip and tighten every time he turns his head towards me, my eyes slide away from his, my jaw clenched, my shoulders rising ever further towards my ears. I never thought of myself as a scared person, but I'm frightened all the time, terrified.

So, I don't even say goodbye when he finally leaves. I don't even feel relief or release when he's gone; I don't even get that. I just feel the same as I did before, which is to say like something burnt and curling up at the edges. But at least with him gone I don't have to worry about someone peering around those burning edges, realizing how fragile they are, how close they are to crumbling.

CHAPTER TWENTY-THREE

CJ's was busier than I thought it was going to be, but I still didn't have any problem picking out Ange in the crowd. She had her head down, hunched over her laptop, a familiar figure of concentration that sent a stab of useless nostalgia through me. I don't tend to look back fondly on my teenage years; Nora cast a shadow so large it obstructed everything, turned it monochrome. But I realized that more than anything I missed the simplicity and the wide-open promise of youth. At that point in time, the future had felt like a trap, something you fell into and were caught by, its teeth wrapped around your ankle, its jaw shaking you back and forth as you held on for dear life. But back then, before all that, the yawning maw had been something to run towards, full tilt, with nothing nipping at your heels but hope.

"Morning," I said, sliding into the seat opposite Ange. She looked up quickly, her brown eyes wide with surprise before seeing it was me and settling back down again.

"Mads, it's you. I was in my own world there."

"What world was that?" I asked, slipping off my coat and scarf.

"One where none of this had ever happened," she said after swallowing her mouthful of coffee. She then swiveled her MacBook towards me so I could see the screen. She'd been feeling nostalgic too evidently, because her browser was open on Nora's Facebook page and Nora herself was staring out at me, a little disdainfully, from her profile picture.

I pulled the laptop towards me, peering into the screen. It wasn't just that Nora's life, and therefore her profile page, was caught in amber, but that it was from another time altogether. She'd only been on Facebook for two years when she went missing. Her profile page was a relic from before Instagram, and Snapchat, before either Twitter or even Facebook itself had become ubiquitous; before all our lives, from toddler to grand-parent, from cradle to grave, were lived out online.

It had been disorientating to see, or at least be reminded of, how far the world had come, how many spins on its axis we'd lived through since she'd disappeared. I felt guilty then, that deep trench of betrayal rising up, as I thought of how much life I'd lived without her. I missed her then not the way you miss another person, but the way you miss another, earlier version of yourself. I wanted to hold her and warn her at the same time of everything that was to come, of everything she would miss, to give her the whole world while holding back everything that could harm her.

The diner went in and out of focus while I stared at her and eventually I had to turn the laptop back to Ange, to reclaim my position in the world, whatever it was worth.

"I did something a little weird a few days ago," I said.

Ange turned sharply towards me, her shoulders rigid. "What did you do?" she demanded.

"I logged into Elle's Facebook," I said, finally telling her all about John Smith. I don't know why I hadn't told her sooner; probably I'd been worried and waiting for her judgement. I was always the one fucking up, after all, but she visibly relaxed at my confession. Clearly I hadn't fucked up too bad with this one.

Her voice was tired, though, when she finally said: "That could've been anyone, Mads. Literally anyone. That's pretty much the point of the internet."

"Yeah, but—"

"What's this really about?" she said, eyes narrowed, her mouth pulled into a firm line.

"What do you mean?"

"Is this about Nate?"

I struggled to see how any of "this" *wasn't* about Nate, so I just said: "In what way?"

She sighed, rearranging herself in her seat, trying to get comfortable. She looked like she was about to explain a simple math problem to a small child. "Are you in love with him?"

"I'm having a vague sense of déjà vu. Haven't you asked me this before?"

"Yeah, only about a dozen times. I still want to know though."

"Why?"

"Because you're … stuck. And I want you to be unstuck."

"I don't know if I'm in love with him. I love him. But then, I love you too."

"Yeah, but you don't want to sleep with me."

My brain felt as though it was encased in cotton wool. I was having trouble accessing it. "I don't want … I don't want to sleep with Nate. I have no idea what I want. From him, from anyone." I hadn't yet told her about the kiss on the night of Elle's memorial, and I wasn't about to. "It's all so messy. What I want more than anything is to know what I want."

"See, this is what I'm talking about. Stuck."

"But that's me. That's not Nate. I'd be stuck even without him in the picture."

"You still don't get it. What you want, how you feel, it doesn't exist on a different plane from what I want or feel, or what Nate feels, or what Serena or anyone else feels. You can't siphon yourself off from your friends and family as a way to figure out what it is you want. Everything you do affects everything I do, because we're here, doing it together. You can't try and figure out whether or not you want to be with Nate without him. If

248

it's a mess, it's both of your mess. You can't deal with it on your own or figure what it means on your own, because it wouldn't exist without him."

I thought about the night of Elle's memorial, and how close I'd come to finally telling Nate how I felt, how I'd always felt about him. But there had still been something holding me back, stopping me from finally reaching out and meeting him wherever he was.

It had been my inability to reach out that had pushed him away, all the way to Texas and out of my life, and that hadn't made me any happier, hadn't made my life any easier, hadn't lightened the load or loosened the stitches that seemed to bind my life together. But he'd tried to siphon himself off too, just as Ange was accusing me of doing and, in the end, we hadn't let ourselves grow and change together, and so whenever we saw each other it was brittle and raw, rather than lived in and familiar, and that shock was too much, too overpowering, so we pulled away again and fell further and further apart until we got to where we were at that point, a place I didn't recognize, a place that tripped me up and pulled me down, a place I couldn't find my way through.

But maybe that wasn't the problem, maybe I didn't recognize Nate at that time because I'd never really known him then; a desperate need for comfort could dull your edges, make you blind to danger and, what if, after Nora's disappearance, I'd searched him out so much because what I was really searching for was *her*? And if that was the case, I thought, had I ever really known Nate at all?

What if Nate hadn't been fueled by grief, but guilt? Then, I still couldn't quite comprehend it, not yet, even as articles and blog posts, and even close friends exhorted me too. I'd known I would have to eventually, but for the time being, the river of fear was too wide and I was too scared to find out what was on the other side. Because, I reasoned, what would it mean if the person

249

I found standing there was Nate? What would it mean for me? That would mean losing not just him, but part of myself too, and I wasn't sure if after that there'd be enough of me to go round. It was selfish and cowardly, I know that now, but sometimes selfish and cowardly are the only tools you have to protect yourself.

"Maddie?" Ange said, bringing me back to the diner. When I still didn't answer she gently rapped her knuckles against the side of my head and said: "Anybody there?"

"Sorry," I said, reaching for Ange's coffee and taking a sip, "didn't sleep well last night."

"I haven't slept in days," she said, and I could hear in her voice how exhausted she was. "I just want this all to be over."

I had wanted it to be over as well, I just still hadn't been sure if I was ready to accept that particular ending. Not yet, anyway. I looked back at her laptop screen, but it had gone dark once again; Nora was gone.

Ruby the waitress was walking towards us, ready to take our order and suddenly my heart clenched, my stomach knotted, the thought of eating anything too much. I asked for a coffee and Ange got a refill, and when Ruby was gone I said: "What if we logged into Nora's Facebook?"

Ange visibly blanched, her whole body stiffening once again. "Why would you do that, Mads?"

"To see if anyone was messaging her the way they were Elle? And we have no idea what was really going on with her and Louden at the end there; what if we log on and there's a bunch of angry messages from him? That could be something."

"Maddie. I get it, okay. You don't want Nate to be guilty of this. Because if he is, then that makes all your complicated feelings about him even more complicated. Even messier."

I had to fight my way through the next few minutes, each one a small war. She was right of course; I was terrified of that: that sooner or later I was going to have to confront my own guilt in

250

believing so blindly in Nate. Not just trusting him, but loving him, even if it was only from afar. But there was something else I was scared of even more.

"Or maybe I can't bear the guilt of letting him rot away in prison just like we've left Nora to rot somewhere for the past ten years."

Ange didn't say anything, but she didn't look away either. She nodded, just once, as if to say, *okay we're done with this now*, and by the time Ruby arrived back with fresh coffee I was ready to order waffles, Ange asking for the same thing when Ruby turned to her.

It took me a little while to get up the courage to log in to Nora's Facebook account. Ange clearly hadn't thought it the wisest of ideas, so I'd waited until I got home, and even then, I felt the only way I could do it was under the cover of darkness. It had never once occurred to me to do this before; I'd continued to sporadically send Nora messages after she went missing, but visiting her profile page was a small torture and I'd given up after a while. Her absence was so present I didn't need to be reminded of her presence to remember it. It was probably the same reason why I'd never found the blogs about her, or the Reddit thread, or the different true crime podcast episodes that had apparently been made about her disappearance, before now. In some ways, she was always with me, and so I didn't need to find her.

But Noelle had changed all that. Like her sister, Nora hadn't been big on internet security or thinking up intricate passwords no one was likely to guess. Her one password had always been "Altman1234" and by entering in those ten characters I was let into the last space she still existed. Every June 18th I was reminded of her birthday and watched as fewer and fewer people each year continued to write on her wall. I had, on a number of occasions, been exhorted to "reconnect" with Nora over the years, an act that no one had bothered to inform the good people of Facebook was near impossible.

As I had done when I first logged into Elle's account I quickly turned chat off, so that Nora's little green dot wouldn't suddenly appear on anyone's sidebar. I breathed slowly, in and out, daring myself to continue, and yet also willing myself to calm down. Despite the darkness and the lateness of the hour, or perhaps because of it, energy fizzed through me, a static feeling trapped just beneath my skin. My nerves shouldn't have surprised me, I suppose. I hadn't been alone in a room with Nora for ten years, after all.

I spent a few minutes just looking through her pictures, which I could have done from my own account, but it gave me time to get used to her, to feel her reverberate through me. Again, and again, as I scrolled through photos, I felt the loss of her rip through me as if it were something new, and not something I lived with every day. She looked so young. I couldn't get over how young she looked. There were photos of Ange and me that I hadn't looked at in years, our faces so much rounder than I ever remembered them being, my hair a completely different color, Ange's eyes brighter than I'd seen them in years.

We were different people then; we would have been whether Nora'd been still with us or not, but it had made me feel every single one of those ten years and just how long it had been really since I'd last seen her.

I bunched up all the courage I had and discarded whatever shred of integrity I had about reading my missing best friend's private messages, and headed to her inbox. I wasn't the only person to have continued messaging her after her disappearance. Hardly a surprise really, considering everything, but what really stood out was that very few of them were unread. Even the ones which had appeared after she went missing. I hovered over my own message stream, which had been one-sided since early 2008, and yet which showed that someone had read them all. Who the hell was reading Nora's messages? Feeling more than a little nauseated I clicked through to Ange's messages, only to find the same thing; a stream of messages sent after Nora went missing, all of which somehow had been read by someone.

It was starkly different to logging into Elle's account, which had been inundated with messages. In comparison, Nora had remarkably few messages in all, and if Louden had sent her any angry messages in the lead up to her disappearance, they weren't there.

In all likelihood, if there had been any they would have been on her phone, which had disappeared along with her, but that didn't stop me logging into her Yahoo account just to double-check there wasn't anything there. I was worried I wouldn't be able to get into the account—not because she would have used a different password, because she hadn't—but because I thought it might have been suspended after ten years of disuse.

Luckily, it was still there, the inbox full of junk, every other email an offer for Viagra or Hot Fun with a Sexy H00kup. I searched Louden's name first but there was nothing to see there, so I just trawled through the inbox, looking for anything that popped out at me, or snagged at my eyes, something that shouldn't be there, but not really expecting to find anything, not after all these years.

I certainly wasn't expecting to find anything from Bright of all people. But there it was—a stream of emails sent in the days leading up to Nora's disappearance. Barely breathing but hyper aware of the sound of my heart pounding against my chest, I clicked on his name:

From: Michael Brightman 01/01/2008 13:14
We need to talk about last night. Call me
From: Nora Altman 01/01/2008 14:11
We never need to talk about it Bright. We're never GOING to talk about it because it will NEVER happen again and I

wish it never had happened in the FIRST PLACE.
From: Michael Brightman 01/01/2008 04:27
I just need to know you're not going to tell Maddie. Because if you tell her than she'll tell Serena and if Serena finds out we slept together I'm dead, you're dead, we're all fucking dead.
From: Nora Altman 01/02/2008 10:07
As if I'd ever tell Mads, the thought of her knowing makes me want to die. Just leave me alone. I'm not going to tell Maddie.
From: Michael Brightman 01/02/2008 10:14
Okay fine, that's all I wanted to know, that you wouldn't tell Maddie. But just so you know Leo saw us and I don't think he'd tell Maddie but I just thought you'd want to know that. I've asked him not to tell Louden though, so don't worry about that.
From: Nora Altman 01/02/2008 10:33
I don't fucking care if he tells Louden. I WANT him to tell Louden.
From: Michael Brightman 01/02/2008 10:46
Well I don't want him to! Jesus he's one of my best friends. Just as long as no one tells Nate either cos he'll tell Mads and then it'll definitely get back to Serena.
From: Nora Altman 01/02/2008 10:50
Why on earth would I tell my brother any of this?
From: Michael Brightman 01/02/2008 10:53
I don't know, just in case. All I care about is this not getting back to Serena. So seriously just don't tell Maddie?
From: Nora Altman 01/02/2008 23:58
What did I just say about not telling Mads? I'm definitely not telling her any of this. But I am planning on telling Louden, not that it's any of your business, so if you're worried about him telling Serena, then you should probably tell her yourself.
From: Michael Brightman 01/03/2008 00:16
Please don't tell Louden I'm actually really worried he might

go crazy and tell Serena or something.
From: Michael Brightman 01/03/2008 00:31
Nora?
Seriously please don't tell Louden
From: Michael Brightman 01/05/2008 11:31
Nora come on
Seriously
Don't tell Louden
From: Michael Brightman 01/06/2008 13:12
Please don't tell Louden, Nora. I'm serious.
From: Michael Brightman 01/07/2008 18:42
Nora? Please

I couldn't breathe. Bright and Nora? My stomach, my heart, my whole goddamn body clenched with fear. Bright? He'd sent his last message a little over forty-five minutes before Nora had left her final voicemail on my cell phone, the message that was considered to be her last. I thought about Bright coming over to the house that morning to tell us her car had been found, and she was nowhere near it. He'd written this email barely twelve hours earlier.

My hand trembled slightly as I reached for my phone and called Serena. I could feel every pulse of my heartbeat, my scalp itched so profusely I swear I could actually feel my hair growing, and the scratchy feeling behind my eyes, the one that made me feel like I was about to cry every goddamn moment I was alive, was well and truly back. I swallowed hard, again and again, as if doing so would push the feeling away, as if I could breathe my way through it, as if I could close my eyes and it would stop, when all the evidence I'd ever accrued pointed to the contrary. There was nowhere for the feeling to go.

I counted the rings until Serena's voicemail kicked in, but didn't leave a message. Then I rang again and again until, finally, on my fifth attempt, she answered.

"Hey," she said, sounding muffled, tired, and even a little alarmed. "What's going on, Mads?"

"Sorry for calling so late. I just needed to ask you a question."

"What's going on?" Serena demanded again, sounding much more awake. Awake and unappeased. "It's almost three o'clock in the morning, what's the fucking emergency?"

"I logged into Nora's Yahoo account."

"Her email? Why the hell would you do that?"

"Well, I started by going on to her Facebook account, but there was nothing there, so I thought I'd try her email."

I could hear Serena's low even breaths but she didn't say anything immediately. "What do you mean there was nothing there? What were you looking for?"

"I thought there might be some messages from Louden or someone that might tell me what was going on with her before she went missing."

"But why would you suddenly be interested in that?" Coming from down the line, her voice sounded stretched and strained with exhaustion, pitching higher than normal. She wasn't just tired from being woke up at 3 a.m., she was tired of all of it, of everything. Of all the calls I'd placed in the middle of the night before, of all the times she'd had to talk me down from something, to take me home, to make sure I was okay. It didn't stop me though.

I ignored her question, but I still wasn't sure how to frame the topic of Bright and Nora, and I had to force myself to say the next few words. "There were some emails from Bright. From right before she went missing. They slept together, on New Year's Eve by the looks of things." Serena was quiet for a long time. Or at least for what felt like a long time. "Did you know?" I asked finally, prompting her.

"Yeah, I knew," she said at last.

"You did? Since when? Why didn't you tell me?"

"One thing at a time, Mads."

"Jesus, Serena, is it possible for you to ever not sound completely condescending?"

"I'm not trying to. Sorry. Whatever. This is hard for me too, you know."

"But you knew?" my voice came out so much more quietly than I'd meant it to. The betrayal stung not because I didn't trust Serena, but because she didn't trust me. Didn't trust me with information which she presumably had always assumed I was too fragile or fucked up to cope with.

"Yeah. Yeah, I knew. He told me right after. He was terrified it was going to come out and he'd be accused of having something to do with her disappearance."

"Did the police know?"

"He *is* the police, Mads," she said, unintentionally sending a shock of pure, cold fear through me.

"I mean did he tell anyone else?"

"I don't know. I'm sorry I didn't tell you, okay? It was just never the right time, and honestly, I didn't see how it was going to help you in any way."

"Your boyfriend cheated on you with my best friend. Weren't you … weren't you mad?"

"Of course I was mad, I was fucking furious! But come on, there was so much more to be worried and scared and angry about back then. To be honest, I think I just buried it and then in the end it didn't matter. We were always going to break up anyway."

"But what about Nora?"

"What about her?"

"Serena, Bright messaged her less than an hour before she went missing."

I could hear Serena suck in a breath before saying: "That doesn't mean anything, Mads. He didn't see her that day. That's why he was emailing her probably, he was trying to track her down."

"And what if he did track her down?"

"Mads, come on. Listen to what you're saying. Bright didn't kill or do anything to hurt Nora. It's absurd."

"As absurd as Nate killing Elle?"

"Maddie," she said very slowly, "I understand what you're doing here. You don't want it to have been Nate. You don't want to believe that he's capable of any of this—that he killed Elle, and in all likelihood killed Nora. But you're reaching, you're twisting everything to suit your own theory."

I was tired of people telling me that. Of asking why I was asking so many questions, and then telling me it was just the guilt talking, or my inability to believe Nate could have done it. So what if it was? What did my motives matter—didn't I at least deserve answers? Didn't Nora? Didn't Elle?

"You really think he did it?" I said at last, meaning Nate.

"What else am I supposed to think?" she asked.

She didn't sound convinced though. She sounded tired, exhausted, just as Ange had done at the diner. It had been so long. We were tired of not knowing. Was that all it boiled down to in the end? We were done. We wanted it to be over. And here, here was an answer, finally. Someone to blame. A place to put all our loss and grief, fear and hatred. It didn't feel the way I always thought it would though, and I couldn't work out if that was just me, or if that was inevitable; that closure when it came, if it ever came, might mean the closing of a gate, but it also meant the opening of yet another door.

"Serena, we've known him our entire lives. This is Nate we're talking about. Nate Altman. How can you think he'd do this to Elle? To Nora? *Why* would he do it?"

Serena didn't answer immediately, and I imagined her gnawing on the nail of her right thumb, as she always did when she was thinking.

"Maddie," she said eventually, very slowly, "everything you've just said, you could apply to Bright. And they don't have a weapon covered in *his* fingerprints."

She was right of course. Or, at the very least, I couldn't find a flaw in her logic. And yet. It wasn't just that I wasn't ready to let go of Nate; I needed the "why" answered before accepting that he had done it. Maybe it was naive of me, childish even, the desire for a reason over reality. Death was often senseless, especially when it was accompanied by violence, and I had wondered if I would have been so set on the idea of a motive if the person they'd slapped the handcuffs on hadn't happened to be Nate.

But I'd grown up with the Altmans, all of them, not just Nate, and it wasn't just him I loved but Elle and Nora too and I couldn't let it all end without knowing why it had even started.

I thought of Nate alone in jail and for whatever reason I couldn't just leave him there. I understood why everyone was so willing to accept his guilt; it let us off the hook somehow, and allowed us to finally continue with our lives. But I needed more than that, more than fingerprints on a knife and someone behind bars. I needed to know not just who had taken Nora and Elle from us but *why* they had, and I was pretty sure I wasn't going to be getting my answers from Nate.

CHAPTER TWENTY-FOUR

It felt as though I'd only just fallen asleep when my phone rang. Reaching for it, I saw it was from an unknown number and I just stared down at it for a minute as it buzzed in my hand, before finally answering.

"Madeline Fielder?" a vaguely recognizable voice asked. "This is Agent Lee, I'd like you to come down to the station to answer some questions, please."

"Agent Lee? What happened to 'call me Steven'?"

"Steven's around here somewhere. I'm sure he'll be back soon. Are you available for a quick chat?"

"It's awfully early."

"We can arrange a time that's more suitable for you, but sooner rather than later would be better. Please."

Light was beginning to stalk the edges of the curtains, trying to crack through, break the day wide open. I could have stayed in bed forever; I wanted to, wanted to wait as the world hurled itself forward and I tried to catch up, but that wasn't what was in store for me. So, I told Agent Lee I'd be down there as soon as I could and got up to have a shower and get dressed.

* * *

The station was quiet, the waiting room only just beginning to warm up, the cold morning managing to creep its way in as I sat there and waited for one of the agents to come and get me. I was still shivering in my coat when Agent Lee finally appeared.

"Sorry to keep you waiting, Maddie," he said.

I raised an eyebrow at him silently and just followed him out of the waiting room, down the hallway and into one of the few interrogation rooms the police station actually had, where Agent Gutierrez was already waiting. The room was airless, dusty, and cold. Lee offered me a coffee, which I accepted, and he disappeared again, leaving Gutierrez and I to stare at each other from opposite sides of a table.

"How are you doing, Maddie?" she asked, her voice smooth, low.

"I've been better."

Gutierrez flattened her mouth and slowly nodded her head, as if she knew exactly what I meant. "You're probably wondering why you're here."

"A little bit."

"We just have a few more questions about the night Noelle Altman was killed. Nothing to worry about."

Lee returned, three mugs of coffee balanced delicately in his hands. He passed me one with a smile before delivering another to his partner. He stayed standing, his back against the furthest wall from me, watching me while he drank his coffee, and Gutierrez leaned towards me, her arms resting on the tabletop.

"So, Maddie," Gutierrez continued once she'd taken a sip of her coffee, "we just wanted to ask you about the night of January 7 again. Be 100 per cent sure of your movements that night."

I looked from one of them to the other and back again. The question was posed perfectly nicely, and Lee smiled warmly at me yet again from the back of the room, but instead of reassuring me, it set me completely on edge. I'd already answered this question, I thought, so why were they asking it again? Was I a suspect

261

now? Or was it possible that they didn't actually have enough on Nate to make it stick?

"Maddie," Gutierrez said when I didn't answer, "where were you between the hours of seven and eleven that night?" She was beginning to sound a little impatient.

"I was at home. I've already told you that."

"Did you see anyone else while you were at home? Or on your way back from the bar?"

"You mean apart from my parents?"

"Apart from your parents."

"No. I walked home, got in, had dinner with my parents and then went to bed. I wasn't feeling great."

"You didn't happen to see anyone on your walk home from Cool's that night?"

I reached for the mug of coffee that I hadn't yet drunk from and wrapped my fingers around it. "I don't think so. Not that I can remember. I mean, there might have been some people on the street, but it was cold and dark and a Sunday night, so there probably weren't that many people around to be honest."

"Could any of those people you may or may not have seen have been Nathan Altman?"

"Nate? No. I didn't see him again that night after leaving the lake house."

"So, he didn't stop by the bar to walk you home?"

I stared at her, something scratching at the back of my memory, something telling me to be careful, to watch where I was going. An image of Nate walking me home flashed through my mind, but it hadn't been on Sunday. Finally, I shook my head and said: "No."

"Are you sure about that, Maddie? You'd had a bit to drink, hadn't you?"

"I'd had some wine. I wasn't drunk. Not really."

"What do you mean by 'not really'?"

"I mean, I wasn't drunk enough to forget running into Nate

that night," I said through my teeth. I watched as the agents shared a look, and forced myself to drink some of the coffee.

"Your recollection of that night differs somewhat from Mr Altman's," Gutierrez said at last.

"What?"

"He claims he picked you up from the bar, walked you home and then stayed to chat."

My mind clenched, frantically. Memories falling in on one another, building up and breaking down. Nate had picked me up from Cool's and walked me home, but that had been on Tuesday, the day after Elle had been found, not the night she was killed. I swallowed hard, trying to rearrange myself and said: "No, not that night."

"Not that night? Can you explain?"

"Well, he did come to the bar and we did walk home together, but it was a couple nights later. Not on Sunday."

"So, you think he might have confused the two evenings?"

"I-I don't know. Maybe."

"Could you have confused them?"

"No," I said too quickly, the agents once again sharing a look. I didn't have a good enough grip on what was going on. I felt ambushed. Why had Nate told them he saw me on Sunday evening? One possible explanation pushed its way through my mind, insistent, persistent, unwanted; he was claiming me as an alibi.

"But you think Nate might have?" Gutierrez asked, her voice even, neutral.

I stared down at the tabletop. It was made of metal, covered in scratches, had probably been there for years. It had probably been there ten years earlier, in fact, when I had sat in that very room and was questioned all about Nora's movements the night she went missing. "I guess it's possible."

"But you had been drinking that night. You'd had a fair amount to drink by the sounds of it, is there a chance you're the one who's misremembering?"

My head shot back up to stare between the two of them, still struggling, desperately to make sense of anything. I knew I had the whole picture right in front of me, but I was only being allowed to see it one section at a time. Every time I learned something new the focus would shift and I'd be left in the dark again.

"Maddie," Gutierrez said gently, "is there a chance you can't be sure of who you saw on the night in question?"

I wanted to say yes, that there was a chance, that I did see him, that I'd simply forgotten, been too drunk to remember as they seemed to be accusing me of, or had got my days mixed up, because I knew that was his way out, maybe even my way out. But I could barely form a thought, let alone a sentence, and as they stared down at me, expecting me to answer, it took everything I had to take a sip from that mug of coffee and swallow it down. I couldn't save him though, not like this, not with a hand reaching out in the dark that turned out to be a fist. I knew if I did this, there would be no going back, I would have crossed a line that I hadn't even realized needed to be drawn. So, I shook my head and finally said: "No, I'm not misremembering. I didn't see him that night."

I could practically hear the doors slamming shut on Nate's innocence. But instead of feeling angry at him for putting me in this position, I was scared for him. Because how fearful must he have been to lie like that.

There was silence for a while as the agents contemplated me. I think I'd given them the information they expected all along; Nate had no alibi for the night Elle was killed, and this was just another box to be checked in the case against him.

"Well, thank you for coming in, Maddie," Gutierrez said, "we really appreciate it."

"Yeah, of course. There's something else though, while I'm here," I said, unable to stop myself.

"Yes?" Gutierrez said.

"I-I logged into Nora's email account last night, and there were messages from Bright that indicate he slept with her a couple of nights before she went missing."

Agent Lee pushed himself off from the wall he'd been leaning against and walked towards the table. "Officer Brightman, you mean?"

"Yeah."

"Maddie, as we told you before, we're not actually investigating Nora's case. If you have anymore information about Noelle's case, then of course we'd like to hear it, but this isn't within our purview at the moment."

There was something about Gutierrez's tone that made me feel like a nuisance, like a child telling her mother her sister was being annoying only to make an annoyance of herself in the process. I wanted to mention the messages Noelle had received from "John Smith" too, but that seemed likely to go down just as well as Nora's messages had done; besides, I thought, surely Leo would have told them about the messages by now, so I just nodded and left the room, leaving my barely touched cup of coffee behind.

Agent Lee caught up with me just as I was passing through the waiting room. "Hey," he said, a little breathless, "do you think I could buy you a drink later?"

I looked at him, my vision swimming a little so that I saw two sets of dark eyes and two smiles that were trying incredibly hard to look sheepish, and failing.

"Why?" I asked, and his eyes widened a little as he let out a bark of laughter.

"I'd like to talk to you about those emails," he said more seriously, once he realized I was actually waiting for an answer.

"So, why didn't you in there?" I nodded my head in the direction we'd both come from.

"This wouldn't be official. I'm just interested."

I stuffed my hands into my coat pockets and clenched my

fists. "Fine," I said. "See you at seven at Cool's?" He nodded and we left it at that, Lee returning to his partner in that airless inter-rogation room.

Across the room I could see Bright, large shoulders hunched over his too-small desk, working on something or other. He looked up, catching my eye, and I must have stayed staring at him a little too long because he stood up and walked over to me, something like concern sketched over his face.

"Maddie, what are you doing here? Everything okay?"

It took a second before I could speak, and even then I sput-tered my way through the sentence. "I was just talking to the agents about something."

He turned to look back at the hallway Lee had disappeared down, and I watched him carefully, trying make sense of him, trying to make sense of him and Nora, trying to make sense of someone living a lie for so long that it almost became the truth.

"You slept with Nora," I said suddenly, unable to hold it in, and his entire body stilled, still looking off down the hallway, before he slowly turned to look at me.

"What are you talking about?"

"I'm talking about how a week before she went missing, you and Nora slept together."

Bright didn't move, as unmovable and unreadable as ever. "Serena finally told you?"

It took me a while to answer; I hadn't expected him to admit it so readily. "No. I found your emails to Nora from ten years ago,"

"What? You went through her emails? From *ten years ago*?" It was the most animated I'd ever seen him.

"Yeah, and you were emailing her right up until she disap-peared."

"Maddie, you need to stop right there. You have no idea what you're talking about."

"Forty-five minutes before her last call to me, that's when you were still emailing her, still trying to track her down. Did you?"

266

"No. I didn't."

"Of course you'd say that."

"Because it's the truth, Mads." Bright raised his eyes to the ceiling, searching for wisdom perhaps. "You're acting a little crazy, you know that, right? What are you doing going through Nora's emails? Logging into Noelle's Facebook? None of this is normal, Maddie. You need to take a step back. Go home, go back to Madison, look after yourself."

"Does anyone else know?" I asked, "apart from me and Serena?" and he shook his head at me, in disbelief and despair. In disgust maybe.

"Yes, actually they do. I went straight to the Chief with it when Nora disappeared. I couldn't have that coming up when they searched her emails and social media, which I knew they were going to do. I didn't hurt her, okay, Mads? I made a mistake, a fucking huge one, but I didn't kill her."

"And that's it?" I asked, my voice beginning to strain, fray at the edges. "You came forward like a good little boy and they just believed you? No further investigations?"

"Well, I did also have an alibi, remember?" He was starting to get frustrated; I'd never actually seen Bright lose his temper—wasn't sure that he had one—but I could see it, the beginnings of it at least.

"Oh, that's right. You and Louden were just chilling out together, weren't you? You really expect me to believe that now? That you were just casually hanging out with the person whose girlfriend you'd just slept with? Please, Bright. Give me some credit."

"If you don't believe me, fine. But I'd think twice before running your mouth about it all over town, because I'm pretty sure, when it comes down to it, people will be more likely to believe me than you." His voice was scathing, his face, normally so placid and immobile and impossible to read, was suddenly twisted and tortured, disfigured by anger and something else even uglier, even darker.

I took a step back, suddenly aware of how close he was standing, how easy it would be for him to reach out and grab me, hurt me. Would he dare do that in the middle of a police station, or would his uniform and the presence of his colleagues embolden him even further? Because he was right, wasn't he? Who would believe me over him?

Maybe it was that that made me realize there was something there. That I hadn't stumbled upon an open grave only to find it empty; there was something more here, I knew, something under all those years of lies, something to be dug out and dug up and finally held up to the light. I think maybe I'd known it all along; that I was the one who had to do it, who had to finally get her hands dirty, to keep digging until my arms ached and my hands shook and I could finally lay Nora to rest.

We were already a beer in when Agent Lee finally deigned to talk to me about the emails I'd found from Bright. He'd bought us a pitcher of beer again and was pouring me a glass as he said: "So I took a look at the case file from Nora's disappearance after you left the station. Officer Brightman told the investigating officers about the emails and their contents the day she disappeared."

"He did?" I asked, a little deflated but still unable to shake the feeling that someone, somewhere, had to be lying.

"Yeah," he said, wiping a little froth from the top of his mouth as he did so.

I looked at him, trying to get a handle on him and failing. "Why are you doing this?" I asked.

"What do you mean?"

"I mean, your partner made it pretty clear that you guys have no interest in investigating Elle's murder in conjunction with Nora's disappearance. So why did you look at the file; why are you even here, talking to me about it all?"

"Look, I can't get into it with you, but it's not as if we came here with the intention of not reopening Nora's case. We all want to find out what happened to Nora, okay? I mean, for Christ's sake, if I can be involved in solving one of the most famous cases in the state, I'm going to be," he ended with a guffaw.

"Because it will help your career?"

Lee kind of tipped his head at me and pursed his lips a little. "Well, yeah, but that doesn't mean I don't also want to find out what happened to your friend. It's a win-win for me."

"A *win-win*," I repeated, unable to meet his eye.

"I realize that must sound a little callous."

"No, it's fine. You're just doing your job, right?"

"Right," he said after a while, and then: "so, you had no idea about any of it? That they'd slept together?"

I shook my head. "No idea."

"And you're thinking either Bright killed your friend to stop her from telling her boyfriend, or the boyfriend killed her once she told him, is that it?"

"Well, it is a little convenient that the two people who had the most obvious motive to kill Nora were also each other's alibis, isn't it?" I said, swallowing down the taste of bile that had suddenly coated my mouth.

Lee raised both his eyebrows. "It does send up a few red flags, yes."

"So, what can we do about it?" I said, before amending it to: "What can *you* do about it?" when his eyebrows began to rise even higher.

"Well, nothing officially. The case hasn't been reopened yet."

I tightened my grip on my glass. "So, then what was the point of this? If you can't do anything about it? Or won't?"

"Calm down, Maddie. I understand you must be frustrated—"

"*Frustrated*? You think I'm frustrated? It's been ten years, *Steven*, I'm more than fucking frustrated."

He held up his hands. "I understand, I'm sorry. I spoke out of turn. But what I was about to say was that we've found some

269

suspicious messages on Noelle's Facebook profile that indicated she may have been watched in the months leading up to her murder."

"John Smith," I said without thinking.

Lee almost choked on the beer he was drinking. "John Smith? How do you?—you logged into Noelle's Facebook as well as Nora's email?"

I looked at him. "Yeah. I was the one who told Leo about him, about the messages. Isn't that how you know?"

"You mean Officer Moody?"

"Yeah."

"That's not how we got hold of the messages."

"So, he didn't tell you about them?"

"Not as far as I'm aware. We started monitoring Noelle's social media accounts as soon as we got here. But that's really beside the point. You can't just log into other people's private Facebook and email accounts, Maddie."

"So, what are you going to do? Arrest me?"

"Jesus Christ." He looked down into the bottom of his almost-empty glass, letting out a bark of frustrated laughter. "I think I need something stronger. And you need to stop trying to do our jobs for us. Or you really will get arrested."

He got up as if to leave, and I reached across the sticky beer-splashed table to grab his arm, pulling him back into his seat. "Can you just tell me about John Smith, please? About the messages?"

Lee sighed, his face morphing into a picture of unease. "I can't discuss any of this with you, Maddie, not really. It's an ongoing investigation. But if there's a connection between those messages and these emails, then I promise we'll find it. Despite what you may think, we've been trying to find a reason to reopen Nora's case since we got here. Now, I'm going to go get myself a whisky. Can I get you anything?"

I stared at him a little too long and his gaze shifted from mine, looking around the bar which had grown busier while we sat there. I followed his gaze, spotting Gloria Lewis a few tables over from us with a basket of onion rings and waffle fries that she was ignoring in favor of staring at Agent Lee and me. She smiled thinly as our eyes met, and I grabbed my coat, pulling it on with stiff arms, fingers fumbling.

"No, thanks," I said at last, "I think I just need to get home."

I could feel Lee watching me as I rushed out of the bar, but it was a woman's voice that stopped me just as I was pulling the door open.

"Cozying up to the guy who arrested your boyfriend, huh? I'm sure Nate will be glad to hear you're getting so close with Agent Lee," Gloria Lewis said.

I turned around to look down at her, desperate to leave, to just get the hell out of there, but unable to let it go. "You know, it's incredibly sad to see a woman of your professional distinction resting on ten-year-old laurels, Gloria. You'd think you'd have moved on from all this by now, but I guess we just don't always get the career breaks we deserve, do we?"

"I won awards for my coverage of Nora's disappearance," Gloria replied with eyes narrowed.

"Oh, I know, and we're all so proud of you. But how many have you won since?" My arms were shaking as I pulled the door open again and walked out, this time without anyone following me.

I paced my room, energy burning through my body in a way it hadn't done in years. Static buzzed through me, insistent but impotent, with nowhere to go. I had to do something; I couldn't just sit here doing nothing when Nate was in jail and somewhere out there was the truth.

Eventually I sat down, opening up my laptop and sending Louden a Facebook message. I didn't have his phone number, otherwise I would have called him, but I knew I had to speak to him. Had he known about Bright and Nora? And if so, what had he done about it? Or alternatively, what had Bright done to stop Nora from telling Louden?

But I was too impatient to wait for his response—or maybe I just knew he wouldn't respond. Louden and I weren't exactly on speaking terms, after all—so after an hour or so of jittery waiting, of scrolling through Louden's wall, looking for something, anything, I picked up my phone and called Hale.

"Maddie?" she said, surprise lacing her voice.

"Hey, Hale. Sorry for calling so late."

"That's … okay. What's going on?"

"I'm trying to get hold of your brother. Could you give me his number?"

Silence filled the room before a long, heavy sigh came down the line. "Why?" she asked.

"I just really need to speak to him, okay? It's about Nora."

"When is not about Nora?" Hale asked, and this time her voice was weary, tired.

"What's that supposed to mean?"

"Exactly what I just said," she said, her voice still heavy with a sigh.

"Look," I said, trying a new tactic, "I know we're not exactly friends anymore—"

"Ha!" Hale barked, surprising me. "Bit hard to stay friends when you accuse my brother of murder, isn't it?"

I swallowed, mind racing, trying to figure out a way to get what I wanted out of this conversation that was heading nowhere fast. "I'm sorry, Hale. Okay? I really am. I'm just trying to figure out if Louden knew about Bright and Nora sleeping together right before she went missing."

I had raced through my lines, getting the words out as quickly as possible before Hale hung up on me, but my sprint was met by a brick wall of silence before Hale said: "Bright slept with Nora?"

"Yeah. That New Year's Eve. You remember you had that party?" I said, suddenly on slightly steadier ground, appealing to a shared memory.

"I remember," she said.

***

From far across the room I can see Nora and Louden talking to each other, or rather talking at one another. Nora is a blur of wild gesticulation, Louden more an immovable mountain. Neither of them really seem to be paying attention to what the other is saying. They're just saying it for the sake of it. I've never seen a couple who scream "we're over" more than the two of them, and yet if Nora's actions over the past two weeks are anything to go by, they'll probably end up sleeping together tonight.

Ange pushes her way through the crowd, too small to see until she's almost upon me and passes me a cup of frothy beer. "They still going at it?" she asks, following my gaze to the Nora and Louden show in the corner of the room.

"They sure are."

Ange groans. "Why don't they just break up already? This is such a fucking charade."

"Yeah, Nora normally likes to keep all her amateur dramatics firmly on the stage."

"Louden's finally unraveled her."

"Don't say that, it's too depressing." I hate the idea of anyone being able to unravel Nora, let alone Louden Winters. I immediately notice Bright as he walks through the door. I watch as he gets himself a drink and takes a look around the room, quietly assessing the damage. No one else seems to have noticed that there's a cop standing in a room full of underage drinkers, which is weird because Bright is six foot three and very noticeable. He catches my eye and raises both his eyebrows in recognition before heading over.

"Hey. What's that in your cup, Mads?"

"Don't do this, Bright."

"Do what?" He's all innocence.

"Don't come to a high school party and bust our chops for drinking. It's your own fault for coming."

"This isn't a high school party, Fielder. Louden invited me, and the last I heard, he was in college."

"Well, Hale invited us," I say, motioning at myself and Ange. Bright leans forward to sniff the contents of both our cups, and shakes his head wearily, faux-disappointment prematurely ageing his young face. "Anyway," I continued, "I thought you were supposed to be with Serena in Madison tonight?"

"Gotta work tomorrow," he says, "either of you seen Nate or Leo yet? I'm meant to be meeting them here."

But Nate's just arrived and has clearly spotted Bright with ease as he pushes through the crowded room towards us and claps Bright on the back in salutation. They exchange gruff greetings and Nate says hello to both me and Ange before turning his attention to the corner of the room. The music's loud, too loud to hear what Nora and Louden are saying, but they're drawing a lot of attention regardless. Everyone within earshot of them is surreptitiously eavesdropping, some dropping the pretense at subtlety altogether and staring, mouths slightly open at the feuding couple.

"How long's that been going on?" Nate asks the three of us.

"Since we got here, pretty much," Ange answers. "So about two hours?"

"You're kidding?"

"Only slightly. I suggested they maybe take it to another room, but I don't even think they heard me."

"Remember when the reason they couldn't hear you asking them to get a room was because they were practically having sex on the couch?" I ask, referring to more than one occasion.

"Gross, Fielder. That's my sister you're talking about."

"Your sister's had sex, Nate. Get over it."

Nate shakes his head and looks around the room, anywhere but at the corner. "I need a drink for this," he pronounces, and wanders off towards the kitchen.

Hale rushes towards us, appearing out of the crowd as if from nowhere, and says, eyes wide, almost breathless: "Nora caught Louden and Natalie Carmichael in the bathroom."

"Natalie Carmichael?" Ange says, incredulity written all over her face. "I didn't even know she was here."

"Yeah, she's still in there. She won't come out of the bathroom," Hale says, looking back towards the hallway. "This is so fucked up. People are using my parents' bathroom! They're going to kill me."

"I'm not sure that's the most pressing problem here, Hale," I say, as the fight in the corner comes to a crescendo and we all turn to watch as Louden stalks off down the hall to where the downstairs bathroom is, back towards Natalie Carmichael, and Nora stumbles off on her own in the direction of the kitchen. All three of us share a look and silently agree to follow her.

She's standing over the kitchen countertop, eyes firmly on her cup, which she's filling with rum, only stopping about three inches from the rim to top up with Coke.

"You okay?" I ask under my breath as Ange, Hale, and I sidle up next to her.

She blinks, very, very slowly while looking down into her cup, before raising it to her lips and turning towards us. "I'm fine," she says shortly, after taking a long slug of rum and Coke.

"What happened?"

Her chin lifts and her mouth is drawn down into a frown, her eyes hard. "He was fooling around with Natalie Carmichael in the bathroom when we got here." She takes another sip of her drink and continues, "Apparently he didn't know I was coming though, so really it's my fault." Her voice is thick with acid.

"For fuck's sake, Nora, just break up with him," Ange says. "This has got to be it, right? His last chance."

Nora just shrugs and takes three massive gulps of her drink before scanning the kitchen. Nate's nowhere to be seen but that's not much of a surprise. He tends to avoid his sister as much as possible when we're all at the same party. If I was her I'd already be out of here, but Nora's never really been one to run away.

"What's wrong with you?" I ask. "Why aren't you more angry?"

"Yeah," Hale says, "I know he's my brother and everything, but if this was one of us, you'd be the first one shouting 'DUMP HIM!' across the room at us."

But Nora isn't really paying us any attention, her gaze has landed on Bright, and Leo, who's just arrived, and waves happily at us hiding in the kitchen, blissfully unaware of the recent drama.

"I am angry," Nora says at last. "I'm fucking livid. But I also really wanna get drunk, so let's just do that, shall we?"

"I remember losing track of her around two o'clock, but I think I just thought she went home with you and Ange?" Hale said.

"Yeah, and we thought she'd gone off somewhere to patch things up with Louden. Guess we were all wrong."

"Oh my God," Hale said in one breath, interrupting me. "That night. The night she disappeared …"

"Yeah?" I said, prompting her, because she seemed to be thinking twice about telling me.

"I can't believe I'm going to tell you this …" she said with a groan.

"Tell me what?"

"Louden and Bright. They lied about their alibis. They were covering for each other because neither of them had an alibi that night and they knew it would look bad."

If someone had told me then that all the air had left the room—literally—I would have believed it. I couldn't breathe, even the thought of it, of taking another breath, felt insurmountable. But then survival and rationality kicked in and I hauled a great gulp of air into my lungs.

"They lied?" I managed to croak.

"Yes," Hale said simply, and in my view, much too calmly.

"Are you … are you sure? How do you know?" *And how could you not have told anyone*, I mentally added.

"He told me. He may not remember telling me, but he told me."

"What's that supposed to mean?"

Hale sighed again. "Look, Louden hasn't dealt with any of this well. I know you think you have the record of dealing with Nora's disappearance the worst, but believe me I'm pretty sure Louden could have you beat."

"What do you mean?"

"I mean, he went from a fairly heavy social drinker to a very heavy drinking-on-your-own drinker, to drugs, to an overdose, to rehab."

"Hale, I had no idea. About any of that," I said, surprised at least that I could still be surprised.

"Yeah, I know. That's kind of the whole point. No way would my parents ever want to make any of this public knowledge. But anyway. There've been a few times when I've had to clean up some of his messes, and one time he told me about the alibi. He was … well, it was awful, let's just leave it at that. But I'm pretty sure he doesn't remember any of it."

"And you've never asked him about it?"

"No. Anytime anyone mentions Nora or that night he just shuts down. But that's not the point. The point is that, yeah, Louden lied about his alibi, but so did Bright, and now you're telling me Bright also slept with Nora just days before she went missing?"

It seemed pointless to point out that both these revelations—Bright and Nora sleeping together, neither Bright nor Louden having a valid alibi—looked bad for Louden too, but I still couldn't help asking: "Hale, what time did Louden leave Forest View on Sunday night?"

She was quiet for a while, and I swear that even after all these years, I could visualize her face perfectly, bronze-brown eyes lit up with anger when she said through gritted teeth: "You mean the night Elle was killed?"

"Yes."

"We left a little after nine. We drove back to Chicago together."

"That's a long drive that late at night. Especially at this time of year."

"Yeah, well. We both had work the next morning and he really hates being in town; he just wanted to get out of there."

"Nine o'clock?" I said, double-checking; but I was barely listening when Hale said: "Yes."

Elle had last been seen around eight o'clock that night.

CHAPTER TWENTY-FIVE

I don't know what it was exactly that sent me back to Nora's Facebook account. I probably would have logged into Louden's or Bright's if I'd had the wherewithal, but I didn't even know where to begin, so I let myself be foolish and selfish, let myself make just one more bad decision and signed in as Nora again.

The ping of the messenger system going off surprised me, and for a second I forgot whose account I was logged into when I saw it was Ange messaging me.

Hey

I replied.

Mads? Is that you?
Yeah of course
You scared the shit out of me
Why?
You're signed in as Nora you idiot. I almost shit myself
Sorry, I forgot to turn chat off

I wrote, realizing as I did so that this might have happened before. What if I wasn't the first person to log into Nora's account? Those read messages that had all been sent after her disappearance had been bothering me, but if someone else had logged in and read them then I could only really think of one person who that would be.

There were a thousand reasons Elle might have wanted to access Nora's account. Maybe it was just to look, to sense her, to see. To wallow a little, to play in a garden where Nora still lived and breathed, even if just virtually.

Who knows what spurred her to do so, but I'd had a feeling it was something to do with those messages she'd been getting. Maybe it was just the fact that she'd turned seventeen the last year. The last time she'd ever be the same age as her older sister. She was about to outrun her, outpace her. Maybe she just wasn't ready to leave her behind. Or maybe getting those messages had made her think all over again of what she'd lost, what we'd all lost, and who had taken it from us. But what could she have found here, I wondered, that led her to a snowdrift on the side of the road?

So, I checked Nora's inbox again, this time remembering that Elle's own anonymous messenger had appeared in the "message request" section rather than in her main inbox. I drew in a strong, sharp breath when I saw the last few messages were from someone calling themselves "John Smith"; the same "John Smith" who'd been contacting Elle. I leaned over my laptop, blood pumping erratically in my ears and opened the message stream.

From: John Smith 12/31/2017 08:14
Who are you?
From: John Smith 01/01/2018 00:36
You're not Nora Altman
From: Nora Altman 01/01/2018 22:44
How do you know that?

I could be
From: John Smith 01/01/2018 22:55
Because she's missing
From: Nora Altman 01/06/2018 23:11
Sometimes missing people get found
From: John Smith 01/06/2018 23:17
Not you
From: Nora Altman 01/06/2018 23:21
What makes you say that?
From: John Smith 01/06/2018 23:24
I just know
From: Nora Altman 01/06/2018 23:31
How?
From: John Smith 01/06/2018 23:34
I just do
From: Nora Altman 01/06/2018 23:45
There's plenty of theories I'm still alive
Living in Canada or whatever
From: John Smith 01/06/2018 23:52
So that's where you are? Canada?
From: Nora Altman 01/07/2018 00:57
I'm here: http://tinyurl.com/hfa6noh3

Ice cold fear gripped at my insides until it broke and shattered, reverberating through me like a bell; *I'm here, I'm here, I'm here.* I stared for so long at those messages, barely able to breathe as I did so, that the screen went black. Waking my laptop up again, I clicked on the link in the last message, but it just led me to a 404 Not Found page and I returned to staring blankly at the messages in Nora's inbox, trying to figure out what it was exactly I was reading.

The thought of Elle sending and receiving those messages haunted me; seventeen years old was too young to confront a ghost, too young to be turned into one. But there were fewer shadows haunting my mind now, less doubt stalking my thoughts. Here was their killer, whoever this person was, they'd reached through that screen and taken both Nora and Elle and now all I needed to do was figure out exactly who they were. I closed my eyes and saw both Louden and Bright at the memorial on Sunday, barely even two weeks ago. Could one of them really have done all this, I wondered: Killed Nora ten years ago and stood by our sides ever since, in grief and in mourning for an entire decade, only to then steal Elle from us too? Even as I edged ever closer to an answer, I still couldn't quite believe it. But then I saw Nate standing by the lake on Sunday afternoon, face washed with such grief, and then, just a week later, being hauled up the police station steps, head bowed against accusations, and something inside me finally snapped into place.

Whoever "John Smith" was, it wasn't Nate. Of that I was certain.

I rang Keegan because he was the only person I could think of who might be able to help me.

We met at CJ's the next morning and I showed him the messages from "John Smith," pointing out the shortened URL in the last message Elle had sent.

"Did you click the link?" Keegan asked, pointing at the screen.

"Yeah, it didn't go anywhere though."

"Was it already purple when you clicked it or still blue?"

"I don't know, I can't remember. Why?"

"I'm pretty sure she was using this to try and track the sender's IP address. It wouldn't bring up an exact hit, but she would've got a general area at least."

"I didn't think you could track Facebook message IPs."

"You can't unless you have a warrant or whatever, but that's not actually what this does. If the other person clicks it, it automatically sends an email to your account, and you can track that. It's really rudimentary but it works. You just have to have someone that's stupid enough to click the link in the first place," Keegan looked up quickly from the screen and made a face at me, "no offense."

I raised my eyebrows. "None taken. Elle was clearly much smarter than I am."

"Yeah, it's a nice easy way of getting it done. She probably just looked up how to do it online to be fair though. It's not rocket science."

"So, the only way we'll know if she got the guy to click that link is if we can get into her email?"

"Yeah probably. You know her address and password?"

I nodded, turning the computer towards me and pulling up Gmail to log in as Elle, reassuring myself that one more breach of privacy was worth it if it meant I could figure who had done all this.

"What am I looking for?" I asked as I scanned Elle's inbox, looking for anything out of the ordinary.

"I don't know really; here let me take a look." Keegan reached for the laptop, swiveling it away from me and peering down at the screen intently. He double-checked the date Elle had sent the link and looked at every email she'd received that day, but there was nothing to indicate John Smith had fallen for her trap.

"I really thought this was it," I said, disappointment weighing down my words. "I thought we had him."

"Well, hold on, don't lose hope just yet. She might have put it in a different file or trashed it or something."

"Well, if she trashed it then we're screwed."

Keegan shook his head, still staring intently at the laptop screen, scrolling dutifully through Elle's inbox. "Nah, Gmail saves trashed emails for thirty days, so if she did it will still be there. Hasn't been thirty days yet."

It was then my phone rang, Ange's name lighting up its screen. "Hey," I said on picking up, "I might have found something pretty good."

But Ange was breathless about something, not even stopping to say hello. "Put on the news," she said instead.

"I can't, I'm at CJ's."

"They're about to release another statement to the press about Elle. I think this could be big. I'm on my way to the police station right now."

I looked over at Keegan, who was still digging through Elle's emails, and said: "I'll be right there."

Keegan refused to stay behind for the press conference and ended up driving us both down to the police station in Waterstone while I searched the contents of Elle's trashed emails. It wasn't all that difficult to find in the end—it was the last email she'd deleted before she died.

"It's just the IP address," I said to Keegan. "How would she have found out where the messages were coming from with just that?"

"Just put it into IP tracker or something, it should come up with a geographical location at least. But don't expect an exact address or anything, it's not that specific."

Keegan walked me through the steps as we drove towards the police station, and by the time we got there—the car park too full of TV station vans, reporters and photographers for us to find a parking space—I had the location.

My heart dropped to somewhere around my knees when I saw it come up on screen, and if I hadn't been sitting down already, I would have needed to.

It was the area covering the lakes between Forest View and Stokely; Witchend, Pine Grove and Fox's Leap. Keegan had pulled in somewhere and turned the car's engine off and was turned towards me.

"Maddie? Did it work?"

"Yeah, yeah. It worked."

"And?"

284

"Fox's Leap Lake," I said, my voice scratching the air.

"What?"

"It's the Altmans' lake house," I said, "the messages were coming from their lake house."

"You mean …?"

Not Bright. Not Louden. "Nate," I said distantly. Nate had been sending those messages. I tried to make this match up with the picture I had of him in my mind, but I was too slow, too sluggish. Stuck. All that energy I'd had just the night before—mere hours earlier—all the certainty was suddenly gone, and once again I was stuck. Immobile and impotent.

I couldn't stop staring at the screen even as the crowd of reporters outside began to assemble more formally, and the doors to the police station opened as the Chief walked out. He was accompanied by Gutierrez and Lee and I realized that they were having to do this outside, in the freezing cold, because there were too many people to fit inside the station.

I barely heard Keegan as he said: "Maddie, we should get out the car, they're about to make the announcement," but I still managed to leave the car and follow him to the crowd of reporters. I was numb, bloodless, reduced to rubble. Someone said my name but I couldn't do a thing, even as I realized it was Ange.

"Mads, are you okay?" she said to me, her voice reaching me from somewhere very far away.

I nodded, unable to speak and then, thankfully, Chief Moody cleared his throat and began to speak, cameras and microphones directed at him. Someone brushed up against my arm and I jumped, pulling away from them, only for them to grip my arm a little tighter.

I looked around to see who it was, and Leo stared down at me, pale blue eyes concerned, his mouth pinched tight. "You okay?" he mouthed at me, although he may have spoken the words aloud and I simply couldn't hear them. Once again I nodded, words stacking up in my throat unable to break free and turned back to Leo's father standing on the steps of the police station, the deep blue of his uniform standing stark against the gray of the day. Stood just behind him and to his left were Gutierrez and Lee, watching calmly as he addressed the press.

The Chief's broad shoulders were rigid, his eyes trained on the paper in front of him almost the entire time as he intoned: "Thanks to the hard work and cooperation of local police officers here in Waterstone and Forest View, along with the expertise of the Wisconsin Department of Justice Special Agents, we have been able to determine that in light of recent evidence, the case of missing person Nora Altman will be reopened, and treated as a murder investigation. After careful analysis, trace DNA evidence from the aforementioned victim was found on the same weapon that was used in the attack on Noelle Altman. I can confirm that Nathan Altman is the only suspect in this reopened case, although he has not yet been formally charged. It is our great hope that we will finally be able to bring some peace to Nora and Noelle's parents, and the community at large, as well as bring justice to the perpetrator." He then finally raised his head to stare straight into the wall of cameras that were trained on him, and said without a hint of modulation in his voice: "There will be no further questions at this time."

It was all over in a second, the Chief turning his back to walk into the station followed by the agents, the reporters dispersing, talking to the cameras, calling in to their editors.

"That's it?" someone said. "That's all we get?"

I walked away from the crowd, pushing past people until I was somewhere alone, staring down at the frozen ground as I threw up the pancakes I'd eaten with Keegan earlier. Someone's hand landed on my back but I shrugged them off, away from me, couldn't look at them whoever they were. There was a boulder the size of Australia crammed inside my chest and even as I tried desperately to breathe, in, out, in, out I hated what I had been reduced to.

I hadn't even realized I was crying until someone gently turned me round to face them, pulled me into a hug and then handed me a crumpled but clean tissue.

"This is good, Mads," they murmured into my hair, "this is the best possible scenario. They're finally going to find out what happened to her."

I pulled out of their arms, blew my nose and finally looked at who was comforting me: Leo. He wasn't dressed in uniform, so he must have just headed down here when he heard the announcement was going to happen.

"Did you know?" I asked. "Did you know they were reopening the case?"

"No. Dad didn't tell me anything. It's all the agents' decision anyway, he's just the media liaison at this point."

"Nate," I said, his name suddenly unfamiliar in my mouth, my throat full of barbed wire, "it was Nate."

"Looks like it," Leo said, then fell quiet for a while. The only sounds were those of the crowd talking and dispersing, shouts punctuating the cold air, the slam of van doors closing and opening issuing a mechanical screech that shuddered down my back and made me jump. Leo looked back at the station steps, now empty, abandoned and said: "I should get you out of here. They're not going to be making anymore statements today."

I was shivering even though I wasn't cold, not really; I wanted someone to tell me how to feel, to give me a rule book to follow, beats to be played out. All I'd ever wanted, for ten years, was to know what had happened to Nora, to finally know by whose hand she'd been taken from us. I knew it wouldn't bring me closure, resolution. I knew I would still have to live with it for the rest of my life, to try and fit whatever shape my life took around the missing piece that had been gone for so long already.

But I hadn't expected it to feel the way it did now that I finally did know. Nate Altman. There was a way for me to make sense of all this, there had to be, I reasoned, but I couldn't find it,

287

wasn't sure if I wanted to. It was that thundercrack of change again, the giant rift that tore through life and demanded we attempt to keep up, and I no longer knew if I could. I'd let everything slip through my fingers, and now there was nothing left to hold on to.

"Come on," Leo said, his voice as firm as the hand at my back, "let's go."

I let him push me back towards the car park as we weaved around still-milling reporters and cameramen. Ange found us just as we were getting to Leo's truck and told me Keegan had left to write up about the statement from the Chief on his blog. I nodded along, hearing her words but barely taking them in. Her face was strained as she spoke, her words brittle and near to breaking point. I wanted to ask her what she thought, how she felt, how any of this was real, what we were supposed to do now, but she had a job to do and I didn't want to hold her back.

"I'll see you later, okay?" she said, and I told her she would.

"You want me to drop you home?" Leo asked as he exited the parking lot. I didn't answer immediately, staring blankly out the window at a day I couldn't get a grip on. "Mads?" Leo prompted gently.

I shook my head. "No. I don't want to go home yet." The thought of being somewhere familiar, somewhere warm and welcoming, felt wrong somehow.

We were coming to the edge of Waterstone when Leo signaled right instead of going straight ahead. "Do you mind if we stop at mine, then? I need to change into my uniform."

"You're heading back to the station?"

"Yeah, my shift starts in a bit."

"Yeah, that's fine," I said, only dully aware of him sitting next to me in the truck. It had started to snow and I stared out through the windshield to where it was rapidly filling up my field of vision.

The world narrowed suddenly, and daylight wiped itself away;

the road was edged by thin figured trees, weighed down by layers of white snow, their branches hung like icy specters above us. My body felt light and heavy at the same time, like a balloon filled with lead was lodged somewhere in my stomach, and I wondered at those bare, fragile branches holding up all that frozen water. We stayed on that narrow road for a while before Leo turned left and I started to pay attention to where we were.

We were out by the lakes, just a few minutes' drive from the Altmans' own lake house. The rough-hewn wooden sign by the side of the road said **PINE GROVE LAKE** and I stayed staring at it, even as we passed by, craning my neck to make sure I read it right.

"Pine Grove Lake," I said, my voice snagging as I sat up a little straighter in my seat. "This is where you live?"

"Yeah, I moved in ages ago, right after I graduated from the police academy. It's my parents' old summer house."

"Doesn't it get lonely?"

The road we were driving down was little more than a track. It had been cleared of snow, but I had found it hard to believe the plough made it down here; Leo must do it himself, I thought. It was banked high with snow, the bottom layers graying with dirt, the trees bent under the weight of snow and ice, stick figures waiting to set off at a run, if only they could get out from underneath their wintry burden.

"I'm used to it now. Every winter I think about moving, but then summer rolls around and I change my mind again."

The truck came to a stop, and I followed Leo into the cabin, trudging through the snow. I stood for a second as he unlocked the door and stared at the frozen lake, its wide expanse sheathed in ice; you couldn't tell exactly where the lake ended and the earth began but there was a small hut out on it for ice fishing that promised refuge of some kind.

"Make yourself at home," Leo said as he opened the door and we walked inside. He turned back to me and shot me a grim smile. "You want a drink? I've got whisky and a couple of beers."

"No, I'm okay. I think it's a little early even for me," I said, drawing out my phone to see if mom or dad had tried to call me.

"Fair enough. You won't get any signal with that out here, I'm afraid," he said, pointing at my phone.

"Yeah, I figured. You got Wi-Fi instead?"

"Sure, the password's on the cork board over there," he replied.

The password was written on a Post-it and stuck to the frame of the cork board, the rest of it covered in photos, overlapping and crisscrossing one another. I examined them while tapping in the passcode and waiting for my phone to connect to the internet. Almost all the photos had Nora in. In some of them she was grinning, but more often than not she was posing or pouting. I pulled one off the board, careful not to tear it, and stared down into her smiling face. It must have been taken with flash, the photo, because Nora's face was ghost white, turned up towards the camera in a wild, ecstatic grin. She was sandwiched between Louden and Leo, and I wondered who had taken the photo, both boys staring down at Nora with laughter in their eyes.

It was a wonderful photo, brimming, bursting with energy, practically fizzing with it. It looked as though flakes of snow were falling through the dark air, but Nora was in summer clothes and both Leo and Louden were wearing T-shirts, so it couldn't have been winter. I took a closer look and realized it was ash raining down on them, blurry and indistinct, but undeniable. There was a noise behind me and I realized Leo was stood behind me, suddenly resplendent in his uniform.

"You took that photo," he said, "remember?"

"Really? When?"

"Oh, the summer after Nate and I graduated high school."

"I've never seen it before though."

"Well, you were using my camera. I've got a bunch of photos

from around that time that I've never got round to putting on Facebook or whatever."

"I don't know how you do it," I said softly, still gazing at all those images of Nora.

"Do what?" Leo asked, his voice a little sharp suddenly.

"Look at these every day. Look at Nora every day."

"Why? Don't you have any photos of her?"

I let my eyes wander over every single photo, tracking Nora, drinking in her face. It had felt okay to do it like this, in one go, but I couldn't have photos of her on my wall or on my desk, or wherever people hang photos, somewhere I walked past every day, getting so used to her image she just became a part of the scenery.

I still had a vital, visceral reaction to her image, even ten years later, because I'd never wanted to get used to the fact that she was just a photo to hang somewhere, rather than Nora. But I didn't quite know how to say all that to Leo or perhaps I just didn't want to, so I simply said: "It's too hard," and left it at that, turning away from the cork board as I did so.

"I get that," he said looking at me as something passed over his face. Upbeat all of a sudden, or simply just trying to change the subject, he asked: "You want some coffee? I don't need to be at the station for a little while."

"Yeah, that sounds good."

I wandered from the kitchen into the living room area, which was small and a little cramped, with a TV dominating the main wall. There was a bookcase overflowing with DVDs and games' cases, the bottom shelf stacked with comic books and graphic novels. I crouched down next to it to read the titles, thankful for the distraction.

I couldn't remember the last time I'd been there, if I ever had been; certainly not while Leo was living there full time.

"Wow, someone's into *Batman*," I said, my eyes roving over his comic collection.

291

Leo turned away from the coffee machine for a second and raised an eyebrow. "The secret's finally out."

"Have you read *Saga*?" I asked, not seeing it on the shelf anywhere.

"No, I haven't. I didn't know you were into any of that stuff."

"I didn't know you were," I said right back.

There was a lot you missed when your whole relationship with someone revolved around one event. My eye was caught by a collection of sketchbooks to the left of the comic book stacks, their black spines making them stand out from the wash of red and white. I pulled one out, glancing back at Leo to see that he was still busy in the kitchen, and settled down on the floor with my back against the wall.

"Hey, have you eaten?" he said, unaware that I was now paging through what I figured was his own sketch book. "I don't have a lot in, but I could probably make a couple of sandwiches if you're hungry."

"No, I'm fine," I murmured, stopping to look at an intricate line drawing of a wolf's head done in black ink, the wolf's fur represented by dots and loops that reminded me of paisley patterns, or those adult illustration coloring books that were so popular for a while. It was so good that, for a second, I thought it might actually be a page from a coloring book, but I could see where the ink had bled.

"This is good," I said, looking up as Leo passed me a mug and stared down quizzically at the sketch book in my lap.

"Oh, man what are you doing?" he said with laughter in his voice. "You found my sketch book?"

"Yeah, did you do all these?"

"Over the years, yeah."

"They're good. You ever do anything with them?" I said, thinking of my own abandoned attempts at cartoons, and comics that I'd long ago decided were a thing of my past.

Leo shook his head. "No. It's kind of my guilty secret."

"What? Why?"

Leo just shrugged. "Oh, you know. It's just not what you expect a cop to do in his spare time."

"That's ridiculous," I said.

By now I'd leafed through most of the book, but there were a few loose pages at the end, obviously ripped from other sketch books or comp books and shoved to the back. I shuffled through them while taking a sip of coffee, not really taking any of them in until one stopped me short. Unsure of what I was looking at, I carefully drew out the piece of paper, which was divided into six panels like a miniature comic strip.

I stared down at it uncomprehending for what felt like several minutes but can't have been, not really, before managing to say: "What's this?" My voice was strangled, mutated; I barely even recognized it as my own. But considering I was holding something I hadn't seen in over ten years I was surprised I managed to get the words out at all.

CHAPTER TWENTY-SIX

"What?" Leo said, standing up from the couch and leaning over me so that he could see what I was looking it. "Oh that's something from years ago. Probably did it when I was still at school." He waved his hand that wasn't holding his coffee at me dismissively and sat back down on the couch.

I stared back down at the cartoon and then back at him, my mind reeling. I wasn't sure what to make of his dismissal, but I wasn't buying it.

"You didn't draw this, Leo," I said, trying to make my voice as even as possible. I didn't want to rush to any conclusions, and at first I thought I might be seeing things, imagining them; it had been a long day, after all. I'd already felt the world smash to pieces around me, what if I was just trying to pick them up and fit them back together again but was missing crucial, integral pieces?

Leo looked at me and laughed. "Of course I did. It's just a stupid cartoon I drew in study hall or something."

I looked down at the cartoon again, double-, triple-, quad-ruple-checking that I wasn't imagining holding a cartoon I'd drawn over ten years before that had turned up in Leo's sketch book. But no—there it was.

It was similar to the one I'd found in Nora's room the previous week, but finding that cartoon languishing in Nora's teenage dream of a bedroom had made sense. Finding it there, in a house I wasn't even sure I'd ever been to before, ten years later, didn't make any kind of sense at all. Not that I could see.

I could have slipped it back into his sketch book, of course, placed it back on the shelf and gone back to sipping the coffee he'd made me. But just like always, I was scrambling to keep up, struggling to find a foothold, so I pressed on, trying not to worry about falling debris.

"Leo, these characters are called Wolfora, Foxeline, Haloe, and Squirange. They're the 'Forest View Furies'," I explained. "I drew this. I drew them. They're my characters."

"What are you talking about?"

"This is mine, Leo. My stupid cartoon, not yours. Where did you get it?" That was the question I really wanted answered, of course. Because the person who last had it in their possession was Nora. It was the final cartoon in a story about Wolfora having to fight an evil wolf who she thought she could trust and ultimately killing him and becoming the alpha. The evil wolf, of course, acting as a stand in for Louden.

I'd drawn it while sitting in CJ's with Nora and Ange, just a few days before Nora went missing. She'd spent the entire time complaining about Louden, anguished and angry, but when she'd seen the cartoon I'd been drawing while she talked she laughed and demanded I give it to her. So she'd taken it and put it in her wallet and, as far as I knew, it was still in her wallet when she went missing. And now *here it was*, shaking in my hands, in Leo's cabin. I felt as if I had fallen into another story, or was paging through someone's diary and suddenly saw my own name.

"Will you just calm down? What's wrong with you?"

"I'm perfectly calm, Leo," I said, lying, "I'm just confused about how you came to have this."

"I don't know," he said, throwing up his hands. "Maybe you gave it to me years ago?"

I gave him a quizzical look and let out a bark of what I hoped sounded like good-natured laughter. "We weren't exactly in the habit of drawing and giving each other cartoons ten years ago. I didn't even know you could draw until fifteen minutes ago."

I was staring at Leo, willing him to make sense of it to me, but he was looking around the living room, basically anywhere but at me, looking as lost as I felt.

"Look, Leo, I drew this and gave it to Nora. I'm not trying to pick a fight with you or anything, I'm just trying to figure out how it came to be here. Did you find it somewhere?"

"Maybe? I can't remember. Maybe she gave it to me or something."

"When would she have given this to you? And *why*?"

Leo sighed, leaning forward so that his elbows were resting on his knees and he could place his face in his hands. "I don't know, Mads. Can't we just drop this? Why is it so important?"

"You know why it's important. She had this in her wallet, Leo. It would have been on her when she went missing."

Leo propelled himself to standing, a flurry of movement, his image of quiet repose suddenly gone. The speed of his movement, and the look on his face—which had slipped from studied confusion to unrestrained frustration—took me aback.

"You couldn't possibly know that for sure," he said, his voice strained, pulled and yet much too loud. His choice of words, the way he said them, finally convinced me he was hiding something rather than simply confused.

I took my time to answer, heart beating heavily in my chest, willing it to slow down. The crinkled cartoon rustled almost silently in my hand, and I tried to think as fast as the blood that was beating in my ears. I knew that the only way this cartoon being here, ten years later, made sense was if Leo had seen Nora on the night she went missing, and if Leo had seen Nora on the night she went missing and never breathed a word of it—not to me, not to Nate, not to his own father who was the chief of police—then what else was he hiding?

I looked up at him, suddenly realizing how tall he was, how quiet his cabin was, how silent and remote that snow-covered lake outside his house had felt when we got there.

Pine Grove Lake.

Something caught at the back of my brain, digging in and grabbing on. Those messages Elle had been receiving on Nora's Facebook could have come from here too.

Leo was staring down at me, demanding a reply. His face was a blotchy concoction of red and white, his eyes somehow glinting hard and silver, even though I knew they were blue. I swallowed, slowing down my breath, trying to catch it, trying to stop my mind from running away with me, and to stop it from shouting "run away" so loudly at me.

"No," I admitted, slowly getting up from the floor, "I can't know that for sure, but I'm pretty fucking positive. She wouldn't have just given this to you anyway. It has nothing to do with you." I was trying to keep my voice light, casual, but I was sure it wasn't working because Leo seemed to react even more defensively.

"Or maybe me having it has nothing to do with you."

"What does that mean?"

Leo sighed and sat back down, crossing one leg over the other at the ankle, giving himself a little more time to rearrange himself in a more casual manner. I felt sure we were both pretending though.

"You didn't know Nora as well as you thought you did, Mads. There was a lot about her that would have surprised you. If you'd known."

I cocked my head at him, and suddenly it was my turn to be angry. I'd lived too long with Nora—both when she was alive and by my side, and when she was gone and yet still right by my side—to let someone undermine my relationship with her. It didn't matter to me that she'd disappeared while still holding onto secrets. Finding out that she'd slept with Bright and never told me hadn't disappointed me in the way you might think; in some ways it had been a relief, that even ten years on there was still more of her for me to know, that even then, she could still surprise me. It made her more real, as if she was still breathing life into our lives, rather than a picture caught in amber, never changing.

"Don't do that," I spat, "don't you dare. You have no idea what I did or didn't know about Nora."

Leo held his hands up, palms facing forward, the universal sign language for *don't blame me*, and said: "All I'm saying is that people have secrets."

"Okay, so explain to me, Leo, what's the secret here exactly? I'm listening."

I was standing over him now, and he leaned forward again, reaching out to grab my wrist and pull the illustration free from my hand.

"Don't get hysterical, Mads, it's not worth it. Just sit down and drink your coffee. It's just a cartoon. Who cares how I got it?" he said with faux gentleness.

I was watching him closely then, trying to read him, trying to understand what was going on. My mind had leapt to a conclusion but I was struggling to join the dots in between. None of it quite made sense, not yet, but I was determined to think it through. I wandered back towards the dining table which divided the living area and kitchen and sat down on one of the wooden chairs, not wanting to sit next to Leo on the couch but not wanting to turn my back on him either. The knowledge of his gun strapped to the side of his hip buzzed at the edge of everything, getting louder and louder.

"Either it's a secret, or it's no big deal and you can't remember, Leo. It can't be both. Can you just please explain to me how you have a cartoon I drew ten years ago?"

Leo shook his head, staring at me, his blue eyes cold and compelling. Or maybe I was just imagining that, recasting him in his new role, in a new image, one that made sense with what I was thinking. One where Leo could have killed Nora and, in all likelihood, Elle as well.

Here was someone I'd known all my life, maybe not intimately, maybe not as well as I knew Nate, but still, I'd known him forever. I knew his father and his mother; I remembered when his granddad died and that his grandmother was still alive. I knew he didn't drink wine and that he preferred rum to vodka, that he played ice hockey and played it well, that he took his coffee black and preferred waffles to pancakes.

How had my mind leapfrogged over all that, all that history, I wondered, and immediately decided that this discovery changed everything? That here, finally, was the person who took Nora. That it wasn't Nate, as everyone thought, but Leo. Was it purely because I didn't want it to be Nate? Because I needed him to be innocent?

It didn't matter. In that moment, none of it mattered because I no longer really had the ability to think clearly. And I desperately needed to, in order to get Leo to admit to me what he'd done, and then get out of there alive.

"Why do you care so much, Mads? Do you want it back or something, because I can give it back to you if that's what you want?" He made to stand up, as if he was going to give me back the cartoon but I raised my hand to stop him.

"You can keep it. I don't care that you have it. I just want to know *how* you have it. *Why* you have it."

"Isn't it obvious? Nora gave it to me."

I stared at him. I didn't believe him for a second and yet he was almost convincing. Everything was moving too fast, and I worried that in my struggle to keep up, I was finding footholds in all the wrong places, catching my breath when I should have been running as fast as I could. Barely an hour earlier I'd finally been forced to confront the fact that Nate had killed both his sisters, and now everything was rushing away from me again.

"Why would she give it to you?" I asked cautiously, trying not to sound too accusatory.

"Because we were ..." His voice trailed off as he refused to continue.

"You were what?" I prompted, getting impatient now, pushing a little too hard, but I felt close, so close to an answer and was worried if I pulled back too much I'd never get there.

Leo sighed and rubbed his face in his hands before finally saying: "We were sleeping together, okay?"

I let out a bark of laughter that seemed to bounce off the walls of the cabin. It wasn't what I was expecting him to say, and yet I shouldn't have been surprised by it. As a lie, it made sense; but that didn't make it true. "You're lying. That is complete bullshit."

"It's not, Mads."

"Okay, fine," I said, pretending to play along, "let's say you were sleeping together; it still doesn't explain why you would have that cartoon. Why Nora would have given it to you. It doesn't mean anything to you, so why would she give it to you?"

"She-she told me she drew it. That I was supposed to be the wolf. The one who wins the fight. I had no idea you actually drew it."

I looked at him. His voice had been hesitant, a slight waver to it, but he'd come up with that easily, smoothly. Maybe it was true. Or maybe it was a lie he'd told himself so many times he'd come to believe it.

Because that didn't sound like Nora. Why would she lie about drawing a cartoon to a guy she was sleeping with? To impress him? Nora already believed she was pretty fucking impressive. On top of which she'd never recast herself in the role of bystander. She loved that cartoon because I'd drawn her winning, defeating Louden, finally taking up her role as alpha female, as she believed she was. She'd never have passed on that role to some guy she happened to be sleeping with.

"That's the truth, Mads. I promise you. I had no idea you drew the cartoon until just now, you have to believe that—I'm as shocked as you are! She was lying to both of us. To everyone. All along."

I nodded slowly, his words filling up my brain, brick by brick. "Okay," I said, hating the way my voice shook and taking a deep breath to steady it, "okay, Leo, I hear you. I believe you."

The words felt wrong in my mouth, the lies like bile, but the relief that swept across his face, all through his body like a wave, pounding across the distance between us, convinced me he was lying. Only the guilty could experience a relief so profound.

I'd thought I was doing a good job of pretending, of convincing him he had convinced me, but just then my phone buzzed on the table beside me, making me jump, startled. I grabbed it, my hand covering the screen but something about my jittery movements must have alerted Leo because he stood up suddenly, tall and broad in his little living room and said: "Who was that?"

I looked up to find his eyes on mine, burning hard, blue fire, and it was that that made me finally think that I was in serious trouble. It wasn't as if I hadn't thought so before, it was that now I felt it rather than thought it, the fear crystallizing not only at the center of my mind, but in my veins, in my blood, lying thick and impenetrable all along my bones.

"It's just Ange," I said, picking the phone up and checking the notification. She was asking where I was.

"Don't answer her," he said stoutly, staring at me.

"Why?"

"Does she know you're here?"

"No," I said, watching as he shook his head and began to pace around the room.

Taking advantage of his distraction, I wrote a quick reply to Ange and then carefully placed the phone back down on the table. "Why would it matter whether Ange knows I'm here, Leo?"

His head whipped towards me, stopping short his pacing, and I almost flinched but managed to stay still.

Everything in that cabin had suddenly changed. It wasn't just Leo who kept flipping from a studied casualness to razor wire energy, the whole place had taken on a new role in my eyes.

Whatever Leo was saying, whatever was the truth, she'd been there; Nora had been *here*, and it was possibly the last place she'd ever been. The force of that ripped through me, tearing everything I knew, everything I'd ever thought I knew apart.

I wasn't the only one struggling to keep up though. If I was suddenly tumbling through airless space, then so was Leo; his face had gone red, his eyes kept sliding towards and then away from me, and his right hand was gripping his gun, still in its holster for now, as if it were his personal talisman.

I looked down at my phone to see that Ange had replied to my message and, making sure to do so just as Leo turned away from me to restart his urgent pacing, I turned the ringer down to silent and pressed the call icon in the corner of our message stream. Then, when Ange picked up without saying a word, I pressed the speaker button.

"Is this what happened with Elle?" I asked.

"What?" Leo stopped mid-pace, once again going completely still.

"Did Elle find out you killed Nora? Is that why you killed her?"

"I didn't … that's not …" Leo's eyes were darting everywhere, looking at anything but me, but I had to keep going, to keep pushing. I could feel how close I was to getting him to tell me the truth, and he seemed so unraveled that I thought I could do it. That maybe I could get him to confess to killing Nora and Elle, and even make it out of there alive.

"Did she figure it out?" I said. "Did she figure out what you'd done and come here to confront you about it?" The thought of Elle appearing at Leo's door that snowy night, of her *here* all alone, trying to get at the same truth I was, turned me inside out.

"That's not … I didn't mean to …"

"You didn't mean to kill her?" I said, standing up, the chair no longer able to contain me.

"She came here—"

"Oh, so it was her fault?"

"She kept digging! She didn't know what she was doing, she wouldn't stop talking, she said she had evidence, I don't know what, but she just wouldn't stop. She shouldn't have come here. She'd still be alive if she'd just never come here."

"She'd still be alive if you hadn't killed her."

Something passed over his face, but I couldn't quite decipher it. Pain? Regret? It didn't matter, not really. He was someone else by then, or maybe he had been the whole time and I had just never recognized him, not really, not until that moment.

"She was going to turn me in. I had no choice. She had evidence. I did what I had to do."

"She didn't have evidence," I said quietly. "She had a hunch. A feeling."

"Maybe. I don't know. Maybe she didn't have any evidence, but I couldn't take that risk."

"So, you killed her? Rather than take a risk?" I didn't know how I was continuing to speak, to make sense, to even stay on my feet. I wasn't sure if what I was feeling was fear or something else, something I couldn't put my finger on, because I'd never felt it before. How do you name something so new to you your first instinct is to run from it when you feel it? Maybe it was fear, fear so intense it was paralyzing, but I wasn't thinking of myself. As soon as I'd found that sketch I'd known. Known I was in the last place both Nora and Noelle had been, and I knew, then, it was full of them. Everywhere I looked, there they were. Maybe that's what a haunting is, at the end of the day, a place we can barely bear to be because it's so full to the brim with those we've

303

lost. And maybe that's what was happening to me. I wasn't afraid, I was haunted.

"It was too dangerous for me. To just let her go thinking I had killed Nora."

"And it was perfect timing for you really, wasn't it? Everyone in town? Nate, Bright, Louden. The whole gang back together. Nate and Louden were both suspects for Nora, so easy to assume they'd be dragged into this as well."

Leo seemed to wince a little, maybe just a bit, but I couldn't tell what was real and what was fake by then. He'd been lying for ten years, staring us all in the face while doing it. "I didn't plan it," he said levelly, in a low, steady voice that scared me more than the panic from before, "she came here, Mads. I never would have hurt her if she hadn't come here."

"And Nora? Was that all an accident too? Did you mean to hurt her?"

Leo turned away from me, towards the cork board layered with photos, almost every one with Nora's face gazing out from it. All of us caught in the same time warp she was forever trapped in. Forever seventeen. I'd thought it a memorial when I first saw it, but was it really a monument to what he'd done? To his real self who lay hidden beneath the layers of normality he so resolutely presented to the rest of us.

My stomach suddenly gripped at me, nausea penetrating right through to my bones so that I felt weak, stupid and weak.

"She ran out of gas," he said simply, "the fuel gauge was broken, and I stopped to help. She was on her way to see Louden. At the Altmans' lake house. But she … she'd lost it. Maybe the car running out of gas was the last straw, I don't know. I'd never seen her like that; she was crying, shouting at me, at one point she actually screamed, yelled at the sky, kicked the tires of the car. Eventually I got her into my truck; I was going to drive to the lake house, but she was a mess and didn't want Louden to see her like that, I guess, so I suggested we come here first so she could calm down a little, and then I'd drive her over later."

He paused, still staring at the cork board full of photos, before turning to face me. "She didn't know the half of it. Of Louden's cheating, I mean. That whole first semester he was in Chicago every text he sent was about some girl he was banging. And then Nora finds out and suddenly he's heartbroken? It was bullshit, all of it. He should've just broken up with her, but it's Louden, right? He has to have everything. She was on her way to break up with him, I think. She was going to tell him about Bright, or at least that's what she told me."

"You mean that she slept with Bright on New Year's Eve?"

Leo's gaze focused in on me, sharp and clear. He'd been looking anywhere but at me while he spoke, avoiding eye contact. "You knew about that?"

I nodded, even though I'd only recently learned about it. I didn't want him knowing that I'd been following the same rabbit hole that had led Elle to him, that I'd read the same messages she had.

"Louden still doesn't know," he said with a short, rasping laugh.

I could have pointed out that that was the least of what Louden didn't know, but I didn't. I couldn't. Leo seemed to have fallen under his own spell and I was worried anything I said would break it and I'd never hear what happened to Nora. I should have been more worried about other things of course. I should have been worried that I was in the presence of a killer, a two-time murderer who had a gun at his hip and a badge over his left breast. But I could feel it, how close I was to finally finding out what really happened to Nora, and I couldn't stop myself from pressing on, pushing forward, even though I should have been running away as fast as my legs could carry me.

"She used the bathroom to clean herself up, wash her face. She was pretty calm by the time she came back out and I gave her a beer. We both had one. She didn't seem like she wanted to leave. At least not at first. We were having a nice time, talking, drinking. I asked her about Louden and Bright, but she didn't wanna talk about any of that. She wanted to be distracted, I think. I think maybe she was a little embarrassed about how she'd been when I found her by the side of the road. She was always so cool, you know?"

He seemed to be waiting for a response this time, so I nodded. He was right, she was cool.

"I'd never seen her like that before. But the more we talked, the calmer she got. The cooler she got. More herself. We had a couple more beers. We were sitting over there," he said, pointing towards the couch where he'd been sat when I found the cartoon.

He paused again, still staring at the couch, and I thought maybe I'd lost him. The cabin was so full, the air breathing in and out with Nora and her last few hours, I could hardly bear it. I could feel her there, her and Elle both, the haunting moving on from something ephemeral, from a gossamer veil to a velvet heaviness that permeated everything.

My limbs felt heavy, like iron, weighting me to the floor but also as though they might melt at any moment, while just underneath my skin, razors whittled away at my defenses. I wondered how long I would last.

"I kissed her," he said, the words punching the air. "And she kissed me back for a while but then she pushed me away, started babbling again, putting her face in her hands like she was going to cry again. I wanted to make her feel better. I'd liked her for ages. I think maybe even Louden knew, which was why he was always bragging about how many other girls he was sleeping with, because he knew how much it killed me. But she wouldn't let me hold her, wouldn't even let me touch her, like I'd done something terrible, you know? She was the one who slept with Bright. She was the one who let me kiss her."

Nausea tore through me again, even stronger than before and

306

I thought I might actually throw up. I had to force myself to stay standing. Leo shook his head, lost to memory, engulfed by time.

"It didn't have to happen the way it did," he continued. "If she'd just gone along with it, none of this would have happened."

"Gone along with what?" I asked. I was practically whispering, physically unable to make my voice any louder, any stronger, but my words still sounded like thundercracks in that quiet, deadly room.

His eyes snapped to me and whatever reverie he'd been in was gone. I'd ruined it. Spoken too soon.

CHAPTER TWENTY-SEVEN

"She wouldn't let me hold her. If she'd just let me hold her, it would have all been okay."

I told myself to breathe, to stay where I was, to keep standing, keep listening, because Nora deserved that at the very least, at the very last; my full attention. I'd waited years to hear this story, to finally hear this truth, but she'd been waiting just as long to tell me, waiting right there for me while the world spun on and she stayed *here*, trapped.

"What did you do to her?" I managed to hiss.

Leo shook his head at me, although he'd gone back to not meeting my eye. His face was awash with something that looked so much like grief I wanted to scream. I'd seen it look like that so many times, at countless vigils, countless memorials, stood solid as rock next to Nate or nodding gravely as someone else spoke words of mourning, words of loss.

I couldn't fathom it, all this hiding, all this covering up. It must have been exhausting. I'd spent my entire life just trying to be who I really was, faults, cracks, fault lines, crack-ups and all, and that had worn me down to the bone. My whole life, everything I'd felt, everything I'd thought, had been a battle, and

I'd tried my hardest, even when it was damn near impossible for me, to show the people I loved and cared about who that person was. My friends and family could find me, even in the dark. No one could find Leo Moody, not even with the brightest spotlight in the world shining on him.

Even at that moment I still wasn't sure I could see who he really was; was he still performing, still pretending? I hated him then for that as much as for anything else. The fact that he could fake it and fool us and none of us were any the wiser.

The back of my eyes began to sting and that boulder was back, building in my chest, my throat. I tried to push them both away, to concentrate on the room, on his face but it was going to be impossible to ignore forever.

"What did you do?" I demanded again, this time louder, forcing my words to stand up for themselves.

"I loved her, Mads. I loved her—"

"No," I said in a strangled growl which I'd meant to be a shout. "No. Don't you dare. Don't you fucking dare. I loved her, Leo, *I loved her*. Ange loved her, Nate loved her. *Elle* loved her. You didn't love her. You wanted to hold her in your hands and when she wouldn't let you, you crushed her."

All the color drained from his face. "I didn't want any of this," he said, voice loaded down with sadness, head shaking back and forth. "I never wanted any of this."

"Well, this is what you have, this is what you did. What *you* did, Leo, not anyone else."

His head snapped back towards me, his whole body stiff with contained energy, as his eyes darkened, icy blue sliding into indigo. I'd never seen anything like it before, would never have believed it possible, his many masks made real, his entire body slipping off one identity and embracing another.

He walked towards me, long strides covering the small space of the cabin in seconds, but it still took me a second to realize what was going on when he reached for my arm, wrapping his hand around my bicep and leaning down to whisper in my ear: "Who knows you're here, Maddie?"

He jerked me towards him, my feet stumbling beneath my weight as he unbalanced me, and my breath got caught somewhere in my throat. I thought I was going to scream but my body wouldn't let me; I could feel fear running, thrumming, thumping through me but it was stopping me from being able to think or do anything. Turned out that when it came to flight or fight, I wasn't capable of either. I simply froze.

"I said, who knows you're here, Maddie?" Leo repeated, his voice as sharp as a razor blade in my ear.

I shook my head. "No one, no one knows I'm here," I said, trying to appease him, to keep him calm, to let me go.

For a second I thought it might have worked. He let me go, his hands releasing my biceps, but my mind was racing with thoughts of Ange, who I was desperately hoping had picked up the WhatsApp call I'd placed earlier and was listening in on everything that was happening.

I probably should have dialed 911, but at the time it had been more important to me for someone else to hear Leo's confession.

But in that moment, all I could think of was survival, of getting out of there, and I had to hope that Ange had called the police for me, and that they were on their way, or at the very least, that she was.

I slid my eyes towards my phone that was still sat on the kitchen table, just to reassure myself it was still there.

But Leo noticed the slip and grabbed the phone before I could get to it, throwing it across the room so that it hit the wall with a metallic crash.

In a moment of sheer panic, blood pumping erratically in my ears and my heart beating so loudly I could have sworn I could hear it, I reached for the gun that was holstered at Leo's hip.

He was so quick though, too quick, and so much stronger

than me that my fingertips had barely grazed the weapon when his hand, strong, firm and hot, wrapped itself around my wrist, pulling it back with such force, hot grumbling pain shot down my arm.

Before I understood what was happening, Leo pulled my arm behind my back, my body angrily shuddering against itself as fear, pain, and anger tore through my muscles.

Turning me against him, Leo threw me across the table and suddenly something smashed into my wrist and every single one of my bones turned to glass only to be shattered with the butt of his gun. This time I really did cry but it came out as a mangled sob, falling dully, hollowly onto the fake wooden tabletop.

"What are you doing?" I managed to gasp. "You won't be able to pin this one on someone else again with Nate in custody. All your careful planning will have been for nothing."

He pulled at my arm again, my shoulder screaming silently against the pain, but his voice was jumpy, jumbled when he said: "So, that's what this is about? Nate?"

"You killed them. You killed Nora and Elle, and now you're making someone else pay for it. Isn't that why you drew the compass? To make it look like it was all to do with the Altmans, with Nate? And the hunting knife," I said, gasping for breath as Leo leaned over me, his body pressed against mine as his lips warmly grazed my ear, filling me with a sick horror. "It's Nate's, isn't it? And you planted it there, knowing it would be covered in his fingerprints? What did you do? Did you drive over there after you'd killed her, hide it somewhere near the body where you knew it would be found—?"

"You don't know what you're talking about," he hissed, his grip tightening on me, even as he spoke, his frustration carried out by his hands and inflicted on me. It burned through my sweater, right to my skin, sinking deep into my bones.

He'd been there before; blind panic, burning anger and a body that could overpower me even as it couldn't overpower that

311

bright, boiling frustration. A dead weight dropped through me, from my chest, through my stomach and right down to my feet.

"And John Smith? What was that, some sick game you were playing with Elle? Keeping an eye on her, following her, messaging her on Facebook to what—to scare her?" The way he told it to me, it was Elle's suspicions that had led to her murder, led her to his door, to that cabin, surrounded by snow and silence.

But those messages had started months before, and who knows, maybe there were more somewhere, going back even further, under a different name, another pseudonym, another mask for Leo to hide behind.

I wondered when the obsession had started, if it had been there all along, ever since he'd killed Nora, or if Elle's seventeenth birthday had sparked it, set something off.

Leo pulled on my arm again, and I cried out, pain screaming from my wrist, all the way up to my shoulder.

"Stop fucking talking," he said through gritted teeth, his face still so close to mine, his voice trembling against my ear, hot and thick. It wasn't a denial though, and I knew I was right: Leo had been John Smith, taunting and tormenting Elle long before she'd arrived at his cabin door. I thought back to the scraps of paper scrawled with sharp-edged words, and dark intentions, that had been shoved into my locker in the months after Nora had first gone missing; had that been Leo too? But he had left high school by then, was already a cop, working, on all things, Nora's missing person case. I doubted he had anything to do with those Facebook messages Jenna had received either. Whatever this was, this obsession, it was about Nora and Noelle, the rest of us were just shrapnel, falling apart in the background of the bloody scene he had managed to create.

I closed my eyes against the surface of the table, focused on the coolness of the faux wood across my left cheek, tried to stop my mind from closing in and closing down.

Leo was still holding the gun he'd just used to smash my wrist;

I couldn't see a way out of it, but as I lay there, my cheek crushed against the table, I could still feel Nora in that room. Noelle too.

They were both there, and they'd both been through it, and the horror and the unspeakable grief I met that realization with made me wake up. Opening my eyes, I stamped the heel of my right foot down onto Leo's foot while simultaneously wrenching my smashed wrist free from his grip in an agonizing move.

The surprise destabilized him a little and despite the sick, swooping feeling of hot, sharp, insistent knives that was coming from what I was now sure was a broken wrist, I brought my elbow back to connect with his groin, forcing him to double over.

Leo staggered back, barely even making a sound, and I smashed my elbow down again, this time onto his lower back. My nerves, muscles, bones, and blood screamed out, but despite how fast everything was going it was like I was moving through water.

I held my right arm tight against my chest, holding onto my broken wrist as I kicked Leo in the crotch again, desperately trying to get him to drop the gun. It fell from his hand, landing with a crash and skittering across the floor.

I reached for it, but with my right arm held against my chest, my left hand had to do all the work, and once again Leo was faster. Our fingers touched as we both reached for the gun, and I sobbed, a gasping, desperate sound as he quickly snatched it out of my reach.

I wanted to give up, to give in. To lie down on that floor and for everything else to go away. But he wouldn't let me. It wasn't going to be that easy. Nothing ever was.

I tried to stand, my legs shivering with adrenaline, but before I could get there a shout of pain rang in my right shoulder, deep, hot and ugly, tearing through everything. I screamed, the sound filling the entire cabin, so vital and so vivid it sounded animal, the high notes hitting the ceiling, and the last guttural gasps falling at our feet.

Leo had shot me.

I dropped back down to the floor, turning to face him again in an achingly slow move that lasted a short lifetime. He'd dropped his arms at his side, the gun still black and strong in his right hand, and he was staring at me, his breathing erratic, his face blank.

My heart beat wildly at my ribcage, as if replaced with the wings of a giant, trapped bird struggling to escape, as the room closed in on me and all I could see was what was directly in front of me. Leo melted away and I struggled to the door.

But he was quicker than me yet again, and he reached for my arm, the same one he'd just shot, and dragged me up with it, urging the pain through me, strong and relentless, so that I was standing again, and pulled it back behind me.

I screamed out again, although I could hardly hear it against the sound of my own blood beating in my ears. Tears lay hot against my skin and nausea rolled through me so strong I retched, surprising myself when nothing came out. His breath was warm, disgustingly intimate, against the top of my head, his cheek resting there, his long body pressed against me and the gun nestling just beneath my ribcage.

When he spoke, it was just a whisper, a lover's confession: "Nora fought back too, you know," he said, and his voice crawled straight through me, digging deeper than any bullet could.

"Where is she?" I asked. "Just tell me that, at least. Just tell me where Nora is, Leo, please. What did you do with her?"

Leo held me against him even tighter, and my body sang with pain, rang with fear. "I'm surprised you haven't figured it out yet. I thought it would be obvious."

I closed my eyes, squeezed them tight and suddenly I could see it. The gauzy white stretch of frozen water right outside the door. "The lake," I said, as loud as I could, forcing the words out of me, despite the fact that I was draining, fading away.

"'The lake,'" Leo repeated, and I let out a deep sigh. It was as if the world had opened up inside of me and everything was rushing out.

But when all that was done, what was left was relief. Because now I knew. I no longer had to live on a high wire; I didn't have to traverse a tightrope anymore. Finally, I could fall.

The gun pressed against my bottom rib shifted a little, and Leo pressed his chin into the top of my head as his left arm held me closer and closer, squeezing the life out of me. His right hand clutched at my shoulder which was torn through with blood and bullets, the pain beginning to lift me through a veil I wasn't sure I was going to be able to come back from.

I was light and heavy at the same time, falling in and out of darkness, rushing towards the ground. I could hear someone calling my name, the familiarity of her voice lost for a second in the sound of Leo's heavy breathing, and the blood pounding in my ears.

Leo's hold on me loosened a little, and I tried to break free, but all I managed to do was stumble against him. I could hear her. Her voice, finally. Calling me.

"I loved her, Maddie," I heard Leo say again, his words a whisper in my ear, although I could just as easily have imagined it. "I loved her but she couldn't see it."

"No," I tried to say, "no, no."

Someone was shouting my name again, so loudly it pierced the room.

And then there was a long, screaming wail, getting louder and louder, an electric scream tearing through the snowy woods. I thought I was imagining it, dreaming of a savior, but it must have been real because suddenly Leo jerked away from me, rushing to the window to look out onto the whitewashed expanse.

Without him to hold me up I fell to the floor, black rising up to meet me. I could hear her voice again, the sweet familiarity, but there was fear there too and I didn't want her to be scared. Not anymore.

I took a second to breathe through it all, and heaved myself up from the floor, a sick, molten swoop of pain charging directly from my shoulder to my chest and stomach, and then my pelvis right down to my legs. My legs shook with the effort of moving, and despite everything, despite never wanting to cry in front of this man again, a sob broke through my body as every part of me filled up with pain.

I pulled the door open, cold air sweeping over me, the white snow almost blinding me, just as another shot rang out, and another. I waited for the rush of bloody pain to greet me again, but it never came, the bullets missing their mark—me—and hitting the open door instead, which acted as a shield as I stumbled and ran.

I could still hear her calling my name again, this time louder, so close.

But when I looked up it wasn't Nora I saw but Ange running towards me, her face just a blur beyond my tears. She grabbed both my arms as I fell on her, my legs buckling, my knees almost hitting the ground before she managed to pull me up.

She was saying my name over and over, but I could barely hear it, barely react to the fact that she was there at all. Why was she *here*? How? My gaze was drawn to the lake, frozen, still, and although my tongue felt fat, hot, and strange inside my mouth I said: "She's in there."

"What?"

"She's in there," I repeated, my voice a flat line.

Several other vehicles started arriving then, pulling up into the little snow-filled clearing. Lundgren slammed the door of her car behind her and ran towards us, her right hand resting on her hip, hovering over her gun. An EMT truck followed and she waved them over towards me and Ange, who was still staring resolutely at the cabin at my back.

"Maddie," Lundgren said when she reached us, alarm tracing through her voice. "What the hell's happened?"

"She's hurt," Ange said before I could answer. "I think she's been shot in the shoulder."

316

But all I could say was: "She's in there."

"Who's in there, Mads?" Ange asked, "Nora? Nora's in there?"

I nodded, mute, still staring at the lake.

"Oh my God," Ange said under her breath. "She's in there." But she was looking in the wrong direction, and her voice sounded strange, almost hopeful.

I finally pulled my gaze from the lake and looked at Ange, Lundgren, even at the EMTs. They were all looking the wrong way, looking at where I'd come from.

"No. Not in there," I said, meaning the cabin. "In there," and I pointed at the lake. "She's in there." The frosted sheet of ice glimmered opaque and treacherous at us, the perfect round circle at the center of the lake put there for ice fishing a perfect bullseye, winking quietly in the milky light of a grey, pearlescent afternoon. There was a small hut next to the hole, painted a cracked, peeling navy that my eyes were drawn to.

I closed my eyes against it, this picture of wild domesticity, and leaned into Ange as she kind of collapsed onto me so that we were holding one another up.

My shoulder pulsed and burned, something beyond pain, and I could feel my brain tripping over itself as it tried, desperately, to get everything in order.

There was absolutely nothing I could do when a pair of strong hands gently prized the two of us apart and lowered me onto a stretcher. I kept my eyes closed, squeezing them tighter and tighter, as tight as they could go, but I could still see the lake, even as they turned me away from it, even as it became little more than a memory.

317

CHAPTER TWENTY-EIGHT

Madison Journal

Local Cop Arrested in Murder of Two Sisters

By Angela Cairney

January 27, 2018

Nathan Altman has been released from custody and all charges have been dropped against him in the murder and suspected murder of his two sisters: Nora and Noelle Altman.

In a recent chain of events that have left the small town of Forest View reeling, local policeman and friend of Nathan Altman, Leo Moody, has been arrested after attacking and attempting to take hostage Madeline Fielder. Fielder is a longtime friend of the Altman family and was particularly close with Nora. Reports say that the 27-year-old had no idea Moody was involved in the murders, but came across something suspicious while at his secluded lakeside home that lies between Forest View and Stokely.

Moody confessed to both murders to her, although not before breaking Fielder's right wrist, and shooting her in the arm with his police issue Glock 22.

Working from information provided by Miss Fielder, the lake outside Officer Moody's house was searched using sonar and the remains of a young woman, who has since been identified as the missing Nora Altman, was found.

The medical examiner has yet to release a statement regarding the teenager's cause of death, but she is believed to have been strangled.

The discovery of Nora Altman's body ends a ten-year mystery that has haunted this town and its citizens. That she has finally been found must bring some relief to her family and loved ones, but the fact that she was eventually found so close by to where she originally went missing calls into question the way this case was handled from the beginning.

That she was apparently killed by a serving police officer calls into question the integrity of the police force and begs the question of who, exactly, they serve.

Chief of Police Patrick Moody, father of the suspect, today released a statement tendering his resignation. He expressed his "overwhelming sadness" at having not apprehended the killer sooner, and although he denied knowing anything of his son's involvement in the murders, he claimed "full responsibility for these senseless and heinous crimes that have horrified and haunted our town." The Chief went onto say that he regarded this the "greatest oversight and tragedy not just of my career, but of my life. My thoughts are with the Altmans and those two girls, as they have been for the past ten years, and will be for the rest of my days."

Speaking outside the police station in Waterstone, Jonathan Altman, father of Nora and Noelle, appeared almost too overwhelmed for words. "We have waited years to find Nora and know what happened to her, and we are grateful that we can finally put her to rest. In the face of losing Noelle, all this feels like very cold comfort, but we know that one day we will be able to mourn them both properly, as they deserve. With regards to Leo Moody, I have no words. In my mind, he is beyond forgiveness. As a lawyer, I know that justice will ultimately be served. As a father, I know that is impossible.'

CHAPTER TWENTY-NINE

There was one more memorial, one more funeral where we finally buried the both of them; more calla lilies and black dresses, inappropriate footwear sinking in the snow, sliding on ice. More tired faces, drawn mouths, sallow skinned and hollow eyed.

There were people missing of course, Leo's absence the most glaring of all. I couldn't think of a single vigil or memorial for Nora—and later for Elle—that he hadn't been present at, and that thought sent more than a shiver down my spine. It sent a wave of nausea and roiling fear so real I thought for a second I was back there, in that haunted cabin.

But the reassuring crush of bodies, the stale air, and crunch of food reminded me of where I was, pulling me back. I thought that away from the cabin, with Leo in custody, without the threat of violence, the feel of a gun against my ribs, the hot crush of fear, and the excruciating scream of pain to obscure and obfuscate, I'd be able to finally put Nora and Elle to rest. That's what we were all gathered there to do, after all, but I couldn't think of everything that had happened in that cabin; to me, to Nora, to Noelle without wanting to turn it all off.

I'd fought so long and hard to get to that place, and now I had nothing left in my arsenal, which had been so barren to begin with, with which to drown out those particular screams. They'd be with me for the rest of my life.

I'd have to testify of course. Be forced to stand up in court and live it all again, repeating the unrepeatable to a crowd full of faces. The stabbing twist of fear that met me as I thought of it grew bigger the closer the day got, coiling through me. I wondered how I'd feel when I saw his face again, and I had to stop myself from retching.

But even if I didn't have to testify, to bear witness, I knew that it wasn't over just because I'd stumbled out of that cabin and into the light. I was beginning to realize that even though we'd finally found her, finally buried her, I'd be saying goodbye to Nora for the rest of my life.

It turned out that Leo had lied about his alibi along with Bright and Louden that night, and then, ever since, he hadn't stopped lying. On the night of Nora's memorial, Elle, no longer able to contain what she was beginning to suspect, had driven over to Leo's cabin instead of to Jenna's and confronted him.

Leo later explained that the hunting knife had been a decoy, that after suffocating Elle with one of his couch cushions, he'd gone over to the Altmans' lake house, just minutes away, and grabbed what he knew was Nate's hunting knife in order to frame him. Then, he'd stabbed Elle's body, making sure not to leave any of his own fingerprints on it, and left it close to where he'd abandoned her, ensuring it would be found by the crime scene team.

All this he'd managed to do while appearing to grieve Nora, and then Elle, to support Nate and his family; the cold horror of the cover-up shocked me as much as the murders.

I didn't believe in turning men into monsters, but I didn't have the words needed to describe just how inhumane his actions were.

On the other side of the room I spotted Sheriff Lundgren, and beside her, Regina from the bar in Stokely. When they'd searched the lake, I'd thought they might find Annalise down there too, finally answering a question Regina and Lundgren had been asking for five years, but she wasn't there, and Leo was categorically denying having anything to do with her disappearance. That hadn't stopped Regina from sending flowers to my hospital bedside though, the card reading: "I'm glad you finally found her." I'd wondered where she found the strength, the grace, for such a thoughtful act, when all she wanted was to know what had happened to Annalise.

There was a part of me, maybe the darkest, sickest, most twisted part, but still a part, that hoped when they finally dredged Pine Grove Lake that they'd find Annalise down there too. At least Regina would have the same relief we had when they pulled what was left of Nora out of the ice. Maybe the darkest part of Regina had hope for that too, I don't know.

What I did know, was that she was still living in that cold, unforgiving place where hope and desperation exist side by side, the same one I'd lived in for so long, and was now, thankfully, free of. Looking at Regina, I hoped for her sake—for Annalise's sake—that Annalise had simply done what everyone had originally thought she'd done: up and left.

I hadn't really been aware of much while I was in hospital, coming in and out of consciousness, pain rearing its ugly head only to subside again when the drugs kicked in. At least I was able to produce a legitimate doctors' note from it, if nothing else, and I'd been reliably informed that my boss was going to grudgingly accept it when I finally returned to my desk the next week.

Nate had come to see me on the last day I was there, arriving with Serena and Cordy who packed up all my things before Serena discreetly led Cordy away, leaving us alone.

"I'm sorry about the alibi," he said, his voice almost drowned out by the beeps and whirs of the hospital machines.

I shook my head, grimacing in pain. "It doesn't matter, Nate," I croaked, "not now."

And I'd meant it. He'd lied to the police, telling them he'd been with me on the night Leo killed Elle, desperate to put some distance between him and a crime he was sure he was about to take the fall for. None of that mattered, though, not now we finally knew the truth and I was able to maybe, finally, face a few truths of my own.

The sheriff nodded at me then, offering me a tight smile. She'd been the one to arrest Leo, to charge him, to take my statement, to order the search of the lake. I wasn't sure if I believed Chief Moody's assurances that he had no idea his son had been responsible for Nora's and Elle's deaths, but at the very least he'd proven himself inadequate for the task of protecting even our small town. There were accusations of corruption, a cover-up, and I wondered how much further, how much deeper all of it might go, and whether or not I had the energy to deal with it.

The press showed no sign of leaving us alone, and I knew enough to expect the flash of cameras when I left the relative comfort of the room. To everyone else it was just another story, and a good one at that, but to the people in that room it was the thing we closed our eyes against at night, hoping against hope that we'd be allowed to sleep, to forget, even if just for a little while.

Because even all those weeks later, I could still feel the frozen lake against my back, pressing in, and I knew it would always be there. I didn't even have to look at it to see it, I could just close my eyes. And underneath all that frozen water, there I was. Even with Nora finally found, there was still a part of me down there, and maybe there always would be.

That precious pane of glass I'd been dreaming about and carrying around since Nora disappeared had finally slipped and shattered and I was trying to slide all the pieces back into place to make it fit. It was like a jigsaw puzzle except that every time I reached for a piece of the puzzle, tried to put it back together again, I drew blood. I was sick of bleeding all over everything, the throbbing in my strapped-up shoulder worsening as if just to prove a point.

I shifted my arm in the sling, but it made no difference. The pain built a little, minute by minute, and it would continue to do so until it stopped. I had no idea when it would stop.

"You okay?" someone said from behind me. Nate was staring down at me when I turned around. "Is it hurting?"

"It always hurts," I said. "All the time. Everywhere."

He nodded, his face a pale mask. "I know," he said.

He slipped his hand into my free one, and it was coarse and cold, the rough skin of his palms pressing against mine. It was enough, I thought, for now at least. Enough just to hold someone else's hand, to feel their life pressing against mine, and to not let go.

Acknowledgements

Biggest and best thanks to my parents and sister for being the most supportive family possible, not to mention major book nerds who love books and reading almost as much as I do.

This is my first book so on some level I basically want to thank every person I've ever known but for the time being I'll keep it to: Katie Reeves, Ciara Halpin, Beth Adamson, Fiona Fultigan, and Emily Marsh for still being the coolest people I've ever met, even all these years later; Alicia Field, Zoe Jubert, Isabel Colbourn, Alice Dean, and James Baker for being the best group of friends to come out of randomly allocated university housing; Corinne Jones and Sophie Meyrick for being constant sources of kindness, support, encouragement, and entertainment (Soph – I promise you'll get your dedication one day, but you know what Ruthie's like); Caroline Crew for endless *Buffy* chats over countless rounds of pilsner, introducing me to the Winchesters, and basically finding friendship in a hopeless place (yep, that's a RiRi ref); and Derica Shields for over half a lifetime's worth of friendship and punctuality.

Thank you to my agent, Suzie Townsend for making this book the best it could possibly be, and likewise to my editor Kathryn Cheshire for doing the same before ushering it out into the world. I'd also like to thank Peter Knapp for holding that query competition all those years ago, for being the first person to really *get* Maddie and her story, and for welcoming me to the New Leaf family.

Finally, many thanks to the women of the Agented Authors on Sub Facebook group for being consummate virtual comrades while wading through the trenches.